flyboy

flyboy

Kasey LeBlanc

BALZER + BRAY

An Imprint of HarperCollins*Publishers*

Balzer + Bray is an imprint of HarperCollins Publishers.

Flyboy
Copyright © 2024 by Kasey LeBlanc
Library of Congress Control Number: 2023943340
ISBN 978-0-06-328435-7

Typography by Julia Feingold
24 25 26 27 28 LBC 5 4 3 2 1

First Edition

For trans youth of all ages—
your existence is the real magic.

PROLOGUE

No one knows where the Midnight Circus comes from—when it began or how. No one knows who pitches the tentpoles or raises the flags. No one knows why it shows up at night, or why it disappears at dawn. No one knows if it's magic or machine, a dream, mirage, or something in between. All anyone knows is why the circus comes.

It comes for those who need it, for those who have been wounded. It comes for the broken and the brave, for those who hide and those who need a home. It comes for those whose dreams seem impossible by day, for those who feel split in two. At nightfall it beckons in field or forest, at daybreak it shimmers away, and in between?

In between it makes wishes come true.

The popcorn is perfect, the rides never break, the Ferris wheel stands tall. See it there on the horizon, flags waving. Hear the music calling to you, feel the gentle breeze brush across your face and know that as long as you're here, you're home.

Open your eyes, Asher.

Welcome home.

ONE

There's a fly buzzing near my ear at the edge of my peripheral vision, and if looks could kill, this fly would already be dead. Sweat drips from my forehead onto the church program as the fly continues to buzz, and I wonder if I'm in hell. It certainly feels like it. My grandmother sits beside me, unblinking eyes trained on the priest, perhaps testing the theory that they're the window to the soul. Not that her soul needs saving. Mine probably does, if God hates queers even a fraction as much as our priest says.

At the front of the church, Father DeMello says something, and we stand for the Nicene Creed. I reach a hand behind my knee and, yup, it's wet with sweat. Knee sweat. This is definitely hell.

I trace my name on the pew in front of me, the wood worn smooth beneath generations of fingers that have done the same. *A-S-H-*. From there I can veer off, two paths. The first leads to the name given to me at birth, the name spoken when I pick up the phone to hear Mom say she's working another double shift at the hospital, the name printed neatly on the base of a figurine collecting dust in the corner of my closet: a little girl in a white gown kneeling in prayer, a first Communion gift from my grandparents. The second path leads somewhere else, somewhere more dangerous, somewhere more *me*. In the safety of invisible letters, I take the second path. *E-R*.

Asher.

1

Grandma nudges me, and I realize that everyone else has sat back down. There must be something in my sweat, because the fly follows me, hovering in front of my eyes. I roll up my program and hold it in my right hand until just . . . the . . . right . . . moment . . .

And *BAM!*

I kill the little bugger, smashing it against the top of the pew where I traced my name. The sound is louder than I anticipated, so loud the priest pauses for a moment. I draw the attention of most of the congregation, but it's my grandmother's gaze that makes me glad looks can't, in fact, kill. She clears her throat. Mass continues on.

Nothing stops Jesus.

After Mass begins social hour, that unofficial time when parents and grandparents linger and chat with other parents and kids look at their phones impatiently. My hands itch for the sketchbook Grandma made me leave in the car. I had the dream again last night, the one about the circus. It's not even a dream, not a full one, at least. It's more like something floating at the edge of my vision, something I can see only from the periphery, but in it I feel peace. I feel like myself—like Asher—for once.

I started sketching the circus after the first dream, trying to envision what it looks like, hoping each day that the next time I dream of it I'll be able to get closer, but I never do. I just wake up with the smell of popcorn and the sound of music in my head.

We make the rounds through the church, inching closer but never close enough to the heavy wooden doors that separate me from freedom . . . and from lunch. My stomach growls audibly as we approach Mr. and Mrs. Baker and their three-year-old daughter, Kinsley. Grandma squeezes my wrist, fingernails digging in slightly, as though cutting off circulation to my hand will somehow make the growling stop. Kinsley brightens when she sees me and tries to wiggle free from her father's arms. He sets her down, and immediately she runs over and gives me a one-armed hug around my legs. Her other hand remains firmly in her mouth as she sucks on her fingers.

"Kinsley, take your hand out of your mouth," her mother chastises. She pulls her back apologetically, but I don't mind. I like kids.

"Mommy, can he give me a piggyback ride?"

Kinsley beams up at me, but Mrs. Baker looks pained. "*She*, sweetie. Remember, we talked about this? When it's a girl, you say *she* and *her*." She glances up, apologetic. "I'm so sorry." She laughs, clearly embarrassed. "You know how kids are."

Grandfather puts a firm hand on my shoulder, an indicator that it's my turn to respond. I know the rules of this game, so I provide a small (but tasteful) smile, a little laugh (to say I am now old enough to understand "how kids are"), and a statement (in this case quite sincere) that I don't mind having been called *he*.

Kinsley, however, isn't old enough to understand the rules of the game, so, fingers once again back in her mouth, asks, "Are you a boy or a girl?"

My heart drops into my stomach, and there's a part of me that hopes Mrs. Baker will step in once again and answer for me, and even though the answer will surely be wrong, at least I won't have to say it myself. But she doesn't, and there's a beat of awkward silence as the four adults, Kinsley, and I stand amid the quickly emptying pews of the church. I feel, or perhaps imagine, Grandfather's hand tightening even more on my shoulder and in a panic say the first thing that pops into my head.

"I'm a horse," I say, making a neighing sound as I pick Kinsley up and set her on my shoulders.

"Giddyup, horsey!" she says with a laugh. I gallop around the church, through the empty pews, and down the center aisle. I know my grandparents won't approve of my running around God's house like an ill-behaved child, but I also know they won't say anything. For they, unlike me, are well-mannered Christians. And because the Bakers are clients at my grandfather's law firm, which is surely something God would understand.

Kinsley laughs, says *faster, faster!* I oblige, glad to be free in this moment from everything else but a little girl wanting a piggyback ride. When we're done she looks at me, head cocked, fingers in her mouth, as if thinking back to her original question, but then she runs back over to her mom without saying another word, and I'm left to say the answer to myself.

I am a boy.

After church is Sunday dinner, though it's served at neither lunch- nor dinnertime but somewhere in between, when I'm so hungry a Communion wafer would make me salivate. My grandparents' house smells of the pot roast that's been cooking in the Crock-Pot since the early hours of the morning, but still, somehow, it's not time to eat. Not before we've set the table, poured the wine (a small amount in my glass, preparation for the socializing I'll do when I take over my grandfather's law firm one day), and said grace. And then, finally, food.

I take a few pieces of meat (not too much, can't look like a pig, that wouldn't be polite) and pass the plate to my grandfather.

"School starts tomorrow," Grandpa says.

"Yes, sir," I say. It's something I've been trying my best not to think about.

He pours himself some water and takes a long sip.

"We're so proud of you, dear," Grandma says. "And for you to finish out your schooling at Our Lady of Mercy, well, it's everything we could have hoped for. Your father—" She chokes up a bit here, reaches for my hand, which I've no choice but to offer up like a lamb sent to slaughter. "I know how proud he would've been to see you walking across that stage in your white dress for graduation. When he passed, your grandfather and I knew we'd need to step in to guide you on your journey with God. I thought your mother might never agree to let us send you to Catholic school, but—" She pauses, takes a breath. "Well, it's not worth rehashing. All that matters now is that we're here, and tomorrow you'll be where you belong."

She smiles, my grandfather smiles. I smile. Inside I want to throw up.

"Need to keep your grades up," Grandpa says after a moment, "if you wanted to be accepted into UNH." The way Grandpa talks about the University of New Hampshire, his alma mater, you'd be forgiven for thinking it's as difficult to get into as Harvard. "They've got a good law program, and the dean's an old friend. It would be nice to have him on your side, even though it's still early."

"Yes, sir," I say again, helping myself to a hefty portion of green beans, glad the conversation has returned to safer territory.

"Sit up straight, dear," adds my grandmother. "Ladies don't slouch."

I sit up. I don't tell my grandparents I'm not a lady. There's a lot I don't tell my grandparents. We finish the meal without any more conversation about college or law school or my dead father, and when we're done, Grandma brings out an apple pie.

"You're welcome to spend the night, dear," she says as we eat. "Your grandfather can take you to school in the morning."

"I should probably get home soon," I say instead. "Mom's taking me out to dinner. It's a tradition."

Another smile. This one pinched, but now that Mom has agreed to their life's greatest dream, she can hardly complain.

"Of course, dear."

Grandpa gets a call on his work phone. "Excuse me," he says, leaving the room to answer it.

When he returns, he's pulling on a coat, car keys in hand.

"Where are you going?" Grandma asks.

"Work," he says. "It's Bill Ross again. There's a reporter sniffing around, and he's insisting I come down to the school."

"I wish you'd tell him Sundays are for God and family," Grandma says disapprovingly.

I normally don't pay much attention to my grandfather's work, but what he's just said suddenly registers.

"Wait, Bill Ross like Principal Ross? At Wilbur?"

"Don't talk with food in your mouth," chastises my grandmother. "And never you mind. We pulled you from that school for a reason. You don't need to concern yourself with their issues any longer."

"I've got to go," my grandfather says. He kisses Grandma and then he's gone, leaving just the two of us, three-quarters of an apple pie, and a sinking feeling in the pit of my stomach.

6

Five minutes from home and the sky opens up like God himself tore it asunder. Our pace slows to a crawl as Grandma turns the wipers to the highest setting, but even that does little against the torrential rain.

Grandma tuts. "I knew I should've had you spend the night."

I don't respond, instead laying my head against the window and tracing a raindrop with my fingertip, wondering what it would feel like to climb out of the car and walk the rest of the way home. To let the rain soak me to the bone until I don't know where the water ends and I begin.

Lightning flashes in the distance, followed a few seconds later by a huge crack of thunder. Grandma slows the car as we approach the dirt driveway in front of my house, now more of a muddy Slip 'N Slide.

I sit up straight in my seat. "I can just get out here!" I say quickly, hand readied to throw open the door and make a run for it before Grandma can have second thoughts and take me back home with her. Fortunately, the vision of her only granddaughter running through the mud in her church clothes must be even more horrifying than driving her white car through it, because without warning, she jerks the steering wheel to the right and floors the gas.

"Well," Grandma says once we reach the front door. For the first time ever, she seems to have run out of words, as she takes in the view through the mud splattered windows, no doubt imaging the damage to the rest of the car. I'm more focused on what I'm *not* seeing through the windows—Mom's car.

And then I glance at the house and—oh, *shit*. I need to go. "I'll see you next week," I say quickly, not waiting for a response before jumping out of the car and sprinting toward the front door.

When I checked the weather forecast this morning, it said it wasn't supposed to rain until later in the night, so I left the windows open in hopes of dispelling the smell of cigarette smoke that has seeped so far into the walls and furniture, I think the house might fall apart in its absence. Instead, all I've done is flood the living room.

I run around the first floor shutting all the windows and throwing down towels to soak up the puddles. Just when I'm ready to crash on the couch and take a breath, I remember I left my bedroom window open.

Shitshitshitshit

I dash upstairs and throw open the door, immediately wishing I hadn't. The wind has blown all the papers on my desk around the room, large droplets of water causing the colors to bleed on at least a half dozen drawings. Everything I'd imagined of the circus that sits somewhere between dream and fantastical musing—ruined. I slam the window shut, then gather all the rogue papers together to dry when I see *it*, laid out across my bed. Taunting me.

White button-down shirt, blue sweater, and the *skirt*. A heavy plaid monstrosity, pleats ironed in perfect little lines. Long white socks lie folded in half beside the ensemble. And to top it all off, the rotten cherry atop this shit sundae, black Mary Janes. My stomach curdles. Immediately I'm six, seven, eight years old again, Grandma forcing a brush through hair the length of my back, hair once again tangled and knotted before church, feet squished into too-narrow Mary Janes because the store didn't have girls' shoes in a size wide and my last pair had been so *unfortunately* chewed apart by my neighbors' dog. It was only when I took a pair of scissors to my hair in the church basement and emerged with a choppy and lopsided haircut, right ear bleeding where I'd nicked it, that my grandparents settled for khaki pants and a polo shirt as acceptable church attire. And even then, I think it was only because Mom made them.

And now. All these years later, and she's the one betraying me.

I throw the uniform to the floor, clearing space to lay out my drawings. Except for the rough sketches I made in my sketchbook this morning before church, everything I've drawn of my circus dreams lies before me now, paper soggy, colors bleeding. I pick up the most salvageable of the lot. A figure doing trapeze, flying across the sky. I remember the fly at church that morning flitting around my face and wonder why God would give wings to such a useless creature. If I could fly, I certainly wouldn't stick around here.

As I leave my drawings to dry out, I watch the storm rage through the living room window, dread building as the minutes roll on and I don't see Mom's car pull down the driveway.

"Historic rainfall," the meteorologist says when I turn on the TV. "Flash flooding is expected throughout the area, and a severe thunderstorm warning is in effect through eleven thirty this evening. The wind looks like it will continue to pick up, creating a risk of downed tree branches and power lines, so, folks, this is not a night to go out on the roads if you can avoid it. This is Jim signing off with your local weather. Now, back to you, Harvey."

I switch off the television. *Screw you, Jim.*

"Hey, sweetie." Those are the first words I hear when I pick up the phone almost an hour later. It's Mom, calling from work.

"You aren't coming home, are you?" I say, voice flat.

"Oh, sweetie," she says, and that's when I know I'm right. "It's just with the storm, the roads are completely flooded, and a lot of folks are having trouble getting in, so when they asked me if I could stay . . ." She trails off, waiting perhaps for me to say something, but I stay silent. "And it wouldn't be any safer for me to go out there right now, but I was thinking maybe we could reschedule. Tomorrow night? And you can tell me all about your first day?"

"Yeah," I say. "Maybe." A beat of silence. "But you know, fancy new school and all. I'll probably have loads of work."

"Right, yeah, course," Mom says. I can hear the exhaustion in her voice, and part of me knows it's not fair to be mad at her, but I am. "Another time."

I hear a faint beeping sound. A pager.

"Sounds like you need to go."

"They need me downstairs," she says. "I'm—"

I cut her off. "It's fine. They need you. I'll see you tomorrow."

I hang up the phone before she can say goodbye, and then I hurl it across the room.

The rain has slowed but not stopped by the time I should be getting ready for bed. Each time I turn on the television, I'm treated to images of reporters in rain gear shouting into a microphone as they stand in puddles that reach their calves and the wind bends the trees around them. Grandma calls twice, the first to ask if we're still planning to leave the house, the second, once she's learned Mom isn't coming home, to offer to order a pizza. I assure her there's food in the house and that if it's not safe for me to go out in this weather, it's hardly safer for a delivery person to go out in it, at which my grandmother scoffs and says, "Well, I would tip him."

At quarter past ten, the wind picks up speed. Between the howling and the banging of the tree branches against the side of the house, it feels like I'm living in a haunted mansion.

That's the last thought I have before the lights flicker and then go out entirely.

I use the dim light of my flip-phone's screen to maneuver my way to the junk drawer in the kitchen, the only place I might find a flashlight, but of course the one I find is a small key chain flashlight with a battery that's completely dead.

Lightning flashes outside, illuminating the house before returning it to utter blackness a moment later. At this point there's nothing left to do but go to bed. As I feel my way through the kitchen to the stairs, smashing my knee against something not once but twice, I realize there's one good thing about the dark.

In the dark I can't see myself.

TWO

I wake to silence. No rain, no thunder, no trees rustling in the wind. I wonder if it's morning already, but the darkness outside tells me it's not. What I don't need to be told is that it's here. I can feel it, rippling electric across my skin, calling out to me with a force so magnetic it's a wonder I'm not pulled through the walls of my house straight to its heart.

The circus has arrived.

I hear it next, the words I know by heart. I say them along with the announcer under my breath.

"Come one, come all! Witness the marvelously magical, the splendiferously stupendous, the enchanting, entrancing, most downright entertaining show you'll ever see! Come experience the Midnight Circus! Show begins promptly at midnight!"

I know how this goes next. The smell of popcorn, the sensation of flying, the knowledge that here I'm Asher.

I wait, but there's nothing. It's different tonight. Somehow, the dream feels more real.

I sit up. I've never been able to do that before. I know I should wake up, that the knowledge this is a dream should pull me from it, but it doesn't. I step forward, tentatively at first, testing out the expanding boundaries of this dream, and then I rush down the stairs and out the back door.

Behind the thin stretch of trees separating our backyard from the empty field that lies beyond stands a Ferris wheel, towering high above the horizon. Beside it, three flags wave in the cool evening breeze.

I grin, running forward to take my first step through, knowing as I do that everything is about to change. Overhead the clouds part and the stars shine through, and I'm here.

I'm at the Midnight Circus.

A woman standing nearly ten feet tall on stilts with rainbow hair stretching down to the ground blows bubbles that shimmer as they drift through the air. A young boy catches one on his tongue, then shouts in delight, "It tastes like watermelon!"

Two girls on unicycles juggle back and forth across a path under which patrons walk; a young woman twists balloons into animals that spring to life, a balloon puppy wriggling out of her hands to chase a balloon kitten that is itself chasing a balloon rat in a dizzying figure eight; a man with a long braided beard scoops popcorn into large bags while a band plays a rousing tune; an old woman breathing fire cooks a marshmallow, then plops it into her mouth; a contortionist crab-walks with his legs bent back over his head, and behind it all is the tent, a three-ringed tent of blue and gold with lights sewn onto the canvas that sparkle like stars.

It's even better than I hoped it would be.

"Hey, 'mano, you're late!"

I turn, face the boy now standing beside me. Somehow, he's even shorter than me, dark hair standing tall in a just-rolled-out-of-bed sort of way, brown eyes wide and bright against his golden skin as he taps his wrist impatiently.

He must have the wrong person. "Sorry," I say, "I don't think—"

"No time!"

The boy grabs my wrist and drags me along, past the crowds and the performers, the stands and the stalls, and the

delicious-smelling popcorn. I want to tell him he's clearly confused and I'm not who he's looking for, but he's got a surprisingly
strong grip and seems quite determined.

The boy stops at the back entrance to the main tent. He
turns, finally releasing my wrist, which I massage a little self-
consciously.

"Name's Seb." He pauses, cocking his head as though actually
seeing me for the first time. "You *are* Asher," he says, "yeah?"

"I—"

He cuts me off before I can answer. "S'pose I should've
checked sooner, but Fizz gave me a description and he's never
been wrong before. 'Skinny white boy, dirty-blond hair, will look
a bit like a deer in the headlights, freckle on his right elbow.'"

Seb grabs my right arm, flips it over, and there it is, a single
freckle. He makes a satisfied hum. "Well then," he says, a grin
lighting up his face. "Are you ready?"

"Ready for what?" I say, finally managing to get a word in.

"Ready to work, of course. Gotta earn your keep if you're
gonna stick around. But don't worry, ol' Seb here will show you
the ropes."

I think longingly of all the things Seb dragged me past. My
dream has finally allowed me to pass through the gates, and
now I'm getting put to work? I want to protest, but I also don't
want to wake up, so I nod reluctantly.

Seb pulls back the fabric separating us from the inside of the
tent and steps forward. I hesitate for just a moment, turning
back longingly toward the excitement outside the tent, when
I spot someone in the darkness. They're wearing a mask, one
of those beaked plague masks from the seventeenth century.

14

Another performer? I wonder what their act is, but not for long, because Seb drags me into the tent and into pure chaos.

Performers run this way and that, some already in full costume and makeup, others in various states along the way.

"Has anyone seen my shoes?" one woman shouts. A moment later a pair of ballet slippers tied together at the laces flies over our heads.

A ball whizzes through the air, and without so much as a glance Seb throws up his hand and catches it. A moment later, I nearly trip over what turns out to be a sword that Seb again avoids almost instinctively.

"Sorry, sorry," a man with a heavy Russian accent says as he picks it up, but there's no time to respond or even introduce myself, because I'm afraid to lose Seb. Finally he stops, plopping down in a canvas-backed chair that reminds me of the ones directors use, and gestures to an empty one beside his.

But I don't sit. I can't, because in front of us is a mirror, one of those tall ones with bright lights all around the edges, and in the mirror *I see me.*

I don't know where to look first, don't know what to do with the image in front of me, because it's everything I ever imagined, but it's real and it's right in front of me. I reach up, run my hands through my hair, watch as the boy in the mirror does the same. And my chest. I put my hands over my chest, hesitant at first and then firmer.

Flat. It's flat. I laugh and turn back to Seb.

"That's me?" I say, and then I notice my voice. No longer the high whiny voice I hate so much. I feel this voice in my chest, and *my God*, it feels good.

15

"Who else were you expecting to see in the mirror, 'mano?" he asks, amused.

I shake my head. I can't explain. Before he can say anything further, a tall white man with black hair and fingernails painted gold comes over and kisses me once on each cheek.

"I'm Marko," he says. "Hair and makeup extraordinaire. And you are?"

"That's Asher. He's mine," Seb says between bites of something he's shoveling into his mouth. He licks an orange powder off his fingers, staining his tongue the same fluorescent shade.

"*Hmmm*," hums Marko. "René gave him to you?"

"'Course. He's here with me, isn't he?"

"It just seems like an odd fit. With a build like that? Seems to me like he'd be better suited for—"

"Don't you dare say it," Seb says, bolting upright.

Marko raises an eyebrow, takes a step back.

"That's the last thing this place needs."

"Well," Marko says slowly, "if René insists. I'm sure he knows best. Am I doing him up as well?"

"Nah," Seb says, calming back down. "Not tonight. 'Mano's gotta train first."

Marko walks away, begins gathering what look like makeup supplies from a cabinet and carrying them over.

"Who's René?" I ask. "And what do you mean he *gave me* to you? I'm not some dog you can give away."

Seb laughs. "I like you," he says. "René leads this whole gig. You'll meet him soon enough. And all I meant was you've been assigned to me. I'm going to teach you how to become a clown."

If I was drinking water, I'd have spit it out. A clown? No, that's not right. That's not right at all.

Seb misinterprets my expression. "Don't worry," he says. "You don't have to perform tonight. New folks rehearse for a month or two before their first show. You'll be well trained by yours truly before your first performance." He grins. "You'll see."

Marko tells Seb to close his eyes and starts doing his makeup, but I'm stuck on what Seb said. I think back to my drawings. I'm not supposed to be a clown.

I'm supposed to fly.

When Seb is all put together, he takes me to see where they'll actually perform. He wants me to see it before Fizz lets the audience in, he says.

"I've been telling René for ages that we need another clown, and he always goes, *Yes, Seb,* and *I'll get right on it, Seb,* but then every few months when someone new shows up he's always like, *It's not the right one, Seb,* and *Have some faith, Seb*—"

Seb continues, but I'm not listening because there's only one thing I can focus on.

The trapeze rig. Stretching upward probably thirty feet, a ladder on one side leads up to a platform from which the performer jumps, a large net maybe fifteen feet below to catch him if he falls. I drift away from Seb, walk closer, head cocked up to see the person high on the platform. He grips a hanging wooden bar with one hand, and then in an instant he pulls the bar closer, grabs on to it with his other hand, and jumps.

I've imagined flying, but to see it up close is something else entirely. Watching the boy fly is like watching a ballet in the sky; body arched back, toes pointed as he makes an arc across the rig, before pulling himself up onto the bar with near effortless grace.

It's beautiful.

Seb notices I've stopped. He turns back and makes a face of disapproval. "Come on, 'mano," he says.

Reluctantly I follow along. He brings me into the center of the ring and introduces me to Maisie, his clowning partner. She's about ten, with pale skin, long ginger hair, and a face full of freckles. She greets me with significantly less enthusiasm than Seb has thus far displayed.

Seb gives me a quick history lesson on the different types of clowns, particularly the whiteface, or white clown, and the Auguste, or red clown. I learn that the white clown is the straight man at the top who sets up the comedic gags, while the red clown is the one the audience tends to root for, the clown who messes everything up and ends up on the receiving end of the jokes. Apparently Maisie often plays the white clown and Seb the red, which, given their age difference, adds to the comedic humor of their performance. With a third clown, they can add the role of the character clown. "But don't worry about that yet," Seb says. "We have time to figure out what character you'll be best at."

I try my best to pay attention to everything Seb is teaching me, though it's hard not to let my gaze wander. I want so desperately to fly it almost hurts.

We start with some basic warm-up exercises, the first of which is called Exaggeration. Seb explains the premise, which sounds simple enough. We'll each draw an action or an emotion from slips of paper put into a hat, then we'll have about a minute to act them out in a comedic manner.

Seb said if I want to stay I have to work. I can do charades if it means I get to stay.

"I'll start," Seb says. He doesn't say what his word is, but it quickly becomes clear the action described is "having cereal." In just a minute he takes us through a whole journey without any words, from waking up and being unable to decide between two different types of cereal to deciding on both, being so eager to pour them into the bowl it overflows, to carefully peeling and chopping a banana and adding it to the top, then adding the milk, and finally, as he's about to carry the bowl to the table, slipping and falling on the banana peel he'd tossed aside and spilling the entire bowl of cereal all over himself.

Seb takes an exaggerated bow at the end as I laugh and clap.

"Your turn," he says, and Maisie holds out the hat. I reach inside and pull out a piece of paper.

Playing basketball.

Behind Seb, I see the young man. He releases the bar, arms outstretched, then he connects with his partner's hands.

Focus. Playing basketball. I know how to play basketball.

I take a moment to collect myself, and then I start, dribbling an imaginary ball up and down a basketball court, chasing the ball a bit when it escapes from me, and then finishing by dunking the ball into the net. I turn to Maisie and Seb to see their reactions.

Maisie's squinting and biting her lip, and Seb has his head cocked, lips pursed.

"Well," he says finally. "Maybe you'll be better at juggling."

An hour later it becomes clear I am even less skilled at juggling, hopeless at riding a unicycle (which, for the record, is nothing like riding a bike), and terrible at remembering lines.

Despite how clearly inept I am at every aspect of clowning,

Seb remains upbeat and optimistic. Maisie hasn't said much, but her face hides nothing. I wish I could tell her I feel the same.

In the background, the young man releases the bar, does a triple flip, and lands in the net below.

Focus.

Seb decides I should take a crack at reenacting his breakfast skit from earlier in the evening rather than letting me improvise, which is clearly not working. He runs through it again, gives me instruction, and sets me to it. I do my best, feel rather good about it actually, and for the first time I even smile upon finishing.

"Well?" I say. "How was that?"

"How does someone trip on a banana and it's *not* funny?" Maisie mutters before shaking her head and walking away.

Seb and I watch her go. He turns back. "Perhaps it's time for a break."

Seb goes off to get some water, telling me not to wander too far. We aren't the only ones rehearsing in the space. Across the ring, a large man with bulging muscles throws knives at a target while a woman dances ballet. Another person balances on one hand some three feet off the ground atop a stack of blocks. It's a veritable zoo and also controlled chaos. Every person has their place. Every person except me.

I look back at the trapeze, feeling pulled to it in a way that feels more like destiny than coincidence. I *know* I'm meant to fly, so why does no one else see that?

I move closer to the trapeze. Up above, the boy still flies. I crane my neck, but from so close the motion makes me dizzy, so instead I focus on the ladder in front of me. I see something resting on it, and as I move closer, I realize it's a blue butterfly.

Slowly, so as not to scare it, I reach out my hand for the butterfly to climb on so I can move it to a safer location. Almost there . . .

"What are you doing?"

The butterfly flits away. I turn, finding myself face-to-face with the young man from the trapeze. He stands, bare arms folded across his chest, hands white with chalk and his shoulders slick with sweat beside the straps of his purple and blue leotard. From his shoulders I can tell that his skin is not much darker than mine, but he's got a significant farmer's tan, as though he lived almost exclusively outdoors this summer.

"Who are you?" he asks. "And what are you doing over here?"

He's my age, only a few inches taller than me, though he's barefoot and I'm still wearing shoes. I'm about to answer, when the butterfly reappears, flying around the boy's face before landing on top of a brown curl plastered against his forehead. I don't know much about butterflies, but I swear this one is looking at me.

"Don't move." I step closer and the boy freezes, brown eyes locked on mine. I can feel his breath and my heart races, but I don't want the butterfly to fly away again. I reach for it, hand hovering in front of the boy's eyes, and as I'm about to touch it, his arm shoots up and he grabs my wrist tightly before dropping it almost as quickly.

I don't know which of us is more shocked, but before I can say anything, the butterfly lands on my still-outstretched hand and I wake up in my bed.

THREE

The sun shines bright through my window, but I don't yet open my eyes. I know I can't bring myself back, but I want to hold on to my dream for as long as I can. I was there, I was *at* the Midnight Circus. I saw the trapeze rig, was so close I could even touch it. And then there were the people. Seb, Marko, the young man on the trapeze . . . what a strange cast of characters. And me, a clown! I laugh as I finally open my eyes and sit up.

A glance around my room brings me back to Earth real fast. My drawings lie scattered, paper bubbled and curled from yesterday's rain. And beside them, the uniform.

First day of senior year at Our Lady of Mercy Academy. I feel sick. The single redeeming factor is finally being at the same school as my best friend, Moira. She's supposed to pick me up this morning, in fact.

I head downstairs, hoping to put off the task of getting dressed for as long as possible. Mom's passed out on the couch, still in her scrubs, arm dangling over a cup of water in which her extinguished cigarette now floats. I throw a blanket over her before going to make breakfast. The stove clock says it's almost seven. Mom must have reset it before falling asleep.

My phone buzzes. Two, a pause, two more, pause, two more. I give it a second to see if it's done, then pick it up and flip it open. My grandparents wanted to get me a smartphone a couple of years ago for my birthday and add me to their phone plan, but Mom refused, which is why I have an actual flip phone more than two freaking decades into the twenty-first century.

I've got three messages, all from Moira, of course. She's the only person who ever texts me.

I open the first, but it makes no sense.

[1/3] snakepit! ☒☒☒ Stopping at Dunks b4 I grab u. Will

I open all the others, hoping that will help me figure out what the hell Moira is trying to say.

[2/3] Hope ur ready to jump into the

[3/3] get ur usual. UR gonna need it ☒☒

I know the boxes are emojis. Moira never remembers that my phone can't read them, so I just get little boxes where they should be. It's always a fun game to guess what she was intending to send me. My phone also has a shit capacity for text length, so Moira's texts often get split into multiple parts that don't always arrive in order, which is the case this morning, and because it's still early it takes me longer than normal to put the pieces back together, but I chuckle slightly when I do.

I rinse my bowl in the sink, and when I can put it off no longer, I head back upstairs to get dressed.

I stare at the clothes on the floor. It should be easy. Top, bottom, socks, shoes. I've done it literally every day since I was a child.

And yet.

I put on the white button-down first over the new sports bra I got my grandmother to buy me a few weeks ago when I told her I might try out for a sport this year. I will not be trying out for a sport this or any other year, but I could hardly tell her my old one had gotten too loose to properly flatten my chest.

I pull on the socks next. I know I must look ridiculous right now, but the thought of putting on that final piece, the thought of knowing that every second, with every glance, people will see me and not really see *me*, well, it really fucking sucks.

A car honks outside, and I recognize it immediately as Moira's. She inherited her older brother's truck when he left for college, and the horn is so messed up it sounds a bit like a dying rubber chicken.

No more time to think. I pull on the skirt. Time to get this over with.

"Repeat it back to me," Moira says as she pulls into the parking lot, bringing us to an abrupt stop. Her overabundance of curly red hair whips forward as my chest slams into my seat belt. I take a moment to collect myself, then do my best to repeat back everything she's just told me about Our Lady of Mercy. A survival cheat sheet, she called it.

"Mr. Dortson is a perv, Sister Johnson is a 'walking corpse'"—Moira nods approvingly—"Mr. Richards will let you sit out of gym class if you tell him you're having *woman* troubles, the middle toilet on the . . . second? floor—"

"Third floor," Moira interjects.

"Right, third floor is constantly getting clogged, never eat the cafeteria tacos, but do eat the chocolate-chip cookies Marge makes, and . . ." I trail off as I try to recall the decade's worth of knowledge Moira has attempted to distill and shove into my head during our twenty-minute ride to school.

"And whatever you do, stick close to me."

"I can do that."

Moira slurps down the rest of her coffee. "Are you ready for this?"

"Hell no."

She grins. "That's the spirit."

Crucifixes. Crucifixes everywhere. Jesus stares down at me at every turn. There's entryway Jesus, locker Jesus, classroom Jesus, even, as I find out way too soon, bathroom Jesus. I wonder if people are more likely to wash their hands with Jesus watching in the mirror. I certainly scrub a lot longer than usual.

Moira waits outside the bathroom for me. She raises an eyebrow, presumably at the length of time I was inside. "Bathroom Jesus?"

"Bathroom Jesus."

She nods sagely. "He'll get you every time. Locker room Jesus has the opposite effect."

I can't tell if she's serious. I'm not sure I want to find out.

As I trail behind Moira, I notice the stares people are giving me, but she never stops to introduce me to anyone, so I don't stop either.

"Don't bother making friends" was another bit of advice she'd given me in the car. "The kids here aren't worth your time. Besides, you've got me. It's all going to be downhill from there."

Given how things ended with my only friend at public school, that seems easy enough advice to follow. Moira's been my best friend since we were kids, and she shoved a boy who

25

was teasing me at the church's daycare. I followed her around the rest of the week and never really stopped.

As we head to homeroom, I notice an immediate difference in the atmosphere of Our Lady of Mercy from Wilbur High in the lack of graffiti, hallway fights, and bathroom smoking. Not having to worry about being shoved into a locker or tripped in the hallway is a disorienting experience.

Moira leads me to senior homeroom, which is another thing I find strange. The school is small enough that each grade fits into a single classroom. I've barely sat down before I'm set upon by a dark-haired white girl with two perfect French braids and perfectly manicured nails.

"You're new," she says, extending a hand, and I wonder if she thinks she's telling me something I didn't already know. "I'm Rebecca-Ann Taylor, senior class president and cofounder of our school's chapter of Women in Christ. I can get you signed up right now. We meet twice weekly. Once during lunch and once before school. What's your name?"

She's already pulled out a purple pen and a notebook embossed with what I presume are her own initials, poised to write my name down. I glance at Moira frantically, but she just looks amused.

"Err, I'm good actually," I say. Rebecca-Ann has already started writing something down before my words seem to fully process, and she looks up.

"Excuse me?"

"I'm good," I repeat, more confidently this time. I don't think there's anything I want to join less than a group called Women in Christ.

"What I believe my friend here is saying is *'Buh-bye,'*" Moira says with a little wave.

Rebecca-Ann purses her lips but puts her notebook into her purse with a huff, then walks away.

Beside me, Moira starts cracking up, and I think she might even be crying a little bit.

"You might have given me some warning," I say.

Moira wipes the tears from her eyes. "No," she says. "No, I really couldn't."

I feel like I'm treading water all the way from homeroom until Moira guides me to a corner table during lunch. It's bad enough being the new kid, but it's worse when you're the new kid in a school where everyone has a decade's worth of history and new blood is as rare as Jesus himself returning from the dead.

"So," Moira says as I take a bite of my lunch. "First day. Thoughts?"

"I think I'm ready to graduate," I say. I adjust my skirt, then try to forget it exists. I imagine the circus instead. Pretend that's my real life and this is just a dream. A very bad dream.

A piercing noise sends the cafeteria into momentary silence.

"And it begins," Moira says when she sees where the noise has originated from. Rebecca-Ann stands at a table by the end of the food line, bullhorn in one hand, clipboard in the other.

"Attention, students of Our Lady of Mercy."

The room quiets some as people turn their attention toward the noise.

"Thank you. In case you don't know me, my name is Rebecca-Ann Taylor, class president and cofounder of our school's chapter of Women in Christ"—Moira rolls her eyes, and I wonder if Rebecca-Ann ever introduces herself with just her name—"and I will be collecting signatures for a petition in support of our brothers and sisters at Wilbur High School. I truly hope that I will get the full backing of the Our Mercy community in this trying time." She turns the microphone off and holds her clipboard out for a handful of students who have already wandered over.

Though Rebecca-Ann never specifically states why the students at Wilbur need our support, I have a sinking feeling in the pit of my stomach.

"What do you think that's about?" I ask Moira, hoping she has an answer that makes this feeling go away.

"Don't know, and couldn't possibly care less," she says. I look back at the table Rebecca-Ann has set up. A small crowd has already gathered, and more students appear to be on their way over.

"Ugh," says Moira when she sees where I'm looking. "She totally did that on purpose."

"Did what?"

"Didn't say what her stupid petition is about. Now if you want to find out, you have to go up and ask her about it. It's very clever." She narrows her eyes. "I hate it."

"Not as much as you're going to hate this," I say next, before standing up. "Sorry."

"Nooooooo! If you go up there, she wins!"

"It's my old school," I say. "And I think whatever's going on involves my grandfather. He got a phone call from the principal of Wilbur last night. I need to know what's happening. I'm not going to sign her petition," I add, though I can tell from Moira's face that detail makes little difference in the perceived betrayal of my actions.

"You're dead to me," Moira says. "Unless you come back with one of Marge's cookies, in which case I might again acknowledge your presence."

I snort, then head over to the table Rebecca-Ann has set up. A few students have already signed the petition by the time I reach it.

Rebecca-Ann perks up when she sees me.

"You transferred in from Wilbur High, didn't you?"

I nod.

She makes a pitying sound. "I know we didn't get off on the right foot this morning, but I just want to say I am *so* glad you are here, and I know it would be a particularly powerful statement to have your signature on my petition. I'm glad to know Our Lady could be here for you to conclude your educational journey in light of what's happening over at Wilbur."

"I'm sorry," I say, "but what exactly *is* your petition for?"

Rebecca-Ann's eyebrows shoot up. I wonder if she's always this extra.

"Oh, it's just awful," she says before honest-to-goodness putting her hand over her heart. She lowers her voice to a whisper, so I have to lean in to hear her.

"They're thinking of letting a boy use the girls' bathrooms and locker rooms," she says, "just because he says he's really a girl." She shudders. "The principal is working to stop it, God bless him, but I can't even imagine." She looks back up at me. "That's why I started Women in Christ. We women need to stick together now more than ever."

I don't say anything. I can't. My throat feels like it's closing up, and I can't get enough air. I feel the edges of my vision going black, and I know I need to get out of here. I need—

I push my way out of the crowd of students gathered behind me, past the lunch table where Moira sits, past the doors separating the cafeteria from the courtyard outside, and once I'm there I lean over the perfectly manicured bushes and empty the contents of my stomach, the bile sour on my tongue.

Moira's behind me a minute later, her hand hot against my back.

"I know," she says as I stand, wiping my mouth with the back of my hand. "I went to see what the petition was about, and you know what? Screw her. Seriously. You're worth a hundred of her."

I know Moira means well. She's the only person in my life who knows I'm trans, and she's been completely supportive from day one. I couldn't ask for a better friend, which is exactly why I don't want her pity right now. Because if she knew the real reason I left Wilbur High, I don't think she'd want to be my friend anymore. And I don't know what I'd do if that happened.

I look up, steeling my gaze. "It's fine," I say. "I'm fine. Let's head back inside."

FOUR

The first thing I do when the bell rings at the end of the day is dash to the bathroom and change out of my uniform. A simple black T-shirt, a pair of overalls I picked out at the Goodwill, sneakers, and a faded red baseball cap under which I stuff my hair, and I finally look like myself again. Or the most acceptable version of myself I've found outside my dreams. I don't spend long looking at myself in the mirror; seeing Jesus staring back at me creeps me out. It's like one of those horror movies Moira's obsessed with. Every time there's a mirror, it's never just a mirror. Something else always seems to be staring back at you.

Moira waits outside the bathroom. "Ready?" she asks. I nod, and we start walking to her truck.

At the front of the school, Rebecca-Ann has set up another table. Though I try to keep my gaze straight ahead, I can't help but notice from the corner of my eye that she's gained quite a few signatures on her petition. I don't know whether all the students signed because they agree with her position or because she's so relentless, but it still stings.

As soon as Rebecca-Ann spots us, she gives us her full attention. Between Moira's dismissal this morning and my running out of the cafeteria at lunch, I would've thought that would be enough to scare her away. Apparently not.

"Moira, Ash—" As soon as she says Moira's name I know my own is coming, and I turn on the internal static I've worked so hard to develop over the years. I let the name pass through me, let it not sit heavy and wrong in my chest. If it were up to me, I'd never have to hear that name again. But it's not. At least not yet.

"We're not signing your petition," Moira says flatly. I'd prefer to keep walking, to make it out into the parking lot and finally pull away from this place. But Moira isn't like that; confrontation runs in her blood. She jokes that it's the curse of being the middle child in a large Irish family, but I think she'd be this way no matter what. Moira can't see an injustice and just keep walking.

Rebecca-Ann moves forward, holds up a picture of a rather sketchy-looking white man with a scraggly beard. He must be in his mid-forties at least. "So you're okay with letting men use the girls' restroom?" she says, thrusting the picture forward. "You don't find that even *remotely* concerning?"

Now Moira stops dead in her tracks, turns back to face Rebecca-Ann. We're so close to the door. So close to freedom, I can just about taste it. My body grows hot under my overalls, and it feels like the walls are starting to narrow in around me. I close my eyes for a moment and I'm back at Wilbur High. Back in the bathroom, trapped between the sink and the two girls, Kaycee looking at me for support, but I can't speak because my throat feels like it's closing up, and all I want is to be anywhere but there. Anywhere but *here*. "Come on, Moira," I say just loud enough for her to hear me. "We should go."

"You know what, *Rebecca-Ann*?" Moira says, ignoring me. "The only person I'm concerned about sharing any type of space with is you, but you haven't seen me creating a petition to ban your bigoted ass from the bathroom."

A few students snicker in the background while Rebecca-Ann glares at Moira. I look around and see a small crowd gathering, hovering on the edge of the doorway, waiting to see what happens next. More than a few look at me with curiosity, wondering perhaps who the kid out of uniform is. I feel anxious. I wish I could step outside myself and draw this moment with a pencil and paper instead of living it.

"And you know what else?" Moira says, not content to leave while her opponent still stands. "I don't think your cause has as much support as you think it does. *I think* people are just too scared to stand up to you. And I'm going to prove it." She turns back to me finally, a look in her eyes I know only too well, and says, "Come on." I follow along eagerly, and I don't look back.

Five minutes after leaving the school, Moira hits the steering wheel hard.

I raise my eyebrows. "Are you okay?"

"Ugh, I can't stand her! Where does she get off acting like she's better than everyone else? Just because she's got her stupid little notebook and her stupid little pen and her stupid little Jesus fan club? I hate anyone who uses religion to justify being an asshole. People like her clearly haven't read the same Bible as me!"

"Yeah," I say, because, well, I don't know what else to say. I don't disagree. I just don't want to think about this, about any of it. I close my eyes for a moment and envision the circus instead, imagine myself standing beneath the lights of the center ring.

"Sorry," Moira says, calming down slightly. She laughs.

"You know how I get when I'm worked up." I do. The light ahead of us turns green, and Moira pulls forward. "You're working today, right?"

I nod.

I spend a couple days a week helping Mr. Roberts at the art store in the center of town. Besides Moira's house, the shop is like my home away from home. He officially hired me a couple years ago, though I've hung out at the shop and done odd jobs for him since I became old enough to walk the twenty minutes into town by myself.

Moira pulls into the parking lot beside the art store and puts the truck in park.

"Do you have to run errands?" I ask, confused. Normally Moira drops me off in front of the store. It's not like there's much of interest on the grand Main Street of Wilbur, New Hampshire. Besides the art store, there's a gas station, church, animal shelter, liquor store, Dunkin' Donuts, pizza place, laundromat, and movie theater. And those are the highlights. Then there's everything else. The antique shop that's almost never open but also never goes out of business. That one shop on the corner that has been, in the past year and a half alone, a children's consignment shop, a gold and silver exchange, a video rental store, and yet another children's consignment shop. Apparently the nine-month gap between the first and the second was long enough to develop a renewed hope of a market for such a thing in our small town. Or, like Moira hypothesizes, the entire thing is a front for some sketchy business, and that's why none of these ideas sticks around all that long. Either way, there's not much here for Moira to do, unless perhaps she's got a particular craving for some greasy pizza.

"I'm coming in with you," she answers. "If this girl thinks she's the only one who can make pretty signs, then she's got another thing coming."

I don't know exactly what that means, but I'm sure I'll find out.

The bell above the door signals our entrance to the small shop on the corner of Main and Greene. There's no one at the counter, which means Mr. Roberts is likely out back.

"Do you need any help?" I ask Moira.

"I'm good! I'll wander."

She sets off down an aisle as I throw my backpack behind the counter. It bulges as much as it did this morning, only this time the extra bulk is from my uniform, not my regular clothing. I figure the bell above the door will let me know if a customer comes in, so I head out back to find Mr. Roberts.

As expected, he's in the stockroom unpacking some boxes.

"Ah, Ash," he says. "Come take a look at these." That's something I like about Mr. Roberts. He's always called me Ash, even from the very first time I met him when I was a little kid, and my grandmother brought me in to buy colored pencils for school. I remember she introduced me to him with my full name, and while she went to look for some stationery for herself, he bent down, green eyes meeting mine, and said, "You seem more like an Ash to me. Do I have that right?" And then he smiled, winked, and has called me that ever since.

He waves me over, and I almost gasp when I see what he wants to show me. Three boxes of the Derwent watercolor pencils, seventy-two count in that sweet, sweet wooden box. The set probably sells for at least $150, probably more at a small local shop like this. Mr. Roberts picks up a set and hands it to me to look at. There's a picture on the cover of the cardboard box the set comes packaged in—two Italian gondolas, one blue and one orange—not quite gold, but close enough that my mind flashes back to the tent in my dreams. Now this is a set suitable for capturing the circus.

I reluctantly hand the box back to Mr. Roberts. He sets it down before standing up. It doesn't escape my attention the way his blue veins have become pronounced beneath his papery-white skin, or how he leans heavier on his cane than he used to, and I wonder whether he might hang up his hat soon. He's certainly old enough to retire, but I can't imagine the downtown without him. I can't imagine my life without him.

"Bring that box out front, would you?" I pick up the box of colored pencils and follow Mr. Roberts out of the stockroom. When I see Moira standing at the counter, I realize I'd forgotten she was still here.

I put down the box I'm carrying and go to ring her up.

"Jesus," I say as I look at her pile. She's got something like half a dozen poster boards, a large pack of permanent markers, glitter, glue, *glitter glue*, a clipboard, a pad of legal paper, a multi-colored selection of pens, and a nice hardcover journal. "Maybe you should ask Mr. Roberts if you can buy the store while you're at it."

Moira flips me off, then pulls a debit card from her wallet and hands it over. She doesn't even blink as I read the total: $94.42. My grandparents are plenty wealthy, so it's not like I'm unaccustomed to folks with money, but I never forget it's theirs. That their money, much like their love, comes with conditions. Moira's family isn't wealthy in the same way my grandparents are, but they're certainly well-off. The fact that she can drop nearly $100 on a whim is evidence of that.

"Will you need a ride home later?" Moira asks as I bag up her supplies.

I shake my head. "It's nice out. I'll walk home."

She nods, then blows me a kiss. "Love ya!"

The bell above the door rings as she leaves the shop, and then it's just Mr. Roberts and me once more.

I return to the box I'd brought out front. "Where do you want these?"

"Over here!"

I go to where Mr. Roberts has cleared some space with the rest of the colored pencils and start unpacking the box. Besides the three Derwent seventy-two-count packs, there are some twelve- and thirty-six-count boxes, as well as a variety of other brands. I arrange them neatly on the shelf, making note of where stock is low so Mr. Roberts can place an order.

"Ah, not that one," Mr. Roberts says, and I pause, the twelve-count pack still in my hand. I look down, not seeing any tears or dents on the box. When that happens, we'll sometimes use those ones as samples for customers to try on the pads of paper that line many of the shelves. And then, when they get worn down enough that they don't look appealing anymore, Mr. Roberts usually lets me take them home. I have quite a selection of mismatched pens and pencils from doing that.

"Take that box home," he says, "and some watercolor paper too." Before I can protest, he holds up a hand. "Don't give me that look—I'm going to make you work for it. I want you to draw something for me, something we can use to show off what these pencils can do. These boxes aren't going to sell themselves."

I look down at the pencils in my hand. Even a smaller set

like this goes for about $30, way more than I've ever spent on so few pencils, even with the generous employee discount Mr. Roberts gives me. Not that I've needed to use it recently with the way he keeps maneuvering art supplies into my hands. I should refuse, but I've got other plans for the money I've saved. I know it's unrealistic to think about any future other than the one my grandparents have so carefully orchestrated, but sometimes late at night I fantasize about going away to an art school, somewhere in one of those big cities, like New York, or San Francisco, or Chicago. A few hundred dollars saved in a box under my bed is nothing compared to the tens of thousands of dollars I'll lose from my grandparents if I don't do what they want me to do, but it still feels like something. It feels like hope.

"Anything in particular you want me to draw?" I ask, but Mr. Roberts just waves his hand as he walks back to the counter. My hands itch to tear open the box and get to work. "I'll have the picture for you the next time I come in," I say. I know *exactly* what I'm going to draw.

I spend the walk home fantasizing about all the things I'll make with my new colored pencils. But mostly I fantasize about the circus. I still remember the first time I dreamed of it. It was the night after Mom declared I would be attending Catholic school for my senior year. But it wasn't until last night that I was able to get more than a glimpse, more than a hint of what lay beyond the trees.

I know it was just a dream, but it felt *so real*. And unlike most other dreams I have, very little of it has faded since waking up. If I close my eyes, I almost feel like I could reach out and touch the cool, slick fabric of the tent.

When I finally get home, I almost miss the turn for our driveway, not because of my fantasizing, but because there's a giant moving truck parked directly in front of it, blocking us in. I squeeze between the back of the truck and a row of hedges and find my mom, all five feet two inches of her, standing on the step, cigarette in hand, peering through the rolled-down window of the truck.

"Mom?"

At the sound of my voice, she hops down and gestures angrily toward our neighbors' house—the farmhouse. "Honestly! If it's not one thing with them, it's another!"

For most of my life the farmhouse was a ramshackle building falling slowly into decay, a total playground for the child of an overworked mom. Moira and I used to spend a lot of time over there, daring each other to do dangerous shit, like climbing up into the loft of the barn and walking across the exposed beam and back again, or scaling the tree that constantly seemed one rogue gust of wind away from crashing into the second story of the house. It's also where I came out to Moira the summer after seventh grade, lying in the shadow of the barn one hot night looking up at the stars.

But then the *neighbors* arrived. Or rather, the construction equipment. Twelve long weeks of digging and tearing down and rebuilding until the house looked essentially the same as before but with a new coat of paint. Six days a week, from seven in the morning until eight in the evening. Mom struggled to sleep for months after working overnights at the hospital, and I still flinch when I hear the sound of a truck backing up.

And now this.

"Don't they have enough furniture?" I look toward the

farmhouse and see Mrs. Bennett standing outside, directing a couple of movers as they carry a bedframe into the house. She seems to be quite pointedly avoiding looking in our direction.

Mom drops her cigarette on the ground and puts it out under her shoe before marching over to confront Mrs. Bennett, for what I suspect is not the first time. I bend down and pick up the cigarette butt, putting it into the front pocket of my overalls to throw away once I get inside.

When I stand back up, Mom is leading one of the movers back to the truck. I catch the end of her lecture ("—difference between life or death!") as he climbs into the truck, looking appropriately chagrined, and I know exactly what speech she's giving him about emergency vehicle response times, survival outcomes, and why you should never block the driveway. I take a step back as the driver climbs behind the wheel to pull the truck forward and out of the path of our driveway, but Mom remains standing beside it, arms crossed in that no-nonsense way of hers.

I don't get it. In so much of her life, Mom takes no shit from anyone. After my dad died, she put herself through nursing school as a single parent while still working shifts as a waitress at a local restaurant. When I was twelve, she dated a guy who came into my room once in the middle of the night, claiming he thought it was the bathroom. I woke up and screamed when I saw him standing there, and I swear I've never seen my mom as terrifying as she was when she marched him out the door at three in the morning, still in his boxers. It didn't matter in that moment that she stood only as high as his shoulder. He looked small compared to her.

So that's why I don't understand why she finally gave in to my grandparents' demands to send me to Catholic school.

When the truck has finally moved out from in front of our driveway, Mom drops her arms and turns to face me. "How was your day?" she asks. Without waiting for an answer, she comes closer, grabbing my chin and turning my face toward the sun. "Your scar is looking a lot better."

I pull away from her grasp and start walking down the driveway toward the house. "I'm fine. It's all fine." The front door is already open when I reach the house—Mom clearly forgot to shut it when she ran out to confront our neighbors, so I walk right through into the kitchen. Between forgetting to pack a snack for work and throwing up the little lunch I had, I'm absolutely ravenous. I pull out some turkey and cheese from the fridge, along with a jar of mayonnaise, and set them on the table.

"You know you can talk to me," Mom says, hovering behind me.

"What's to talk about?" I tip the nearly empty mayonnaise jar upside down over a slice of bread and smack it a few times until a small splattering falls out.

"How about your first day at school? Or perhaps why you look ready to murder that jar of mayonnaise?"

I look up, meet her eyes. "School sucked, and the mayonnaise had it coming." I return to the jar, smacking it even harder to make a point.

Mom rubs her fingers under her eyes. She looks exhausted. "I'm sure it can't have been that bad. And you know why I needed to move you to Our Lady."

41

"Do I?" I say. "Because it seems to me like I slipped on some water in the school bathroom, you freaked out, and now I'm stuck at Catholic school for my senior year."

"That's not what the school says happened," Mom says calmly. She grabs a knife, takes the jar from my hands, and scrapes the rest of the mayonnaise onto my bread.

"Didn't realize the school was in the bathroom with me." I pile the turkey and cheese onto the bread and shove another slice on top. I'm not having this conversation again. If Mom wants to know what really happened, she can come out and ask. Or better yet, let me drop out and go live in the woods as a hermit. Because at this point, I want to return to public school almost as little as I want to go back to Our Lady.

"What about Moira? I remember when you used to cry because you didn't go to the same school."

"Really? I'm not seven anymore." I rip off a large chunk of sandwich with my teeth and start chewing. Loudly.

Mom winces, which brings me some small pleasure. "Well, maybe I should've done this when you were seven," she says. "Wilbur was falling apart when I went there, and it's no better now. Our Lady of Mercy can help you get into a good college. And there are more scholarship opportunities for you there."

College? That's the defense she's using now?

My reaction must be clear on my face, because Mom frowns. "College is expensive. I've been putting money aside where I can, but it's tough."

"Grandma and Grandpa will pay for my college. I don't need scholarships." What goes unspoken in that statement are the many stipulations that money comes with. And the growing feeling that the path laid out so nicely for me might not be one I can follow.

"I can't let your grandparents pay for everything."

My phone buzzes at the same time, that three-part buzz of a text message being broken into parts because my phone can't handle even such a simple task, and suddenly it's all too much. All of it. This entire day from the skirt and the shoes to Rebecca-Ann and bathroom-fucking-Jesus and I can no longer keep it in.

"Right," I say, throwing my phone down onto the table. "No, not everything. Not even a real fucking phone. Whenever it's anything I actually want you'd rather stand in the way. But for the one thing, the *one thing* I asked you not to do, you're suddenly okay with spending my grandparents' money."

Mom purses her lips. "You know what? I'm done with this conversation. You don't like it? Tough shit. Turn eighteen and move out. Otherwise, go to your room. I'm sick of talking to you."

"Way ahead of you."

I grab my phone and storm up the stairs, slamming my door for good measure.

One day down. A hundred and seventy-nine more to go.

FIVE

The moon shines above the Midnight Circus.

I remember going to my room, remember pulling out the colored pencils Mr. Robert gave me and slipping away into that headspace where time has no meaning. I remember making a late dinner after Mom went to bed and climbing into bed myself, hoping, *praying* I'd come back, but I don't remember falling asleep. Only I must have, because I'm here now, Ferris wheel before me like a pool of cold water in the desert. For the first time all day I can breathe.

"Welcome back, 'mano!" Like last night, I have barely taken a step into the fairgrounds before I'm set upon by Seb. Tonight he's juggling two balls in his left hand, one red, one blue. He's not even looking at them as he does it. I trip when I'm not looking at my own feet, and he thinks I'm going to become a clown? Besides, funny is the *last* thing I feel after the day I had.

"Catch!" He tosses a ball at me, and my immediate reaction is to duck. The ball bounces once on the grass behind my head, then rolls down toward the trees. "We'll work on that," he says, frowning.

"Look," I say, "you seem like a nice guy, but is there someone I can talk to about this whole clown thing? I just think that maybe, *perhaps*, it's not the right role for me."

Seb dashes behind me to pick up the ball he threw. "I'm supposed to take you to meet René first," he says, "and then you'll get to watch the full show, since you didn't have a chance last night. And after, I'll introduce you around." He steamrolls past everything I said with such skill, I might have suspected he hadn't heard me had I not known better.

All I know is as long as Seb takes me to the man in charge, I *will* learn to fly.

I follow Seb past the food stalls and performances I still haven't had the chance to visit, past the main tent, where yesterday I failed at clowning, all the way to a long train resting in the grass, despite a lack of tracks nearby. The train isn't sleek and modern like the one I rode with my grandparents on a trip to Washington, DC. These are wooden boxcars, bright red like the one on the cover of my favorite book from when I was a kid. Seb scales a ladder on the side. I follow closely and start to wonder if he's actually bringing me to meet this René fellow, or if my dream is about to take a dark turn and end with a strange clown murdering me in the woods.

Then we reach the top. Seb steps aside so I can see what lies beyond the boxcar—a tent village. Fabrics bright and muted, polka-dotted and striped, cloth patched and torn and patched again spread like an oversize quilt across a valley. Strings of lights crisscross narrow pathways where folks gather for conversations before disappearing beneath another tent.

"This," Seb says, "is where the real fun happens." He scurries down the other side of the train, and I hurry after him, lest I lose him in the maze ahead. It becomes clear I needn't worry about losing Seb, since he's incapable of moving more than a few feet without introducing me to one performer or another.

After almost tripping over someone folded so far over himself that just looking at him makes my back ache, I meet Vikram, one of the circus's contortionists.

"Pleasure," he says, extending a hand for me to shake. With the way he's all folded up like origami, I have to bend down to reach it.

"Before you ask, I've already claimed him. He's mine," Seb says, making a two-fingered motion between his eyes and Vikram as though to say he'll be watching him. I'm amused by the idea I could ever be a contortionist. I can barely touch my toes.

Seb introduces me to about a dozen more people, none of whom is René, and it's hard to keep all their names straight. With each one, Seb repeats his claim on me. I feel like a stray dog adopted by the class clown, literally.

Finally, we stop at a single caravan at the edge of the camp. Seb raps on the door until a man opens it. He's younger than I expected, mid-thirties perhaps, with reddish hair and green eyes. There's something familiar about him, but I can't quite place it.

"Thank you, Seb," he says, studying me for a moment. "You can run along. I'll give him to Fizz when I'm done."

As much as Seb has been a tad overbearing, him leaving me alone with René is a little unsettling. I remind myself this is a dream (no matter how little it feels like one), and it's time to take control. I steel myself and extend a hand.

"Asher," I say.

"René," replies the man. "Come inside. Sorry it's a little tight."

I step inside and look around. There's not much to see. A desk and a worn-down chair, a couch covered in blankets. Photos plastered everywhere and filing cabinets against the back wall. René takes a seat and gestures for me to sit on the couch.

"One moment," he says. I wait as he pulls something from his desk drawer. It's a notebook. An old one by the looks of it, leather bound with a brass clasp. René opens it and grabs a pen. With his left hand, he scribbles something on one of the pages. When it dries, he closes the notebook. "There," he says.

"What was that?" I ask.

"That," René says, "was me officially welcoming you. Now, tell me, how are you finding the circus so far?"

How am I finding the circus? I glance down, taking a deep breath into my flat chest. I think of how I've been treated, as Asher, as a guy, as myself. No one here is surprised by what they see in me. Nobody here knows any different.

"It's perfect," I say.

"Excellent." René says. "I can see Seb's taking his mentorship role seriously. I think you'll be good for him. Unbridled energy needs an outlet. A good project for the both of you, I think."

"Right," I say. "About that—"

"You should have seen him when he first arrived." He chuckles. "Ah, he was such a little troublemaker. Still is, if we're being honest, but he's a good kid."

"He seems great," I say. "But—"

"Goodness! Look at the time! Here I am reminiscing, and I've got a show to run. I'll have Fizz take you back, and we'll chat more later. I have a good feeling about you!"

Before I can say anything else, René jumps up, throws open the door, and shouts for Fizz, whoever that is. A minute later, a young white man appears in a fantastic outfit—a tuxedo the color of lapis lazuli with black satin lapels, eyes like robin's eggs sparkling from behind a shimmering mask of sapphire, emerald, and amethyst feathers, golden-white hair shining in the starlight.

"Ah, Fizz, excellent. This is Asher."

"Seb's new one, right?"

René nods. "Can you walk him back, get him settled for the show? I need to prepare my remarks."

"Sure thing, boss," he says, then to me, "You can come with me."

I stand but don't exit. "There was something I wanted to discuss," I say, finally managing a complete sentence.

"Yes, yes," René says, "plenty of time to discuss things later. But now I've got a show to put on, and you've got a show to enjoy! You should have just enough time to get some popcorn from Gino. I guarantee you've never tasted popcorn this good. Now, allez-vous!" He shoos me out the door, then shuts it behind me.

"Welcome to the circus," says Fizz with a chuckle.

We walk back to the main tent, stopping to get some popcorn like René suggested. And it is the best damn popcorn I've ever had. It's hot and buttery, with just the right amount of salt. None of the pieces is soggy, or too dry, and there aren't any kernels trying to break my teeth like at the discount theater I go to with Moira. As I shovel popcorn into my mouth like there's no tomorrow, I decide the only way it could be better is if it was mixed with caramel popcorn, and then I taste that sweet, slightly sticky flavor with my next bite. Fizz laughs as I stare in wonderment.

"What is this place?" I ask, more rhetorically than literally, but Fizz responds anyway.

"An escape," he says. Before I can ask what he's escaping from, he continues. "Come on," he says, "there's someone I want you to meet."

Fizz leads us toward the young woman who I had spotted making balloon animals last night. Her dark brown hands move deftly as she twists long balloons into anything and everything a person could dream of. Her hair is buzzed short on both sides of her head, with cool swirled patterns shaved into it, while her curls sit atop her head. Gold earrings line the length of her ear, which I notice as she bends down to allow a young child to whisper a request. She smiles, squeezes the child's shoulder, and gets to work. In less than a minute, the child is driving around the grassy field in a small clown car made of balloons, enchanted by whatever magic this place holds. There's even a working horn, which squeaks each time the child squeezes it. I can't look away, nor can I stop grinning.

Fizz makes his way closer to the balloon woman and pulls her close for a chaste kiss. Her face lights up, and she's still smiling, exposing a small gap between her top two teeth, as she turns toward me.

"This is Asher," Fizz says. "He's the newest performer."

"Gemma," the balloon artist says. "Welcome to the circus!"

"Thank you," I say, taking her outstretched hand in mine. Just then, fireworks erupt above the tent.

Five Minutes, the fireworks spell out in impossibly clear lettering. *Please take your seats.*

"That's our cue," Fizz says to Gemma.

"I'll see you after the show," she says, before kissing Fizz one last time. "Both of you."

I wave goodbye, then follow Fizz to the front of the tent.

This is further into the evening than I got yesterday, and I hope tonight I won't be pulled prematurely from this dream. I'd certainly like a chance to see the show.

"Tickets! Tickets, please!"

Fizz pulls a ticket out of his pocket, then hands it to me. Like the tent, it's gold and blue.

Midnight Circus, it reads in bold swirling letters across the top. *Admit One, Asher Sullivan.*

I hand it to the man standing at the entrance to the tent. He looks down and then hands it back without ripping it or anything. I look back down and am surprised to see the ticket has now changed. Where it had once read *Admit One*, it now reads *Admitted*. And below my name is a seat number I swear wasn't there a moment ago.

"And this is where I leave you," says Fizz. "Seb will come fetch you after the show."

My seat is located in the middle of the front row. I'm not sure there is a better seat in the whole arena to see everything perfectly.

The lights dim, and the crowd goes silent. From the back of the tent the ringleader comes out. It's René, here to introduce the show. I mouth the words to his introduction along with him.

When René is done the performance begins, and it's like nothing I've ever seen. The acts weave together to tell the story of a young girl lost in a strange jungle. Seb and Maisie are her only guides. Trees grow onstage as though by magic, and water pours from the roof of the tent in a waterfall onto which fantastical images are projected. When she reaches an orange grove, the tent fills with the scent of oranges, and through the trees performers dressed as monkeys do acrobatics while an aerialist performs, suspended in the air by a single rope wrapped around her wrist as though swinging through the trees on a vine.

The show continues. Acrobats dodge flying knives and jump through rings of bright blue fire. A ballerina dressed as a fairy flits across the stage and bestows small globes of light upon the young girl and her two guides to guide them home. Seb swallows the globe of light and immediately begins floating in the air. He tries to reach the ground unsuccessfully to much laughter from the audience, prompting Maisie to swallow her ball of light and begin floating as well to try to grab on to him. The skit continues for a bit, and by the end tears are streaming down my face from laughing so hard. Seb truly is meant to be a clown.

Finally, just as the young girl is about to reach home and part ways with Seb and Maisie, there's one last performance. The young man I met yesterday scales the ladder to the trapeze. My heart leaps in my chest.

Watching him perform tonight is on a scale that can't even be compared to the one trick I saw yesterday. He soars through the air, his body twisting and turning, spinning and stretching with both power and grace. I would do anything to fly like that.

When the act ends, the two performers take a bow before scrambling back to join the rest of the cast for one final number. In it, the young girl says one last goodbye to each of her friends before the sun rises and she climbs into her bed, safe at last.

The audience jumps to its feet with a thunderous roar of applause, and all I know is I never want to leave.

SIX

I stay in my seat after the show ends, waiting for Seb. I reach into my pocket, pull out my sketchbook and a pencil, never far away even in my dreams. My fingers itch to record what I've seen, to transcribe it into the language I know best. I flip open to a blank page, and my hand begins its own flight, across the page, turning graphite into images. I draw everything: Seb juggling onstage, Fizz in his mask, Gemma with her balloons, René in his caravan, and the boy who flies across the stage. The boy whose name I still don't know. When I close my eyes, I can see him standing in front of me the way he was last night, brown eyes inches from mine, lips parted slightly . . .

"That's a pretty good likeness, 'mano, but you haven't quite captured my roguishly handsome good looks."

In my concentration, I didn't notice Seb sitting down next to me. I clear my throat, wondering if my face is as red as it feels. He grabs the sketchbook from my hands before I can protest and starts flipping through it.

"Hmm," he says. "Well, you certainly didn't spare any effort capturing *his* looks." He gives me a pointed look, and I know if I wasn't blushing before, I certainly am now. "Everybody loves a flyboy, but nobody spares a second glance for the clown. Normally I'd say it's my lot in life, but we clowns need to stick together!" He drapes an arm across my shoulder and sighs dramatically.

I decide to take my chance.

"Can you introduce me?"

Seb cocks an eyebrow. "To Apollo?"

Apollo. That's his name. I nod, trying not to seem too eager. The way he flew through the air . . . I need to learn, and I need *him* to teach me.

"Nah, vato, you don't want that," Seb says. "That boy has got a stick up his ass. Look, I'll introduce you to anyone else, but trust me when I say he's not going to give you whatever it is you're looking for."

I feel the desperation sink into my voice. "Please," I beg.

Seb sighs. "Well, luckily for you, unluckily for the rest of us, you'd be hard-pressed not to meet him where we're going. Now, come on!"

I follow Seb more confidently this time, recognizing the path back to the tent village where I'd met René before the show. Instead of taking us down the center of the fair where all the action is happening, we bob and weave behind stands and stalls, even ducking inside the tent of a fortune teller I hadn't known was there, just so Seb can pretend to be a ghost and spook one of the patrons inside. He cackles as we're chased from the fortune teller tent by Madame Zostra, whose real name is apparently Celeste.

"She loves me," he says. I'm skeptical.

He seems to know everyone and everyone knows him, but it's a relief when I finally see two people I already know.

"Fizz! Gemma!"

They turn, and Fizz gives me a big grin and comes over and pulls me into a hug. "Asher!" he says. "How did you like the show?"

"It was . . ." I feel like a fish as my mouth opens and closes, but I can't seem to find the words to describe how I felt. How do you describe the moment you know your life has changed forever and irrevocably? What words could possibly be sufficient?

Fizz laughs. "Seems about right."

"What was your favorite part?" Gemma asks.

"The flying trapeze," I say without hesitation.

"Ouch," Seb says, stumbling back as he pretends to take an arrow to the heart.

"And the clowns," I add quickly, to laughter from Fizz and Gemma.

"I was hoping to meet him," I say. "Apollo, I mean. Seb says he was the one flying on the trapeze."

"Are you talking about me?" a voice says, and from a tent nearby pops out a young man I recognize instantly.

"No," Seb says at the same time Fizz says, "Yes."

"Who's the stray?"

Seb steps forward, stands in front of me possessively. "*Stray?* As I recall, you're practically still a stray yourself."

Apollo's mouth cocks up. "'Course he's yours."

"What's that supposed to mean?"

I step forward, stick out my hand. "Asher," I say, feel the tiny thrill that rises up when I introduce myself. When I say my name and it's not a whisper, not in front of my mirror in the dead of night, when the lights are out and it feels safe to say out loud. "I'm Asher."

He glances at my hand, then looks away without taking it.

I drop my hand, ignore the phantom sensation of his hand grabbing my wrist the way he did last night. I push forward, ignoring the daggers Seb is shooting at Apollo.

54

"I saw you in the show," I say. "You were . . ." I pause, try to find the words. "Well, incredible, though that hardly seems strong enough of a word. I mean, it was amazing, and anyways, I wanted to meet you because I thought maybe you could teach me. How to fly, I mean."

Shit. Could that have been any more awkward?

Apollo looks at me with an expression that might best be compared to the one you'd make when your roommate's new puppy shits on your rug.

"Well, I'm pleased you enjoyed the show, but we aren't really looking for new aerialists. But I'm sure Seb would be happy to take you under his wing. Well, metaphorically." Apollo leans in, smirks, then says in a mock whisper everyone can hear quite clearly, "He's afraid of heights." He glances at Fizz and Gemma, gives them both a nod in acknowledgment, and walks away.

"I'm not afraid of heights," Seb mutters as I watch Apollo disappear between the rows of tents. "God gave us two feet for a reason. Not so we could fly around like birds."

"Sorry about him," Fizz says, wincing.

"He's still pretty new," Gemma adds. "I'm sure he'll come around."

Once Seb has moved (mostly) past Apollo's parting comments— he decides I need to experience the full wonders of the fair, or the midway, as he calls it. "Just this once, mind you," he says. "I can't be seen wandering around all starry-eyed by the Ferris wheel like some First of May, no offense or anything." I don't take offense, because I don't understand a word of what he said, but as we eat our way through the midway, it seems to me he's enjoying himself plenty, despite all the talk.

We stop to get more popcorn and candy apples, and then Seb drags me to the top of the railcar with two bottles of a fizzy soda that seems to change flavor with each sip as we sit and watch the crowd, performers on one side and everyone else on the other. I focus my attention on two old men not too far away from us. Unlike many of the other circus goers, they aren't running back and forth, spinning and twirling like children in a candy store. Instead they sit, backs against a tall oak tree, holding hands as they pass a chocolate ice cream cone back and forth. The shorter man says something to the taller one, a cheeky grin on his face, causing the taller one to double over in laughter. It's so tender it makes my heart ache. I wonder if I'll ever have that.

"Does everyone come back?" I ask Seb. I gesture to the midway, to all the other patrons of the circus enjoying their evening without sparing a second glance for the soon rising sun.

"Nah," he says. "I mean, maybe once or twice for some of them, but most of them won't be back again."

"Then how can you be so sure that I will?" I ask, struck with a sharp and sudden pain at the thought of having to leave this place behind. At never getting the chance to fly, regardless of what Apollo said.

This makes Seb pause, and he looks a little surprised. "I thought you already knew that, vato," he says. "People like us"—he gestures here to us and the folks on the tent side of the train—"we come back because we need to."

We come back because we need to.

I look at Seb, and I wonder for the first time who this boy is, underneath all the jokes and the laughter. Wonder what he sees when he looks at me.

"All right, all right, enough with the serious face," Seb says as he throws some popcorn at me. I laugh and throw some back, as behind us the sun completes its journey back across the horizon and my second night at the Midnight Circus comes to a close.

SEVEN

Mom's making breakfast when I wake up on Sunday morning. I don't know which part is weirder, Mom being awake while I get ready for church or Mom making breakfast, but I know a reconciliation attempt when I see one. We've barely spoken since our fight on Monday, and despite my making it clear at every moment that I'm displeased at my new school, she still hasn't budged.

But that's going to change today, because I have a plan.

"Morning, sweetheart," Mom says as I sit down at the table. "How did you sleep?"

"Good."

She sets down a plate in front of me. "Your grandparents called, said to remind you to take a jacket since you'll be stopping at the cemetery after your father's Memorial Mass."

Dad's Memorial Mass—we have one each year near his birthday. Other than his name being printed in the church program, it's really no different than any other Sunday Mass, but we always stop at the cemetery after and then go out to eat. And this year, Mom's going to join us.

She just doesn't know that yet.

"Will you come?" I say. I take a bite of the bacon. It's burned. I try not to grimace as I wash it down with some water.

"Come where?"

"Come to Dad's Mass," I say casually, as if Mom has stepped foot in a church even once since his funeral. As if she's ever spent time voluntarily with his parents, my grandparents, in all these years.

She fumbles the pan from which she'd been shoveling eggs, dumping nearly all of them onto my plate in the process, her discomfort apparent. I'd feel worse, but if she truly wanted to experience discomfort, she should try being a closeted trans guy at a Catholic school.

"Oh, hun, I don't think—"

I push ahead. "So you get to send me to Catholic school, but you won't even come to a Mass for your husband? For my father? How is that not hypocritical?"

"I don't think your grandparents will want me there."

"*I* want you there."

There's silence. We're in a standoff, but I know how to play this game.

A minute passes, two. She sighs, looks down at the ripped jeans and faded band T-shirt she's wearing.

"I should probably go get dressed in something nicer."

I've won. I try to hide my grin as she stands and heads to her room to get changed.

Check and, soon, mate.

If my grandparents are surprised when I tell them Mom will be joining us for Mass this morning, they do a good job of not letting it show. My plan seems doomed from the start, when my grandmother rolls down her window and tells my mom she has a few minutes if she'd like to run inside and freshen up before church. I look at what my mother's currently wearing, a spaghetti-strapped floral dress that comes down a few inches above her knee, and black flats. I know for a fact Mom is already wearing her most church-appropriate outfit, but she thanks my grandmother politely before heading back inside. She returns five minutes later smelling of cigarettes but otherwise looking exactly the same.

"You look nice, dear," my grandmother says without looking up.

We ride to church in silence, interspersed only with terse pleasantries. Mom fidgets beside me as though unsure what to do with her hands. She twists her wedding ring on her finger, twice to the right, once to the left, then does it again. My dad's been gone fourteen years, so many years I'm not sure the memories I have of him are even my own, but she still wears her wedding ring every day. I wonder if I'll ever know love like that.

We reach the church, and as we step inside, Mom looks around, eyes wide as she takes it all in. Spending as much time here as I have over the years, it's hard for me to appreciate how intense the physical structure is, but as I watch Mom look around it's like I'm seeing it for the first time. The vaulted ceiling stretches toward the heavens, gold leafing painted onto each of the ribs, while tall stained-glass windows line the sides of the nave, the early morning light decorating the pews in fractured rainbows. A large mural depicting two angels covers the wall behind the altar, a large crucifix hung in the middle, while above, the ceiling is painted to look like a starry night. Even the layout of the building itself is in the shape of a giant cross. No one does ostentatious quite like the Catholic Church.

Once inside, Grandma steers us to a pew, much farther back than we'd normally sit, and without any of the socializing she would normally engage in before Mass. I catch Mom studying the Stations of the Cross hung on the wall as we slide into the pew, the series of wooden reliefs depicting Jesus's crucifixion so helpfully hung around the nave to remind us that to live is to suffer.

"Pretty fucking grim, isn't it?" she leans over and whispers, and I have to choke back the laugh threatening to escape because I'm still pissed at her and making her feel comfortable is not the way to convince her to pull me from Catholic school. But also, yes, they're pretty fucking grim.

Grandpa joins us a minute later, passing down a handful of programs. I turn to the back, to the part that has Dad's name, and I show it to Mom. She runs her finger over his name, then puts it down on the bench beside her.

Peter John Sullivan. My father. A man I hardly remember, and yet his legacy looms over so much of my life. The prodigal son who graduated high school at sixteen, who was so smart he got into every college he applied to, but chose to stay close to home to raise his newborn child and marry his young girl-friend. A family man destined for career success, groomed to take over his father's law firm from the time he was a child. But I don't remember any of that. Those are just stories I've heard time and time again from my grandparents, reminders of all I have to live up to. There's a picture I have, which I keep in my room and look at from time to time, of me and my dad when I was a baby, probably only six months old or so, still young enough I fit in the clothing my parents purchased before I was born, before they knew whether I'd be a boy or a girl. My hair's short, just beginning to grow in, and I'm dressed in blue over-alls, a knit sweater, and a pair of black-and-white Nike shoes.

It's my favorite picture, because when I look at it I can imagine he knew, when he was holding me there, that I was really his son.

I wonder how much would be different if he were still here. Would he have already taken over his father's law firm? Would he expect me to take up the mantle from him, the third generation of the Sullivan family to go into law, or would he know that isn't me? If I didn't feel so much pressure to fulfill his dreams, would I be less afraid to pursue my own?

Unfortunately, that's a question I'll never have the answer to, because he's dead, and I'm still here, the only family my mom and my grandparents have.

Mass begins as the priest approaches the altar. We all stand, Mom a half beat behind everyone else.

The first hymn is one I know well, one I've sung probably hundreds of times in my life, which is why it's strange to remember that Mom wouldn't know any of the words. I watch her flip through the hymnal to the page listed on the board in the front of the church and begin to sing along. Each verse has the same melody, so by the time we reach the second, she's picked it up and has begun to sing with confidence. Fortunately for Mom, she has a lovely voice. Unfortunately, she has no way of knowing we only ever sing the first three verses of this particular hymn, so her voice echoes through the church on verse four before she realizes she's singing alone.

Everyone in the church turns around to look. Grandma sucks in a sharp breath while my mother slowly closes the book and sets it back down. Father DeMelo clears his throat and begins the sign of the cross, at which point everyone turns their attention back.

"They shouldn't print the fourth verse if you aren't supposed to sing it," Mom mutters beside me.

Mass continues, and Mom keeps her mouth shut during all future songs, which is probably for the best. The only real indication she's still here is the fact that she is perpetually a half beat behind the rest of us when we transition between sitting, standing, and kneeling, which happens quite frequently. I take pity on her and start gesturing right before a transition. I think perhaps we might make it through the rest of Mass without anything else happening, until Father DeMelo begins the eucharistic prayer.

"Take this, all of you, and eat of it, for this is my body, which will be given up for you."

Mom sits up straighter beside me.

The priest continues. "Take this, all of you, and drink from it, for this is the chalice of my blood, the blood of the new and eternal covenant, which will be poured out for you and for many for the forgiveness of sins. Do this in memory of me."

"Jesus Christ," Mom whispers, which, yes. Actually. "They *ate* him?"

A snort bursts out of me before I can stop myself, and though I try to disguise it as a cough, Grandma still squeezes my hand like she's actively trying to break all my bones. When we stand to take Communion, Mom slides out on the right to let me out, and I think Grandma is afraid Mom is going to get in line, because she begins frantically waving her hands from the left-hand aisle to get her attention. Mom raises an eyebrow as she slides back into the pew. "As if I want any part of *that*."

After Communion are the announcements, which is where

the priest dedicates the Mass to my father, and then, finally, it's over. I have a feeling my grandparents, my grandmother in particular, would like nothing more at this point than to flee from the church, taking my mother far away from this place, but the very reason my mom is at this Mass is the very reason they can't do that.

A crowd, larger than usual, gathers in the aisle near our pew to greet my grandparents and politely ask about my father, a man none of them have ever met. My grandparents introduce my mother and then break into their regularly prescribed commentary on my father, and on me.

Yes, he died much too young.

Oh, she's the spitting image of him.

A senior, can you believe it? Feels like just yesterday she was toddling between the pews.

She'll be taking over the law firm soon enough. She's ambitious, like her father. A talented artist too. We're so proud.

Oh, and this is her mother, Abigail. It's so nice to have her here to remember our son.

Mom stays largely quiet through all these interactions, shaking hands and greeting folks politely before retreating back into silence, but her flaring nostrils tell me that beneath her cool exterior, she's ready to blow. I knew she'd be uncomfortable here, counted on it in fact, but each time my grandparents introduce her as though she's an afterthought, as though Peter was only their son and my father rather than her husband, I find myself joining in her frustration, until I can't take it anymore.

"You know, Mom asked if she could come today," I say to Mr. and Mrs. Kelly, who are talking to my grandmother. Mom looks at me curiously but doesn't say anything. I lean into it. "Yeah," I continue. "She even had Dad's service marked on the calendar so she wouldn't forget." My grandmother glances at my mother, surprised, while Mom squeezes my hand, grateful. The rest of the conversations go by more pleasantly after that, until finally we're able to leave and head to the cemetery to lay flowers on my father's grave before going out to lunch.

Dad's buried in a Catholic cemetery at the edge of town. I've only ever come here with my grandparents, never before with Mom, and for the first time as we approach, I find myself wondering whether she's ever come here by herself. The cemetery is small, so we park outside the gate and walk in. You can spot Dad's grave almost as soon as you walk inside; the large stone angel beside his headstone is a dead giveaway.

My grandparents make the sign of the cross when we reach his grave, then lay down the flowers they brought for him. Though I've been here plenty of times, the part that never ceases to feel strange to me is how both my grandparents' names are on the neighboring headstone, blank spaces left for their eventual dates of death. I know it's not uncommon to secure your grave years in advance, particularly if, like my grandparents, you care about which plot you end up in, but I still think there's something unsettling about visiting your own grave.

"It's such a lovely plot, isn't it, Abigail?" my grandmother asks my mom.

Mom stands to the side, staring at my father's name. I see her rubbing her wedding ring with her thumb, lips pursed. "Lovely," she repeats.

Grandma continues, oblivious to the strain in Mom's voice.

"I'm glad we were able to secure a second plot; it's getting harder and harder these days to find good spots. I know Peter would have wanted to be where his family will be."

"No," Mom says, finally breaking. "No, I'm sorry, but I can't do this any longer." She shakes her head. Her whole body shakes. "*I'm* his family. Peter would have wanted to be buried with me, not here in a Catholic cemetery."

Grandma reaches out to lay a hand on my mom's shoulder, but Mom flinches away. "Of course you're his family, but you were both so young when he died. When you meet someone else, I'm sure you'll want to be buried together."

"Meet someone else?" Mom laughs. "Right. Well, I'm glad to know you were thinking of me when you buried my husband here. Certainly, it would have been nice if you had asked me what I wanted. Or if you'd ever asked me what *he* would have wanted, because I could have told you he certainly wouldn't have wanted *this*. He didn't want a tombstone; he wanted a tree. We were going to be buried under a great oak tree, that was the plan. The plan wasn't to take over the law firm, and it certainly wasn't to send our child to Catholic school. None of this was part of the *fucking plan*!"

She stops, and I don't know who is more shocked by her outburst, my mom or the rest of us, but I'm not missing my chance.

"I could go back," I say quickly. "Back to public school. It's only been a week, I wouldn't have missed much."

"Abigail—" my grandmother starts, but I keep going. This is it. The final push. I'm going to win. I have to win.

"I can start back on Monday. I already know what classes

I want to take, so I'm sure they can make me a schedule in no time and—"

"No."

Everyone stops.

"What?"

"I said no," Mom says, looking at me. "No, you won't be going back to Wilbur. You'll be finishing the year at Our Lady of Mercy Academy."

Grandma beams while my stomach sinks through the floor. "But you said—you *just* said it wasn't the plan."

"Plans change," Mom says. "You're staying at Our Lady of Mercy, and that's final."

There's a beat of silence. Grandpa clears his throat. "Lunch, perhaps?"

Grandma takes his hand, still beaming, every other thing Mom said or did today forgotten in that rare moment of solidarity. They head to the car, Mom following along behind. And as I stand alone by my father's grave, I think this is the first time I've ever truly been angry at him for abandoning me.

EIGHT

"Yo, 'mano, where's your head at today?"

I glance up right in time to see the ball Seb throws at me, but I can't be bothered to try catching it. It lands by my feet, bouncing a couple of times before coming to a stop. I haven't stopped thinking about the cemetery since we left. I don't think I've ever seen my mom and my grandparents get along as well as they did at lunch; it was like aliens had come and replaced my entire family, and I was the only normal one left. And now I'm here, in the one place I should feel good, no, the place I should feel *freaking incredible*, and instead each missed ball and unfunny joke has me feeling like even more of a failure.

Seb comes closer. "Yo, whatever shit you're carrying around with you, you've got to leave it out there." He gestures vaguely toward the entrance of the tent, but I know that's not the *out there* he means. He means the unspoken out there, the daytime world we all leave behind for a few short hours each night, and I wish I could leave it behind, but I can't.

Seb claps his hands together once. "I'm calling it for tonight. What you need is some popcorn, and after the show everything will be better. You'll see."

What I need is for Mom to side with me. What I need is for someone at this damn circus to see that I'm not a clown, that I'll never be a clown, that I was always only ever meant to fly.

"Right," I say. "Popcorn, sure. Sounds good."

"That's the spirit! Tell Gino I sent you!"

I don't even wave goodbye as I exit the tent. Instead I wander around the midway until the exuberance of the crowd annoys me enough to seek solitude. I end up sitting on the grass beside the train car, far away from anyone else.

A memory pops into my mind as I sit. My seventh birthday. There was only one thing I wanted: a bicycle. But not just any bicycle—a black and lime-green Mongoose bike, seven speeds with handbrakes—a definite upgrade from the too-small, too-rusty secondhand bike my mom had grabbed from a yard sale when I was just learning to ride. I pointed it out to my grandparents every time we walked by the bike shop in town, being sure to emphasize just what it was I loved so much about the bike, particularly how cool the green and black looked together. Subtlety was not in my vocabulary.

On the day of the big party (big, of course, because it was my grandparents, and small was not in *their* vocabulary), I waited patiently for my grandparents' gift. My mom got me art supplies, and Moira got me a cool pirate-themed Lego set, but otherwise the gifts were the standard sort of gifts you get for a seven-year-old you've reduced entirely to stereotypes about their perceived gender: dress-up clothes, play makeup, Barbies and baby dolls, and so. much. pink.

And I smiled through it all, thanking every guest for their gift, because my grandmother had told me how excited she thought I was going to be with their gift, and because I'd spotted a suspiciously bike-shaped package wrapped in their bedroom earlier that afternoon.

When the big moment came, my grandparents made me close my eyes as they wheeled out my gift and set up the video camera to record the big moment. It's one of my grandparents' favorite videos of me, and one of my least. There's a moment, as I'm pulling off the wrapping paper and thanking my grandparents profusely, that I always think they'll notice, but they never do, so blinded are they by their own perceptions of that day. It's just a small moment, as I spot the first flash of color on the bike—bright pink and sparkly, rather than lime green and black—when my face falls, before I recover and plaster on a new smile, fake this time.

Being a clown at a magical circus is a lot like that pink bike. Almost perfect, yet completely wrong.

"Penny for your thoughts?"

I look up, startled to see the person in the plague mask hovering over me. Without prompting, he lowers himself down and sits beside me. I don't recall seeing him in the show the other night, or staffing one of the stalls outside, though he's surely got some sort of role if he's here again now.

"What seems to be the matter?" the man asks. He holds up a finger as my mouth opens and says, "And don't say nothing's wrong. I've been at the circus a long time and hardly ever see a face so glum."

I chuckle. "It's my assignment," I tell him. "I'm supposed to be a clown. Or so everyone else says anyways."

"And you're not?"

"No more than I'm supposed to be a girl," I say, not bothering to explain what I mean by that.

"Ah," the man says, nodding as though he understands. The hooked nose of his mask bobs up and down, exaggerating the motion. "And what are you supposed to be doing?"

"I'm supposed to fly."

The hooked nose bobs again. "You could change that."

My heart races. "How?"

"There's a book—a notebook—perhaps you've seen it. René keeps it in his trailer. Control the notebook, and you can control the circus. Control the notebook, and . . ."

"I can fly," I finish for him. I know the notebook he's talking about. The old journal that René wrote my name in the first time I met him.

"You could fly."

A breeze drifts across my face. I close my eyes, and I can see it, can almost *feel* it. The smell of the chalk, the feeling of the ladder beneath my hands, the sensation of soaring through the air . . .

"I couldn't do that," I say, opening my eyes. "It wouldn't be right."

"Or perhaps it would be. This is your dream, isn't it?"

Without waiting for an answer, the man stands and strolls off.

I find myself wandering the empty midway while everyone else enjoys the show. It's also the time when the stall workers are able to enjoy the evening, which means that many have retreated to the tents behind the train car for games of cards or to exchange stories and jokes and all those other things that come with the ease of friendship. Two people who haven't retreated from the midway, however, are Fizz and Gemma, who I spot up ahead, sitting on the ground by her balloon stall.

Gemma smiles and waves me over upon spotting me.

"Not enjoying the show tonight?" Fizz asks.

I shrug. "Figured I'd see what you all get up to instead."

"Well, this is it!" Gemma says, then gasps as though remembering something. She jumps to her feet. "I never got to make you anything! So tell me, what do you want? What do you most desire?"

I know we're talking about balloons, so her question is likely at least partially a joke, but I answer truthfully.

"I want to fly."

Gemma thinks for a moment, and then her face lights up. "I've got it."

She works quickly, selecting different-size balloons, blowing them up, and connecting them with such speed and dexterity that it's almost as impressive as whatever the final product turns out to be. And the final product is certainly impressive.

A hot-air balloon large enough for one person, complete with a basket and a red balloon at the top the size of a small car.

"So?" Gemma says, holding out a hand, "would you like to take a ride in my hot-air balloon?"

I rise higher and higher until I'm floating above a circus that shouldn't exist in a balloon that shouldn't be able to fly. Below me, the show comes to an end, the audience streaming out of the show with glee palpable even from fifty feet above the ground.

And as I stand in this balloon and look over this midnight carnival of magic and wonder—

As I watch children laughing and performers dancing and musicians playing—

And as I look down at this body that finally makes sense—

I know what I need to do.

Back down on the ground, I thank Gemma, then head straight for the tent village and the trailer that lies at its farthest edge.

The area is mostly empty, the midway staff having returned to their stalls and the performers still changing backstage. I keep to the edges, not wanting to be seen, even though I tell myself that I'm just going to talk to René. Which isn't anything I need to hide.

I halt as I see René's trailer in the distance.

This is your dream, isn't it?

It is.

I walk forward, climb the stairs, and knock on the trailer door, knowing somehow as I do that there won't be any answer, and further knowing that the door will open when pushed.

"Hello?" I say as I step into the dark trailer. It's silent.

I fumble in the dark for a light. The notebook probably isn't here anyway, or if it is, it's surely locked up tight. But when I switch on a lamp, it's there. On top of the desk—René's notebook, all that stands between me and flight. I don't think, I simply take, heart racing as I shove the notebook and the pen that lies beside it beneath my shirt and flee the trailer.

Outside it's still quiet but I can hear the approach of voices as many of the performers make their way back postshow. I need to get out of here before someone stops me and tries to make small talk. At some point I'll need to use my hands, and under closer examination I'm fairly certain my square stomach will raise questions. Head down and hunched over, I make my way along the edge of the tent village as quickly as I can.

And plow straight into another person, nearly toppling over as my head meets a firm chest. I scramble not to drop the book or pen as a hand grabs my arm to steady me.

"What are you doing?"

I finally look up, and my voice catches in my throat. Apollo is looking at me with a mixture of curiosity and disdain, and I'm terrified he's going to figure out what I'm up to and ruin everything. Especially since he seemed pretty clear the other night about his thoughts on me flying.

"I—"

"Actually, you know what?" Apollo says. "I don't care." He drops his hand from my arm and walks away.

I breathe a sigh of relief.

Time to get out of here.

I make it out of the tent village without being stopped by anyone else or dropping the notebook, and settle down at the edge of the woods behind a large tree. I wait a moment to make sure I wasn't followed and then pull out the pen and notebook, though it's more like a journal than anything I'd really call a notebook. Thick and old, it's bound in leather and tied shut.

I untie the strap and open it. It's filled with names, each page list upon list of names in small, precise writing. As I look closer, I notice other things written between the names— *300 balloons*, *20 lbs popcorn*, *Ferris wheel*. It's like a grocery list for the circus, where the grocery store lets you buy not only food and supplies but entire carnival rides. Though I don't understand the exact mechanisms by which this journal works, I begin to form an understanding of how it can be used to shape the circus. Right now, however, there's only one thing I need it to do.

I scan through the pages in reverse order until I come across my own name. Scribbled next to it is the word *clown*. I cross it out and write *aerialist* in its place, and I swear something changes right then and there, nearly imperceptible, like the light breeze that blows each time I cross the border into the circus and arrive in my true skin. Perhaps it's nothing more than wishful thinking, but I feel like I *am* an aerialist now.

I hide the notebook and the pen in the crook of a hollowed-out tree and let myself be drawn back—through the midway, around and between the crowds of people, past the popcorn and the balloons, the cotton candy and the Ferris wheel, until only the tent remains, looming large before me, blue and gold flags waving from its blue and gold canvas.

I step inside. The seats are empty. Even the popcorn spilled by the enthusiastic audience is gone, cleared away, the space now ready for tomorrow night, for another performance. I walk forward, down the rows to the center, stopping only when I reach the trapeze rig. I don't know what it is that compels me to want to fly, to *need* to fly. Perhaps it's something beyond explanation. All I know is I've spent a lifetime trying to escape the weight of gravity upon a body I never asked for, and I feel like if I could just break free, I might be able to see the world more clearly.

Hand on the rung, foot over foot, hand over hand. I climb the ladder, and no one stops me. This time there's no one to tell me this isn't for me, that this isn't who I'm meant to be. When I reach the top, I step up to the bar. I don't look down, don't want to look down, don't want to see the world below. I should be terrified, but instead all I feel is an overwhelming sense of *correctness*.

I grab the bar and then I

JUMP.

I soar through the air, fingers curled over the wooden bar as I throw my legs forward, gaining height, so much height, before swinging back toward the platform, then forward again, and only when I've reached the highest point do I TWIST, spinning around, hands letting go of the bar for a brief second before reconnecting on the other side. I swing back to the platform and then again I

JUMP.

This time I fly higher, higher with more power, legs and arms doing things that should be impossible, but I do them, and as I throw my body through the air time stops. As I throw myself through the air

I

Am

Free.

I go, again and again, moving between the bar and the platform until my arms burn, until I've taken all the pain that's inside and brought it outside, tacked it onto my left arm, my right leg, my abs and chest. I go until the voice shouting inside, the voice telling me I'm not enough, that I should be satisfied by what I have, is quieted, and then I drop to the net, climb down, and do it all over again.

NINE

After the disaster that was church on Sunday, it's almost a relief to go back to school for the week. *Almost* being the key word.

"I've got a surprise for you," Moira says as we begin the drive to school.

"Oh?" I say. I've known Moira long enough to express only cautious enthusiasm when she uses the term *surprise*. Sometimes it means she's brought me a coffee from Dunk's (fun surprise). Other times it means she found some new clothing item or piece of fabric at the consignment store and wants to use me as a living mannequin as she pokes me with pins and modifies it into something much cooler (a not-so-fun surprise). Knowing we are officially two months out from Halloween, my horror-movie-aficionado best friend's favorite holiday, I'm worried the surprise will be the latter.

"You'll have to wait and see!" she says between sips of her morning coffee. "But I'll give you a hint. I'll be near the bleachers on the left side of the gym."

Strange hint, but I don't push for more. When Moira has a plan, I've found it's best not to interfere.

I almost forget entirely about Moira's cryptic hint until an announcement is made during second period calling for all club leaders to come to the gym to set up for the activities fair. I'm not shocked to see Rebecca-Ann immediately stand up, but I am surprised when Moira grabs her backpack and follows behind, until I remember what she said in the car.

What club could Moira have started? A horror club? Probably not something a Catholic school would approve of. Way too much blasphemy and misuse of religious iconography, though bonus points for the number of exorcisms. As I listen to Sister Johnson drone on, I think she could benefit from a good exorcising. Maybe I'll draw that as a birthday gift for Moira. It would be appropriate given that she was born just minutes after the end of Halloween.

Finally, it's our time to go to the activities fair. The first table I see when I enter the gym is Rebecca-Ann's. A large cloth in a deep shade of purple is draped over the table, the words *Women in Christ* printed in silver. She's got about fifty purple pens on the table, plus about as many purple lanyards. I steer clear, worried she'll try to drag me into her group again if I get too close.

There are about twenty other tables set up in the gym, though none with quite the polish of Rebecca-Ann's. I finally spot Moira in the back of the gym by the bleachers, about as far away from Rebecca-Ann's table as can be. Probably for the best.

On the way over to Moira, I see a boy I recognize from class doing caricatures, and I realize there's an art club. Because Our Lady of Mercy has a class requirement called Foundations that I wasn't able to do earlier, on account of my being new to the school, I wasn't able to sign up for an art class this semester. But joining art club could be a way to get access to the school's art resources.

As the boy staffing the table finishes the drawing he's working on, I take a look at some of the art on display. One of the pieces appears to be his self-portrait done in oil pastels. What interests me most is the way his normally tan skin is shaded with cooler undertones at the top left of the portrait, and subtly shifts to warmer ones as you follow his gaze down to the lower right of the page. He does something similar with his black hair. It's really interesting and impressive.

"Hey! Interested in having a caricature done?"

I look up just in time to see the boy behind the table hand off the caricature he's just finished to its subject—a girl who skips off to show her friends.

"Actually, I'm interested in the club," I say. I offer my hand. "Ash."

"Julian," he says. "I recognize you from my Foundations class. You're a senior, right? Must suck to have to take a class with a bunch of juniors."

I shrug. "That part's fine, it's not being able to take the art elective that sucks."

"Well, the art club would love to have you! We meet Tuesdays right after school, and Ms. Sanchez, the art teacher, is really cool."

Finally, something in this school I can get excited about. And Tuesday is one of the afternoons I have free from working at the art store. I go to sign up but then pause.

"Do you have a question?" Julian asks.

"No, I just— My best friend has started a club, and I should check in with her before signing up for this."

"Oh, which one?"

I gesture toward Moira, who is speaking to a couple of students.

"Oh, the social justice club! I saw her setting her table up earlier. My girlfriend, Zoe, is over there now signing up."

He points to a Black girl I also recognize from our

Foundations class. Julian calls her name, and she spins her wheelchair toward us, face lighting up as she gives him a wave. I notice her hair has changed since I last saw her—it's now braided into tight cornrows with blue, pink, and purple beads hanging from the ends. Bisexual-flag colors? I wonder if that's a coincidence.

"Right," I say. "I'll come back."

I drop the pen I'm holding and head over to Moira's table. Immediately it becomes clear what has become of the art supplies she purchased the other day at Mr. Roberts's store; the table is decked out with a half dozen posters filled with large sparkling bubble letters.

SOCIAL JUSTICE CLUB
NO JUSTICE, NO PEACE!
QUEER RIGHTS ARE HUMAN RIGHTS
BLACK LIVES MATTER
WANT CHANGE? JOIN US!

Moira's face lights up as soon as she sees me, and she comes around the table to drag me closer. "Surprise!"

Yes, surprise indeed. When Moira bought all those posters, I thought maybe she'd set up her own petition after school one day, not start a whole damn club. Moira never does things halfway. Also, I'm rather surprised the school let her not only start the club, but hang a poster advocating for queer rights.

"So? What do you think? I already signed you up, and before you ask, it won't interfere with your job. I made sure to request a Tuesday slot so you could come!" She looks so pleased with herself that I do my best to smile, even though I can feel my dreams of art club slipping away.

"So," I say. "A social justice club, huh?"

"Yeah! And we've already got another member. Zoe, meet Ash . . ." She stumbles as she says my name, fortunately trailing off after the Ash part, which is what we agreed she'd use as a compromise between my given name and my chosen name. I turn and see Zoe and give her a little wave.

"We're in Foundations together," Zoe says to Moira. "It's good to see you again."

"Great! This is perfect." Moira claps her hands together. "I've already got so many ideas. First things first, I think we need to show support for the girl at Wilbur." She snaps her fingers. "I don't know her name, though. That's important. Do either of you know?"

"Kaycee," I say before I can stop myself.

"Oh, right," says Moira. "I keep forgetting you were in school with her. Did you know her?"

I know what she's asking. Two trans kids at the same school in the same small town. We must have known each other, right?

Of course we did.

She was new, like I am now. And she found me right away, some sixth sense perhaps that I was like her. Or maybe it was because even at my old school, a school I'd attended for eleven years, I didn't have many friends. Any friends, really. But then there she was, sitting with me at lunch as I sketched, following me to my locker between classes and doing homework with me in the library until she'd fit herself so seamlessly into my life it was as if we'd always been friends.

Like Moira, Kaycee was—is—everything I'm not. She was out and proud, unafraid and unapologetic. And it scared me. It scared me so much that I never told Moira we were friends, never came out to Kaycee as trans. I was afraid they'd both want me to be more like her. Afraid they'd know just how much of a coward I really am.

"No," I say finally. "I didn't really know her."

Moira seems disappointed, and I feel bad for lying to her, but I can't tell her the truth, because if I told her the truth she'd probably hate me as much as I hate myself, and I don't think I could handle that.

"No matter," she says. "We can discuss what we want to do at our first meeting. First, I need to recruit some more students. Ash, can you handle the table?"

She doesn't wait for an answer before she grabs her clipboard and walks away to poach students from the other clubs.

"She's a go-getter, isn't she?"

I turn to face Zoe. "That's definitely one word for her."

By the end of the period, Moira has managed to recruit another five students for a grand total of eight. Not a huge group, but not insubstantial either, especially for a small Catholic school. I pass Julian on my way out, and from the look on my face he seems to understand I will not be joining art club.

"Hey," he says. I turn back. "Maybe I can still show you around the art space another time. I'll talk to Ms. Sanchez about it."

"Thanks," I say. I assume he's being polite, but I appreciate the thought.

Moira and the other club leaders miss lunch to clean up after the activities fair, so I end up eating alone. As I pull out my sketchbook, I'm reminded of all those years of lunches at Wilbur before Kaycee arrived. I wonder who she eats lunches with now. Probably a better friend than me.

"So, I was thinking, we should get club shirts made—show Rebecca-Ann she's not the only one who knows how to order from a professional printer. You could even design them for us!"

"Hmmm, yeah." I look out the window, watch as the trees pass by. If I squint, I can almost imagine the circus lying just beyond; can almost see the flashes of blue and gold. I finished the drawing of the circus tent for Mr. Roberts. It might be the best work I've ever done.

"Hellooooo, Earth to Asher!" Moira takes her right hand off the steering wheel and waves it in front of my face. I pull my attention back from the circus in my head.

"I'm listening."

"What's wrong? I thought you'd be more excited about the club. It took me all week to find a teacher who would agree to serve as faculty advisor, and I'm pretty sure Sister Johnson's head was going to explode when she saw the signs I posted. Like actual ka-boom-level explosion." Moira grins. "It was awesome."

I laugh. "You should put that in your college applications."

"Ha! No, better yet, a college interview. I'll set the scene: Mr. Bob—"

"Mr. Bob?"

Moira waves a hand in my direction. "Hush. This is my story. Anyways, as I was saying. Imagine this. Mr. Bob, a fuddy-duddy alum of St. Ignatius College for the Perpetually

Powerless. And little miss Moira, prim and proper, curly red locks tied back tastefully like a good Catholic girl."

I snort, both in response to the name of the school and that image of Moira.

Ignoring me, Moira continues. "We'll skip past the initial introductions and the part where I naturally wow him with my impeccable transcript."

"Naturally."

"Naturally. Anyways, we have a wonderful interview; I'm a shoo-in for admittance and then Mr. Bob says, 'I have just one more question for you. You've accomplished so much for someone so young. You might be the most impressive candidate we've ever seen, but I wonder: What do you think is your most impressive achievement?'"

"What do you say?" I ask, almost forgetting for a moment where this fake story started.

"I say, 'Mr. Bob, what an excellent question. It's so hard to choose, of course, but I really think my greatest achievement might have been blowing the mind of Sister Johnson. It *was* a little messy; I had to scrub to get all the brain bits off my uniform, but ultimately worth it.'"

I laugh as Moira pulls up in front of the art store. "And were you accepted?"

"To St. Ignatius College for the Perpetually Powerless?" She sighs. "Alas, it was not to be."

"Oh well, guess you'll have to settle for Yale or Harvard or one of those other safety schools."

Now it's Moira's turn to laugh. "Yeah, right, that'll be the day."

I grab my backpack and start climbing out of the truck.

"Don't forget! First meeting of the social justice club is tomorrow after school!"

I wave as she drives away and then head inside the shop. If the circus is where I belong in my dreams, the art store is where I belong in the real world. When I enter, I find one of our regular customers, Mrs. McGee, perusing the latest pen selection. She comes in about once a week to test out the new supplies and say hi to Mr. Roberts and me.

I greet her before heading over to the counter to say hi to Mr. Roberts.

"I've got something for you," I say. I pull out the picture I drew and set it on the counter.

Mr. Roberts puts on his glasses and picks it up gently. He doesn't say anything, and I'm starting to wonder whether he even likes it when he sets it back down and says, "It's perfect." It might be my imagination, but I swear there's a tear in his eye. I look to the side, blinking away the ones threatening to form in my own. But then he clears his throat and tells me to grab one of the precut window mats to display my picture, and the moment passes.

I take a moment to admire the picture once I've set it up above the colored-pencil display.

"Oh, that's just lovely," Mrs. McGee says. "Did you draw it?"

I tell her I did, and she asks if I'm a fan of the circus.

"It's a recent interest."

"You know," she says, "I once had the most wondrous dream about a circus. It was not long after my husband, Roger, passed away. This was, oh goodness, almost thirty years ago? I don't

85

usually remember my dreams, but I remember this one so clearly. Your picture reminds me of it." She smiles pleasantly, before patting my arm and walking away.

I watch her go, then look back at my drawing. It couldn't be . . . ?

Right. Of course not. Still, as I head back to the counter and watch Mrs. McGee leave the shop, I can't help but wonder whether she once visited the Midnight Circus too. But of course that's not possible. It's just a dream.

Mr. Roberts waves me over to the front counter, and I think he has something he wants me to do, but instead he pulls out a large stack of catalogs.

"What are these?" I ask as I pick up the first one. Rhode Island School of Design. I set it down and look at the others: School of the Art Institute of Chicago, Pratt Institute's School of Art, Massachusetts College of Art and Design.

"Schools with a solid art program," he says. "You've got real talent. You should do something with it."

I think of the stash of money under my bed. Nearly $1,000 the last time I counted. More money than I've ever had in my life, and only pennies compared to the cost of any of these colleges. And there's no way my grandparents are going to pay for me to go to art school.

"These are great," I say, "but—"

"But what? Your dream is to become a lawyer and stay in this small town forever?"

"This town's not so bad," I lie.

Mr. Roberts raises an eyebrow, clearly calling me on my bluff.

"Fine," I say. I can pretend with my grandparents, pretend

with my mom, pretend at school, but I can't pretend here. Not about this, at least. Not to Mr. Roberts. "I can't afford art school."

"I'm not suggesting you mortgage your future children to afford school," Mr. Roberts says, "I'm just saying—take the brochures. Apply for scholarships. Worst case, you end up following your grandparents' plans. But the best case? I think that's worth a shot." He pauses, a faraway expression on his face before he refocuses on me. "Word of advice from an old man? Sometimes the risk is worth it. Keep your options open."

He holds out the brochures again, and this time I take them.

When I get home after work, I find a note on the counter along with a $20 bill. *Picked up a shift. Order yourself a pizza. Love you, Mom.*

My expression softens. Mom tries, I know she does. I know the long hours she works are for me—for us—so that she doesn't have to rely on my grandparents for support, but sometimes I wonder—would it truly be so bad if she did? If, instead of picking up extra shifts at the hospital, she took a week off and came to Nantucket with us in the summer? Or took the job at Grandpa's firm that I know he's offered her? At least she'd be home for dinner every night. But the one time I brought it up to Mom, she shut that idea down so firmly that I've never brought it up again.

I order a large pizza, half plain cheese for me, half pepperoni for Mom, which I wrap and put in the fridge for her and take the rest up to my bedroom. While it cools on my desk, I remove the fan from my window and set it on the ground. Outside my window there's an overhang just large enough for me, the pizza, and the stack of college brochures I promised Mr. Roberts I'd take a look at. I like to come to come out here sometimes and sketch or look at the stars. Mom hates when I sit out here; she thinks I'm going to fall to my death. Which is why I do it when she's not home.

One of the things I used to love about this ledge was that it faced the old farmhouse. There was something beautiful about the way the sun would set over the derelict property. A couple of years ago, I did a series of watercolors of the property: one for each of the four seasons. I mounted them and gave them to Mom as a Christmas present. She hung them above her bed. Of course, half the time she falls asleep on the couch, so I'm not sure how often she actually sees them.

Tonight, there's a light on in one of my neighbors' upstairs bedrooms. One I've never seen before. And there appears to be someone inside. Against the light of the setting sun, it's hard to see too well, but it appears to be a young man, and oh. Oh. He's shirtless now, and if those back muscles indicate anything else about him, he's very attractive. He's standing directly in front of the window but facing away, so I can't see what he looks like or how old he is, but he's got to be around my age, maybe a little older. He starts stretching and I can't look away. I'm debating whether it's unethical to grab my sketchbook when the guy turns around. In a panic, I dive headfirst back into my bedroom, knocking a stack of textbooks off my desk.

I wait a couple of minutes before risking another look out the window. Fortunately, the light is off, and the young man is gone, though my embarrassment remains. After picking up the textbooks, I turn my attention to the college brochures. I've looked through plenty of these before, for Kaycee and for

Moira. They're all the same when you get down to it; shiny paper, smiling college students standing on perfectly manicured quads, beautiful brick buildings behind them. There's always a picture of a student in a lab, safety goggles on, pipette in hand; another of an a cappella group mid-performance, or a Bollywood dance group, or a production of Shakespeare. Every picture is perfect and polished; no one wants to see a picture of a student having a mental breakdown or trudging through the New England snow and slush to get to class after waking up hungover.

I always thought I was immune to the charm of these propaganda packets. UNH has been in the cards for me pretty much my entire life. It's where my grandparents met, where my dad was studying before he died. I'll study something practical, like economics with a minor in law, take as many art classes as I can for elective credit. When I graduate, I'll move back to Wilbur and work for my grandfather until he retires and passes the law firm on to me. And maybe once he and my grandmother pass away, I'll come out and transition. There are worse futures to have.

But as I look over these art school catalogs, I imagine something different. Something so much better it hurts. I close the pamphlets. Time for bed.

TEN

As I walk into the circus later in the evening, I can hardly contain my excitement. No more juggling, no more whoopee cushions, water squirting flowers, never-ending silk handkerchiefs, or pies to the face. No more trying to be funny. No more failing spectacularly. This clown is officially out, good riddance.

"Ah, Asher, good—a word, please?" René pulls me aside just before I make it to the tent. I see Apollo standing not too far behind him, arms crossed, a scowl on his face.

I try to keep my face neutral, but inside I'm panicking. Did Apollo tell him he saw me sneaking around yesterday? Does he know I took the notebook?

"Yes?" I say, much more calmly than I feel.

"Small change—I'd like you to switch over to the trapeze rig. I think it will be a better fit. You don't mind, do you?" I quickly shake my head, relief washing over me. I definitely don't mind. I've never minded anything less, in fact. "Great! Apollo will show you the ropes," René says, then walks away, checking a watch on his wrist and muttering to himself.

I turn to Apollo, who sighs loudly and turns to walk into the tent without a single word. I race to keep up.

"I'm really looking forward to working with you," I say.

No response. Okay, so the feeling isn't mutual. That's okay. I'm sure once he sees me fly, he'll realize that this is what I'm meant to do. I'm not going to hold him back.

We reach the main ring, me just a step behind Apollo, when I spot Seb and Maisie practicing their routine.

"Ah, there you are, 'mano!" Seb says, jumping in between Apollo and me. "I've got a new plan for today. It involves pie." He squints. "You aren't allergic to blueberries, are you?"

Apollo turns back with a smirk. "Ooh, awkward. Guess you haven't heard that your boy is abandoning you. But, uh, hey—perhaps you can save me a slice of that pie?" He winks and walks off. Asshole.

Seb furrows his brow. "What's he on about?" Apollo's little dig was not at all how I intended to break the news. He looks between me and Apollo and without my having to say anything, connects the dots. "Flyboy, huh?"

"René—"

"And that's what you want?" He nods toward the trapeze rig. "To fly?"

"I do. I want it more than anything," I say almost pleadingly, needing for Seb to understand that I'm not rejecting him or his friendship, that this is something I need to do. "Besides," I say, trying to lighten the mood, "I was a really shit clown."

It takes a moment, but Seb laughs. "A *really* shit clown." We both laugh. "Hey," Seb says as I turn back toward the trapeze rig, "go show him what a real flyboy looks like, yeah? And if he's ever standing too close to the edge, feel free to give him a little—" Here Seb makes a small shoving motion, and I grin.

Apollo is already flying when I approach the ladder. I guess it was too much to expect he might wait for me, give me some sort of direction, or perhaps introduce me to his current flying partner. But he can't get rid of me that easily.

I climb the ladder and step onto the small platform at the top, where Apollo stands rewrapping his hands.

"We don't need you," he says, not even bothering to look at me. "Our act is fine with Tessa and me." He nods to the older woman swinging on the catching bar across the rig. "We don't need anyone else."

"Yeah? And does Tessa feel the same as you?" I ask. "Because it looks like maybe she doesn't to me."

I nod back to the woman, who is waving over at me with a smile on her face. She looks small from way over here, her white hair tied up in a bun behind her head, but she must be stronger than she looks if she's the catcher. Apollo frowns, then makes a series of hand gestures to her, which I realize a moment later is him using sign language. She signs something back, and his frown deepens further.

"She's deaf?" I ask.

Apollo slow-claps, and I swear I've never been so tempted to shove somebody over a ledge as I am right now.

Then Apollo does something unexpected. He steps aside.

"She wants to see what you can do. But don't think I'm going to help you out."

I think of my performance last night. "Oh, I don't think I'm going to need it."

Stepping forward, I grab the bar with my right hand, take a deep breath to steady myself, and then I let that instinctual part of myself, the part with wings, take control and I jump.

I don't know how long I fly. By the time I land in the net it feels like there's never been a me that existed outside the air, and like I spent no time there at all. I crawl over to the side of the net and lie down on my stomach, grabbing the netting and somersaulting off as I've seen Apollo do so many times before. Seb's waiting for me, cheering as though he himself has triumphed in my flight.

"You showed him up big time, 'mano! Watch him try to stop you now." Seb slaps me on the back. "Gotta go, but you've got this," he says before dashing off, presumably to find Maisie.

A moment later, I watch as Apollo drops down into the net, followed shortly thereafter by Tessa as Apollo climbs down onto the ground. Apollo's expression is still dark, but Tessa immediately comes over and pulls me into a spine-crushing hug, then pulls back and begins signing something.

I start to shake my head. "I'm sorry, but I don't—"

"You're a natural."

I turn, bewildered, as I hear Apollo say those words, but he juts his chin toward Tessa, and I realize he's not saying it, he's interpreting. I turn back and sign the one phrase I still remember from some early elementary school lessons in ASL.

"*Thank you*," I mouth along with the gesture. She smiles, and behind me I hear Apollo huff and stomp off.

I turn back to Tessa, not sure what we do now. She signs something, but without Apollo to interpret, I have no clue what she's saying.

"I'm sorry," I say, unsure if she can read lips but hoping my facial expression at least makes my meaning clear. I don't know what Apollo's deal is or why he seems to hate me so much, but I feel bad for Tessa that I'm the reason he's stormed off.

"I'll go," I say. "Uhhh, right . . ." I pause, then point to myself a few times and use my pointer and middle fingers to mimic legs walking away. I want to fly, but maybe René was onto something when he stuck me with the clowns, because I kind of feel like one right now. None of this is going according to plan. At least Seb was always happy to see me, and I was awful at clowning. I don't know how this is supposed to work when Apollo seems determined to hate me.

I start to walk away when I feel a hand on my arm. I turn and see Tessa. She shakes her head, and I stop. She gestures back toward the net, then starts walking in that direction. I follow a moment later.

I stop a few feet away from Tessa, then watch as she begins stretching. She looks up, then points to me and back to herself and I realize she wants me to copy what she's doing. I breathe a sigh of relief. I can do that. Maybe there's hope after all.

I'm not sure how long we work together, Tessa demonstrating some kind of stretch and me attempting to mimic. Occasionally she'll come over and, with a nod of permission from me, use her hands to adjust my posture or help me sink deeper into a particular stretch. By the time we're done, I feel a little like a piece of overstretched Silly Putty, but already I can see how these exercises might help me in the air. I sign my thanks repeatedly when we finish, and Tessa smiles and nods.

Apollo's attitude toward me notwithstanding, my mood is much improved as I wander the midway while Tessa and the other performers prepare for the show. I take in everything: children with faces painted with animal expressions that seem to shift and come alive as they run and play, adults laughing joyously as they consume cotton candy larger than their heads or fight with balloon swords lovingly crafted by Gemma. I watch an old woman perform ballet with the grace of someone sixty years younger, and a young couple holding hands as they stare up at the stars in the night sky. The circus makes anything seem possible.

There's nothing I desire more at this moment than to take out my sketchbook and record everything I'm seeing, but then I get a better idea. Overhead, the five-minute-warning fireworks go off, but instead of joining the crowd as they head toward the tent, I move in the opposite direction, toward the woods and the tree where I hid René's notebook. If the notebook can make my time at the circus even better, why can't it make everyone's time here that way?

I remove the notebook and pen from the hollow where I left them and settle down at the base of a large oak tree. From my pocket, I pull out a fabric-wrapped bundle of colored pencils, as though the circus knew that even here I shouldn't be far from my trusted companions, and I get to work.

I sketch straight through the entire show performance and slightly thereafter, and when I'm done my pencils are just as sharp as when I started. How I wish I could carry that over to the daytime world! As a final touch, I use René's pen to outline my sketch, then take a moment to admire my work. Much like my own transition to the flying trapeze, I don't expect my change to take place until the following evening, so I close the notebook and return it to its hiding spot.

With the rest of the night ahead of me, I head back toward the tent, hoping to find Tessa up for some postshow lessons, but as I approach the trapeze rig, I realize I'm not the only one interested in practicing after the show. I watch as Apollo jumps from the platform, trying a trick I've seen him working on before while I was still training with Seb. It looks complicated;

there seems to be both a forward somersault and a full twist involved. Occasionally Apollo makes contact with Tessa's hands, but more often he misses entirely.

I take a seat about five rows back and watch as he climbs down from the net, scales the ladder, and tries again. Over and over again he fails, and over and over again he gets back up and tries again. Who is this boy who can be such a jerk on the one hand and such a determined performer on the other? If he's frustrated by his inability to get the trick right, it shows only in the steely expression on his face as he climbs down from the net. He never yells, never throws his hands up in frustration. He just gets back up and tries it again.

After another failure, he and Tessa switch places. Apollo climbs up to the catcher's bar, while Tessa takes his original spot on the platform.

I'm transfixed as I watch her fly. She must be in her mid-seventies, judging from her white hair and the wrinkles on her face, but you wouldn't know it from watching her. She performs the trick Apollo was struggling with so effortlessly it takes my breath away. At the end, catcher and flyer connect perfectly, and afterward Apollo throws her back to the bar, which she catches right as it completes its arc back toward her. It's only a healthy sense of restraint and my lingering dislike of Apollo that stop me from jumping up and applauding as Tessa lands back on the platform.

Though I want to fly, I find I can't stop watching. I stay until the sun rises, and when I wake up in my bed it's with the determined expression on Apollo's face still fresh in my mind.

ELEVEN

The first thing I do after opening my eyes is run over to my desk and pull out my sketchbook and a pencil.

There's something calming about starting my day this way, something that centers me almost enough to endure the eight hours that follow. I take a moment to flip through the work I've already done; pictures of Seb, Fizz, Gemma, and René are interspersed among drawings of the tent, the midway, the Ferris wheel, and the trapeze rig. I've got one of Gino, the popcorn seller, and Maisie juggling. I've got Ivan throwing his knives and Vikram lying on his stomach with his legs folded back over his head. I've got drawings of almost everyone I've gotten to know at the circus. Everyone except for one person.

I've tried not to draw him, but today it's like my hand has a mind of its own, and his face is all I can see as I close my eyes. I start with his curls, sketching the one that hangs over his forehead, the ones that curl around his ear, then I move on to his face, sketch the rough shape, add in the eyes, dark and intense, and the freckles—one right outside his left eye, another near his ear, and the small triangle near his nose. I add in the mouth last. I start to sketch it, angry like he always seems to be with me, but I don't get far before I'm erasing, changing the angle. Not angry, determined. Determined like he was when he was working on that trick. By the time I'm done, my hand is cramping, but it's worth it. Somehow my picture of Apollo is the best of all the ones I've done so far. I don't know what that means, but I do know I need to get dressed or I'll be late for school, so reluctantly I shut my sketchbook and put it into my backpack.

Moira and I make it to homeroom just before the second bell rings. Rebecca-Ann stands gathered with a small group of girls, hands joined, heads bowed in prayer. Seeing her Women in Christ club reminds me that today is the first meeting of Moira's new social justice club. It's hard not to feel disappointed that I'll miss art club, but I know this is important to Moira, so there's no question about my being there.

I pull out my sketchbook as Sister Johnson begins her morning announcements and turn back to the picture of Apollo as I try to decide what to work on next. Probably Tessa, though I haven't figured out how I want to do that yet.

The door to the classroom opens as Sister Johnson finishes her announcements.

"Ah, you must be Mr. Bennett. You are late. Take a seat."

Bennett? That's my neighbors' last name. I immediately flash back to last night: the boy and the window, my face-first dive back into my room. I'm mortified. Maybe he didn't see me? Sinking down in my seat, I hazard a glance up and immediately gasp because I don't just recognize the boy.

I spent the morning drawing him.

I slam my sketchbook shut, heart racing as I take in the boy who has walked straight out of my dreams and into my classroom. It doesn't make any sense; the circus is a dream, the people in it figments of my imagination. Apollo doesn't get to just walk into my classroom and take a seat. I glance around, half expecting

Seb to come through the door juggling a set of Bibles, but no one else appears. Moira's looking at me, head cocked, brows furrowed, and I realize I'm slouched so far down in my seat that I'm practically under the desk. I sit up, wondering if it's possible to make another escape via window, but quickly rule that out when I remember we're on the third floor.

The bell rings, and it's only when Moira nudges me that I realize and stand up. We walk by Apollo on the way out. He's already been cornered by Rebecca-Ann with her petition in hand. His eyes meet mine briefly, and I panic that he's going to recognize me. He excuses himself from Rebecca-Ann, running to catch up with Moira and me as we head to our next class.

I brace myself, but all he says is "Is she always like that?"

"Unfortunately," Moira says flatly. "On the plus side, she's at peak perkiness whenever there's a new kid. On the downside, you're the new kid." Moira turns and looks at me. "Congrats, you're no longer the new kid."

Apollo looks at me, and it takes everything in my power not to say or do something I'll regret later. But it's hard when this is the most surreal experience of my life and I'm the only one aware of it.

"Haven't I seen you before?" he asks.

"Have you?" I say, my voice shooting to its highest register. To the side, Moira crosses her arms and smirks. I know what she's thinking, but it's not because Apollo resembles his godly namesake that I'm such a mess.

I'm about as relieved as I am embarrassed when he says with a grin, "I think we're neighbors." He winks, and I about melt into the floor, but he doesn't say anything about the circus. He doesn't know I'm Asher. "Next time you can just wave."

I chuckle, rubbing the back of my neck. "Right," I say.

Perhaps hoping to save me from myself, Moira interrupts. "I'm Moira," she says, offering out a hand to shake. "And that's Ash."

"Apollo." He shakes Moira's hand, then reaches out to do the same with me. This doesn't make any sense; none of this makes any sense. Moira clears her throat, and I realize I'm still staring at Apollo's hand. I shake it, half expecting my hand will pass straight through it like air, that I'll discover Apollo is nothing more than a ghost, but it doesn't. He isn't. His hand is warm and solid in my own. The bell rings and I drop it.

We head to our next class, and the conversation comes to an end as we take our seats. Moira leans over, grinning. "It's okay," she whispers. "I get flustered around cute people too." She winks and leans back.

God, Moira really has *no* idea.

Somehow, I make it through this class and the next two without exploding. I pinch myself a few times to make sure I'm truly awake, but it does nothing but leave me with a bruise. I even excuse myself to the bathroom at one point to splash some water on my face. I don't know for certain, but it definitely feels like bathroom Jesus is judging me when I look in the mirror.

Finally, miraculously, we make it to lunch. I try not to look like I'm staring, but it's difficult not to keep my eyes on Apollo. He disappears into the lunch line, and I turn back to Moira, who is staring at her food in disgust. It looks like her stepmom is on another health kick, judging from the contents of her lunch box. Moira's parents divorced when she was only a couple of years old, and her mom moved to be closer to family

100

in Georgia. Her dad got remarried when Moira was ten, and her stepmom, Tanya, is nice, but she's constantly trying some new exercise regimen or diet. Moira takes after her father—their shared sweet tooth resulting in a hidden candy stash rivaling a child's post-Halloween haul.

"Apollo," I say to her. "Does he look familiar to you?"

Moira thinks for a moment, then shakes her head. "I don't think so," she says. "Why?"

I shake my head. "No reason."

Moira turns back to her meal, making a face when she takes a bite of her sandwich. She spits out a bunch of small leafy greens that look a bit like grass. "Yuck. I think I'm going to buy lunch today."

She leaves, and I look around for Apollo. As scared as I am that he might figure out who I am, there's another part of me excited by what it would mean for the circus to be real, to be something that exists outside my imagination. Could I go there and perform for real? And if I could, which version of me would show up once I've passed through the gates?

I'm not the only one watching Apollo, and I feel some sympathy having been the new kid myself last week. A boy I often see with Rebecca-Ann, Jackson Rhodes, approaches Apollo, clearly looking to invite him to join their lunch table. I tense as the conversation quickly turns sour. I can't hear what's spoken, but Jackson's face says enough. As Apollo turns to walk away, Jackson extends a leg, and Apollo and his lunch go flying.

The entire cafeteria comes to a complete halt at the sound of Apollo's tray hitting the ground. Barely a second passes before he jumps up, shirt covered in tomato soup, and tackles Jackson to the ground. The chants to fight start almost immediately, though not everyone participates. Rebecca-Ann bows her head in prayer while Jackson's friend Ricky jumps into the fray. By the time the three boys have been separated, they look like they've been through much worse than a cafeteria brawl with their white shirts stained by the red soup.

Moira returns as the three boys are marched out of the cafeteria. "Aww man," she says. "I missed the entire thing!"

I don't see Apollo the rest of the day, and I wonder what kind of trouble he got into. Can you get expelled on your first day? Maybe that's why he started classes later than the rest of us. Maybe he was expelled from his old school. Though that doesn't explain why he hasn't been living with his parents for the past few months. Boarding school maybe? Either way, that's the least of all the mysteries surrounding Apollo and his sudden entrance into my daytime life.

After school, I change out of my uniform in the bathroom before joining Moira in the empty classroom we'll be using for club meetings. I say hi to Zoe and take a seat on top of a desk next to her. She's reading a comic book, bright pink glasses sliding down her nose as she does.

"Do you know America Chavez?" she asks. I don't realize she's talking about a superhero until she holds up the comic and I see the cover.

I shake my head. "The art's cool, though," I say.

Zoe grins. "I want to be a comic writer someday. America is my favorite. A queer Latinx badass. Let me know if you ever want to borrow some—I have pretty much every issue of hers."

"Thanks," I say, "I will." I want to ask her more, but then Moira walks in and calls the meeting to order. Zoe puts her comic book away, and it's hard not to think of the art club meeting right now. I wonder if Julian is there.

Like me, Moira has also changed out of her uniform into more casual attire. I'm grateful not to be the only one, and I think that was probably the point.

We do a round of introductions, and then everyone quiets down as Moira speaks again.

"Thank you all for being here. I know I started this club, but I really want this to be a place where everyone feels comfortable contributing ideas for projects we can work on. That being said, I did want to propose the first thing I hope we can do. As I'm sure you all know, there's a trans girl at Wilbur High suing the school right now for fair and equal access to the bathroom and locker room. This weekend she'll be holding a press conference in front of City Hall, and I think it would be really great if we could be there to show our support. I've brought some supplies for making signs and I also have these—" Moira dumps out a bunch of pins from a bag and spreads them across the teacher's desk. "For those who are queer and comfortable sharing, I've got a bunch of different pride-flag pins. For everyone else, there are ally pins and some that just have rainbows on them that I figure anybody can wear. If you have any questions about what the different flag colors mean, let me know!"

I wait with bated breath for the backlash; for someone to storm out or the teacher to tell us we can't do this, but neither happens. Instead, slowly, a couple of students stand up and grab ally pins and pin them to their shirts. Zoe wheels herself closer and grabs the bi pride pin, confirming my earlier guess about the colors in her hair.

Moira takes two for herself. The bi pride flag and one with

black, gray, white, and purple stripes that must be the asexual pride flag. There are a few I've seen before but don't know the meanings of, and then there's mine. Baby blue, pink, and white. The trans pride flag. It rests in between a pin with a rainbow on it, which is different from the rainbow flag pin, which has stripes and matches the rest of the pride flag pins, and the pin that says *Ally* against a background of rainbow stripes. I wait until everyone else has had their turn picking; one boy chooses a gay pride flag, but otherwise it's just ally pins and regular rainbow pins, and finally it's my turn. My hand hovers over the trans pride flag and my heart races, but it's the regular rainbow I pick up and pin to my shirt. I don't look to see if Moira is disappointed. I know I am.

How is it everyone else is so confident in sharing who they are with the world? Even here, inside a Catholic school in a small conservative town in rural New Hampshire, there aren't just one or two, but *three* people willing to be openly queer. But being trans isn't the same as all those other identities, because it's not just about who you love, it's about who you *are*. A gay person doesn't inherently look any different from a straight one, but as soon as people know you're trans it's like you're put under a microscope. I know because I saw it happen to Kaycee. People who used the correct pronouns suddenly started messing up as soon as they found out she was trans. Or their eyes would fall; down to her throat, to her chest, her hips, her hands, anywhere they thought they could see signs of who she "used" to be, as though a person's fundamental self could ever live in a single body part.

As an artist, I'm used to observing. But I don't want to *be* observed. I just want to live.

With the pins distributed, Moira takes out a bunch of craft supplies. Some I recognize from her trip to the art store with me the other day; others I know are pulled from her stepmom's crafting room. Someone pulls out their phone and starts playing music, and soon everyone is in the zone making signs in support of Kaycee. I don't know how I feel about seeing her again. I'm not sure how she'll feel about seeing *me* again, but still, it feels good to be doing something to support her. It may not be art club, but as I look over the poster I'm designing, it's something, and I'm . . . well, if not *happy*, I'm satisfied for the moment.

The hour passes quickly. I help Moira clean up her supplies when we're done. As I scoop the extra pins back into the bag, I pause on the trans pride flag. It's just us in the room now, so I let myself linger over it for a moment.

"You can take it, you know," Moira says. "Keep it in your bag or something."

I rub my finger over the smooth surface and almost take it, stick it in my bag like Moira suggests, but I can't do it. I'm just not ready. "Maybe next time," I say.

There're only a few other cars still in the parking lot when we get outside. One of them, a beat-up green boxy sort of car, is parked a few spots over from Moira's truck. Its owner rolls down the window when he sees us, and I realize it's Apollo. I try not to stare, but it's hard because he's sporting a large black eye. I guess that fight at lunch left a mark. It's unfair that he's so attractive even when he's been beaten up.

"Hey!" He smiles and waves. I guess he wasn't expelled after all. It's so weird to see him smiling, and doing it in my direction. "Are you heading home? I can give you a ride if you want."

I'm about to tell him no, Moira will take me, when she interjects.

"That would be great," she says.

"What are you doing?" I say under my breath. I know a sneaky Moira plot when I see one.

"What?" she says. "It makes sense. He's your neighbor. You know I love you, but you don't exactly live on my way home. It saves gas, and saving gas saves the planet. You want to save the polar bears, don't you?" Moira gives me a wide-eyed look of innocence, which confirms that saving the environment is not, in fact, her main motivation. "Have fun with the cute boy!" she whispers, and then she pushes me forward and it's too late and too awkward to protest any further.

I give her a final glare before climbing into the passenger's seat of Apollo's car. While the outside is pretty beat-up, the inside is completely clean; the mark of a car someone takes pride in. Or the mark of a complete neat freak.

I buckle up as Apollo pulls out of the parking lot. We drive in silence for a minute, before he finally says, "Ash, right?"

I nod.

"And Apollo?" I say in response, as if it's possible for me not to know his name. As if by pretending, I can unsee him flying through the air, unhear every cold or snarky thing he's said to me, undraw each line that brought his face to life on my paper this morning.

"My father was a classics major." He snorts. "If he'd had Apollo's talent for prophecy, he probably would've chosen a different name."

I rack my brain trying to remember what I know about the Greek god Apollo other than that he was the god of prophecy.

106

He had something to do with music? And archery? And the sun? There must be something about him I'm forgetting that would make that comment make sense.

We reach a stop sign, and he turns to look at me. "So, what do you do for fun when you *aren't* diving through windows?"

I groan. "I'm not going to live that one down, am I?"

"Nope," he says, grinning. I notice his dimples for the first time. Were it not for the black eye to remind me of his lunch-time brawl, I'd seriously doubt that this is the same Apollo from the circus. "So," he says again, "fun?"

Oh, he was actually asking, not just making fun of me. "I draw," I say, "and I work at the art store downtown."

"So you're an artist?"

"Trying."

"What does that mean?" Apollo asks. "Either you make art or you don't, right?"

"Well, when you put it that way, then yes, I suppose I am an artist."

"See?" Apollo says. "Have some confidence."

I decide to volley the initial question back, feeling uncomfortable with the focus on my art, and also with this weirdly affirming version of Apollo. "What about you?"

"I am definitely *not* an artist," he says.

I laugh despite myself. "No, I mean, what stuff do you like?"

He hesitates. "I like animals," he says finally.

Not what I was expecting. I wouldn't have pegged Apollo for an animal lover. Although maybe he's one of those people who likes animals better than humans. That would explain a lot actually.

"Do you have any pets?"

A shadow seems to pass across his face. "No," he says, "but I do volunteer at the animal shelter." The shadow passes, and his voice brightens. "You should stop by sometime when I'm there. You can meet the dogs." He pauses, sounding a little self-conscious as he adds, "I mean, if you wanted to."

"Yeah," I say. "That sounds cool."

"Okay," Apollo says, smiling. "Cool."

We reach our street and pull into Apollo's driveway.

"Cool," I repeat. I bite my lip, look out the side window so Apollo can't see my face. I'm just glad Moira isn't here to see the flush creeping into my cheeks. The only thing I need less than catching feelings for a boy who seems to hate the true me is Moira's smug I-told-you-so.

Apollo puts the car into park as I unbuckle my seat belt and grab my stuff. "Thanks for the ride," I say quickly, needing to put some space between myself and whatever *this* is.

"See you in the morning?"

I give him a thumbs-up as I hurriedly exit the car, but don't say what I'm really thinking.

See you in my dreams.

TWELVE

The circus comes for me while I'm in bed. It isn't always this way. Sometimes I open my eyes and find myself already standing at the edge of the wood at that amorphous border between here and there, or at the edge of the tent, the blue and gold stripes welcoming me back. For a brief moment after opening my eyes, I fear the circus has left me behind—that, having finally gotten what I want, it's decided to eject me for not accepting my role as a clown, for wanting to choose my own destiny for once. But then the fear subsides, and I finally hear the sounds and let them wash over me.

After climbing out of bed I pause, then walk over to the window overlooking my neighbors' house and peer outside. I still don't know how to reconcile the Apollo from my dreams with the Apollo who now lives right next door, whose locker is two rows down from mine at a school I've only just transferred to myself. How can it be possible to dream of someone you've never met? Can you dream a person to life?

There are no lights on in the house, and I wonder if this is how it worked for him the first time too. Did he wake up in bed, hearing the sounds of the music through an open window? Did he have flight in his bones the same as me?

But above all else, why did it have to be him? It could have been any number of other people. Seb, or Fizz, or Gemma. Having Seb for a neighbor could be fun.

Well . . . perhaps that might be taking it a bit far. A nighttime's worth of Seb seems like the appropriate dose for any particular twenty-four-hour stretch. But even still, it would be less complicated than *this*.

I glance at the clock, then pull myself away from the window. No use dwelling. It's time to go.

Outside, the night is dark, the moon blocked by a large stretch of clouds. There's a slight chill in the air I know will fade away once I've crossed the threshold into the circus. Just before I'm about to pass my neighbors' driveway, a light comes on inside one of their cars.

Shit. I immediately drop to the ground like a character in a bad spy movie as Apollo steps out of his car. He starts walking toward the woods, and when he's out of sight I pull myself up. That was too close. The last thing I need is for him to find out who I really am. The circus is the one place I can actually be myself. I don't need him ruining that for me.

When I'm confident he's passed through the trees, I allow myself to approach. My heart races as I step through the trees, but my fear is assuaged when I see that he's not waiting to catch me on the other side. Who I do find, however, is Seb, bouncing excitedly on the balls of his feet while he juggles a trio of balls absentmindedly, just on the edge of the regular hustle and bustle of the midway. I take a deep breath. I'm home.

"Finally, 'mano!" He tosses one of the balls at me, and without thinking, I reach my hand up and catch it. He tuts. "Why couldn't you do that when I was training you?" He doesn't let me respond before continuing. "Never mind. Check it out!" He steps aside and—oh. My breath catches.

The carousel. It's exactly as I imagined it when I drew it, no—it's even better. The top canopy is blue and gold, just like the colors of the circus tent, with a ring of lights that shimmer, like fireflies or twinkling stars. And the animals! Not just horses but tigers and lions and zebras and giraffes, all inspired by the children I saw with their faces painted. A child with a rainbow painted on their face approaches a unicorn, but rather than climbing atop it, the unicorn lowers itself to the child's level. Each animal does something similar. The giraffe folds down its large neck to nuzzle its passenger, while the lion roars ferociously before allowing its rider to climb on board. When every animal has been boarded, the carousel starts turning, but rather than the up-and-down movement of a traditional carousel, each animal leaps or trots or jumps of its own volition.

It's *magical*.

"Does this happen often?" I ask, trying both to mask my involvement and also gauge whether it's rare for new attractions to be added to the circus.

Seb shakes his head. "Pretty much never," he says. "But it's awesome! And right in time for Masquerade too."

"Masquerade?"

Seb spins to face me so quickly I nearly get whiplash.

"Has no one told you about Masquerade?"

"No?"

He sighs dramatically, shaking his head as he throws an arm around my shoulder. "What would you do without me, vato? Masquerade is *the* best night of the year. It's when we welcome all the newcomers to the circus, which in this case means you."

"Just me?" I ask, eyes growing wide. I mind the attention less in the circus than I do in the daytime world, but still the idea of an entire party to welcome me feels particularly overwhelming.

"Well, no," Seb says. "Apollo's new too, unfortunately." His expression brightens up. "But on the plus side we'll all be wearing masks, so at least we won't have to see his smug face!"

I laugh, but all I can see when he says that is Apollo's black eye. And his dimples when he smiled. I shake that last thought out of my head. Absolutely not.

I take one last proud look at my contributions to the circus, before we head to the tent together and split up for our respective preshow rehearsals. I don't see Apollo when I head over to the trapeze rig, though I do spot Tessa stretching on the ground. She smiles and motions for me to join her, which I do. Like my skill on the trapeze, which seems to have arisen as a natural consequence of whatever magic this circus holds, my body has also acquired a flexibility I know it does not regularly possess. Apollo wanders over as we're finishing, then has a brief conversation with Tessa in sign language. I watch, wondering more about this boy I can't seem to escape. How does he know sign language? Why is he here? I notice there's no sign on his face of the fight. I guess that sort of stuff gets left behind in the daytime world.

Tessa signs one last thing and Apollo nods, then begins stretching. He hasn't said anything to me yet, but he's here at least, so that feels like progress. I follow along with Tessa as I did last night, wondering if I'm going to get to fly tonight. I certainly hope so.

We don't stretch for nearly as long tonight, and when Tessa cuts us off, I feel hopeful. She and Apollo have a brief conversation, and then he sighs and walks away, returning less than a minute later with a beat-up book.

"Catch." He tosses the book at me, and I do, much to my own surprise.

"Hmm," Apollo says. "We just might make a clown out of you yet." He grins and I glare. *Asshole.*

Tessa takes the book from me and begins flipping through it until she reaches the page she's looking for. She hands it back to me, pointing to the words at the top.

Bird's Nest.

It's a trapeze trick, and the book is a guide, complete with diagrams. I grin. This might just work after all.

Apollo and I trade off practicing tricks on the trapeze, Tessa watching from down on the ground, until she decides it's time to try catching us. As I wait for her to scale the rope up to the catch bar, I find myself looking down. Most everyone else is rehearsing their own material and not paying any attention to what we're doing here, but Apollo stands to the side of the rig, arms crossed as he looks up. I can't see his expression but I can imagine it, and I want to know what his deal is with me. Why is he such a jerk here but so nice in the daytime world?

I'll think about that later. For now, I grab on to the fly bar with my right hand, holding on to the side of the platform with my left. Tessa begins swinging on her side, and then calls out as she gets into the catching position. I bend my knees, and when she yells *Hup!* I hold the bar with both hands and jump.

Everything starts off right, but somehow my timing is off. Even with Tessa cuing my movements, I miscalculate and struggle to swing my legs over my head. To make it worse, I'm not able to recover and instead fall into the net below. Once I've stopped bouncing, I lower myself to the ground, annoyed.

"You're jumping the cues."

I look up, surprised to see Apollo talking to me. Voluntarily. "What?"

"You're anticipating when Tessa will cue you and moving too soon. Trapeze is all about timing. Move too soon and you're working against gravity instead of with it. Makes it harder to pull your legs up."

That's the longest stretch of words I've heard Apollo speak at the circus without being rude. It feels like a trick, except I think he's being genuine.

"Thank you," I say. He nods, looks away quickly. I get the feeling that sustained eye contact bothers him for some reason.

Tessa climbs down from her perch and joins us. She starts signing and Apollo interprets. "I'm going to have Apollo catch for you this time, and I'll cue you from the other side." Apollo looks ready to balk at the idea, but then Tessa signs something and he nods. Tessa gives me a smile as though anticipating I might not be so keen on being caught by someone who has never said a kind word until about thirty seconds ago. And even that might be stretching the definition of "kind."

She gives me a nod that I assume is meant to be reassuring. At least the net doesn't seem to hold a grudge against me.

She lets me climb the ladder first and follows closely behind. When we reach the top, she uses a long hook to pull the bar close enough to grab, and when I've taken hold, she gestures across the rig to Apollo.

Apollo begins swinging, and when he calls out the cue, I'm ready for it. I jump, cognizant of the advice he gave me before, and I hold my position until Tessa cues me. This time my legs swing easily above my head. I hold the position as I swing back

114

toward Apollo, and when I'm close I hear him call out and I let go of the bar, stretching out my arms and connecting with his. We stay connected for only a few seconds before he releases his grasp, and I fall down into the net with much more grace than I did last time.

When everyone is back on the ground, Tessa pulls me into a big hug. Afterward I reach out a hand to Apollo. He hesitates for a moment, then takes it. It's a small handshake and he disengages quickly, but I'll take it.

We have to stop rehearsing so Tessa and Apollo can get ready for the show, and as I take a seat in the audience, I feel for the first time like maybe the universe is finally on board with my plans.

THIRTEEN

After the show, Seb grabs me and brings me backstage to the dressing room to prepare for the Masquerade. He's refused to tell me any more about it than he's already revealed, but his excitement is contagious.

"Here," he says, shoving some clothes into my hands. It's a silky navy-blue collared shirt and mustard-colored chinos. He starts stripping off his own clothes without a second thought before changing into a ridiculous burgundy suit. He looks over once he's dressed. I'm still standing, holding the outfit. He frowns.

"Can you maybe turn around?" I ask.

He sighs but spins around. I pull off my shirt and look down, my heart leaping in my chest as I see the flatness I knew I'd find, but still worried I wouldn't. I can't help it. I grin, stupidly, run my hands across it, take a deep breath. God, I can *take a deep breath*. When's the last time I took a deep breath? I laugh as I pull on the shirt, button it up. The buttons are on the wrong side and it's weird, but I love it. I want all my shirts to button on the wrong side. I want all my shirts to button up.

"Okay," I say, once I've switched into the pants Seb provided. We both turn around.

"You're an odd duck, 'mano, you know that?" he says, stepping forward and sticking a mustard-colored handkerchief into my shirt pocket. "There," he says, patting my chest once. "Perfecto."

"Where to now?"

"Now? Now I do something about that hair of yours," Seb says, frowning and eyeing my head like it has caused him personal offense.

"My hair looks fine!"

"You want to be alone for the rest of your life? Flat hair like that is how you spend your life alone with a dozen cats. Now shut up and let me work my magic." He begins muttering under his breath in Spanish.

I shut up.

"There," Seb says a few minutes later. I look into a mirror and am impressed by the volume my dirty-blond hair seems to have acquired. It looks . . . good. I look good. I reach up to touch it, but Seb swats my hand away.

"No touching," he says, "Now let's go."

We stop and pick up Fizz and Gemma along the way. Fizz is already wearing a mask. It shimmers in tones of blue, purple, and green, and around the edge is a plume of brilliant gold feathers. Beneath it his golden-white hair sparkles under the light of the moon and stars. He and Gemma are wearing coordinating outfits of forest green. Hers a one-shoulder dress with a long tulle train, his a silk suit. Gemma's bottom set of earrings has been replaced by long gold feathers that match Fizz's mask. I *have* to sketch them later.

"Asher!" Gemma pulls me into a tight hug. "You look so good!"

I grin. "Thanks. You two look incredible!"

"Are you excited?" Fizz asks me.

117

"Clearly not as much as you," Seb jokes, likely referencing the fact that of the crowd all headed in the same direction, Fizz is the only one already wearing a mask.

Fizz extends a middle finger toward Seb but otherwise ignores the jab.

"Definitely," I say.

We join up with the rest of the crowd, all of whom I recognize as performers from the show. We're at the woods at the edge of the fairgrounds, and the crowd swells around us. There's a buzz in the air, an electricity I let myself get caught up in. With every step forward, Seb's grabbing my shoulder and shaking it like he's trying to dislodge a bar of candy from a jammed vending machine.

"It's gonna be great, 'mano," he says. "Masquerade is *the* best night of the year."

The crowd moves forward, and we let ourselves be carried along with it. Just past the trees, a person is handing out masks, and as I get closer, I recognize the plague doctor mask and the man beneath it.

"You!" I say, but he just holds up a single finger to his mouth as he hands me a mask. I want to thank him, but now isn't the time. I take my mask, a butterfly with wings like stained glass, and continue forward, checking out the masks given to each of my friends. Seb's is an intricate piece that covers his forehead and the right side of his face in what looks like a cross between ivy and a spiderweb, while Gemma receives a delicate ivory cat's-eye mask.

Beneath the masks, we exchange grins and step forward onto a forest path covered in leaves of the most brilliant shades of red, orange, and gold, floating globes of light bobbing up and down and illuminating our path forward. The night smells like pine trees and spiced cider, like a million possibilities and a million ways to achieve them. I think of the daytime, of a world that seems intent on beating me down, and I know that won't happen here.

We continue on, reaching a clearing in the woods that feels like it formed itself just for tonight. Thick, soft grass carpets the ground. Around the perimeter, trees bend their boughs to form a canopy of leaves that makes me feel like I've entered an autumnal snow globe.

My friends slip off their shoes before stepping forward onto the cool and springy grass. I let the feeling of it ground me as I listen to the sounds of the crowd and the string quartet playing a melody that is simultaneously bright and melancholy.

Just when I thought the circus couldn't get any better, it produces this.

"Wow."

My friends laugh, and then Gemma's grabbing my hand and pulling me forward to dance. I drag Fizz and Seb along, and soon everyone else begins dancing as well. Seb's dance moves are as goofy as his personality, and it's just what I need to lose any inhibitions I may have carried over from the daytime. I spot Tessa dancing, and as I might have expected, she's with Apollo. He's wearing a deep purple shirt that hugs his chest, the top button undone, and a pair of black slacks. He looks . . . well, he looks damn good, though I hate to even think it.

Gemma notices my staring and leans over. "He does clean up quite nice, doesn't he?"

I clear my throat, pull my gaze away, embarrassed.

"It's okay," she says. "I won't tell Seb."

"I don't care," I say. So Apollo is attractive. It's not exactly a secret.

"Okay," Gemma says.

"Okay." I clear my throat. "I'm going to get a drink." I slip through the crowd until I find a waiter holding a tray of brightly colored drinks that fizz and steam and bubble. I take a blue fizzy drink that comes in a tall glass and sip it as I sit on a seat shaped like an oversize toadstool and watch the crowd. As I'm watching my friends dance and enjoying the brief respite for my weary feet, I feel a tickle on my hand.

"Oh, hello, friend," I say to the blue butterfly that has again returned. I move my hand up slowly, but the butterfly doesn't fly away.

Suddenly the music stops. I look up and see René standing on the small stage where the band sits. He clears his throat, and everyone quiets down.

"Thank you," he says. "Wow. It's hard to believe it's that time of year again, but here we are for another Masquerade."

The crowd cheers, and it takes a few seconds for it to quiet down enough for René to continue speaking.

"Every year we come together to celebrate where we've been and where we're going, and this year is no different. The Midnight Circus is more than a show, more than a performance or a single act. It's a culmination of the magic each and every one of you brings each night. It's a bright spot in a dark world. For those of us gathered here tonight, it's a family. And it's a home." Folks cheer and snap their fingers at this line.

"And so, tonight it is my distinct pleasure to officially welcome our newest members to the Midnight Circus. Apollo and Asher, would you come up here, please?"

The crowd erupts as Apollo and I make our way to the front of the crowd. I lift the butterfly up and let it climb onto my shoulder. My friends whoop and whistle as I pass, and as I look at the other performers and listen to them cheer for me and Apollo, I realize this is the first time I've ever been celebrated as myself. The first time anyone has ever looked at me, actually looked, and said, *Yes, you belong here. You belong just as you are.*

I'm suddenly glad for the mask covering my eyes.

I sneak a peek at Apollo standing beside me and see that even he isn't immune to this moment. He meets my eyes and smiles. It's only for a second and then he pulls away, but it's progress.

René clears his throat, and the crowd quiets down again. I notice Tessa standing in the front of the crowd, looking at Apollo, who begins signing as René speaks. "There's a quote I've always liked, from T. S. Eliot. He said: 'For last year's words belong to last year's language. And next year's words await another voice. And to make an end is to make a beginning.' I think of that each year as we come upon Masquerade and as I reflect upon the ways in which the circus, like life itself, is a place of renewal. I think about this quote because the next part of the evening is always the hardest. But as this quote reminds me, there's no such thing as a simple ending, only new beginnings."

He pauses, and I'm confused. What is he talking about?

"And so, as we welcome our newest voices into the circus, so too must we say goodbye to some of our dearest friends. But how fortunate we are to be welcomed here for the time we're able to stay, and may the lessons we've learned here allow us to turn our endings into new beginnings. Jenni and Tessa, would you please step forward?"

Everyone claps loudly as the two women step forward. Everyone except Apollo and me. Tessa steps forward and stands between Apollo and me, taking both our hands and squeezing them, and that contact is the only thing keeping me standing right now because my legs feel like jelly. When she lets go, it takes everything I have not to fall as the world drops out from beneath my feet.

René turns now and looks at the four of us, standing together on the small stage. "Jenni and Tessa. As is our tradition, your time at the circus has concluded. Would you do the honors of bestowing our newest members with these pins, to signify the start of their journey here with us?"

He waits a moment for Apollo to finish interpreting, and then hands Jenni and Tessa each a pin. Jenni, the Ferris wheel operator, comes over to pin me, while Tessa pins Apollo.

Perhaps seeing my expression beneath the mask, Jenni gives me what I assume is supposed to be a reassuring smile, but I'm not having it.

"How can you be okay with this?" I ask. "He's kicking you out!"

Next to me, I see Apollo signing something to Tessa. I assume it's in a similar vein to what I'm saying now.

"I felt like you at my first Masquerade, but it's my time to move on." Jenni squeezes my hand. "Besides, you'll see us again. Look."

She turns to face the audience as René speaks again.

"And now, before I let you all return to your dancing and merriment, there's one final thing to do. It is my pleasure to officially welcome back former members of the Midnight Circus. Please join me in giving them a round of applause!"

The crowd of current performers begins to holler and cheer as a group of nearly one hundred people comes streaming in through the woods. I spot an older gentleman with blue hair who I recognize from the audience tonight, and I watch as Seb nearly bowls him over with a hug. So that's it? Get kicked out and come back, what? Once a year? And that's supposed to compare to the freedom of being myself every night?

René cues up the music again as Tessa and Jenni leave to go mingle with the rest of the crowd. I turn to Apollo, rendered speechless, but he storms off the stage and pushes through the crowd until he disappears from sight.

Gemma spots me standing onstage and motions for me to come and join them. I do, but it doesn't seem to matter since no one is paying any attention to me anyway.

"I'm going to go get a drink," I say, but there's no response because no one is listening. Before I couldn't move a foot without someone slapping me on the back and welcoming me to the circus, and now I'm a ghost.

I slip away from Seb, who's currently being given a piggyback ride by the old man with blue hair, slip away from Fizz and Gemma, slip away from the smiling and the crying and the laughing, slip away as easily as I slipped away from my old school. With no one noticing and no one caring.

It's not fair. You can't give someone something and tell them you're going to take it all away in the same breath. How can everyone else act like that's okay? I rip my mask off and throw it to the ground. It doesn't matter that I haven't been here long. I'd rather spend my whole life in the closet than be shoved back into it by the same people who helped me out.

A chill in the air settles over me as I step out of the clearing back into the trees. I hear the sounds of the Masquerade behind me, but where they felt welcoming before, now they feel oppressive. I'm drawn instead to another sound, and I soon find its source—Apollo. Specifically, Apollo's hand, punching a tree. Over and over he slams his fist into the tree even as his knuckles scrape and bruise and bleed, and I stand and watch because I understand the impulse to let physical pain numb the rest. But then I see his face and the tears running down his cheek, and something seizes inside me. Hesitantly, I take a step forward and take his hand in mine, half expecting for him to come swinging at me instead, but he doesn't. My heart races as I uncurl his fingers and turn his hand over, eyes lingering over his calloused palms for just a moment before I remember what I'm doing and with whom. I reach into my front pocket and pull out the handkerchief Seb stuck in there, then wrap it around Apollo's knuckles, tying it just over his palm.

Apollo stays still the entire time, letting me work, and when I'm done, I'm the one who lets go first. He re-forms his fist around the handkerchief, then lets it fall by his side.

"I can't do this without her," he says, then leans against the tree and sinks down to the ground. For the first time I see a bridge between the rude and distant nighttime Apollo and the daytime one who swings between aggression and kindness. It's fear, and very likely some trauma I can only guess at. And perhaps for the first time, I really understand that I'm not the only one here with demons.

More confident now, I squat down and join him on the ground. Neither of us speaks. I watch Apollo from the corner of my eye. He rests his injured right hand on his lap, and with his left he picks up a stick and starts doodling aimlessly on the ground, making a cross pattern that reminds me of a tic-tac-toe game.

I reach out and take the stick from him, then draw an *X* right in the middle square. It takes him a second to understand, but then he takes the stick back and adds an *O* to the top right. We pass the stick back and forth until the game ends. A draw because, well, tic-tac-toe isn't exactly the pinnacle of strategic games. But then Apollo takes a deep breath and mumbles his thanks, and while it's not much, it feels good to be able to make things slightly better with just a stick and some letters.

If only fixing the circus were that easy.

If only . . . *Oh!* I jump up. "I'm sorry, but I've got to go!"

I don't wait to see Apollo's reaction. I know exactly what I need to do.

I pull René's notebook and pen from its hiding space in the hollowed-out tree and flip through it frantically, scrolling through pages of names until I find first Jenni's and then Tessa's. Each has been crossed out by a line. My heart races. Could it really be that simple?

I rewrite each name clearly and wait for the ink to dry. At first it seems to be working, but then I realize the ink isn't just getting dryer—it's *fading*. Soon the names are completely gone, as though they'd never been written in the first place, and all that remains is the original crossed-out names. I try again, writing each name fresh on a brand-new page and waiting, but again they fade from the page entirely.

Okay, new strategy then. I put away the pen and pull out my colored pencils. If I could draw a carousel to life, then surely I can draw two people back into the circus. I put everything I have into my drawing, hoping that if I can somehow imbue the image with the *essence* of Jenni and Tessa, the circus will understand what I'm doing and allow them to stay. I don't know how long I draw, but I do it with such intensity that my hand starts to cramp by the time I'm finished. No one is going to leave the circus on my watch.

I sit back once I'm done, putting the colored pencils back into their case and into my pocket. Maybe I'll be able to enjoy the rest of the evening after all. I take one last look at my drawing and—

NO! I run my fingers across the page frantically, uselessly, as though I can reach through the page and grab the drawing, force it to stay, rather than fade as it's doing now, slowly then all at once.

FUCK!

I hurl the notebook as far as I can, then immediately regret it and start searching for it in the dark. I don't understand why it's not working. It should work! I need it to work! If I can't keep Jenni and Tessa here, how will I make sure that I never have to leave?

"I think you may have dropped something."

I look up, startled by the man with the plague mask. He glances down pointedly, and I follow his gaze, finding René's notebook at his foot.

"Thanks," I say, picking it up and brushing it off. I'm embarrassed to be caught in the middle of what is essentially a temper tantrum, when I realize that this is exactly who I need to be talking to.

The man starts to turn and walk away. "Wait!" I say. He turns back. "I need your help." I share everything—what I've done with the notebook since taking it, what I learned tonight about the circus, and all the ways I've tried to stop Jenni and Tessa from being kicked out.

The man listens quietly until I've finished speaking. "I've always thought it was cruel, the way René kicks people out of the circus," he says.

"René did this? But I've had the notebook."

"Mmm, yes, but this was in the works much longer than the time you've had the book. It'll be quite difficult to undo."

I seize on that last sentence. "But it *can* be undone?"

"Oh, yes," the man says. "Little is permanent."

"And you can do it?" I ask, hope rising inside me.

"I can," he says. "For a price."

Like a balloon popped by a pin, I'm quickly deflated. I think of the money under my bed, money I've been saving for something bigger, saving for a way out. Is this it? Is this what I've been saving for? Perhaps I'm only ever meant to be fully free in my dreams. There are worse fates.

"I can pay," I say. "I've got money." I just hope it will be enough.

"Not money," the man says. "The notebook. You aren't the only one who has been wronged by René. Or who has plans for this circus."

"Oh," I say. I look down at the notebook in my hands, feel its power. It's already done so much for me; why won't it do just one thing more?

"Or you could return it to René," the man suggests, picking up on my hesitation. "Perhaps he'll be sympathetic. Or perhaps he'll kick you out instead."

My heart races. That is *not* an option. I can't do anything to jeopardize my place here. And that includes being caught with René's stolen notebook. I don't need to bring more carousels to life. All I need is to fly. And to stay forever. And if this man can also bring back Tessa and Jenni, that will be icing on the cake.

"Okay," I say. The man holds out a hand to take the notebook, but I'm not ready to turn it over yet. "I want Jenni and Tessa brought back. And for no one to have to leave."

"Of course," the man says. "That can be arranged."

"And I don't ever want to be a clown again!" I add for good measure.

"Noted," he says dryly.

Before I can change my mind, I hand the notebook over. The man takes it, secreting it beneath the black cloak he wears with his plague doctor costume, and turns to walk away.

"Wait!"

He turns back.

"I don't know your name," I say.

The man pauses, as though debating. "Jean," he says finally. "My name is Jean." Then with a tip of his head he disappears into the darkness, leaving me to wonder if I've made a terrible mistake.

FOURTEEN

I wake up knowing that the day cannot possibly pass fast enough. Tonight, I'll know if Jean kept his deal. Or if I've made a huge mistake.

Second period is a free study today, so we're in the library, Moira and I at two of the computers. A quick glance at Moira's tells me she's deep into reading fan fiction. I do a brief scan of what she's reading and raise an eyebrow because wow, that is not school appropriate. Across the room Apollo is reading a book, far enough away to risk what I'm about to do.

I open a new browser tab and google *Apollo Bennett*. Being an uncommon combination of names, the first few entries are all about my new neighbor. His name comes up repeatedly in the *Wilbur Gazette*, which covers local news. Seems he was a frequent name on the Principal's List at North Leicester High School, which also explains why he transferred schools his senior year. The school burned down earlier in the spring. Wilbur High got a pretty large influx of students right afterward. Maybe Apollo was one of them before his parents decided to move him to Our Lady. What doesn't make sense is where he was all these past months when he clearly wasn't living at home.

I open one article about the fire that also tags Apollo's name in a separate window, and then I return to the main search page. Before I can stop myself, I type another name into the search bar. I've been trying not to think about Kaycee and the lawsuit, but between her upcoming press conference and my grandfather's involvement in the case, it's been hard not to.

Lawsuit Moving Forward over Wilbur High Bathroom Policy

By Ramona Durling

WILBUR—When Kaycee Reynolds transferred into Wilbur High School, the last thing she expected was to be taking the school to court for a "discriminatory policy against transgender students." Kaycee Reynolds, a transgender female, says the school's policy, which limits her to a restroom in the nurse's office, has had a significantly detrimental impact on her education.

"When I have to trek across the school to use a bathroom, that impacts my education. When I have to separate from my friends because they can use the girls' room, and I can't, that impacts my education. All I'm asking is for Wilbur High to allow me to use the same bathroom as every other girl."

Local law firm Sullivan & McKinley Associates has been retained by the high school to spearhead its defense. When reached for comment, lead attorney John Sullivan stated, "Wilbur High School is committed to providing alternative private facilities for students with gender identity issues in full accordance with New Hampshire laws. We are confident that this lawsuit will be dismissed on the merits."

Students at Wilbur are divided in their response to the case and current school policies.

According to Kayla Perkins, a member of the junior class, "I don't know any girls who want to share a bathroom with someone just because they say they're a girl. Bathrooms are supposed to be safe spaces. We divide them for a reason."

Student-body president James Hawthorne disagrees, stating that "Trans rights are one of the biggest civil rights issues of our generation. No student should feel singled out for being who they are."

Discourse on the issue has spread to nearby Catholic school Our Lady of Mercy Academy, where class president Rebecca-Ann Taylor began collecting signatures in support of Wilbur High School's current policies.

"The students of Our Lady of Mercy stand with our brothers and sisters at Wilbur High as they fight to protect the sanctity of their bathrooms. I recently met a student who transferred to Our Lady because of this issue. I'm just glad she'll be able to finish out her educational journey without further disruption."

I hit the print button then and jump to my feet, seeing red. Moira looks up, her face a mix of curiosity and alarm, but I don't care.

Where is she?

I look around. There. Sitting at one of the round tables with her posse, writing in her journal with a purple pen.

I storm over to the printer and snatch the paper, still warm, then march it over to Rebecca-Ann. "What the *fuck* is this?"

She glances up, her face the picture of ignorance. "I'm sorry, but I don't know what you're talking about." Her friends glare at me, but I ignore them, smashing the paper down in front of her.

"You know nothing about me and you know *nothing* about why I transferred here. You want to have a petition? You want to talk to reporters? Fine, but leave me the hell out of it."

I leave the paper behind as I storm out of the library and run straight into Sister Johnson.

"Ms. Sullivan! In-school detention, now."

In-school detention at Our Lady of Mercy is very much what it sounds like. Sister Johnson leads me to a small room with no windows and tells me to take a seat at one of the desks. A teacher sits at a desk at the front of the room, and other than a single Bible on each desk, there is nothing else in the room, not even a clock, and I'm not allowed to do anything other than read the Bible or sit in silence.

Apparently however, it's my lucky day, because we have Mass at the school chapel after lunch, and I'm to be let out to attend.

Yay.

By the time Sister Johnson returns to collect me for Mass I feel like I've aged five years. It should be considered torture to deprive someone of both windows *and* a clock.

Sister Johnson leads me to a pew near the front of the chapel and proceeds to sit next to me. The rest of the students file in a few minutes later. I spot Moira, but she ends up a few rows behind me. There's some quiet whispering as we wait for the priest to arrive, but since I'm trapped between the wall and Sister Johnson, I have no one to talk to.

As I sit and stare at the clock (the beautiful, glorious clock!) there's a shift in the whispering. I turn around and see everyone either reading something from a piece of paper or gesturing to their neighbors to pull out the pew Bibles. I turn back and grab my own Bible, and as I open it, a piece of paper flutters down onto the ground. I reach down and pick it up, then unfold it and begin reading.

It's a screenshot of an article from the *Wilbur Gazette*, and it's an article I immediately recognize, because my school username is at the top of the page. And that's not the only thing I recognize.

Early Morning Fire Destroys North Leicester High School

By Ramona Durling

NORTH LEICESTER—Firefighters were called to the scene of a blazing inferno around 1:30 Thursday morning after local resident Mack Thorn called in a report of smoke. When Fire Chief Graves arrived on the scene, he found the local high school engulfed in flames.

Two boys found near the scene were brought to the hospital and treated for smoke inhalation, but were later released. Nearby residents say the late hour and the remote location of the high school may have contributed to the delayed response to the fire.

Fire Chief Graves says that no determination as to the cause of the fire has been determined, but foul play was not being ruled out.

The line about foul play is circled in black ink, and an arrow links it back to the picture at the top of the page. It's Apollo, wrapped in a blanket beside an ambulance. The caption beneath reads: *Apollo Bennett, 17, receives treatment from EMTs for smoke inhalation*. Beside that someone's written in *wonder where he spent the summer . . . juvie?*

The whispering grows louder, and I turn to see if I can spot Apollo. Clearly everyone else had the same idea, because all eyes seem to be on him. Cackling from a few rows away tells me the culprits behind all this are, as expected, Jackson and Ricky. Apollo seems to realize this too, because he climbs over his pew and punches Jackson right in the face, just as the priest enters the chapel.

Sister Johnson rushes over as the priest pulls Apollo off Jackson, and she picks up one of the pieces of paper that's fallen to the ground. I happen to catch Moira's eye as Sister Johnson turns back to me.

She's so apoplectic she can hardly speak, but the pointing gesture is very clear. It seems I will not be attending Mass after all.

Sister Johnson marches us straight out of the chapel, bemoaning the loss of corporal punishment the entire time.

"In the Lord's House of all places!" she wails. "Whatever could have possessed you!"

Apollo rolls his eyes, and I try not to laugh. When we reach solitary, Sister Johnson doesn't stop like I expect. Instead, we keep walking until we reach the principal's office.

"Sit," she says sharply. Apollo and I take seats outside the office while she goes inside and shuts the door.

I try to meet Apollo's eye, but he looks steadfastly ahead, avoiding my gaze. I wonder if there's any truth to what Jackson and Ricky suggested when they stuck that article into the Bibles. Some pieces definitely fit. Who goes to their high school at 1:30 in the morning?

But then, why would he start a fire? I feel like Seb as I try to mentally juggle all the different sides of Apollo I've encountered. How can this boy who loves animals and encourages me to call myself an artist be the same one so quick to anger and violence?

Finally, Principal Walker comes out and beckons us into his office. Sister Johnson tries to linger, but he tells her she should return to Mass.

Apollo and I exchange glances, then head into Principal Walker's office and take a seat.

"Mr. Bennett and Ms. Sullivan. Tell me, do you know how often we accept new students in the last two years of our program here?"

I shake my head, but Apollo doesn't even react, just stares straight past Principal Walker with a blank expression.

"Almost never," he continues, clearly not waiting for a response. "Our Lady of Mercy prides itself on many things, among them being our small and closely knit cohorts of students—"

I have to stop myself from raising an eyebrow at that statement. Small? Yes. Closely knit? Hardly.

"And someone joining the class in the last two years risks upsetting that careful balance. However, in some *rare* circumstances, exceptions are made."

I presume a large donation is what he's talking about. I know why my grandparents would give generously to get me a spot here for my senior year, but what could make Apollo's parents want to do that for him?

"That being said, we take incidents such as this quite seriously, and as such, I have no choice but to suspend you both for two days."

"What? But I didn't do anything!" I can't keep my mouth shut any longer. Apollo remains silent.

Principal Walker holds up the newspaper article. My username is circled at the top.

"This is you, is it not?"

"Yes, but—"

"It can be a longer suspension. Whatever it takes for the message to sink in."

I shut my mouth.

"Excellent. I think it best you both leave for the rest of the day. The two days will begin tomorrow, which means I expect both of you to be nowhere near this campus until Tuesday morning, after Labor Day. Do either of you need to call someone for a ride?"

Who would I call? Mom? She's either asleep or at work. My grandparents? They're the last people I want to know about this. I shake my head.

Apollo shakes his as well.

"In that case, I expect when you return to class not to have any further issues. Is that clear?"

"Yes," we both say.

I'm almost surprised not to find Sister Johnson with her ear pressed against the door when we exit Principal Walker's office. We both stop at our lockers on the way out of the building to collect our things. Neither of us says anything until we get outside.

"Do you want a ride?" Apollo asks.

I pause for a moment. Do I want to ride with someone who may have burned his old school down?

"Sure, thanks," I say. I guess not wanting to walk home trumps riding with a potential arsonist. And you know, he didn't stab me with the stick at the circus last night, so that's a point in his favor. "Actually," I say, "could you bring me to the art store?"

Apollo shrugs. "Sure. Guess I can get in some extra hours at the shelter."

I follow him to his car, then wait while he unlocks the door. Given what I can now presume about his family's income, I'm surprised he has such a beat-up car. Then again, if my son burned down a school, I'm not sure I would give him a nice car either.

"I didn't put those articles into the Bibles," I say to break the overbearing silence and then wish I didn't, because what if he asks why I was searching his name in the first place?

"I know," he says. I wait for the inevitable follow-up question, but it doesn't come.

"Okay," I say, relieved.

"You haven't asked me if I did it," Apollo says a moment later.

I turn to look at him, surprised. "Do you want me to ask you?"

"No."

"Okay."

He doesn't say anything else, and neither do I. I notice at no point does he volunteer that he *didn't* burn his old school down. Maybe it's just me, but that feels like the sort of information I would volunteer if it was true.

We reach the art shop and Apollo parks in front. "Thanks for the ride," I say as I climb out. He nods but doesn't exit the car. I shut the door, and as I walk toward the entrance, I glance back. I don't know what force brought Apollo and me together, or why there's a part of me that feels drawn to him.

I just hope it doesn't end up hurting me.

FIFTEEN

I enter the shop and throw my backpack down behind the counter. "It's me!" I shout back to Mr. Roberts, who is likely in the back room. "Got out of school early." Not technically a lie.

The shop is empty. Now that the back-to-school rush has passed, I expect it will be empty more often.

Sometimes I wonder how Mr. Roberts keeps the business going at all, but he seems to manage. I open my bag and pull out my sketchbook. I've made some more drawings of the circus I want to show him. There's one of Seb that I'm particularly proud of. It's all about the eyes. Capture those, and the rest comes easy. I learned that from Mr. Roberts. Before I officially worked here, he'd let me sit in the back room and sketch after school while Mom was working hospital shifts. When there were no customers, which was often, he'd join me, give me tips on drawing, sometimes set up an easel next to me and work on a piece of his own. He's still the first, and sometimes only, person I show my own work to.

"I've got something to show you," I shout as I pull out my sketchbook. "I was inspired by the circus drawing I made for the display and did a few more that I wanted your thoughts on."

I turn the corner and immediately freeze. Mr. Roberts stands, leaning against a wall, sweat dripping down his face, cane lying beside him. We make eye contact for a brief moment before his face goes gray and he collapses onto the ground.

✦✦✦

Everything seems to happen in slow motion after Mr. Roberts collapses—calling 911, waiting for the paramedics to arrive, watching as they use a defibrillator to restart his heart, standing alone on the street after they've put him into the ambulance and driven away, the small crowd that gathered dispersed now that the action is over.

My legs carry me to the animal shelter before I can stop to think what else to do.

The woman behind the front desk must see the shell-shocked look on my face, because she jumps up when she sees me and helps me down into a seat, pouring me a glass of water that I take small sips from.

"Is everything okay, hun?" she asks, concern evident in her voice. "Can I call someone for you?"

"Apollo?" I manage to get out.

"He's right out back," she says. "I'll go fetch him for you."

She heads behind a set of doors, coming back a minute later with Apollo. He looks briefly like he's seen a ghost. I pull off my beanie and hold it in my hands. He hesitates for a moment and then comes to sit next to me.

"Thanks, Margaret," he says to the woman behind the desk. "Can you go finish feeding the dogs? I only made it to Bentley."

The woman nods and then heads into the back.

"What's going on?" Apollo asks when she's gone. "Are you okay?"

I shake my head. One minute he was standing there, looking at me, and the next he was on the floor. I can't get it out of my head. Somehow, I manage to get the words out to tell Apollo what happened.

140

"I'll be right back," Apollo says. He walks away, says something to the woman in the back, and then returns and he's helping me stand. I follow him out of the shelter, down the street, into his car. We don't speak. I sit in the passenger seat, right hand clutching my sketchbook, the left digging into my leg.

There's a moment of hesitation, and then Apollo reaches across the center console and lays his hand on mine. It's warm, and I look up, surprised. The moment doesn't last long, and he pulls away looking awkward as he starts the car, and for the first time, I wish he saw me. Like really saw me, and knew I was Asher. That the boy who flies alongside him each night is the same person who sits behind him in class each day. I don't know why it would matter. I'd hardly call us friends, but we share something bigger than either of us, and right now I could really use the comfort of that shared life.

"Do you want to go home or to the hospital?"

"The hospital," I say. Mom's there. She'll know what to do. I need to know he's going to be okay.

Apollo starts the car and begins driving. I rest my head against the window, watch as we pass the art shop, watch as it fades into the distance.

When we get to the hospital, Apollo parks the car and walks with me inside. When we get to the front desk, I ask if they can page my mom for me. I take a seat as we wait.

Mom comes down a few moments later, and I run into her arms like I haven't done since I was a child. She holds me tightly as the shock and adrenaline that've kept me standing come crashing down. I struggle to breathe as sobs rack my body and my legs go weak.

I hear Mom instructing Apollo to help me sit, feel his hand warm against my back as he helps guide me down, and then she's there, kneeling on the ground in front of me. "We're going to take deep breaths together now, okay?" she says. She takes my hands in hers and places one on my chest and one on my belly. "Deep breath in through your nose," she says. "Good, that's good—now hold it for a moment, and out slowly through your mouth." We repeat that until my breathing returns to normal and the world refocuses in front of my eyes.

"What happened?" Mom asks once I've calmed down.

I stare at my hands as I talk, focusing on anything other than the image of Mr. Roberts pale as a ghost. I don't even realize I've trailed off until I hear Apollo picking up where I left off.

"Oh, sweetie," Mom says when he's done, "I'm so sorry. I'll check in on him for you, and I'll see what I can do about getting you in to visit, okay?"

I sniffle and nod as I wipe my nose with my sleeve.

Mom's pager starts to beep. Biting her lip, she glances between me and a clock on the wall. "I can get someone to cover," she says. "I'll tell my boss it's an emergency."

I shake my head. "No," I say. "You don't have to do that. I'll be okay, I promise."

"I'll take her home," Apollo says, and still, *still*, after all these years of hearing it, I feel the acute sting of that word. *Her.*

Mom's pager goes off again, and this time she kisses me on the forehead and stands up. "Okay," she says, still looking conflicted, "but call the hospital if you need me and I'll come home, okay? I love you."

"Love you too," I say, but she's already gone.

✦✦✦

"Thank you," I say to Apollo when we've climbed back into the car.

"I'm sorry about Mr. Roberts," says Apollo.

I wipe my nose on my sleeve. "Can we not go home yet?" I say suddenly. I think of being alone in my house for hours while I wait for the circus to come, and I can't do it. Not right now. Not after watching Mr. Roberts nearly die right in front of me.

"Any place in particular you want to go?"

I shake my head.

"Hmm," Apollo says, and then he smiles shyly. "I have an idea. How do you like dogs?"

Twenty minutes later we are back at the shelter. Now that I've emerged from the fog I was in before, I can take a proper look around as Apollo speaks quietly to the same woman behind the desk who helped me before. There are a few chairs for sitting, and pictures line the walls of dogs and the people who adopted them. A small shelf beneath a window holds some basic supplies and other dog-friendly items for sale, and on the counter is a jar collecting donations for the shelter. I can hear barking in the background but can't see any animals from the front room.

Apollo comes back with permission to take a few of the more social dogs to a back room for us to play with, which is how I find myself sitting on the floor surrounded by a handful of energetic pups all demanding my attention.

Apollo sits beside me, laughing as a particularly energetic terrier jumps up and licks my face, while a pit bull mix named Honey with a face full of freckles brings a rope toy over to me to play tug. I'm overwhelmed by dog tongues and furry ears and soft bellies, and it's exactly what I needed. I twitch my head as the terrier tries to stick its tongue in my ear.

"I can see why you like volunteering here," I say. "I used to beg my mom for a dog as a kid, but she said it was too much work, and my grandparents think they're dirty."

Apollo wrinkles his nose. I laugh.

"Do you have a favorite?" I ask, gesturing to the dogs.

Honey has abandoned me for Apollo, tail slapping the concrete floor with gusto as he scratches her behind the ear.

Apollo covers Honey's ears and leans forward. "Don't tell the other dogs, but there's a blind rat terrier named Shakespeare who's my favorite. He's missing about half his fur and teeth, but he's the sweetest thing. His owner was a retired English professor, but when he passed there wasn't anyone to take the dog, so he ended up here. I sneak him extra treats when no one's looking."

I want to ask more questions, get answers to the list of questions burning in my mind, but I'm also afraid that if I answer too many he'll connect the dots and figure out who I really am.

"You were holding something earlier," Apollo says suddenly. "Your sketchbook, right?"

I hesitate, then nod.

"Do you think . . ." He trails off, shy, then shakes his head. "Never mind."

"You want to see something I've drawn?" I meant it as a question, but he takes it as an offer and immediately nods. Shit. The sketchbook is filled with drawings of the circus. If he sees any of those, it's game over.

I stand, shooing the puppies from my lap, and head over to my backpack. I should've just said no, it wasn't a sketchbook, or no, I'd rather not show you, but there's a part of me that wants to show him my art. Wants to blur the line between day and night, to let in the one person who, even more than Moira, has seen the real me.

There's one drawing I can show him without revealing my nighttime identity—a drawing of his house from my window. I flip through the pages until I find it, sandwiched between a picture of the circus tent and one of Apollo himself, flying through the air. My heart races as I bring the sketchbook over to him.

"Okay," I say. "But—only this one."

I feel light-headed as I watch Apollo holding my drawing in his hands, knowing all it would take is for him to the turn the page and that would be it. He'd know I'm really Asher. He'd know my secret, and there wouldn't be anything stopping him from telling everyone.

But he doesn't turn the page. In fact he holds the sketchbook almost *reverently* as he examines the picture. It's not even one of my best drawings. There was a particularly nice sunrise one morning I wanted to capture, and the window overlooking his house happens to face east.

After a few minutes that feel like much longer, he hands the sketchbook back. "You're really talented," he says.

"Thanks," I say, a little surprised. Pleased, but surprised.

Apollo clears his throat. "The shelter's closing up soon. We should probably go. My parents will be expecting me for dinner."

I give each of the dogs a final bit of petting, and after helping Apollo return them to their kennels we head out. The *thumpthumpthump* of my racing heart doesn't slow the whole ride home.

SIXTEEN

It's hard to hide that I'm a bundle of anxious excitement as I enter the circus hours after leaving Apollo. Tonight's the night I'll know if my gamble worked. After the day I just had, I could use some good news.

Seb meets me at the edge of the woods, and I try to judge from his face if anything's different yet. Maybe it's too early.

"René's called a meeting. Come on, 'mano."

I follow Seb, trying not to reveal more than I want to as I ask if he knows what the meeting's about.

"Dunno. Guess we'll find out soon!"

It seems everyone except for the fairway workers is gathered in the back of the main tent. No one knows why René has called us together. I don't spot Tessa or Jenni, though I expected that. If any of them were here, the atmosphere would likely be considerably different.

I find Apollo near the back of the crowd and walk over.

"Hi," I say.

He looks at me suspiciously. "What?"

"Nothing, I was just saying hi."

"Okay." He looks away and says nothing else. I don't know why I expected it to be any different. Don't know why I'm disappointed that it's not. Last night was clearly a fluke, and it's not like his daytime behavior is going to have any bearing here. I suppose I should find it validating; he only ever seems to be an asshole to other guys, but I still can't stop myself from wishing

146

for the Apollo who drove me to the hospital, who put his hand on mine and sat next to me at the shelter so I wouldn't be alone.

Fortunately, the awkwardness of standing silently beside Apollo is soon abated by René entering the space. The crowd goes quiet.

"Well," René says, clapping his hands together. "I'm sure you're all wondering why I've gathered you together. Don't worry, I'll soon let you get back to your training. First, I have a pleasant surprise for you all. It seems that Tessa and Jenni will be gracing us with their presence for a bit longer. I don't know how long they will be here with us, but I know we'll treasure their company while they are."

Everyone exchanges glances and begins whispering as Tessa and Jenni come in through the back of the tent. Apollo's face lights up when he sees Tessa, and I bite my lip to contain my smile.

It worked. I did it.

Tessa makes her way through the masses until she reaches Apollo and me. She looks confused as she begins signing with Apollo. Then suddenly she stops and pulls both of us into a big hug. I can't stop grinning as she pulls back.

I spot Jenni in the crowd. She smiles and gives me a wave, though she too looks a little bit overwhelmed.

"Well," Apollo says. I turn my attention back to him and Tessa, who has already started ahead. "You coming?"

It's like it was before Masquerade. Better even. Apollo's so grateful to have Tessa back that he's nicer than ever. Because no one but me knows how long they'll be back, Tessa focuses

147

on getting me ready to perform with Apollo. I feel a little jolt of electricity every time I connect with Apollo during a trick that I try not to think too much about.

I'm sad when our rehearsal time ends, but Tessa thinks I might be ready to start performing in the show in a few more weeks, which is really exciting. I'll miss the freedom of being able to sit and watch the show or enjoy the fairgrounds while they're empty, but the prospect of being fully part of the show outweighs any of those things.

"Good job tonight," Apollo says to me as I unravel the wraps on my hands. I look up, surprised.

"Thanks," I say. "You were a great catcher."

He looks like he wants to say something else, and I wait for him to speak but he just shuts his mouth again and nods.

Well, it's progress.

Later in the evening, after rehearsal and after the show, I find myself back atop the platform of the trapeze rig. Seb and Maisie are working on a new addition to their act, and while I enjoy watching Gemma make her balloon creations, it's not how I want to spend tonight.

I'll probably practice a bit later, but for now I appreciate the silence and the view.

"Hey."

I turn my head, surprised to see Apollo standing beside me. Maybe he came to practice. I go to stand up, but instead he sits down next to me, legs dangling over the side. I scoot over to make more room, but the platform isn't particularly wide and our knees touch. I think of him driving me to the hospital after Mr. Roberts collapsed, think of the way he looked surrounded by puppies as he sat next to me on the floor of the animal shelter, and suddenly it feels much hotter up here than it did before.

"I know what you did," he says suddenly.

My mouth goes dry.

"I saw you leaving René's trailer last week. And then last night when you left . . ." He trails off momentarily. "I know you stole René's notebook."

I turn my head, force myself to meet Apollo's eyes. "You can't prove it," I say forcefully, hoping that's true. Just when I thought maybe we could be friends. I should've figured.

He shakes his head. "No," he says, "that's not what I . . ." He reaches his left hand up, grabs a fistful of curls atop his head. He swallows, and I watch his Adam's apple as it rises and falls. "I'm trying to say thank you," he says quickly. "For bringing Tessa back."

That is . . . not what I expected him to say.

"Oh."

His eyes are still on mine, and I notice his eyelashes for the first time. They're so long. Have they always been that long? He's got an eyelash right at the corner of his eye. I reach out to brush it away without thinking, and then his hand is around my wrist, like when I reached for the butterfly the first time I met him, except this time it's gentler. I don't know what to do as he hesitates and leans in, and suddenly I feel light-headed, like I've forgotten how to breathe. Which isn't fair, because if anyone is going to make me feel that way, it shouldn't be *this* asshole.

"How do you know sign language?"

The moment ends. Apollo releases my wrist and leans back. Leave it to me to ruin the moment.

149

"My older sister's deaf, so she taught me some. But mostly a *lot* of hours on YouTube watching deaf creators."

I didn't even know he had a sister. "What about your parents? Can they sign?"

He snorts. "Yeah, no. My parents sent my sister away to boarding school pretty much as soon as they could. It's their, uhh, *preferred* method of parenting. Outsource it to someone else. No 'problem' in their children that can't be fixed by some money and a thousand miles of distance."

Right now, gaze trained at some point far in the distance, Apollo seems a thousand miles away, and I'm pretty sure he's no longer talking about his sister. I want to ask him more, but it feels unfair when I know who he is in the daytime world and he can't say the same.

Gently, I touch Apollo's arm, and he's shaken from his reverie. He clears his throat.

"Do you have siblings?" he asks, shifting the focus back to me.

I shake my head. "It's just me and my mom. And my grandparents. Sort of. It's complicated."

"I've got time."

I hesitate, worried that I'll say something that Apollo will be able to connect back to my daytime self, but after what he shared, it only seems fair. And maybe, sitting here beside him feeling like my true self for once, I might finally be ready to take a little risk.

"Okay, well, my dad died when I was a little kid, and my mom was disowned by her parents when she got pregnant with me, so it's just been us for pretty much as long as I can remember. Except then there's my dad's parents. My dad was

150

their only child and I'm their only grandchild, so they've got a lot of expectations for me. Which isn't bad, I guess, except—"

"Except their expectations don't fit who you are?"

"Yeah. Pretty much."

Apollo nods, looks out over the rig, and I get the sense he understands.

"I wish we could meet in the daytime."

I look up at Apollo; he's staring out over the net as if to avoid meeting my gaze.

"In the daytime?" If only he knew what he was really asking.

He shakes his head. "I don't know; it's stupid, I guess. It would be nice to know that all this"—he gestures around the tent— "is real. That I didn't just dream you all up."

"Hey now," I say, bumping my shoulder against his. "It's awfully bold of you to assume you dreamed me up. From where I'm sitting, it seems like the other way around."

Apollo cracks a smile, perhaps the first time I've ever made that happen here at the circus, then he clears his throat and stands up. He reaches out a hand and helps me to my feet. "We should practice."

I don't know why, but I'm disappointed as the conversation ends.

We spend the rest of the night flying until the sun rises over the horizon, and when I wake it's with the sensation of his hand wrapped around my wrist.

SEVENTEEN

Kaycee's press conference is scheduled for Sunday
afternoon, late enough that I'm still able to attend
church and Sunday brunch with my grandparents.

Grandpa doesn't usually talk about cases he's working on, so
I've almost been able to pretend he isn't involved in this one,
but with this afternoon's event on my mind, I can't help but ask
about it.

"How's the case going?" I ask as casually as I can manage
while Grandma serves the brisket that's been in the slow cooker
since the morning. "The one at Wilbur, I mean."

My heart races as Grandpa looks at me closely, perhaps
wondering where this sudden curiosity about his work has
come from.

"I understand if you can't talk about it," I say quickly, already
regretting bringing it up.

"Well," my grandfather says, "I can talk about it broadly.
We're still in the discovery phase. Cases like these often proceed slowly, but I expect this one to be dismissed by the judge."

I think about Kaycee. Feel disappointed on her behalf.
I wonder if she expects to win this case. Knowing her, she'd
fight it anyway.

"I heard there's supposed to be a press conference today,"
I say. "With the girl from Wilbur."

Grandpa reaches for the dinner rolls, begins buttering one.

"Not too much, dear," Grandma says. "You know what the
doctor said."

"The good Lord will take me when He wants to, and until then I'm going to enjoy a hot buttered roll with my Sunday dinner."

"The press conference?" I say again. "Why would she have one if the case is just going to get dismissed?"

"Because the case can't stand on its merits, so the opposing counsel is hoping to appeal to emotion. Don't worry too much. It's just a stunt." Grandpa reaches for a second roll, but Grandma pulls them away.

"The good Lord will take you when He's good and ready, but there's no need to send Him the message that the time is now."

While my grandparents bicker about bread rolls and butter, I think about what Grandpa said. I hope he's wrong. I hope Kaycee wins.

It seems appropriate in some perverse way to go from my grandparents' house directly to the press conference. My grandparents don't live too far from downtown, so I walk, telling them that I'm headed to the art store to work. I never told them about Mr. Roberts, so fortunately it doesn't set off any alarm bells.

When I arrive at City Hall, I spot a podium set up on the steps, and it hits me that I'm about to see Kaycee again for the first time since the incident. My palms begin to sweat. I don't think I fully thought this through.

"Oh, good, you're here," Moira says when she spots me. She's with the rest of the club on a patch of grass to the right of the main path leading to the building. Julian's here with Zoe. He's wearing one of Moira's ally pins on his baseball jacket. I wave to them both. "Hand these out," Moira says, shoving the pile of signs we made into my hands. "And tell everyone to spread out a little. I want us to have a bigger showing than those assholes over there." She nods toward the group across the path from us. I take a good look at them for the first time. They've got their own selection of signs.

KEEP OUR GIRLS SAFE!
THERE ARE ONLY TWO GENDERS!
RESPECT GOD'S DESIGN
"A WOMAN SHALL NOT WEAR THAT PERTAINETH
UNTO A MAN, NEITHER SHALL A MAN PUT ON A WOMAN'S
GARMENT: FOR ALL THAT DO ARE AN ABOMINATION
UNTO THE LORD THY GOD" (DEUTERONOMY 22:5)
GET YOUR AGENDA OUT OF MY RESTROOM!

The last one is being held by a girl who can't be more than three years old. Too young to even understand the hate she's inheriting.

"Hey," Moira says. "Ignore them."

I pull my attention away. It's nothing I haven't seen or heard before.

Moira and I distribute the posters among our group, and then we wait. I see a local reporter from the *Wilbur Gazette*, which makes sense, but it's the news cameras that leave me a little startled. I guess some part of me realized that a press conference requires *press*, but I didn't realize it meant actual big-time news reporters. It suddenly occurs to me that if they turn their cameras on us, I could end up on TV. My grandparents could see me. I slowly slink my way to the back of our

154

group, hoping I can block my face with the sign I'm holding if it comes to that.

"She's coming out," Julian says, and my heart skips a beat. At first I think she's grown taller, but then I see the heels and I remember how she wanted to wear heels to the dance last year. I wonder if she ever did. I wonder if she wore these same ones.

Kaycee's lawyer comes out and takes the podium.

"Thank you so much for coming out today. My name is Sandra Wareck, and I'd like to speak with you today about a girl." She pauses, looks around with a commanding expression, seeming to focus just a moment longer on the protesters, as though daring them to contradict her before continuing on. "Kaycee Reynolds is a seventeen-year-old girl like any other. A straight-A student at Wilbur High School, she loves going shopping with friends, taking trips into the city, and, like every true New Englander, grabbing coffee from Dunkin' Donuts before school." That draws a chuckle from the crowd. She keeps talking, but my attention shifts to Kaycee, standing to the side. Her brown hair has gotten longer. It's parted in the middle and hangs down on either side of her face, reaching almost down to her chest. She's wearing a dark blue peacoat and mustard-colored scarf, and were it not for her fingers tapping frantically against the side of her white jeans, she'd be the picture of calm. She scans the crowd, and before I can look away, her eyes meet mine, and I flash back to the day that started this entire mess.

"I think I want to do it."

The table shudders beneath me, and my pencil flies across the page as Kaycee drops her stack of books down on the table:

textbooks, just-for-fun books, SAT and ACT and college-essay prep books, and at the top, her bullet notebook, meticulously laid out and color coded with every detail of her day planned down to the minute.

I lay down my pencil, trying to ignore the line that now bisects the head of my self-portrait, an assignment for art class I'd rather not be doing.

"You think you want to do what?"

Her voice drops to a whisper, though there's no one else in the library.

"You know," she says, "*it*. I'm ready. I mean, I think I'm ready." She's nervous. I've never seen her like this. She's not afraid of anything. It's what I admire so much about her. I'm afraid of pretty much everything.

"We can do it tomorrow at lunch. You can go in first, and then I'll be right behind you. I'll go in, and I'll pee, and I'll wash my hands, and I'll leave. And that will be it."

"Kaycee—"

"And once I've done it once, it will be done. It will have been a thing I have done, and if I've done it once, then I can do it again and it will be no big deal."

"What about the bathroom in the nurse's office? Hasn't that one been okay?"

"I'm sick of the bathroom in the nurse's office. I'm sick of having to take the nurse's pass instead of the bathroom pass and not being able to use the bathroom at lunch because the nurse is on her break, and I'm so sick of feeling singled out, and I don't think I can keep doing it Ash, I don't think I can. Look, I know you don't get it, that's okay, but it's important to me."

She pauses, takes a breath. I don't say anything. I can't. There's a clenching feeling inside my chest, like someone has reached inside and is squeezing my heart, my lungs, my stomach, everything. I have to tell her. I don't know why I haven't told her, but I just can't.

I hear a vibrating sound, and Kaycee pulls out her phone. "Shit, look, my mom's pulling up front, so I've got to go, but we're doing this tomorrow, yeah?" She bends down, gives me a hug, and then she's gone.

Kaycee looks away, back to the podium, where her lawyer is finishing her remarks. There's polite applause when she's done, and then it's her turn to speak.

"Hi," she starts. "As you just heard, my name is Kaycee Reynolds."

If it were me up there, this is the point when I would awkwardly clear my throat, take a sip of water, possibly even throw up. But not Kaycee. She doesn't shy away from the cameras; like a sunflower, she seems to stretch taller in their light. I can't take my eyes off her.

Her statement is short and well rehearsed, just long enough to thank her parents and friends for their support and express her hopes that one day soon, New Hampshire will find itself on the right side of history.

When she's done, Moira turns back to our group, buzzing with excitement. "Come on," she says. "Let's go meet her. Show her she's got our support."

I freeze. That wasn't part of the plan. Showing up, holding a sign . . . those I can do. I can't talk to her, not right now.

157

Not here in front of everyone. What if she tells them what I did? And Moira—she thinks we don't know each other. She'll find out that was a lie too.

The group starts to move toward City Hall, but I don't follow. Moira waves the others ahead and comes back to where I'm standing.

"What's wrong? We're just showing our support. You don't have to share anything about yourself."

"I know that," I say.

"Okay . . ." Moira says, looking confused, "then what is it?"

God, that question is so much bigger than she even knows.

"Umm, my stomach," I say, putting a hand over my stomach and grimacing slightly for effect. "Mom ordered sushi last night, and I think it might have been a little off. I should go."

Moira frowns. "Okay, well, if you wait ten minutes I can give you a ride home, and you can still meet Kaycee."

I hold up my phone. "I already texted my grandparents while she was speaking. They think I'm working at the art store today, so they're going to pick me up there."

Moira looks disappointed. "All right, well, I hope you feel better." She turns to rejoin the group while I, like the coward I am, flee the scene.

EIGHTEEN

Three more former circus members appear tonight, and this time I am just as surprised as everyone else. More so, perhaps, because I was anticipating only Jenni and Tessa's return. It's clear as René speaks that he's trying to project an aura of confidence, but I'm not fooled. I wonder what Jean's endgame is, but so far I approve. Why stop at bringing back Jenni and Tessa? Anyone who was sent home before their time should be allowed back.

Among the returned circus members is Peter, the old man with blue hair who was Seb's original clowning mentor way back when. As soon as he steps forward, Seb runs and practically bowls him over, and it makes me happy to see him so happy. This is what the circus should be about.

As soon as René leaves, Seb pulls me over. He's got the energy of a kid in a bouncy castle hyped up on too much cake and ice cream.

"Asher! Have you met Peter? Peter, Asher. Asher, Peter. 'Mano, isn't this wild? The last time Peter was here I was just a little kid."

A few other folks, including Fizz, are gathered around as Peter extends a hand for me to shake. I'm quickly surprised by a jolt that makes my hair stand on end, and when he breaks the handshake, he flashes me a quick look at the hidden buzzer in his hand. Seb is laughing so hard he can hardly breathe, and I'm starting to get how Seb became the way he is.

"Tell Asher the story of your first night at the circus," Fizz prompts. This elicits a round of laughs and whistles from the gathered group, and I can tell it's a story that's been told before.

Seb grins. "Okay, so it's my first night, and I'm like seven, this shy little kid"—everyone laughs at the thought of Seb as a shy little anything, and he glares before continuing on—"and René decides to have Peter show me around. So here's this man, probably late sixties by this point—"

"Whoa!" Peter interjects. "I was hardly pushing forty." At the look everyone gives him, he amends that. "Fine, fifty."

Seb rolls his eyes, but continues. "*Anyways*, he's showing me around, this little kid who is terrified of pretty much everything, and I ask him why there aren't any animals, like lions and tigers and shit like that. I mean, it's a circus, and circuses have animals, right? And Peter here crouches down and says he'll share a secret with me. He says they *do* have animals, but they were recently kidnapped and the circus just managed to get them back, so they've been resting and that's why they haven't been in the show, but he could show them to me if I'd like."

Fizz is already doubled over in anticipatory laughter.

"So he takes me, right, and brings me to this train car and tells me to be really, really quiet so I don't spook the animals. And inside the car, it's like pitch-black, and he says I've got to stand completely still so the animals can smell me and decide if they'll let me approach or not. And as I'm standing there, viejo goes and puts on a tiger mask—"

Here Peter interjects, "And when he says tiger mask, you've got to know this is like a thirty-year-old rubber monstrosity—"

"Absolutely horrifying," Seb says with a shudder. "Anyways— I'm standing there hoping none of these animals is in the mood for Mexican when this motherfucker gets right up in my face, throws on the lights, and—"

"He damn-near pissed himself!" Peter finishes, and everyone including Seb bursts out laughing. "Aww, damn, kid," he says, pulling Seb into a headlock and rubbing his hair, "it's good to be back."

Seb wriggles away, and they get into a faux wrestling match. It's good to see Seb so happy. He deserves it.

I think I'm the only one who notices Maisie, in the background, lips pursed until she shakes her head and walks away. I pull away from Seb and Peter and the rest of the crowd and follow her into the ring, where I find her practicing her juggling. She's good—really good. Almost as good as Seb, which is impressive.

"He'll calm down in a few nights," I feel compelled to say. Maisie glances up but otherwise stays focused on her juggling. I try again. "Peter seems really cool. I'm sure you two will connect in no time."

"Totally," she says. "Best of friends, I'm sure."

I'm embarrassed to say it takes me a second to realize she's being sarcastic. I don't know why I feel compelled to defend Peter's return. After all, it wasn't my decision to bring him back. But even if it was, is it really so bad?

"Just give it some time," I say.

"I need to focus," is all Maisie says in return. I can tell she's skeptical, but I decide to chalk that up to a bit of youthful envy. She'll adjust. She has to.

I'm off my game during rehearsal tonight. I can't quite seem to get Maisie out of my head. I decide to watch the show rather than wander the midway, hoping that it'll remind me of the magic I fell in love with.

And it does.

At least until I see her performing with Seb. I glance around at the rest of the audience. I don't recognize most of them, which makes sense as most only get to come once, but a few rows over, I spot a shock of blue hair. Peter is watching the show—no, he's watching *Seb*.

I don't know what it's like to have a dad, but if mine were still around, I hope he would look at me like that.

I sniffle and clear my throat, then look away.

After the show, I go find Fizz. As expected, he's over by Gemma's stand, eating popcorn as he watches her make balloon animals for a group of children.

"What a night, huh?" he says. He's not wrong. "You know, I've never really thought much about how the circus picks people to come and how it decides when it's time for someone to leave. Jenni and Tessa coming back, I sort of get. I mean, they hardly left. But why these three? Peter's been gone for years. Like, so long I'm pretty sure Seb was the only person here when he was still a performer. It's weird." He shrugs, then takes a handful of popcorn and throws it into his mouth.

"Good weird, though," I say quickly, thinking of Peter in the audience, getting to see Seb grow up. Getting extra time. "Right? I mean if they want to be here, they should be here."

Fizz considers that, his face thoughtful in contrast to Maisie's clear skepticism. "Perhaps," he says. "Or perhaps knowing there's an end makes our time here all the sweeter."

I'm starting to feel frustrated but do my best not to let it show. What I need is to find someone who will side with me, someone who can appreciate how great it is to bring people back. What I need is someone like Jenni.

I first head to the Ferris wheel, but she's not there. A bald white man with a long red beard is running the ride. I wait until he finishes loading a couple in and spots me. He starts the ride and then pushes the joystick on his wheelchair toward me, the ground in front of him changing automatically from grass to a smooth, solid surface, and then back again as soon as he's passed. It's pretty cool actually.

He introduces himself as Jeremy and points me in the direction of the tent village when I ask about Jenni. "Follow the music," he says.

Strange, but okay.

Jeremy's meaning soon becomes clear. As I scale the ladder and climb atop the train car, I hear some kind of bass-heavy electronic music that reverberates in my chest. I follow the music until I reach a small crowd gathered around one particular tent.

In the middle is a makeshift poker table, around which four people are crowded—three players and one dealer. A large set of speakers rests behind the dealer, pulsing with the beat of the music. I feel the vibration as a full body sensation, and it might feel good if my eardrums weren't ready to explode.

Someone hands me a pair of earplugs, which I put in. The relief is immediate. I turn my attention back to the game and realize that one of the players is Tessa. And if the pile of plastic coins in front of her is any indication, she's crushing the others. I only vaguely recognize the other players, but as I watch Tessa signing back and forth with one of them, and the hearing aid in the right ear of the third, I realize why the music is so loud.

I feel a tap on my shoulder and turn to see Jenni. She says something, but I can't hear her. We walk away from the tent and I remove my earplugs.

"Pretty neat, isn't it? I've never been back here after the show before. I was always working the Ferris wheel."

"Wait, why *aren't* you working the Ferris wheel?" I ask. They weren't even gone a full night. Tessa is still flying with Apollo.

"Someone else runs it now," Jenni says. "It's what I expected when René assigned me a shadow a few weeks ago. Can't leave the Ferris wheel without an operator after all!" She glances over toward the ride. "Still," she says, sounding wistful, "it's a strange sight watching someone else run the thing." She laughs. "But hey! Now I get to really enjoy this place. Speaking of— I think I'm going to go ride that new carousel."

Jenni wishes me a good night and heads off. It never occurred to me that Jenni wouldn't have the same job when she came back, but like she said, now she really gets to enjoy the circus. It seems almost cruel to have to work every night and then get kicked out before getting a chance to just play. And Tessa! She belongs here. I saw how the other players looked at her, how happy she seemed. René, Fizz . . . they're wrong.

There's nothing sweet about being taken from your family.

NINETEEN

Tuesday is my first day back at school after being suspended. Mom's given no indication of receiving a call from Principal Walker. Knowing her, there's probably an email sitting in an inbox she won't remember to check anytime before my graduation, so I decide to deal with that if and when the time comes.

Mr. Roberts is still in the hospital, in a coma with no sign of waking up. Mom checks in on him when she can and says that he's breathing on his own, so there's hope. But it's hard to pass by the shop and see the lights off. His face, pale just before he collapsed, is still fresh in my mind.

I sketch him during my post-lunch study period while I'm in the library with Moira. He's standing at his easel, paintbrush in his left hand as he concentrates on the image in front of him. This is how I want to picture Mr. Roberts. Not hooked up to a dozen machines in the hospital on the edge of death. It's why I haven't visited him yet, even though I know I should. I'm not sure I could handle it.

"So, I wanted to run something by you before the club meeting today," Moira says, breaking my concentration. She pulls a piece of paper from her pocket and smooths out the wrinkles as she places it in front of me. "There's a rally this weekend at the statehouse."

Rally for Trans Rights
Saturday, Sept. 12
New Hampshire Statehouse
11:00 am

There's some other information and some images, but I've seen enough. Going to Kaycee's press conference was one thing; it felt like the very least I owed her. But this? Traveling to the statehouse? Joining hundreds, possibly thousands of other people, many of whom are probably also trans? Something like this is sure to be televised as well. Just the thought of all that attention focused on trans people, on people like me, makes me start to sweat.

"Well?" Moira says, and I realize she's waiting for me to say something.

"I dunno," I say. "It's pretty short notice. And how would we get everyone there?"

"I've already got that figured out," Moira says excitedly. "I spoke to Zoe, and she says her mom would be willing to drive her van, since it can fit her wheelchair and another five students, and then Kaycee is going to borrow her parents' minivan, which should be able to fit the rest of us plus a couple of her friends, assuming everyone is able to go."

It takes me a moment to realize what she's said. "Wait, Kaycee?"

Moira suddenly looks shy—a foreign emotion on her face. "She's the one who told me about the rally actually. She thought our group might want to come."

My stomach drops. "When did you start talking with Kaycee?"

"We exchanged numbers after the rally and started texting. Actually, there was something I wanted to—"

I interrupt. "You haven't said anything about me, have you?"

"No," Moira says, frowning. "You know I'd never do that." She reaches over and takes the poster back. "Speaking of Kaycee," she says. "I'm actually really excited for you to have a chance to meet her. I think—"

"It's not a good idea," I say.

"What's not? The rally or meeting Kaycee?"

"Both." I see the hurt flash across Moira's face, but I can't stop. Everything feels on the verge of unraveling, and I don't know how to reel it back in. "For me, I mean. My grandpa is defending Wilbur in the lawsuit, and I don't think I should get wrapped up in that, you know?"

"No, I don't know," Moira says coldly. "You *are* wrapped up in it already." She lowers her voice. "I'm not saying you have to come out, but you can't pretend this doesn't impact you."

"I'm sorry. I just, I can't."

Moira nods once, sits back in her chair. "Don't worry about coming to the club meeting today. We'll be discussing logistics for this weekend, and I wouldn't want to bore you."

She stuffs the poster back into her backpack and pulls out a book, signaling the end of the conversation. We spend the rest of study period working in silence, and when it's over, Moira walks out of the library without saying another word.

"Not a word from you," I say to library Jesus as I exit behind her. He doesn't respond, but I can tell he wants to.

After lunch I have Foundations. I'm excited to tell Julian I can finally attend art club. At least one thing might come out of this shitty day.

"Oh, sorry," he says when I finally get to talk to him. "Ms. Sanchez is out sick today, so she had to cancel. Next week, though?"

"Right," I say through a forced smile. "Next week."

My last class of the day is back with Moira, who hasn't spoken to me since she walked out of the library. I corner her just after the final bell rings.

"What, Asher?" she says, sounding tired.

"I just wanted to apologize," I say. "I think it's a good idea—going to the statehouse. I'm just not ready for that kind of thing. Please don't be mad."

She sighs. "I'm not mad. It's fine. Look, I need to get to the club meeting, but I'll see you tomorrow morning, okay?"

I nod, swallowing the lump in my throat, and let her go. She says she's not mad, but even if that's true, she's clearly disappointed. I feel like it's only a matter of time before she learns the truth from Kaycee of what happened in the bathroom that day, and I lose her entirely.

After changing out of my uniform in the bathroom, I begin the long walk home. I decide to take a shortcut through the woods that Moira showed me once, years ago. I'm grateful for my overalls and boots as I brush up against brambly bushes and trample through the tall grass.

About ten minutes in, I start to worry that I'm lost. I decide to cut my losses and turn back, but there's no sign of the trail I'd followed to get here.

In fact, despite trampling over plenty of plants and leaving a trail of broken branches in my wake, everything behind me looks completely untouched. Not only untouched, but somehow thicker than before. I pull down the sleeves of my hoodie to protect my arms as I stumble through bushes that seem to rise up around me, brambles clinging to every fiber of clothing, poking their way through sleeves and pant legs, leaving raw skin in their wake. I stop, listening for the sounds of traffic to guide me out of this hellish forest, but no such sounds come.

I stop moving; stop fighting and just breathe. And listen. I close my eyes. Everything goes silent, even the chirping of the birds and the chittering of the squirrels. But even though it's the wrong place, the wrong time of day, the wrong *every-thing*, I know somehow what's about to happen.

I hear it first. A soft melody but a familiar one, and as I stand in the woods eyes still closed, it grows, swelling until it fills my ears. The smells come next; spiced cider and caramel apples, fudges filled with nuts, and the popcorn, of course the popcorn. And then I see it: the Ferris wheel standing tall, the flags of the tent welcoming me in.

I don't know why it's here, but I grin because it's exactly what I needed. Forget secrets and fights and rallies and canceled clubs. The circus is here.

TWENTY

The forest opens up before me, thorny branches retracting as if to confirm that yes, I am welcome here. Yes, I belong.

It takes me a moment to notice that inside the boundaries of the midway it's grown dark, despite having been the middle of the afternoon when I stepped inside. I suppose I'm so used to it being nighttime at the circus, I didn't realize how strange it is.

Then again, this is a magical circus, so strange is par for the course.

I don't see anyone I know as I walk inside, which might mean they've already made their way into the tent. I head toward the performers' entrance, but before I can go in, I'm stopped by a young man I've never seen before.

"The show starts at midnight," he says. "This entrance is for performers only."

"I know," I say, confused. I don't recognize him. He's white with brown hair and blue eyes and looks to be about nineteen or twenty. Someone else Jean brought back? "Who are you?" I ask. "Where's Fizz?" If anyone should be guarding the performers' entrance, it should be him.

Now he looks confused. "Who?" he asks. "Why don't I walk you back to the midway? You should explore a bit before the show; I highly recommend the popcorn. No one does it better than Francis!"

Francis? There's no Francis at the circus, and certainly not one who runs the popcorn stand. That's Gino's job. I don't understand what's going on, but I follow him back to the midway anyway.

All I need to do is find *one* person I recognize. Just one. Then I'll finally know what's going on. That shouldn't be hard.

Turns out it's impossible. I recognize absolutely no one, and no one recognizes me. And the person in charge of the popcorn stand is indeed Francis, whoever that is. I want to keep looking, but once the fireworks go off, I'm herded like a cat toward the entrance of the tent. It would be funny if I wasn't so worried about *my* version of the Midnight Circus.

My ticket places me dead center in the front row. An amazing seat, which I immediately trade with someone in the back row. I don't plan on sticking around for very long.

The lights dim and the music starts. A lone trumpet swells from the darkness before the entire orchestra joins in, the tent erupting in music as the performers stream out in two lines from backstage to form a giant circle. They move to the melody, a combination of salsa and other Latin dances, and then, moving through the middle, a man in a ringleader's outfit who I'd recognize anywhere.

René. A barely-out-of-his-teens René, but definitely René.

I do the math—the René I know now is probably in his late thirties or early forties, some twenty years older than the version I'm looking at now. Which explains why I haven't recognized anyone until now. This isn't my circus.

I've traveled into the past.

✦ ✦ ✦

René welcomes the crowd to the circus with words I've known since before I ever stepped foot onto the soft grass, when the circus was nothing more than a wisp of a dream. I whisper them in tandem, then slip out of the tent as René turns the show over to the actual performers. Time to follow him and figure out why I'm here.

It doesn't take long before René comes out of the performers' entrance. He doesn't head for the tent village as I might have expected, but toward the woods. I stay a safe distance behind until he disappears behind some trees, and then I approach more quickly, crouching down as I get close enough to hear voices.

"—still in your costume." I don't recognize that voice. Must be whoever René came here to meet.

"Mmm, I wanted more time together. And there're so many buttons." That's René.

"Now we can't do anything or you'll get it wrinkled," the first person says. He sounds frustrated.

"Orrrrr, we do things anyways," says René and then—oh. They're kissing. Let that be a lesson for me on eavesdropping.

I start to extricate myself, when they start talking again.

"Jimmy, wait. Did you hear that?" René says.

Shit. I stop moving, hold my breath.

"I don't hear anything, including the sound of you kissing me."

"No, really," René says. "I could've sworn—" I hear him start to move, and I know I'm going to get caught, but then it stops. Jimmy must've pulled him back down.

"You know," Jimmy says, between the sounds of kissing, "if

172

we met up in the daytime, we wouldn't have to worry about sneaking away during the show each night. And we'd have a lot more time together."

"We've talked about this," René says. "I know the circus isn't perfect, but at least here we can be ourselves without worrying. I thought you agreed with me."

"I do, or I did." He sounds frustrated. "I don't know. We've been doing this for a year now, but where is it going? I spend all day waiting to get back here. I want to wake up next to you in the morning and fall asleep with you each night. I want more."

"I do too," René says, "but you know it's not that simple. Why rock the boat? Everyone else dreams to pass the time until the next day, and we pass the day waiting for our next dream. So it's a little backward. So what? This is the best guys like us can hope for."

There's a moment of silence and then a sigh, as though this isn't the first time they've had this discussion, and finally a resigned "Okay," followed by what is clearly more kissing. I take that moment to finish sneaking away.

I head back toward the midway, but something shifts. The world rocks beneath me for a moment, and as I stumble out of the woods, it's not back onto the midway at midnight, but into the field behind my house in the middle of the afternoon.

"Whoa." That was next-level weird. It's hard to know where to start processing—is it the circus appearing in the daytime? Is it the time travel? Young René? Or how about the fact I appeared right in my backyard despite being nowhere close to it before?

What I can take away from that experience is this—once

upon a time, René didn't want to leave the circus either. And now that he's gotten his wish, he's determined to take it away from the rest of us, one by one. It's just like everybody who's ever had power, and it's exactly why he doesn't deserve it. And why I made the right call in stealing the notebook.

TWENTY-ONE

After my impromptu daytime visit from the circus, I'm prepared for just about anything to happen next. But nothing out of the ordinary does. The circus returns again that night, filled with only its normal cast of characters, something for which I'm quite grateful. If I'm going to have any chance of being ready to perform for real, I'm going to need as much rehearsal time as I can get. Fortunately ever since our conversation atop the trapeze rig, the Apollo in my dreams much more closely resembles the Apollo from my waking life—aka not an asshole. At least, not to me. He even acknowledges Seb with a polite head nod one night, which freaks Seb out so much, I later catch him holding up a small wooden cross as he passes the trapeze rig.

"He's not a vampire, Seb!"

"I'm just saying—have you ever actually seen him in the daytime?" He raises his eyebrow as though he's made some kind of gotcha statement, until I remind him that he's never seen me in the daytime either.

"Don't say I didn't warn you!" he shouts after me as I scale the ladder of the trapeze rig.

Meanwhile, in the daytime, Moira and I find our way back from the frostiness I'd felt after telling her I didn't want to attend the rally at the statehouse. She's in such a good mood upon returning that apparently all is forgiven, and soon the rest of September and then October fly by in a blur of college essay writing and so much homework I almost feel as though

Our Lady secretly wants us all to fail so they can charge us for another year's tuition.

A bright spot finally appears in the form of an invitation to Julian's Halloween party taped to my locker one morning.

I spot Apollo standing at his locker down the hall, holding something in his hands. An invitation? I hate how my heart leaps each morning when I see him for the first time, fresh on the heels of a night spent rehearsing together, knowing that the me he sees is only a shadow of my true self.

I begin to walk over, when Jackson suddenly appears, snatching the envelope straight from Apollo's hands.

"Look who got an invite," he says to Ricky, who, of course, trails right behind him. "Guess we're gonna have to go as firefighters, just in case arson boy gets any ideas." Ricky starts cackling, and Jackson looks way too pleased with himself.

Apollo grabs the invitation back out of Jackson's hands. "If I was going to burn a house down, I have a few better ideas of where to start."

"Is that a threat?" He steps close to Apollo, and while he has a few inches on him height-wise, Apollo has a sturdier build.

"Apollo!" I call out, desperate to stop this before it becomes physical. "There you are. Sister Johnson is looking for you." She's about the only person at this school scary enough that Jackson might actually back off.

I finally reach the pair, and perhaps now that there's a witness, Jackson takes a step back. "Go off with your girlfriend then."

Apollo looks ready to throw a punch, and I'm not far from wanting to do the same, but another suspension is the last thing either of us needs, so instead I grab his hand and pull him away.

"What a dick," I say when we're clear of Jackson and his

annoying shadow. "Don't let him get to you." I realize I'm still holding on to his hand and quickly drop it, hoping he can't tell how flushed I feel inside.

Apollo gives me a small smile but still seems bothered by Jackson's comments. I knew there was still some whispering about the fire and Apollo's alleged role in it after Jackson spread those articles around, but I'd thought it had died off after a week or two. Even a rumor as juicy as that one is interesting for only so long in the absence of new details.

"Thanks," he says. "I should get to class."

He walks away before I realize I never got to ask him if he's planning to go to Julian's party.

As it turns out, the entire junior and senior classes are invited. Halloween is Moira's absolute favorite holiday, as well as the day before her birthday, so I'm looking forward to attending together, especially since things have been so busy lately.

Moira makes our costumes every year, and this one is no different. We're going as Frankenstein's monster and the Bride, from the 1935 horror classic *The Bride of Frankenstein*. I am *not* Frankenstein, who was apparently the doctor and not the monster. All this I learn as Moira makes last-minute alterations on the morning of the party and monologues about how frustrating it is that people still get it mixed up even though Mary Shelley's book was published in 1818 and jump-started the modern horror genre. "Trust me," she says, "if *Frankenstein* had been written by a man, no one would ever get it mixed up."

My excitement grows as we approach Julian's house that evening. The line of cars starts well down the street, and I'd be lying if I said part of the excitement didn't have to do with the beat-up green car I spot close to the driveway.

We're greeted at the door by Julian, who's dressed as a vampire, complete with fake teeth and what looks like ketchup in lieu of blood dripping from the corner of his mouth. "Sweet costumes!" he says when he sees us. "Zoe's manning drinks in the kitchen. If you drove and want to drink, you've gotta hand over your keys first. Other than that, have fun!"

We thank Julian, then head inside. His house is absolutely massive. The entry is basically its own room, with a large staircase and a giant chandelier hanging down from a ceiling that reaches to the top of the second floor. To the left is a living room, couch pushed up against the wall and an open space where a couple of people are already dancing. The room on the right features what looks to be a very nice pool table covered by a piece of plywood doubling as a beer pong table. I wonder where Julian's parents are, but then I figure the type of people who can afford a house like this are probably the type of people who work a lot.

On the way to the kitchen we make our way past a group of girls who look like they raided the "sexy" job fair section of a Spirit Halloween. I spot a sexy nurse, sexy firefighter, sexy teacher, and a sexy *sanitation worker*? I'd love to have heard the marketing meeting where that one was proposed. But then again, someone clearly bought it, so they must have been on to something.

A couple juniors are milling around the food table in the kitchen, while Zoe's got her wheelchair parked between the alcohol and the bowl of keys. It takes me a moment, but then her costume clicks.

"America Chavez!" I shout, remembering the comic book she was reading at the first meeting of Moira's club.

"You remembered!" she squeals, then frowns. "Ricky asked me if I was supposed to be sexy Captain America."

I pretend to gag, and she laughs. "I know, right? I wish Julian hadn't invited him and Jackson, but he hates making anyone feel excluded. Anyways," she says, "if you're going to drive, keys go in the bowl here."

"Just a passenger," I say. "Moira drove. And speaking of Moira, where did she . . ." I trail off as I glance around, finally spotting my best friend over by the food table. She's texting someone, a small smile on her face as her phone buzzes and she reads the response. "Excuse me," I say, but Zoe is already talking to someone new.

"Hey," I say once I make it over to Moira. She puts her phone away. We grab some pizza and head back to the main area of the house. "So, birthday girl," I say, though we're still a few hours from its official start, "where to?"

Moira grins, then drags me to the living room to dance. I groan but follow along, beginning to wish I *had* decided to drink. I scan the room for Apollo. I'm sure I spotted his car outside. Perhaps there's another party room we missed? It wouldn't surprise me in a house this large.

I turn back to Moira. She's texting again. She's been doing that more and more lately, since the rally, come to think of it. I remember she mentioned Kaycee was bringing some friends of her own along with her. Maybe Moira hit it off with one of them? While I don't love the idea of her dating one of Kaycee's friends, I don't want to jeopardize our friendship by prying.

Moira puts her phone away, then grins and takes both my hands, forcing me to do more than sway back and forth, which had been about the extent of my "dancing" until now. Julian joins us for a time, and then Zoe, having been relieved from her duties at the drink table. It's fun, but there's still no sign of Apollo. At least it's early, not even nine. I'm bound to spot him eventually.

Just as I'm about to excuse myself to get a glass of water, Moira's phone rings. "Be right back!" she shouts over the music. I mime a drinking motion and point toward the kitchen so she knows where to find me.

The temperature in the kitchen is a solid ten degrees cooler than the living room. I didn't realize how warm I was, or thirsty, until I down a glass of water and immediately fill my cup again. Julian's on drink duty. I give him a nod and am about to head back into the party when I notice a sliding-glass door leading out to the backyard. The door is open, providing a welcome breeze in a house overheated by the sweaty bodies of horny teenagers.

Well, Julian knows where I am. I'm sure he'll point Moira in my direction.

Outside, the music, which had been almost unbearably loud, loses much of its harshness, until all I can feel is the bass reverberating in my chest. It's a nice night, cool but not freezing. Like my own, Julian's house borders the woods. Unlike mine, his backyard is more than bumpy rocks and uneven patches of grass. A large in-ground pool with an attached hot tub is locked behind a gated fence. I'm standing on a large stone patio that in the summertime is probably used to host all sorts of events. Right now the furniture is covered by large tarps, ready for a typical snowy New Hampshire winter.

I seem to be the only person out here, and I'm about to head back in when I hear a noise. I pause, keeping close to the door just in case. It's probably another partygoer, but we're rural enough it wouldn't be crazy to see a bear out here.

A motion-detecting spotlight floods the backyard with light, and someone stumbles into view.

"Oh, hey. Guess you found me." It's Apollo, and he is very, very drunk. And dressed as . . . René? Or at least that's what I assume he's going for with the red coat and black top hat. He takes a step forward, nearly toppling over his own feet. Liquid sloshes over the edge of the red Solo cup he's holding. "Cheers." He lifts his cup, takes a large drink, then frowns when he realizes it's empty. I don't know how he got so drunk. I can't imagine Zoe or Julian pouring him another cup if he looked even half as hammered as he is now. "Want some?" Apollo holds up a bottle of vodka he must've either brought himself or pilfered from inside, which answers that question.

I frown, then take the bottle from him and set it down on the patio. "You need water." Apollo doesn't resist as I take him by the arm and start leading him toward the door. He almost knocks the both of us over as he stumbles into me, but fortunately I'm sober and sturdier than I look. I've never seen Apollo like this before. Something must have happened.

We take a step back toward the kitchen when I feel a jolt, the earth shifting suddenly beneath me. Earthquake? Except this is New Hampshire. We don't get earthquakes.

Apollo doesn't even seem to notice. The ground stops shaking. We're about five feet from the kitchen door now. I guide us forward another step, and this time I'm nearly thrown to the ground from the impact of the quake.

What the—

I straighten back up once the second shock has passed.

Apollo leans heavily on my arm, and it's hard to tell if he even noticed in his drunken stupor. I see the kitchen door in front of me, and through it the party continues, but there's something new. A reflection in the glass. Something that looks an awful lot like—

I spin around and see it. For the second time, the circus has come while I'm awake. And this time I'm not alone.

TWENTY-TWO

Once the initial shock has worn off, I turn back around. Unlike last month in the woods, the house is still behind me. It doesn't feel like I've been transported into the circus, so much as the circus has been transported to me. I've gotten used to seeing the Ferris wheel standing high above the trees in my backyard, but to see it now through the woods behind Julian's house is unsettling. What if my classmates come outside and see it? Can they even see it?

I take a step forward, toward the woods, when I remember I've got Apollo with me. There's a part of me that wants to leave him here, bring him inside, and have Julian sit him down with a gallon of water, but I can't do it. It's his circus as much as it is mine. And because a quick glance tells me he's noticed its arrival as well.

"Asher?" he asks. Apollo lets go of my arm and takes a step backward. "What's going on? How did you get here? Where are we?"

He looks back at Julian's house, confused, then groans. "Shit," he says, massaging his temples as though he's suddenly got a massive headache. "I feel like I was hit by a truck."

He sounds different, more like his normal self, by which I mean he doesn't seem to be drunk anymore. If anything, he sounds, and looks, as though he was thrust suddenly into sobriety and has the hangover to show for it. He's also no longer dressed as René but as himself. His circus self.

A quick glance downward shows me I'm no longer dressed as Frankenstein's monster either.

Apollo seems genuinely confused about where we are, which means he might have had so much to drink he doesn't remember coming to Julian's party at all. Which might mean he doesn't remember me coming outside either. Certainly he hasn't seemed to put my separate identities together yet.

"Come on," I say, avoiding answering any of his questions. "Let's go check it out."

Apollo says little as we walk through the backyard and toward the forest, just moans softly every few feet. He's slow, and I'm anxious to get into the circus. I don't understand what's happening.

We pass through the first of the trees and emerge into the regular clearing. Everything looks . . . well, relatively normal. Folks are dressed like they're from this decade, and I recognize the people working the booths. Still, something isn't right. I don't know what it is yet, but I can sense it.

"Come on," I say to Apollo. "Let's head to the tent."

He follows without saying much as we head straight for the performers' entrance. I hear everybody before I see them, and when I do see them, I stop dead in my tracks. Dozens and dozens of people, a mix of those I recognize and many more I don't, are not just crammed into the dressing room at the back of the tent, but spilling outward onto the grass as well. I leave Apollo and push my way through, hoping to find someone who knows what's going on.

I don't see René anywhere, and it seems like everyone is asking the same question. What is going on?

I spot Fizz up ahead carrying a clipboard and pen and looking rather harried. It takes some maneuvering before I reach him. He says something to an elderly woman with a hunched back, then guides her to the makeup chairs. I follow, waiting until I can jump in and figure out what he knows.

I've made my way so close, I'm practically on top of Fizz. He jumps a little as he turns around and finds me standing there.

"Asher," he says, "great." He looks around. "Have you seen Apollo by any chance?"

"Yeah," I say, "he's outside. Look, what's going on?" I reach out and grab his clipboard to stop him from moving on.

Fizz looks up. Beneath his mask and makeup, I see a rare serious face from him. "Everyone is back. And I mean literally everyone." He points to the old woman he just sat down. She's looking around her with a mix of deep confusion and wonder.

"Irene Herrington," he says. "She was a ballerina at the circus. In 1953." He holds up his list of names. "So far I've got fifty people on this list who used to be part of the circus in some way or another, and I'm not even finished counting."

Fizz starts speaking more frantically, and it feels a little like opening a bottle of soda after shaking it up. "Do you know how many clowns we've got in here right now?" he asks. He doesn't give me time to respond. "Ten," he continues. "Ten clowns! What are we supposed to do with ten clowns? We've got five contortionists and I don't even know how many flyers. And at least a dozen of these people have got to be seventy-five or older, and I've got probably five who aren't quite in their right minds anymore. And everyone wants answers. Answers, answers, answers! Do I look like I have answers? It's this damn clipboard. I should've never let René hand it to me. I'm going to explode Asher, I swear it."

Someone tugs on Fizz's sleeve. He spins around and snaps, "What!"

I don't stick around. I've heard enough.

Pushing my way out of the tent is somehow even harder than making my way in. More people have arrived, and even though no one inside the tent knows anything more than those who are stuck outside, everyone wants to be as close to the front as possible.

The temperature outside the tent is at least ten degrees lower than it is inside. I take a deep breath and then head toward the midway, where I run into Seb.

"Yo, 'mano," he says. "This shit is crazy! One second I was walking home from the bodega, and the next thing I knew the circus was staring at me through an abandoned alleyway. I almost dropped my tortas!" I must look concerned, because he adds, "I didn't, though." He nods toward the tent. "It's a mess, isn't it?"

It is a mess, but René's been sending folks home for years before their time with no consequences. Fixing that is bound to be messy. Right?

"Maybe it's a good thing," I say, mostly hoping to convince myself. "Having Peter back has been good, hasn't it?"

Seb rubs the back of his head. "At first, yeah, and don't get me wrong, I love the man, but I think there's a reason the circus doesn't stay forever. I mean, all these people had their time here, and now we're supposed to share it with them? There're like a dozen clowns back there, 'mano. I don't care so much about myself, but what about Maisie? She's just figuring herself out, but what happens when she's one of a dozen? She's already started retreating since Peter arrived." Seb frowns. "I dunno. René needs to figure this out fast."

I don't say anything.

"Anyways, I should go find Maisie. The show must go on, right?"

Seb leaves, and I wonder if I too should find Apollo and rehearse. But something still doesn't feel right. What I need to do is find Jean.

I head to the woods where I saw him last. I don't know what I expect to find—Jean standing there waiting for me? I feel stupid standing there when I should be rehearsing. It's not like Jean needs me for anything anymore. He has the notebook. He can make his own decisions. But still, I feel responsible, and Seb's words did give me pause. Maybe bringing *every* person back wasn't exactly the right call.

I'm about to call out Jean's name when there's another jolt, the ground once again shifting beneath my feet. I exit the forest half expecting to be back at Julian's house, returned to the party as suddenly as I was taken from it, but that's not the case. The circus hasn't gone anywhere, but it's definitely changed. It takes me a moment to put my finger on it, but then I realize—this is the past version of the circus. I don't know if it's the outfits or simply some sixth sense, but I know I've been transported back to the circus of my last daytime visit. Young René's circus. I don't spot anyone from my era. I wonder if they're all still waiting for René to turn the chaos into order. If he even can.

There's something different about the atmosphere of this circus tonight. Something more festive?

It seems I've arrived as the show is ending, judging from the crowd streaming out of the tent. A man grins as he passes by. "Already got your mask, I see?" He laughs. "Good man."

As he continues walking, I reach my hand up to my face, where I'm both surprised and unsurprised to find a mask. And not just any mask, but the same butterfly mask as at the Masquerade.

The circus must want me to see something. I haven't spotted René yet, but if he's anywhere, it'll be at the Masquerade. Though I know I'm not really here to attend the party, I'm quickly swept up in the excitement. Between the mask and the scores of past performers who have returned for this one special night, no one questions my presence. A young man even grabs my hand and pulls me over to dance with him and a group of his friends. I scan the faces of the folks around me, but it's hard to see anything from the middle of the crowd.

I extract myself from the group I'm in and make my way to the edge of the clearing, and that's when I spot them—René, and I assume, Jimmy—a few feet into the woods. I move closer so I can hear what they're saying.

"Take this." That's Jimmy. He slips something small into René's hand.

"I've got to go, Jimmy. It's time to make the announcement." René kisses Jimmy, then starts to pull away, but Jimmy holds tight to his hand.

"I love you, you know that, right?"

René looks a little confused but smiles. "I know," he says. "Is everything okay?"

"Of course. I just wanted to make sure you knew."

René finally pulls away and makes his way toward the stage,

dropping something along the way. It's a piece of paper, presumably the thing Jimmy handed him. He doesn't see it, so I pick it up and open it. It's an address and the words *Come find me*. Strange.

Unlike at my last, and first, Masquerade, I know what's coming as I watch René take the stage. He'll welcome the new folks in and kick others out, despite his own obsession with never leaving. What a hypocrite.

The announcement of the newest arrivals isn't too interesting to me, as I don't recognize either of them. Cheers rise from the crowd as the new folks take their place on the stage, and then it's time for the part I hate most.

René gives another trite speech about the seasons changing, blah blah blah, and then unfolds a piece of paper from his pocket. "And now, it is again time to say goodbye to a few members of our beloved family. But as this night reminds us each year, no goodbye needs be forever. And so with that in mind, will Michael, Rebecca, and—" He pauses, stumbling over his words for a moment before looking out at the audience—no, not the audience, at Jimmy—and then mouthing the word *no*. Just that. *No*.

Jimmy pushes his way through the crowd, finishing for René what he couldn't say for himself.

"And Jimmy, come to the stage."

Michael and Rebecca, the other two members called to the stage, linger awkwardly behind Jimmy, who appears to be having a silent conversation with René as the rest of us stand and watch it happen. To call the moment uncomfortable would be the understatement of the year.

Finally, Jimmy takes to the stage, followed by Michael and

Rebecca. René concludes the ceremony before storming off toward the midway, Jimmy chasing after him.

It's only as I watch them go that I realize what the paper in my hand means. It's Jimmy's address. His daytime address.

The circus didn't kick Jimmy out. And René certainly didn't either. Jimmy chose to leave, and he wants René to follow. I may be angry with René, but he deserves to have this paper back.

"Wait!" I yell at the fleeing couple, but they don't hear me. I start to chase after them but struggle to make my way through the crowd. I finally make it out and have nearly reached Jimmy when the world once more shifts beneath me, and I'm thrust back to my own time.

TWENTY-THREE

I stumble out of the woods, the scrap of paper with Jimmy's address written on it no longer in my hand. I search the ground around me, but it's gone, left—I presume—in the past along with Jimmy and the younger version of René.

What is the circus trying to tell me? Am I supposed to pity René? Forgive him? Because I don't. You reap what you sow, and Jimmy leaving feels like the exact definition of karma.

Despite knowing I spent almost an hour at the Masquerade, it seems almost no time has passed since Seb left me in the woods. The entire crowd is now consolidated in the field behind the tent, waiting for René to speak. I spot Fizz, clipboard under his arm, pacing back and forth at the edge of the crowd. I head toward him, noticing as I get closer that he's holding his left wrist in his right hand.

"Hey," I say. "You okay?"

Fizz immediately drops his wrist, wincing as he does. I don't see much before he angles his body just enough to hide it from view, but I do spot what looks like a large bruise.

"Yeah," he says. "I'm good."

I decide not to press further for now, but I'm definitely concerned. I've never seen any sort of injury at the circus. Even the black eye Apollo had from school disappeared once he arrived here. Did Fizz injure himself in the time it took for me to search for Jean? Or is there something more going on?

The crowd goes silent, and I realize René has come to speak.

"I'm sure you are all wondering what is going on. The answer is that I don't know."

A rumble of murmurs rises from the crowd, but I stay silent.

René raises a hand, and everyone quiets back down.

"I've long said the circus has a mind of its own. It's one of the first things I said to many of you when I welcomed you for the first time. I know many of you see me as the one controlling the circus, but the truth is I am merely a temporary caretaker of its wondrous magic. And so I make a promise to you all tonight: I will find a way to fix this. Until then, I ask for patience. To those returning here tonight, we welcome you back as members of the audience. Please enjoy the show we have prepared. And to those who are current members of the circus, we have a show to put on. That is all. You are dismissed."

That's all? There was no mention of the notebook. Just more typical René bullshit.

I know I need to rehearse, but first I need some fresh air. My walking takes me back toward the woods, the one place I can get away from everyone else, except someone has already beaten me to it.

I hear them before I see them. Fizz inhales sharply, pained.

"I know, I know," Gemma replies. She holds a cold compress up to his face, and I stop dead in my tracks.

What was a small bruise on his wrist earlier in the evening has become a patchwork of black, blue, green, and purple, spread across nearly every visible part of his body like some cruel inverse of his normal costume.

"I can't go out there like this," Fizz says.

"We'll figure it out. René will figure it out." Gemma says it so calmly, so confident.

I feel suddenly nauseated. None of this is right. This isn't what was supposed to happen. I need to get out of here. I turn, nearly tripping over my own feet as I flee the woods and crash straight into Apollo.

In the backyard of Julian's house.

"Wait—" I say, but it's too late. The circus is gone. Apollo's still on the ground, doubled over where he fell when I crashed into him. My phone is buzzing in my pocket. I pull it out and see ten missed calls from Moira and about a dozen texts.

I answer the current one. "Moira?"

"What the hell? Where are you? Why haven't you been answering my calls?" I've heard Moira pissed off before, but she's never been like this with me.

I'm so confused. "I'm in the backyard. I just stepped out for a minute while you took your phone call. I was about to come back inside. What's going on?"

"What's going on? What's going on is you've been gone for two hours! What's going on is I was ready to call the fucking police! I'm coming to you. Don't move."

She hangs up, and I look at the time on my phone, confused. Two hours? But sure enough it's nearly eleven. That doesn't make any sense. But then, nothing about the circus makes sense.

I turn to Apollo, but he's clearly in no fit state to have noticed anything. He's sitting on the cold tiles, knees pulled up to his chest, head in his hands as he rocks back and forth, groaning. I don't know what kind of freaky circus magic nonsense is going on here, but it clearly doesn't interact well with alcohol.

Moira comes busting out through the back door a minute

later, stopping dead in her tracks when she sees me and Apollo. "Oh," she says. "So that's it, then. You know, I never took you for the jealous type. Just because I'm texting someone who's not you doesn't mean you get to act like this."

"What are you talking about?"

She laughs. "Really? You're going to do this? Disappear for two hours then reappear in matching costumes, and what? I'm supposed to pretend I don't see it? Has this been the plan the whole time? Did you do it for a laugh, like ha-ha look at Moira, spending a month on these costumes. Isn't she dumb? Well, I guess maybe I am."

I feel like I entered the circus and was spit out in an entirely different version of my life. Matching costumes? The only person my costume matches is hers. I go to grab on to the sleeves of my jacket, the jacket *she* made me, when I realize I'm no longer wearing it. In fact, just as Moira said, I'm no longer wearing any of the costume she made. My mouth goes dry with the sudden realization that I'm in my circus costume. A quick glance over at Apollo confirms my worst fear. The only possible consolation is that he might be too out of it to realize what's going on right now.

"Babe, maybe I should head out."

I recognize that voice. Why do I recognize that voice?

The person to whom the voice belongs steps out of the shadows, huddles up beside Moira, and I realize why I recognize that voice.

"Kaycee?"

"Ash?"

"You know each other?"

"What are you doing here?" I put two and two together

194

nearly as soon as the question is out of my mouth. The way she's holding on to Moira's arm, the way her body is angled toward my best friend, head resting on her shoulder. This is who Moira's been texting. And it's clearly much more than that. I don't know I missed it before. Or maybe I just didn't want to see it. "Oh," I say finally.

Moira gives me a look, a mix of deep confusion and betrayal, then turns to Kaycee. "Don't go," she says softly. "I want you to stay."

Behind us, Apollo vomits violently, then makes another groaning sound.

"You should go, though," Moira says now to me. "And take him with you."

I want to protest, want to say something in my own defense, but what is there to say? I was whisked away into the memories of a magical circus? I can't say that. And with Kaycee standing there I can hardly speak at all. I go over, drag Apollo up to his feet. He slumps over but lets me help him back into the house, where Zoe's once again watching the drinks station.

"Where are Apollo's keys?" I ask.

She looks between us, Moira outside, me suddenly in a totally different costume, but fortunately says nothing as she fishes out Apollo's keys and hands them over.

"C'mon," I say to Apollo. We make our way through the crowd, most of whom are too drunk or self-absorbed to pay us any attention. It's the first bit of luck I've had all night. I see a closet near the front door, lean Apollo against a wall, and tell him to stay, like a dog. He doesn't topple over, but his eyes are closed as though he's about to pass out. I find a jacket I recognize as Julian's in the closet and put it on over my outfit.

I'll return it to him at school. Maybe if I'm lucky, Apollo will be too out of it to connect the dots between this version of me and the Asher he knows from the circus. So far, he's given no indication of having noticed anything amiss, or really anything much at all.

"Okay," I say once I've zipped up the coat. Apollo opens his eyes, squints at me as though he doesn't quite know what's going on.

"Asher?" he asks.

Shit.

"I can explain." I can't really, but it seems like the only thing to say.

He shakes his head, looks around, as though realizing for the first time where he is. "You're not Asher. Am I back at the party?"

I breathe a sigh of relief. "Yes, you're at Julian's party and you're drunk. I'm going to drive you home. Now come on."

Apollo looks suddenly panicked. "I can't go home," he says. He starts muttering to himself, and I can't quite make it all out, but it sounds like he's saying *can't go back* and *won't go back there*. I don't know what he's talking about, but frankly I don't care because he can't drive, and I have no other way of getting home.

"I won't drive you home," I say. "But we can't stay here. Come on."

Reluctantly, Apollo follows me to his car. I climb into the driver's seat and wait for Apollo to figure out the seat-belt situation. He looks miserable, and still somehow, I think I feel worse. We drive in silence, Apollo's head resting against the passenger-side window while he periodically groans. When I get close to our street, I pull over into the woods slightly and park the car.

"Come on," I say. "We need to walk."

The night is quiet as we walk back to my house. All the trick-or-treaters are long gone, plastic pumpkins and pillow-cases filled with candy their parents will raid once the children have gone to bed. When did life become so complicated?

We reach my house, and Apollo panics as he finally realizes where we are.

"You can stay here tonight," I say. I put a finger to my lips as we come inside. Mom's asleep on the couch, and I don't know what she would say about me sneaking a boy back to my room. She might be impressed. My grandmother would probably have an actual heart attack.

Fortunately, Mom sleeps like the dead, because Apollo trips not once, but twice, as he attempts to climb the stairs.

I grab blankets and a spare pillow from the hallway closet and throw them down on the floor for Apollo, who immediately sprawls out across them. It's an odd sight, this boy in his trapeze outfit lying on my floor. I take my own change of clothes to the bathroom, and when I come back, he's already asleep.

As I climb into bed and shut off the light, I thank God I still have the circus.

TWENTY-FOUR

I don't remember falling asleep, but I must have, because the next thing I know I'm standing at the edge of the woods, the circus already bustling around me. I'd hoped the issues from earlier in the night would have just . . . disappeared, but no such luck. Between the returned circus members and the regular audience, the midway is more crowded than ever.

But at least I'm back in the present day. That's something.

Someone taps my shoulder and I turn around. It's Vikram, the contortionist. "Looking forward to your performance tonight!" he says.

A laugh bursts out before I can stop it. Of course that's tonight. Of course the circus and the rest of my life would fall apart on the night I'm supposed to perform for the first time.

I take a deep breath and look around, force myself to see the dozens of people here for the very first time, to see the circus and all its wonder through their eyes.

Something lightens inside me. Perhaps everything will be okay after all.

I'm still smiling as I step into the tent and into chaos. Silent chaos. A crowd is gathered in the middle of the dressing room, other performers standing off to the side, eyes wide as though unable to process what they're seeing. No one says a word. Marko, the makeup artist, steps back, and I'm finally able to see what everyone is looking at.

Or rather, who.

It's Fizz, looking somehow even worse than when I saw him

a few hours ago in the forest with Gemma, lip split and bleeding on top of the patchwork of bruises that cover the entirety of his body. Beside him, Gemma crouches down, holding his hand in hers while Marko focuses on working magic with his makeup.

"Enough gawking. We still have a show to put on." René enters the tent behind me, claps his hands so loudly I flinch. Slowly, everyone returns to what it is they should be doing. René walks over to Fizz, says something to him I can't hear. He and Gemma help Fizz to his feet and out the back of the tent, and I swear René looks at least five years older than he did a few hours ago.

Seb steps up to me, an uncharacteristically serious look on his face. "I can't find Maisie," he says. "Have you seen her?"

I shake my head. Seb frowns. "'Mano, I've been here longer than just about anyone, and I've never seen anything like this. First Jenni and Tessa come back, then everyone else, and now this . . . what's next?"

It's a good question.

"Do you think he'll be okay?" I ask, not needing to specify who I'm talking about.

"I think that's his normal," Seb says. "And there's nothing okay about that. I need to go find Maisie." He walks away, leaving me to contemplate what he's said.

Until now, the circus has been a place where we could leave behind the parts of our lives we didn't want to carry with us. I know what those parts of myself are, but I've never really stopped to think about what they might be for my friends. Or about what would happen if we could no longer leave them behind.

✦ ✦ ✦

I stand in front of the mirror in the dressing room as I take in the sight in front of me. It's my first time in full costume and makeup. I wear an iridescent leotard, which looks alternatingly blue or purple depending on the light. Shimmery wings extend from my back, and my makeup resembles my Masquerade mask. *Le Papillon*, Marko said as he dusted gold across my eyelids. *The butterfly*. It suits me, I think. Speaking of, I haven't seen my butterfly friend since the night of the ball. It flew off when I was speaking to Jean.

Apollo and I are on deck. Tessa's in the audience, so it's just the two of us. He stretches next to me, twisting his torso and extending each arm across the other shoulder, right, then left. He seems calm, but it's hard to tell. I've never seen him at this part of the performance before.

He glances over. "Nervous?"

"A little," I say honestly. Tonight's a night I've been dreaming of, literally, for months. When I'm in the air, I feel free. Flying gives my body purpose, meaning. Instead of weighing me down, it allows me to take flight.

But now, between Moira being angry at me and seeing Kaycee, and Fizz showing up battered and bruised . . . I swallow. I don't know how I'm supposed to let all that go.

As if reading my mind, Apollo says, "Fizz'll want us to do well. You gotta take that stuff, all of it, and put it somewhere else. You can't take it up there with you, understand?"

I nod. I can do that. It's no different than what I do every day to survive.

"Good." He nods toward the front of the tent. "Because that's our cue." Then, without any more words, he runs through the curtain and into the ring.

The crowd cheers, though I can hardly see them beneath the bright lights shining down onto the ring. The music pulses through me, energizing me as I chalk up my hands, scale the ladder. My body's a live wire, fiery and electric. My senses heightened beyond measure. Toes grip the edge of the cool wooden board; fingers wrap around the fly bar. Miles away, the audience claps along to the beat of the music. I feel it pulsing in my chest.

Apollo begins his swing, strong legs pumping. I bend my knees in anticipation, give myself over to the feeling of being here in this moment, in this body.

Tonight belongs to me.

Hup!

I jump, stomach swooping, legs back, grip firm.

And then I fly.

Moments pass in a flash. The audience falls away. Hands meet hands, chalk plumes and floats away like smoke in the wind. We lock eyes and I could stay here forever, but then I'm thrown back, bar in my hands, muscles aching, burning. Weightless.

Free.

I did it. *We* did it. The audience jumps to their feet, but I don't look at them. I look at Apollo instead. His dark curls are plastered to his forehead, his shoulders shiny with the sheen of sweat, but he's smiling. He glances over, takes my hand in his, then lifts them both into the air as we take a bow for the audience. Then it's backstage to rejoin the rest of the performers for the finale.

When it's over, when we're backstage after the performance,

Tessa runs over and pulls me into a hug, and I hug her back, grateful for all she's done for me—and for Apollo. I don't see Seb, which is strange, but I forget about it quickly as someone pops a bottle of sparkling cider to make a toast.

"To Asher!"

"And Apollo," I chime in, looking over at my flying partner, who's standing off to the side, part but not quite part of all this. "First show as a catcher." He glances over at me, surprised perhaps at my choosing to include him.

"To Asher and Apollo!" Everyone cheers. Someone grabs the bottle of cider and pours it over my mouth like a water fountain. I think my costume ends up drinking more of it than I do, much to Marko's chagrin. Tessa pulls me into another hug, this time along with Apollo. For such a tiny woman, she's got powerful arms.

I feel the heat of Apollo's body against mine, and I think about that night, sitting up atop the trapeze rig, his leg touching mine. I flush as Tessa releases us and we pull away. Apollo avoids my gaze, and I wonder if he's thinking about that night too.

Marko calls me over to check on my costume. From the corner of my eye, I see Apollo slip out the back of the tent.

"I've got to go," I say, pulling away despite his protestations that I at least change out of the costume first.

When I exit the tent, it takes me a moment before I spot Apollo in the distance, heading toward the train cars and the tent village. I watch as he scales the train, but rather than descend onto the other side, he stays up top alone, knees pulled to his chest as he looks out over the midway.

"Room for one more?" I climb the ladder on the side of

202

the train, pull myself up beside Apollo. "Why'd you leave the celebration?"

"Crowds aren't really my scene," he says. "Why'd you leave? They were celebrating you."

"They were celebrating *us*," I correct him. "I wasn't up there alone."

"You don't need to try to include me. It's fine no one here likes me."

"People here like you!"

He raises his head, makes an expression like, *Really?*

"Okay, maybe not everyone," I concede. "I won't pretend Seb is your biggest fan."

He snorts.

"But Gemma definitely likes you. And Tessa." I pause. "And me." I suddenly feel self-conscious. I don't want him to think I *like* him, like him. I mean, I don't *not* like him, like him, but I wasn't trying to tell him that.

"How does Fizz do it, d'you think?" he says after a moment.

"What do you mean?"

"I mean . . ." He pauses, collects his thoughts. "I mean the way he showed up tonight. If that's what his life is like when he's not here, how can he show up every night and smile? How does he not want to scream all the time? I want to scream *all the time*."

"So why don't you?"

"Why don't I what?"

"Why don't you scream?"

He scoffs. "Yeah, like that's an appropriate thing to do."

"You know what?" I say. "Fuck appropriate. Just fuck it.

Come on, get up." I jump to my feet, gesture emphatically until Apollo reluctantly joins me. "Where else are we going to scream if *not* at the circus? Watch this."

I plant my feet flat against the top of the train, shoulder length apart, as I face the midway. We're far enough back that the crowd doesn't pay us much attention. That's going to change in a moment, but I don't care. I inhale deeply and then— "Aaaaaaaaaaaaaaahhhhhhhhhhhh!!!" I scream out at the top of my lungs until I'm out of breath, but it feels good. Cathartic.

A few people turn to look, curious perhaps about the strange boys making strange noises, but they don't stare for long before their attention is drawn away by the popcorn and cotton candy, balloon swords and juggling clowns. The circus has no shortage of distractions.

"Now it's your turn."

I expect him to have more hesitance, but like a dam bursting past its walls, Apollo lets out a scream as loud as anything I've ever heard. I grin, then join in. We scream until our voices are hoarse, until our lungs have exhausted every last bit of air, until our bodies are ready to collapse. We scream for ourselves, scream for a world that holds us back, for a world that wants to squish us into small boxes and pretty packages, a world that sees a baby and says "It's a girl!" then spends every moment it can reminding the baby, now a child, now a teenager, now someone on the cusp of adulthood, that he'll only ever be defined by those words said by a doctor or a nurse to an exhausted mother, that no matter how hard he tries, his future has been written since the first moment he came screaming into this world, will be written until he leaves it with a final dying gasp of breath. I scream for that boy and the boy next to me, the boy whose story I don't know but want to, and when we're done, when we collapse back onto the roof of the train car, lying on our backs, staring up at the stars, I turn and face Apollo and I say, "I think I'd like to kiss you now."

And he whispers *okay* and so I take his face in my hands, fingers tangled in his curls, heart racing, and I kiss him.

TWENTY-FIVE

I still feel the ghost of Apollo's lips on mine as I wake up in my bed. I don't open my eyes yet as I let myself linger in that moment. When I remember he spent the night asleep on the floor beside me, my heart skips a beat, but when I finally open my eyes, he's gone. The blankets I gave him are folded neatly beside the pillow. I climb out of bed, disappointed even though I don't know what exactly I was hoping for. The me who kissed Apollo only exists at the circus and in my head.

I go over to my closet, where I left my circus costume last night after the party. I still don't know what happened to suddenly bring me into the circus and spit me back out two hours later in a completely different outfit. Or how I'm ever supposed to explain that to Moira.

When I open the closet door, my circus costume is nowhere to be seen. In its place is the costume Moira made for me, folded neatly with even the wig on top. It doesn't make any sense; none of this makes any sense. I don't understand how so much can happen in such a short amount of time. I don't understand why the circus is choosing now to start doing weird shit, now when I've just had my first real performance and my first real kiss. It would be nice if maybe, just once, some part of my life didn't feel like it was actively conspiring against me. I shut the closet door and head downstairs.

"Your friend left," Mom says as I come down the stairs. She's standing with the front door open, smoking a cigarette. "He was up quite early."

I stop dead in my tracks. "He got locked out after the Halloween party," I say quickly. "He didn't want to wake his parents up."

Mom raises an eyebrow but doesn't call me out for what is clearly a lie. "I thought you'd spend the night at Moira's. Do your grandparents know to pick you up here for church?"

I pause, wait for her to say something more, but she doesn't. Nothing else about Apollo, nothing about a boy sneaking out of my room. "Wait, that's it? That's all you're going to say? I brought a boy home last night. Grandma would probably kill me if she knew." That's the sort of thing that would get any number of my classmates grounded for a month at least. She should be shouting, crying, *something* that shows she cares.

"And is that what you'd like? For me to kill you?" She takes a large drag from her cigarette, then exhales, the tendril of smoke drawn out the open door. I can see she's amused by this conversation.

"You got pregnant at my age! Shouldn't you be more concerned about this?"

"Are you planning to get pregnant?"

"Well, no, but—"

"And you know where I keep the condoms?"

"Yes, but—"

"And you haven't noticed any issues with your IUD?"

That question makes me squirm. I try not to think too deeply about my IUD or its insertion, even though I know it's

207

the only thing keeping me from having to deal with that awful monthly issue on any regular basis. I shake my head.

"Well, then, no, I'm not particularly concerned with you having a boy spend the night. And as you said, I got pregnant at your age, so I know better than anyone that teens who want to have sex will find a way to have sex."

I'm quickly becoming incredibly uncomfortable with this conversation, despite having led us into it. That's one problem with having a nurse for a mother. There's no hesitation in having incredibly frank conversations about the body. And now she thinks I'm having Apollo spend the night so we can have sex.

"Apollo's gay," I blurt out before I can think about whether that was a good idea. I don't even know if it's true. I know he kissed me last night at the circus, but that tells me only that he's probably not straight. And even if he is gay, it's not my mother's business, but I can't take back what I've said.

Mom raises an eyebrow. "Then this conversation seems particularly moot, doesn't it?" She steps outside and stubs out her cigarette against the concrete steps. I don't know why, but that statement somehow makes me feel even worse. It's a reminder that when my mom looks at me, she doesn't see a boy. She doesn't see someone Apollo could fall for.

I think about telling her, but after last night, I don't think I'm ready to rock any more boats.

When I enter church with my grandparents later that morning, I realize that Apollo is here with his parents. My stomach flips more than it did in last night's performance. He smiles when he spots me and raises a hand in acknowledgment. I smile and give a small wave back. His father notices and frowns disapprovingly,

208

whispering something to Apollo, who lowers his hand in response. Even my grandparents don't act like greeting someone in church is a sin. Jeez.

As I take my seat, I wonder what Apollo's thinking about. If he's thinking about our kiss. Or if the circus is something separate for him. Maybe he thinks it's just a dream. After all, he doesn't have me as proof of it being something more the way I do with him. And he was pretty drunk last night. Easy enough to chalk up the missing hours and the change of costume to the alcohol.

I wonder what he would say if I told him. Probably nothing good. Finding out the boy you kissed is actually the girl next door probably wouldn't sit well with most people. Even if he's not really a girl at all and never has been.

I think about my first real kiss. I wish I could erase it from my memory.

His name was Jason Reed, like the Reed farm that sits up the road and across the street from our house. Every summer he'd come up from Georgia to stay with his aunt and uncle. Other than Moira, he was my best friend. We'd spend the summers playing together, running wild through their acres of land, sword fighting with broken branches, filling our stomachs with warm berries plucked straight from the bushes.

It was the summer after seventh grade, the summer after I told Moira my secret, that I wasn't a girl, but a boy. Jason showed up at the end of June, as he did every year. And like every year, things fell right back into place.

Everything wasn't exactly the same, of course. It never was. Jason was taller, he'd had a growth spurt since the summer before, and I had too. A smaller one, of course. But it was the other changes in my body that had been more noticeable. My hips getting wider, my chest growing larger. Where before I'd run around carefree in shorts and an old T-shirt, I now wore pants and an oversize sweater, even on the hottest days.

And there were the butterflies. Figurative butterflies, though there were literal ones as well, swarming near the wildflowers that grew on the edge of the Reed property. But these butterflies were in my stomach, and they appeared only when I hung out with Jason.

It was July 4. Easy to remember. Our town holds a parade every year in the morning and does fireworks in the evening. I always went with the Reeds. We'd pack a picnic for the fireworks, arriving hours earlier, when the sun was still high in the sky, Jason and I joining all the other kids whose families had done the same, hoping their children would run around enough to wear themselves out and fall asleep early. Moira's family was on vacation out of state, so it was just Jason and me, and there was a part of me glad for that.

We ran around for a while, playing tag, and sardines once it started to get dark. Sardines was like hide-and-seek, except one person hides and the rest seek, and once a seeker finds the person hiding, they join them in their spot until there's just one seeker left.

Jason was the first to hide, which meant almost inevitably I'd be the first to find him.

"It's hardly fair," he said when I found him not thirty seconds after the game had started. "You know every place I know."

"Not my fault," I said, gesturing for him to scooch over. "You're too predictable."

The spot he'd chosen, a small clearing carved out between a

patch of wild blueberry bushes, was small, so we huddled close together. The butterflies had come back, the wild ones that awoke in my stomach every time he was near. And this time, he was really near. My shoulder brushed up against his, and in the quiet of the night, I wondered if he could hear my heart pounding the way I could hear it.

"Predictable, huh?" he said a few moments later, long enough after my last comment I'd almost forgotten what he was responding to. "Is this predictable?"

Then he kissed me.

It was my first kiss. My real first kiss.

It was short, hesitant, as though Jason was as scared as I was, and when he pulled away after I was glad it was too dark to see the flush I could feel on my face. There was a light suddenly, just for a second, another one of the seekers, but it passed right over us and continued on its way. But in that flash of light I could see Jason looking at me, and I knew I had to tell him.

And so I did.

And I didn't need a light to see the look of revulsion on his face.

He got sick the next day. Or at least that's what I was told whenever I came knocking at the Reeds' house after that night. So eventually I stopped knocking. And he stopped coming, first to hang out and then altogether, spending summers at baseball camps, hockey camps, football camps, the kind of camps where you could forget that the girl you kissed was actually a boy.

I never told Moira what happened. I don't know why. Embarrassment, perhaps, though I think that's not really the reason.

I think the real reason is this—I was afraid, even as supportive as she'd been of me, that she would understand where Jason was

211

coming from. That she'd give me a look as if to say, *Well, what were you really expecting?* And I didn't think I could handle that. It's ironic. Just as I finally realize how misguided that fear was, I find myself unable to tell Moira about my second kiss.

After Mass, I drive back to my grandparents' house with them for Sunday dinner. Our route takes us past Julian's house. I spot a handful of cars still parked in the driveway and along the street, but there's otherwise no sign of the party he hosted last night. I wonder when Moira ended up leaving. I wonder what she said to Kaycee about me.

I wonder what Kaycee said to Moira about me.

My appetite is virtually nonexistent by the time we reach my grandparents' house, a fact that is quickly picked up by my grandmother.

"Are you sick, dear?" she asks as she puts the back of her hand against my forehead to check for a fever. "Hmm, you're a little warm." She frowns. "Maybe I can get you in with my doctor this afternoon."

"You know my mom's a nurse," I point out.

She perks up. "Of course, dear! She could definitely get you in with a doctor. Good thinking."

I pull back from her hand. "I'm fine."

She tuts.

"Leave the girl alone," my grandpa chimes in. "If she says she's feeling fine, she's feeling fine."

I smile gratefully.

"Now," he says, "I wanted to get your opinion on something. You know the case I'm working on at your old school?"

I nod. As though it were possible for me to not be aware of it.

I already dislike the direction this conversation is taking. I contemplate telling my grandmother I was wrong, that I am sick, incredibly sick, and need to be rushed to the ER, posthaste.

"Well," he says, "needless to say, this has stirred up some broader discussions, and there's a group of parents pushing for Our Lady of Mercy to formulate an official response."

"An official response?"

"Well, more to clarify their own policies. There's a push to add language into the handbook clarifying expectations around who may use which restroom, and I was asked to add my input."

If I wasn't sick before, I definitely am now.

"Oh?"

Grandpa picks up a chicken wing, tears the meat from the bone, then licks his fingers before wiping them clean on the linen napkin beside his plate. Every bit of this is surreal.

"So, I'm curious," he says. "You're there every day. What do you think?"

What do I think? I *think* I'd like to drop dead right about now. Just, *boom*. Collapse on the floor, very dramatic. Might even die with my arms already crossed to save the undertaker the trouble.

Both of my grandparents look at me expectantly. "I don't know," I say. "I guess it seems a little unnecessary."

"Hmmm." Oh God, maybe I shouldn't have said that. Maybe I should've said I thought it was a good idea. "That's exactly what I said."

What? That's not what I was expecting him to say.

"Why would it be unnecessary, dear?" Grandma asks, and while I don't say it, I'm also curious why my grandpa thinks that.

"Well," he says, "the student handbook already lays out a comprehensive standard of conduct that makes it clear students are to live in accordance with biblical standards of right and wrong. Try to add too many specific examples, and you're bound to leave others out." He pauses to tear off another chunk of chicken from the wing in his hand, then washes it down with Grandma's sweet tea. "And that," he says, gesturing toward me now, "is why you'll make a great lawyer. You've got the mind for it."

"May I be excused?"

I stand before either of my grandparents can respond and rush toward the bathroom. Once inside, I slam the door. I grip the sides of the sink, knuckles white as I squeeze the porcelain, physical pain all that's keeping me tethered to reality. My breaths come hard and fast, the world dimming around the edges. It's wrong, everything is wrong. I'm consumed by a terror with no name, and I tell myself it isn't real, none of it is real, but it doesn't stop the world from closing in around me, doesn't stop my racing heart.

You're okay. You're okay. You're okay.

I repeat this until the blackness at the edge of my vision recedes. Until my breathing slows and I'm able to loosen my grip on the sink.

I splash water on myself, staring into the mirror at a face I don't recognize. She looks back at me, eyes and hair the same color as mine. She raises her hand, and mine lifts just the same. I touch the glass, and she meets me there, trapped on the other side but staring back with haunted eyes.

"You are me," I whisper to her. "I am a girl."

I hear myself say the words. I see her say them with me, but the words don't have meaning.

I try it again, willing them to stick.

"I am a girl."

The person on the other side of the mirror doesn't seem convinced, and neither am I.

There's a knock on the bathroom door and a voice asking me if everything is okay.

"Be right out!" I reply. I finish washing my hands. Then, with one final glance behind me, I leave the girl in the mirror behind.

TWENTY-SIX

I struggle to fall asleep that evening even though I want desperately for the circus to come. All I can think about is my kiss with Apollo last night. I don't know what it means for us now or what it makes us, if it makes us anything at all. All I know is I wouldn't mind doing it again.

When I finally find myself at the circus, I realize that my excitement has turned into nervousness. What if Apollo has regrets about last night? And if he doesn't, what then? What do I even say to him?

This is where I wish I could talk to Moira. She'd say, if he likes me, a bit of awkwardness isn't going to mess it all up. And if he doesn't like me, he's a loser who never deserved me anyway. Though after my disappearing act at the party, she'd probably have a few other choice words for me as well.

On the way to the tent, I pass some of the newly returned circus members. They're gathered around René looking quite displeased.

"—send us home."

I catch only the end of what one woman is saying, but a few others nod in agreement.

"I don't want to go home," another person says. "But I should be able to perform. You don't even have anyone on the Cyr wheel!"

A couple others seem to hold similar positions. René rubs his forehead, clearly frustrated.

"I am working on sending you home," René says. "You

need to have patience. As for performing, it wouldn't be fair to those who are currently part of the show. We can revisit this if your stay becomes prolonged, but for now I would ask that you please give me some time." René looks up, and before I can hurry away, he meets my gaze. "Ah!" he says. "I must talk to one of my performers. If you'll please excuse me."

René extracts himself from the gathered crowd and makes his way toward me. I try to keep a neutral expression on my face as René approaches, though it's difficult. There's a part of me pleased to see him in hot water and another that feels guilt over how far things have gone.

"Ah, Asher. Just the man I was looking for," René says loudly. He puts his arm around my shoulder when he gets closer and lowers his voice. "Walk with me, please."

"Thank you," he says when we've moved a sufficient distance away. "I wasn't sure how I was going to remove myself. Your appearance was well timed."

I try to smile. "Happy to help."

"That was quite the performance you and Mr. Bennett put on last night," he says, and I flush before realizing he's likely talking about our trapeze routine and not the postshow kiss. "You're a natural in the skies." He pauses for a moment, staring off into the distance as though recalling some memory from the distant past, then returns his gaze. "It seems you and Mr. Bennett have—hmm, how should I put it—reconciled your differences as well." He winks, and this time I know he is talking about our kiss. René laughs and claps me on the shoulder. "Ah, don't be embarrassed. You're hardly the first performers to share a moment atop that old train car. And it's nice to see something going right around here these days."

René must interpret my expression as one of worry, because he is quick to reassure me. "Nothing you need to be concerned about. I'll sort it out soon enough and get everyone back to where they belong. I won't let it impact your time with the circus."

"Do they have to leave?" I find myself asking.

René, who had begun walking away, stops and turns back. "Everything must end, Asher." He nods once and then continues on.

I'm thinking about my conversation with René as I head to the tent and run smack-dab into Peter, Seb's old mentor, standing right at the front entrance. He's not looking so hot tonight.

As Peter moves out of my way, he steps into the light shining in through the front of the tent, and I realize he's looking worse than I'd thought. He tries to smile, then breaks into a coughing fit that has me worried he's going to hack up an actual lung.

"Are you okay?"

When he's able to catch his breath, he takes a seat in the back row. "No," he says. "I'm dying."

I wait for the punch line, for him to get to the part where I can laugh, but it doesn't come and I know it won't. I take a seat beside him and wait for him to say more.

"Cancer," he says finally. "They say if you live long enough, it's not if but when you'll get it." I don't know how to react, but Peter chuckles. "Ah, you've gotta loosen up, kid. Death comes for us all. If you can't laugh at it, what can you do? But still, it sucks. I mean, I've pretty much made my peace with it. I plan to go out high as a kite when my time comes, but it's Seb I'm worried about." His face becomes more serious. "I never thought I'd come back, you know, when my time was up the first time around. Made my peace with that too. Did always wonder how that goofy kid turned out"—here we both laugh— "but I knew he'd be fine. And I won't say I wasn't glad when the circus came back for me again, especially as the cancer's got worse. Makes you feel young again, and trust me, there's a day you'll know the worth of that. But then it came for me here. You can run, but you can't hide. It was just a cough at first, small, but it's getting worse. I don't want Seb to have to watch that. No one needs to see an old man dying. Especially not here. So here I am, hiding like a coward."

I wonder why Peter has chosen me to reveal this to, until I realize it's not about me. I was just the first person he saw.

"You do have to tell him."

"Yeah, I know." Peter sighs. "I thought maybe I could avoid it. I even asked René if he could make the circus stop coming for me. Thought it'd be less painful if I just disappeared one day."

"But you changed your mind?"

"But he couldn't do it. Said he didn't have the power, that maybe at one point he could have but not so much these days. So now instead of dreaming, I get to watch my body deteriorate twenty-four hours a day, seven days a week. Anyways," he says, "this isn't your problem, and I shouldn't be burdening you with it. I know I need to tell Seb. I'll do it after the show tonight."

"Is there anything I can do for you?"

He shakes his head, then seems to reconsider. "Look out for Seb, would you?"

"I will. I promise."

"You're a good kid. Now go on, get going. You've got a show to do."

I want to stay, to say something more, or useful, but there are no words. I did this. This is my fault. I gave the book away, and I'm the only one who knows who has it.

I need to find Jean.

I decide to do it after the show. I hope to avoid Seb in the meantime, since I'm afraid I won't be able to keep the news Peter shared with me from slipping out, but he finds me first, the look on his face dire.

"Seb—" I start to say before he interrupts.

"—gone. Just gone. I can't believe it, 'mano."

"I know," I say. "But at least you can be there for him in his final days at a place he loves more than—"

"I mean, I thought last night when she didn't show that it was just a fluke, you know? Like because we were all pulled in earlier something got messed up later in the night, but I've searched everywhere and nobody can—wait, what are you talking about?" Seb asks, eyes furrowed in confusion.

I stop quickly, realizing we aren't talking about the same thing at all. "Uh, nothing," I say. "What are you talking about?"

"Maisie!" he practically shouts. "She's gone. She wasn't here last night for the show either. I've looked everywhere for her and can't find her."

"And you've checked—"

"Yes! I've checked everywhere. She's not here. Asher, what am I going to do?" Seb looks so despondent, and all I can think is that his night will only get worse from here. I feel sick to my stomach but need to hold it together for my friend.

"Seb," I say, placing my hands on his shoulders to stop his anxious bouncing. "Take a deep breath. We'll figure this out. It must happen, right? Someone takes a few nights off perhaps? Doesn't fall asleep on time?"

He shakes his head. "No. People only leave after Masquerade, or if they just don't want to be here anymore. But that's really rare." He pauses. "You don't think Maisie stopped *wanting* to be here, do you? I mean, I know I've spent a lot of time with Peter since he came back, but she's my partner, you know? And she's so talented, Asher, *so* talented. I don't know if I told her that enough."

"No," I say firmly, even though I have no basis for my confidence. "It's not that. We'll figure out what happened, and I'm sure she'll come back. Have you tried talking to René about it yet?"

Seb shakes his head. "Okay," I say. "Well, you should start there then, and I'll ask around some more to see if anyone's spotted her. We'll figure this out," I say. Seb nods, sniffling, then wipes the back of his nose with his hand.

"You're right," he says. "I should talk to René. That's a good idea." He manages a weak smile and then walks away in a daze, leaving me with a sinking feeling in my stomach. I definitely need to find Jean.

I end up back in the woods, as I always seem to. But this time I have no intention of leaving until he shows his face. I'm gearing up to shout his name till my throat goes raw, when Jean strolls out from behind the trees, as though he'd been there always, waiting for me to summon him.

"Ah, Asher," Jean says, "a lovely night for a stroll, isn't it?"

221

"You need to fix this," I say, skipping over any pleasantries.

Jean frowns. "I'm not sure what you're talking about."

I wave generally behind me. "*This!* Fizz is covered in bruises and Peter's dying and who even knows where Maisie went and even I know that we can't handle a dozen clowns. I get what you're trying to do, but—"

"Do you?" Jean says, raising an eyebrow.

"Do I what?"

"Do you get what I'm trying to do?"

"Yeah," I say. "You're bringing people back who René never should have kicked out."

"Wrong," Jean says. "That is what you were doing. I'm doing what should have been done years ago. I'm showing the circus for what it really is. You think the Masquerade is the only time you wear masks in this place? No, it's just the only time you admit it to yourself. I want to show what's left when you strip away the veneer."

"You can't!"

"I can't?" He looks at me with what could best be described as pity. "Oh, my boy, I've already done it. I'm doing it right now. Look around! I'm only doing something René should have done a long time ago."

"But what about all the people the circus helps? You want to take that away?" My voice cracks, and I blink away the tears that have gathered at the corner of my eyes.

"You think the circus is a place that helps people? It's a place that *hides* people. Tell me, how many people here know anything real about you? Hmm? I've seen you with that boy of yours. Does he know the truth? Does he know the real you?"

222

"This is the real me," I say reflexively, but inside I feel a cold dread washing over me.

"Then why are you hiding it away in a dream?" There's a beat of silence. "When you can answer that, then you'll know the truth about the circus."

Without another word, Jean turns and disappears into the woods. I feel a sharp pain in my chest that I'm terrified is more than just a reaction to Jean's plans.

TWENTY-SEVEN

I wake with a lingering nausea, further exacerbated by the text I receive from Moira. Unlike every other text she's ever sent me, this one comes in one singular message.

I think you should ride to school with Apollo this morning.

No emojis. No blank boxes I need to decipher but tell me we're okay. And the period at the end of the sentence. Everyone knows that's serious. Even me, and I have only one friend who ever texts me.

I don't have Apollo's number, don't even know how to ask him for a ride short of standing outside and waiting for him to exit his house, so that's what I end up doing. He looks surprised when he sees me standing there but has the good sense not to mention Moira when I ask him for a ride.

There're a few times along the way when he looks like there's something he wants to say. He keeps taking that little breath in and glancing at me out of the corner of his eye, and I have a headache and all I want is for him to be the Apollo who knows I'm Asher, the Apollo who I can stand on top of a train car and scream with and then kiss, but he's not and that's my fault but it still makes me angry.

"If you have something to say, you should say it."

"Right, yeah, sorry. I just had a question about the party the other night. You didn't notice, anything, I dunno, weird, did you?"

"Weird," I echo.

"Like, did I leave in a different costume than I arrived in? Sorry, strange question, I know. I just feel like I remember that happening and thought I'd ask."

"You were pretty drunk," I say truthfully. "Did you wake up in a different costume?" I'm doing everything I can not to tell an outright lie, but it's difficult.

"No, I guess not," he says. "Guess that was a pretty ridiculous question."

Apollo pulls into the parking lot and parks the car. Moira's truck is already here. I suppose that makes sense. If she doesn't have to pick me up, she can get here earlier. Still, there's a part of me hoping maybe she couldn't give me a ride for a different reason, however unrealistic that hope is.

Moira ignores me when I come into the classroom, confirming what I suspected. I've known her to hold a long grudge in the past, but this is the first time it's ever been aimed at me. I see her check her phone periodically when the teacher has her back turned, smile, then put it away again, and I know it must be Kaycee.

Even though it's clear she's not going to want to sit with me at lunch, I still go over.

"Hey," I say. I don't sit down. Moira ignores me as she unwraps her sandwich.

"I know you don't want to talk to me right now," I say. She continues ignoring me. "But I just needed to ask—you haven't said anything to Kaycee about me, right? About my being . . . you know."

She looks up, lips pursed. "I can't believe you even think you would have to ask." She shakes her head. "You know, Ash, not everything is about you all the time." And with that, she goes back to eating her sandwich.

"Right," I say. "'Course. Sorry."

I walk away before my eyes can betray me, wipe at them furiously as I find Apollo sitting alone at a table in the corner.

"You okay?"

I nod, but it's a lie like everything else in my life.

"I met Mr. Roberts's niece today," Mom says when I get home from school. "She came by to visit him, bring him some flowers. When she learned who I was, she asked about you."

"Me?" I ask, confused. I think I remember Mr. Roberts mentioning a niece once, but family wasn't something he really talked about, and I never asked. I got the sense there was some pain there.

"Mmm," Mom confirms. "She says he always talked about you whenever she called. How talented you are. How proud that made him."

I clear my throat, blink rapidly to clear the tears gathering at the corners of my eyes. "How is he?" I ask, trying to change the subject, though I already know the answer.

"The same," she says, and while I didn't expect any different, it still hurts. Mom pauses, clearly debating what she wants to say next. "She's going to be cleaning out the shop this weekend and wanted to know if you'd like to help."

"Cleaning out the shop? But what about when he wakes up? What's he going to do then?"

"It's been two months, kiddo," Mom says gently, reaching

out a hand to rest on my shoulder, but I jerk away from her touch.

"He'll wake up," I say stubbornly.

"If"—I glare and she rephrases—"*when* he does, I'm sure he'd prefer you were there while his niece packed the shop up. Think about it, okay?"

Mom drops me off at the shop on Saturday morning. Mr. Roberts's niece is unlocking the front door as I walk up to her. She's tall, with dark hair pulled back into a ponytail. She introduces herself as Samantha and then steps inside. I follow closely behind. Other than the two months of mail that has collected underneath the slot in the door, everything looks like it did the last time I was here. Samantha places the mail on the counter and then looks around, hands on her hips as though sizing up what an immense task this will be.

"What will you do with everything?" I ask. "Mr. Roberts will want to have it back when he's awake and able to reopen the shop."

Samantha turns, and I see the look in her eyes. Pity. And kindness. Just like my mom, she doesn't think Mr. Roberts is going to wake up. I stare her down.

"My husband and I will keep it in our garage, for now," she says. "We'll need to look for a wholesale buyer if, well . . ." She trails off for a moment. "But that doesn't need to happen right away," she adds quickly. "We can't afford to keep covering the rent." She spins back around, facing the many shelves of art supplies once again. "Right," she says. "I think I'll get a professional company in here to pack most of this up, but I'd

227

like to gather any of my uncle's personal belongings first. And of course, if there's anything you want, you should feel free to take it. Of my uncle's personal effects and the art supplies both. I wasn't, well, I'm sorry to say I wasn't as close to my uncle as I would have liked."

She must see the unspoken question in my eyes, because she continues. "He never married—my uncle. Never found the right woman, I guess. No kids either. And my mother's too old to deal with this, so that leaves me. But the few times we spoke he mentioned you. He was—is"—she corrects herself when she sees my expression—"quite proud of you."

I turn away before my eyes can betray me again.

We start in the back room, gathering and tossing trash as we go, and setting aside anything personal of Mr. Roberts's to take before the professionals come in. It's amazing the amount of clutter that gathers when you work in a space for years and years, and soon enough we break for lunch.

I wander the shop as I eat the pizza we've ordered, looking over the shelves I once stocked and trying not to think too hard about the last time I was here. I pause before the shelf of colored pencils. My drawing, the one I made of the circus tent to advertise the Derwent watercolor pencils, still rests above the shelves. Carefully I remove it and set it on the counter.

"That's lovely," Samantha comments. "Did you draw it?"

I nod. Beside the picture is the stack of mail she'd gathered up when we first entered. I spot a familiar logo and pull it out from the stack. It's a large envelope from SAIC, one of the art schools Mr. Roberts had sent away for information on for me.

"Can I take this?" I ask, ignoring the lump in my throat. Samantha gives it a glance and, upon seeing it's not a bill or something equally important, nods. I place it beneath the picture I drew.

Pizza finished, we return to tackle the rest of the back room and the area behind the front counter. As I'm pulling objects from drawers—paper clips and rubber bands, old receipts and half-dried pens, I feel something wedged all the way in the back, a notebook or something. It feels familiar, and when I manage to finally extract it, I drop it in shock. It's not just a notebook, it's *the notebook*. Or at least that's what I think until I pick it back up and realize, no, of course it isn't. This isn't the notebook from the circus, though the leather-bound book looks remarkably similar. It must be a sketchbook. Mr. Roberts's sketchbook. I open it up to take a look. On the first page is a message, drawn in thick black pen.

SKETCHBOOK OF J. R. ROBERTS. PRIVATE! KEEP OUT!

I contemplate turning the page anyway. They seem like the words of a much younger Mr. Roberts, and it's not like he'd know, but I've destroyed enough relationships recently, so I shut the sketchbook and, along with the mailing from SAIC and the picture I drew of the circus tent, slip it into my backpack. Samantha already said she wasn't close to her uncle. She won't miss this.

We finish for the day as it's getting dark. Samantha tells me to take home whatever art supplies I'd like as payment for helping, and while I feel slightly like I'm robbing Mr. Roberts,

I allow myself to take one thing. A seventy-two-count wooden box of Derwent watercolor pencils. Somehow I know Mr. Roberts would approve.

Back at home, I take my backpack to my room and unload the items I took from the shop. I place Mr. Roberts's sketchbook on the corner of my desk, shut tight, and then I open the packet from the School of the Art Institute of Chicago. There's a paper application and a list of deadlines for various scholarships, which I set aside. The rest of the large envelope contains something like five separate booklets, which I spread out across my bed. Though I know my grandparents expect me to attend the University of New Hampshire in the fall, it's hard not to flip through the packets and dream about a different life.

I could start fresh, start over somewhere so far away no one knows who I am and, more importantly, who I'm not. I could be anyone, do anything.

For curiosity's sake, I read through the portfolio requirements, envision what I might submit, if I was going to apply.

Which I'm not.

In the section called "Advice for Developing a Merit Scholarship Portfolio," they write, "Build a portfolio of thematic work" and "Show us what makes you different, and the things about which are passionate."

What makes me different? Well, I suppose not everyone travels to a magical circus in their dreams each night and gets to soar high above an adoring audience. Nor, I would suspect, do most people have two separate personas the way I do. I'm like Clark Kent, if he really hated one of his two identities.

As for a portfolio of thematic work, well, I already have

dozens of sketches of the circus. That would be a pretty cool theme.

I move to my desk, dig through my supplies until I find a piece of scrap paper and a pencil, and I begin sketching something out. An idea for a graphic novel of sorts, about a boy and a magical circus. Really, a story about me.

It would have to be shorter, obviously, and I wouldn't want to include all the details of my life. That feels like too much, too personal, but still . . .

Mom calls me down for dinner, and as we eat, I can't quite vacate the idea from my brain the way I want to. When I return upstairs I move back to my desk, clear off all the crap I don't need.

Even if I don't apply—and I'm not going to—there's no reason I shouldn't see where this project leads me. Judging from the silence of my phone this evening, I suspect I'll have some free time in the near future.

I pick up my pencil and get to work.

TWENTY-EIGHT

I return to the circus with the anxiety typically reserved for school, Jean's words echoing in my ears as I wait for the other shoe to drop. Only it turns out not to be a singular shoe but a whole truckload.

The midway is in complete chaos. To my left, Gino dumps an entire batch of burned popcorn, an unpleasant odor wafting across the grass, while on my right a child screams as their balloon puppy jumps from their arms and starts aggressively nipping at their legs, and Gemma wrestles with a balloon snake that has wrapped itself around her waist and begun squeezing. Gino drops the popcorn bag he is filling and runs over, first trying to pull the balloon snake away and, when that fails, using his fingernails to split it open. Gemma doubles over, trying to catch her breath.

I'm about to check on Gemma when I hear Seb's voice rise up above the crowd, clearly sounding on the edge of a breakdown. I find him surrounded by a half dozen people jostling for his attention as they juggle and ride unicycles and slip on fake bananas.

"—not looking right now," I catch Seb saying to the group.

One man, a rather angry-looking fellow, steps forward. "She ain't coming back, pal, so if you're not going to pick a replacement, maybe we'll have to have a word with René about shaking things up, yeah?"

A few other folks step forward, crowding Seb as they agree with the angry man.

"What's going on?" I ask, stepping between Seb and the group.

"Who are you?" asks the man.

"I'm his friend," I say, not bothering to keep the sharpness I feel from my voice. "Who are you?"

"A clown out of work," he says. "And if your friend knows what's good for him, it won't stay that way." He nods once as though we've come to some sort of understanding, then turns and walks away, the rest of the group following him.

As soon as they're gone, I turn to face Seb. "Are you okay?" It's a ridiculous question—Maisie hasn't shown up in days, and as of last night, he knows that his mentor is dying and has to watch it happen before his eyes. And now a group of clown thugs seems to be cornering him for a spot in his act.

Seb forces a smile. "Never better," he says before walking away. I want to chase after him, tell him that I know that can't be true, but what would that do? I can't bring Maisie back, can't save Peter, can't do anything except fly and hope for the best.

Since flying is one of the few things still within my control, I head into the tent to practice before the show. From a rack near the mirrors, I grab my workout clothes and head into one of the changing areas. I may have a flat chest at the circus, but that doesn't mean I'm suddenly comfortable with showing it off. I wonder whether I'll feel differently once I get top surgery for real. Assuming I ever do.

I pull off my shirt, my arm brushing against my chest, and I feel a soreness that sends a shock wave through my system. Hesitantly I place my hand on my chest, this time purposefully, and feel it again. *Not here. Not now.* My chest still *looks* flat, but

I remember this feeling from the last time my body failed me. Jean's words take on a new light. Showing the circus for what it really is. Stripping away the veneer. Fizz's bruises, Peter's cancer . . . am I next?

My legs feel unsteady, and I want to lean against a wall, except I'm surrounded by curtains in a tent with no real walls. I don't know what I'll do if my body betrays me here in the one place I can feel safe. The one place I can be *me*.

"Asher, you in here?" That's Apollo. I take a deep breath, finish changing, and exit the dressing area. "Ready to rehearse?" he asks.

Screw this. I march over, stand on my tiptoes, and pull Apollo forward into a kiss. If the circus is going to fall to pieces beneath my feet, then I'm going to go out with a fucking blaze.

I hear a whistle and pull away to find Marko snapping his fingers in approval. Apollo blushes, and I'm sure I do too.

"Is that okay?" I ask, realizing that perhaps I should have sought permission before, rather than after. He responds by kissing me again, and I'm not sure why I ever thought flying was necessary to soar.

"Would you maybe want to hang out with me tonight?" Apollo asks after the show. Even though we've now kissed, more than once, he seems worried I might say no. It's cute.

"Are you asking me on a date, Mr. Bennett?" I tease. He flushes and I laugh. "I'd love to."

"Okay," he says, a shy smile revealing the dimples I wish I saw more.

"Okay." I bite my lip while he chuckles and runs a hand through his curls, but neither of us moves until someone clears their throat loudly behind us, and we turn to find Tessa watching us, amused.

"We should probably go," I say.

"Yes, right, definitely," Apollo replies. "Was just going to say that myself."

We exit the tent and then stop, neither sure where to go next.

"Do you want to—"

"Should we—"

We both speak at the same time, then laugh awkwardly. I gesture for him to go ahead.

"Do you want to ride the Ferris wheel?"

"I would love to."

Apollo hesitates, then takes my hand in his, and for a moment, despite where we are and what we're surrounded by, I feel normal.

We walk through the midway, hand in hand. Everything appears to have returned to normal. Gino serves unburned popcorn, Gemma's balloon animals don't attempt to kill her or anyone else. I even spot Seb laughing over something with one of the musicians, unbothered by the group of clowns from earlier. Best of all, there are still hours before the sun rises and sends the circus packing for another day.

There's only one person ahead of us in line for the Ferris wheel, and then Apollo and I climb on, letting Jeremy pull the safety bar down in front of us. We start to rise up, and I survey the midway, reminded as I do of the view from Gemma's balloon way back when I was first brought here. Back when I thought the circus was solely a dream, before Apollo walked out of it and into my life for real.

"Do you ever wish you didn't have to wake up?" I ask Apollo as we reach the top of the Ferris wheel. "That you could stay here forever?"

He turns to look at me. "All the time," he says. "Though there are some things I'd miss about the daytime."

"Like what?"

"Like animals," he says. "Balloon animals are nice, but not the same. And food other than popcorn and sweets. They're great, but sometimes all I really want is a salad."

I laugh. "What about people?" I ask. "Friends, family?"

"My sister," he answers immediately. "And maybe one friend."

I wonder if he means me. I hope he means me. I notice he didn't say his parents.

"What about you?" he asks. "Are there things you'd miss? Or people?" Though he's just returning the question, the way he asks the last part makes me feel like he means something more specific, like whether I have a boyfriend in the daytime.

What would I miss? It's a good question. Sometimes I think nothing, that I would give up everything to stay at the circus and not wake up, but I know that's not entirely true.

"My best friend, M—" I start to say Moira's name, then cut myself off when I realize that would give away my identity. "My best friend," I repeat. "I'd miss her. My mom," I say. "Sometimes. Pizza." I grin. "I'd definitely miss pizza." Then, because I can't quite resist: "And the view from my bedroom window. I think I'd miss that too."

"It's a good list," Apollo says. He leans his head on my shoulder. His curls tickle my neck, but I don't want him to ever move.

The Ferris wheel begins to slowly rotate, and I look out at

the carousel as it does. My one addition to the circus before turning the book over to Jean. A young girl approaches the unicorn, which turns its head and nuzzles against her, before lowering itself down to allow her to climb on. The girl appears to have her face painted like a unicorn, complete with a silver balloon horn crown, courtesy of Gemma. I smile, glad to know I did at least one thing to change the circus for the better, then close my eyes, taking a moment just to enjoy the feeling of Apollo next to me.

Not ten seconds later, a scream rings out into the night and my eyes pop open, just in time to watch as, almost in slow motion, the unicorn on the carousel whinnies and violently bucks the young girl into the air. With a sickening thud, she lands on the grass, unmoving.

Everything grinds to a halt as attention shifts toward the carousel. A man runs over to the girl, shouting that he's a doctor, and I wonder if he is in the daytime or just in this dream. A few people help other patrons off their carousel animals and lead them away from the ride, clearly fearful of other animals enacting a repeat.

I want to jump out of my seat and run over, do something, *anything*, but the Ferris wheel stops, forgotten about, leaving me trapped fifteen feet in the air with nothing to do but bear witness. I don't realize how shallow my breathing is until I see the young girl sit up, and I gasp for air. The doctor helps the young girl to her feet and the crowd cheers. I can't join in, even though of course I'm glad to see her standing. All I feel is horror. I did this. This is my fault.

As if reading my thoughts, Apollo takes my hand and squeezes it. "She's okay," he says. "It's okay."

But it's really not, and I don't know whether it ever will be again.

René finally arrives on the scene and, with the help of some other workers, manages to disperse the crowd. He looks over to the Ferris wheel and raises a hand in acknowledgment of Apollo and me, then sends someone over to let everyone off. Once we're down on the ground, I notice that neither the Ferris wheel nor the carousel lets anyone else on. It seems that for at least the rest of tonight, the rides have gone dark. The mood on the ground feels noticeably different than it did before we boarded the Ferris wheel, as though we went up in one world and came down into another.

"So . . ." Apollo says, breaking the silence, "what do you want to do now?"

The only thing I can still do. "I want to fly." I turn and start walking toward the tent, leaving Apollo no choice but to follow. The circus is falling apart, my body is betraying me, and I can't fix it. So instead, I fly. I fly until I can't catch my breath, until my muscles scream and my joints ache, and when I can't fly anymore, I lie in the net, head resting on Apollo's chest until the sun rises.

TWENTY-NINE

After the disaster that was Halloween night, I get into the habit of driving to school with Apollo each morning. It honestly makes sense. He's my neighbor, we're going to the same place, and Moira lives all the way across town. Still, I wish those were the only reasons for his driving me. A little over a week into this new arrangement, and a little under a week since I last spoke to Moira, we manage to pull into the parking lot at the same time as she does.

"You should try to talk to her again," Apollo says, and I know he's right. I miss her, and besides, the whole thing feels ridiculous anyways. I'll just apologize, beg for forgiveness if I have to, and we can move on.

"Right, yeah, okay," I say, trying to gather the courage to run over and start the conversation.

"Hey," Apollo says, "you've got this."

My heart skips a beat, but I can't focus on my feelings toward him now. The only reason I still have any semblance of sanity is my ability to keep daytime Asher separate from nighttime Asher. And daytime Apollo separate from nighttime Apollo.

Apollo gives me a small smile, and I nod.

"Moira, hey!" I call as I get out of the car.

"What do you want?" she asks when I reach her.

"I just . . ." I stumble over my words, but then I remember Apollo's words of confidence and know that I have to at least try to fix this. "I want to apologize. Please."

Moira finally stops, sighing, but I'll take it. "I'm sorry about

Halloween," I say. "I don't—I won't excuse any of it. I'm sorry for disappearing and for the costumes. I wasn't trying to worry you or upset you. I miss you and I hate that you're mad at me and I just want this to end." I'm pleading by the end, but I don't care.

"I appreciate the apology Ash, I do, but the fact that you think it's the costumes I care about most is exactly the problem. You never seem to share anything with me anymore. When Mr. Roberts had his heart attack, I didn't even know until Apollo told me at lunch the next day! And I still don't know why you lied about knowing Kaycee. She told me you were friends at your old school. If it was just so that that you didn't have to join the social justice club, you could've told me. I'm sorry if I made you feel you needed to choose it over art club, but I don't think you even understand how much it matters to me too. Yeah, you're trans, and it's tough and you can't tell your grandparents or anyone else and that's fine, that's your choice and I respect that. But it's not all about you. I'm bi and ace and my girlfriend is queer and trans, and you aren't the only one impacted by all this stuff, but you've been so adamant about burying your head in the sand trying to avoid anything difficult that I couldn't even talk to you about her or half the stuff that's been going on in my life, so yeah. Okay, you're sorry for Halloween. That's great, but I think I'm going to need some space for a bit longer."

Moira turns and walks away, and all I can do is stand, rooted to the ground, as I watch her go.

I barely notice Apollo's hand on my arm until he moves and stands directly in front of me. My eyes are dry for once, and at least I won't have to suffer the embarrassment of having a total breakdown in front of Apollo. I feel numb. All I want to do is

240

climb back into bed and sink beneath the covers forever, but I can't do that.

"Hey," Apollo says softly. "The first bell just rang. We should get inside."

I nod, and my brain does the work of guiding my feet in following after him.

After church the next Sunday, Grandpa insists I work on my UNH application at their house so he can "assist" in the process. More like micromanage. It's ridiculous. UNH has an acceptance rate of like 80 percent. I'm no Moira or Kaycee, but I'm pretty certain I won't be in the bottom 20 percent of their applicant pool. Plus, our English teacher already made us work on an essay for the Common App in class, so I'm pretty much done. But Grandpa wants me to sit beside him while he reads through everything I've written, printed out on actual paper, and marks it with a red pen.

The whole idea of college essays is so weird to me. Thousands of college kids mining their lives for personal traumas or profound experiences just to impress a bunch of random adults we'll never meet. Grandpa didn't like my essay about working for Mr. Roberts, so now I'm sitting here trying to bullshit an essay about my dead dad and wanting to follow in his footsteps.

I tell Grandpa I'm going to the bathroom and excuse myself from the table. Instead I head to their bedroom and pull a thick, leather-bound photo album from their bookshelf, flipping through until I find childhood pictures of my dad. There're the typical baby pictures, Dad in the white Christening gown that was later used on me, blurry baptismal photos, Grandpa with a particularly thick mustache and those ugly eighties serial-killer glasses, as Moira always calls them. First-day-of-school pictures, holiday pictures, Dad learning to ride his first bike, Dad opening Christmas presents and birthday gifts, Dad at his first Communion. The picture quality improves slightly as time goes on, but otherwise these are the pictures of a completely average upper-middle-class family. It tells me nothing about the person he was, not really.

I'm about to put it away, when the door creaks open and Grandma steps into the room. "There you are," she says. "Taking a break from your grandfather? He can be a monster with that red pen. I remember him taking it to every essay your father ever wrote. I think he's missed doing that." She takes a seat beside me, looking at the photo album. I turn the page, and she chuckles. "Oh, I remember that Halloween quite well." She points to a picture at the top of the page of my dad dressed in a rather impressive dinosaur costume. It's not like one of those inflatable ones you can buy now—it looks fully homemade, papier-mâché head and all.

"Your father was obsessed with that dinosaur movie. *Jurassic Jungle* or whatever it's called. He spent months on that costume. Made the entire thing himself." Grandma must see my expression, because she continues. "You don't think you're the only creative one in this family, do you? There's a long streak of artists on my side. Doesn't pay the bills, mind you, which is why your grandfather and I care so much about getting you ready to take over the firm. And your grandfather isn't getting any younger. I swear, he'd work himself into the grave if I let him. Case in point," she says as Grandpa calls out from the other room. "I'll stall him," she says before leaning in and giving me a kiss on the side of my head. "Take your time."

She leaves the room, shutting the door behind her. I turn my attention back to the picture of my father. It's hard to tell his age, but I'd guess he was around ten.

If he'd lived, would he have shown me this picture himself? Would we have curled up on the couch, lights dimmed with a big bowl of microwave popcorn, as he introduced me to the movie that inspired this incredible creative feat? Or would he be too busy working with Grandpa, preparing to take over the law firm?

I think it would be the former. I let myself linger over the Halloween picture a little longer before putting the album away. By the time I return to the table, Grandpa has been placated by some fresh-out-of-the-oven apple crisp, and I know how to write the essay he wants. It won't be an essay about me or about my dad. Not the real us, at any rate. And I think I'm okay with that. Some people don't deserve to know our deepest selves. At least not before we're ready to share them. Grandpa can have the future-lawyer versions of me and my dad. I'll hold tight to the kid in his homemade dinosaur costume and the father he never got to be.

THIRTY

W hy does time always move so slowly the day before a holiday?" Apollo asks me as we walk into the school auditorium the morning before Thanksgiving. It's a fair question. Somehow the past month slipped by in the blink of an eye, but it's this final half day that seems unlikely to ever end. I spot Moira a few rows in front of us. I'm giving her space, like she asked. I just wish I knew how much longer she's going to need it.

Apollo and I take our seats, and I try not to yawn. Since the night of the carousel accident, things have only gotten worse at the circus. Out of an abundance of caution, the rides have remained dark. Instead of being a shining beacon of the circus's magic, the Ferris wheel looms like a specter of its impending death. Other changes are less obvious, except to those of us who are there every night.

Gemma's balloon creations have lost their magic. Gina's popcorn more often than not contains burned pieces or unpopped kernels and his machine has been known to stop working halfway through the night. No longer is the sky always clear and the weather the perfect temperature. Two nights ago it even rained, and when I woke up in the morning, I still felt a chill that no amount of warm clothes could shake.

And I don't even want to think about my changing body. Each night it's something new, something small, but added all together the changes are too much, too devastating. I've taken to binding my chest in the nighttime and noticed my voice slipping into a higher register when I talk. I'm terrified of what will happen if it continues. Terrified especially because only two parts of the circus keep me going—flying and my growing relationship to Apollo. While he hasn't connected my nighttime self to my daytime self yet, at this rate it's bound to happen.

I don't know what will happen if he does figure it out. I don't know if we're dating, not just because it's not a word we've used, but also because I'm unclear what the rules of relationships are when they only exist in your dreams, and one of the two parties isn't fully aware of the other's identity. But it's also the closest word to describe what Apollo and I are doing at the circus. This also means our daytime relationship has become more complicated. I have to think of him as a separate person, like circus Apollo's identical twin brother, otherwise each time I see him I'm tempted to do something I know isn't a good idea. Such as kissing him.

I *very* much want to kiss him.

I flush as his leg bumps against mine, the narrow seats of the school auditorium making it difficult not to. I don't pull away, but Apollo does with a quick apology, and I'm disappointed.

Twin brother, twin brother, twin brother, I repeat to myself, though I'm pretty sure a few parts of my body don't get the memo.

The lights dim as two rows of children dressed as Pilgrims and Indians shuffle onto the stage. I raise an eyebrow. I'm pretty sure most other places would consider this offensive, but I'm not sure Our Lady of Mercy cares. Auditorium Jesus stares down over the crowd above the stage. I wonder what he thinks of all this pageantry.

Between the lower- and middle-grade performances, we're allowed a bathroom break and time to stretch our legs.

"How do we still have two more hours of this?" I groan after looking at the clock.

"I wish we could make a break for it," Apollo says, and I stop, a smile spread across my face.

"Why can't we?" I say mischievously. Apollo laughs, but I'm serious. "No really, let's get out of here."

Our plan is simple. With Apollo's help, I pretend to have twisted my ankle. I lean on him for support as I grimace in pain. With the lower grades transitioning from the stage back to the audience, the teacher on hallway duty has better things to do than worry whether we're actually heading to the nurse's office, so she waves us past without a second thought. Then, as soon as we're out of sight, we make a run for it, laughing hysterically as we bust through an unmonitored side door.

It's snowing, the first of the year. Apollo's car is dusted in a thin layer, which also coats the trees and the sidewalk beside the school. He wipes off the door handle with his sleeve before unlocking the car. I shiver as he blasts the heat to warm up the car and the cool air, not yet heated up, hits my face.

"Sorry," he says, and reaches across the center to reposition the vents. He smells good, clean, like whatever soap or shampoo he uses. It takes every bit of willpower I have not to climb over the center console and straddle him right now.

I clear my throat as he turns on the windshield wipers. "Where should we go?" I say. "My mom's home, so we can't go there."

Apollo thinks. "I've got an idea."

246

We drive to a place Apollo says he discovered last year. It's an abandoned housing development at the top of a large hill. One of those that were probably started when times were good, then abandoned when the economy shifted. He parks the car in front of a partially completed model house, and I follow him as he leads us to a hill behind the house. To the east you can see our town, while to the northwest you can see some of the White Mountains. With the snow still falling gently, the view is incredible.

Apollo lays out a blanket I hadn't noticed him grabbing and spreads it out across the ground. I take a seat next to him, then pull my knees into my chest as I look out toward the mountains. "This is amazing."

"I came here a lot earlier in the year, back before . . . well." He doesn't say it, but I'm assuming he means before his school burned down. It's not something we've ever talked about. By now, the other students have gotten bored of gossiping about the new kid and moved on, but it still sits there between us. His knowing I read the article that was passed around, my not asking about it.

I think maybe there was a point at which I cared more whether it was true, but since I've come to know him better, that desire has gone away. I think of telling him sometimes, but when's the right time to tell your friend-slash-sort-of-secret-dream-boyfriend that you don't care whether he burned down his old school? That's the sort of question I would ask Moira if we were still talking.

"Do you miss your old school?" I ask.

Apollo stares ahead, not answering, and I wonder if he heard my question. Or perhaps simply doesn't want to answer.

"No," he says finally. "I don't. But I think I miss the me I used to be back then."

Apollo lies down and closes his eyes, and I don't get the chance to ask him what he means. Perhaps that's the point. A snowflake falls onto his eyelash. I look at it, commit the image to my memory. I'd draw him if it wasn't snowing, but I don't need him to be in front of me to be able to conjure his face. I could draw him a million different ways. I could draw him with my eyes closed. I could draw him on the roof of my mouth with my tongue or with my fingers in the air.

I lie down next to Apollo and close my eyes, and I can almost imagine we're together at the circus. I somehow manage to fall asleep, because I'm woken sometime later with a pile of snow on my face that my body is threatening to inhale. I quickly realize that I'm not the only one who's fallen asleep, as I feel Apollo's chest rise and fall slowly beneath my head, his arm wrapped around my shoulders. Even if I couldn't feel it from his breaths, I know Apollo is asleep because he'd pull away if he was awake. I should move—I know that much. But every fiber of my being wants to stay wrapped up in his arms.

"Asher."

Apollo murmurs my name in his sleep, and I hate how my name on his lips can simultaneously break and soothe my heart. I disentangle myself, and immediately Apollo pulls his arm back across his own chest. His eyes move back and forth beneath his eyelids, and I wonder what he's dreaming about. He looks so vulnerable, and I wonder what part of life hurt him so badly to bring him to the circus. I'm grateful for it, and I hate it for causing him so much pain.

The wind picks up, and the snow with it. Apollo starts

shivering, so I reach over and shake him awake. He blinks the snow away and pulls himself up.

"I can't believe we fell asleep," I say.

"How long have you been awake?" he asks.

"Just a moment," I lie. I stand and reach out a hand to help him up. He picks up the blanket and shakes it off.

It's beginning to snow much harder now.

"We should probably go," I say.

We head back toward the car. Apollo throws the blanket into the back seat and is about to sit down, when he stops and shuts the driver's-side door, with him still on the other side.

"What are you doing?"

Apollo doesn't answer. He bends down, and I think maybe he's retying his shoelaces until he stands up and lobs a snowball straight at me. It hits me right in the chest, knocking me back a step.

"Oh, no you didn't."

He laughs. It only takes a second before I've made a snowball of my own, lobbing it across the hood of the car. It catches Apollo on his shoulder. He sticks out his tongue at me before running back to the field. I laugh as I chase after him, already readying my next one.

We chase each other, throwing snowballs back and forth, hiding behind trees and bushes as we stockpile ammunition in piles that are depleted almost as fast as they're constructed. Apollo sneaks in a hit while my back is turned, and I get him back with a well-placed snowball to the back of his knee that takes him down. Once down, he rolls over onto his back, begins making an angel in the snow, which has accumulated almost half a foot in the couple of hours since we arrived. I trace a halo above his head with my foot, then carefully walk around and help him to his feet.

"Careful," I say as he wobbles, threatening to fall over and ruin the picture. He grabs hold of my hand, hops forward, then topples right into me, knocking us both flat onto the ground. My face is inches from his, his breath warm on my face. From here I can see every droplet of water on his eyelashes, can see every variation of brown in his eyes as they stare into mine.

We lock eyes, and for a moment I think that just maybe he sees me. Sees *me*. And suddenly my worst fear has become my greatest hope.

"Sorry, I can't," he whispers. "I just, I can't."

He pulls himself off of me, and I wonder if he can see the disappointment that's almost certainly written across my face.

"We should go," I say as I stand up, and this time when we get to the car, we climb inside, and we drive away.

THIRTY-ONE

I feel like death when I wake at the crack of dawn the next morning. Perhaps falling asleep in a snowstorm wasn't my smartest move. I wish I could curl up beneath my covers and never leave, but my grandparents have tickets for all three of us to attend UNH's Thanksgiving Day game. I wonder how Apollo is feeling after yesterday. What was fun in the moment was much less fun on the ride home, as our teeth chattered and our feet squelched in our wet shoes.

My grandparents show up just past eight, decked in an absurd amount of UNH gear. The ride to Maine takes a couple of hours. It's a chilly day outside, temperatures in the low forties, and I'm at least grateful it gives me an excuse to wear sweatpants and a hoodie.

The tailgate is packed with probably a thousand people, and yet it seems at every turn Grandma and Grandpa know someone, and I'm introduced to every one of them. "A future Wildcat!" my grandpa says proudly. I shake hands with what feels like at least a hundred people, mustering a smile and a "Go Wildcats!" Finally we make it to noon and then head up to our seats in one of the suites. My grandpa's partner at their law firm is an alum of the University of Maine and a big donor to their football program, which is how we managed to score such great seats. I recognize a couple of the other people in the sixteen-person suite—Mr. McKinley and his wife of course, since it was their suite. They've brought their nephew, a boy close to my own age named Connor. We're the only two people here who aren't adults.

Fortunately lunch is catered, because I'm starving. I fill a plate, and Connor does the same.

"So I hear you'll probably be going to UNH next year," he says to me between bites of food. "I'll be at Dartmouth. My uncle"—he nods to my grandpa's law partner—"is golfing buddies with the dean of admissions, so I got interviewed over the summer. They can't officially accept any sooner than Ivy League decision day, but I expect I'll get a likely letter before that." I nod as though I have any idea what he's talking about. "My uncle and aunt don't have kids, so they see me as next in line to take over the law firm. Hey! Maybe we'll take it over together someday." I haven't said a word in this conversation, and I'm beginning to wonder if I'll ever get to.

Thankfully Connor becomes distracted as the players come onto the field, and I'm able to slip away.

"Ah, come here, kid! Let me see you!" Mr. McKinley, who I've known since I was a child, pulls me in for a big hug. His wife greets me the same way.

"Have you had a chance to meet my nephew, Connor? He's also graduating this year, but from Wilbur. Let me call him over and introduce you."

"No!" I say quickly. "I mean, I did meet him and we had a great conversation. He seems lovely."

This response seems to satisfy Mr. and Mrs. McKinley, who beam in the direction of their nephew, still busy stuffing his face by the food table. I've realized as long as I steer clear of that area, I might be able to avoid him the rest of the game.

"Oh, look, they're about to do the coin toss."

We stop and watch as the toss is called for UNH, who choose to receive in the first half. "How about a friendly wager?" my grandpa says to Mr. McKinley. "Winner pays for the other's Christmas dinner."

They shake on it. "I like my ham honey glazed!" Mr. McKinley says.

"That's great. Just make sure you pick us up a nice plump turkey while you're at the butcher's!"

They laugh, and I imagine this being my life. I'll go to UNH. Connor will go to Dartmouth. We'll become lawyers and spend the annual Thanksgiving game in this box, maybe bringing our own families someday, then taking over the law firm in our mid to late thirties. Then we'll stand here making our own wager on the results of the game.

What a horrifying future.

Maine scores first, and the cheers from most of the box hurt my ears. All I want to do is sit in the corner and sketch, but I know my grandparents would have a literal conniption, so instead I play what feels like a slow-motion game of tag as I try to avoid Connor.

Finally, the game reaches halftime, which is the only part of the game I'm even halfway interested in, so obviously as soon as I sit down, Connor comes over and begins talking.

"What a first half, huh?" he says. "Obviously I'm rooting for Maine, but a close game is more exciting."

I say nothing, just lean forward in the hopes that Connor will take the hint and shut up. He doesn't.

"My uncle says you go to the Catholic school," he says. "I used to be over at North Leicester till it burned down.

"Arson. Some juvenile delinquent in my grade." I grit my teeth but stay quiet. "Anyways, now I'm over at Wilbur. Your old school, I hear. So tell me, what do you think about all this ridiculous drama?"

The Wildcat band finishes their first song and transitions to their second one as I turn to Connor.

"What?"

"The drama at Wilbur. You know, the case your grandpa and my uncle's firm has taken on. Good for business I suppose, but a bit ridiculous."

"Very," I say. "Imagine having to sue your own school because they refuse to let you use the right bathroom?"

It takes Connor a little too long to realize I'm not siding with him. I don't want to hear anything about Wilbur, about Kaycee, about this case. I wish my grandfather's firm had never taken it, and I wish people would find something better to concern themselves with than where a high schooler wants to pee.

I turn back to the band, and this time Connor seems to take the hint and leaves me alone.

The second half of the game drags on, and I'm trying to calculate how many times I can sneak away to the private bathroom before someone starts inquiring about my health, when everyone jumps up from their seats. I'm still trying to figure out what's going on when half the group begins screaming, "Go, go, go!" including both my grandparents.

There is nothing weirder than seeing my normally uptight grandparents behave like screaming kids because a bunch of college kids are running around with a ball, but as much as I dislike football, I have to say it is rather satisfying watching Connor's face fall when our team scores the winning touch-down.

"I'll take my turkey with all the fixin's!" my grandpa shouts, a grin spread wide across his face.

"Hell of a game," Mr. McKinley says. "Hell of a game! This is one your granddaughter will be telling her grandkids about someday. Congratulations."

I shake Connor's hand on our way out of the suite. He's remarkably sullen as he mumbles his goodbye. At least something good could come out of this day.

THIRTY-TWO

It's late when I get home, and there's a faint glow coming through the windows of the living room. Mom probably fell asleep with the TV on again. I let myself into the house quietly, but the sound I'm greeted by isn't the evening news or an eighties sitcom.

It's Mom, tangled in Christmas lights, swearing so profusely she'd make a sailor blush.

"Would you like a hand?"

Mom spins—well, tries to spin, but it comes out more like an awkward hop—until she's facing me, face scrunched in a mixture of embarrassment and gratitude.

I chuckle and walk over to assist, first getting Mom untangled, and then looping the lights around the fake tree she's set up by the window.

"I remember when your dad got this tree," Mom says. "We'd just moved in together. I was pregnant with you and thought we should save the money since you weren't even born yet, but your dad insisted, said it wasn't Christmas without a tree. Said it wouldn't 'smell right' without one." She snorts.

"But you finally gave in?" I ask as I drape the lights between two branches, one of which is missing most of its needles, has been missing its needles for so many years I'm not sure I remember a time when it wasn't.

Mom laughs. "No," she says. "I stood firm. Told your dad I'd buy him a candle if he was that concerned about the smell and that I wasn't going to go and cut down a tree just so we could have it up for a few weeks."

"So what happened?" I try not to show how I'm hanging on every word. Mom talks about Dad so infrequently that I'm afraid of scaring her off the topic.

"Well, I was taking classes at the community college in the day and working night shifts at the Blue Moon Diner, so I wasn't home much, and there was one night, I think I'd just come off of a double, when your dad greets me at the door, so excited like a golden retriever that I was immediately suspicious. He told me to close my eyes even though I could smell the tree as soon as I walked inside, but I did it anyways." She pauses, chuckles. "He walks me into the living room, and what do I see when I open my eyes? This damn fake tree, no lights, no ornaments, covered entirely in those car air fresheners. Says he found it on the side of the road—someone was throwing it away, could I imagine that! At least he bought the air fresheners new. The house smelled like pine for months after we took the tree down." She chuckles. "I think I might still have one of them actually." Mom lets go of the lights and rifles through the ornament box until she finds what she's looking for. She cradles it in her hand for a moment before lifting it to her nose and inhaling deeply.

"Can I hold it?" I ask.

She hands it over and I take it gently in my hands, bringing it to my nose as though whatever scent remains might stir up some memory deep inside me. But nothing comes, and I'm left trying to imagine the scene instead, trying to overlay images of the buttoned-up man from photos at my grandparents' house with the one from my mother's memories. They don't seem to match, but then, I know a bit of something about that. About the masks we wear and what lies beneath.

I hand the air freshener back. Mom sniffs and wipes her nose with the back of her sleeve, and I look away awkwardly, giving her some privacy. Neither of us has ever been good with displays of vulnerability.

She exhales deeply. "Lights are looking good. I think we'll save the ornaments for tomorrow, yeah? I'm beat."

I nod. Mom kisses me on the forehead and heads to her bedroom, placing the air freshener back in the box before she goes. I wait until she's gone, then take it back out and hang it on the tree.

Happy Thanksgiving, Dad.

Church on my Friday off from school is the last place I want to find myself, yet here I am just before lunch with my grandparents. Apparently, there's been a development in the lawsuit at Wilbur High that's turned the tide of the case in Kaycee's favor, and now the parents of Our Lady are demanding action. Leading the charge, unsurprisingly, are Rebecca-Ann's parents. She's here as well, along with a few of my other classmates, including Jackson and Apollo. One of the parents has set up a table in the basement with sandwich platters and individually sized bags of chips. I make a plate and take it to a table at the back of the room, where Apollo's already sitting.

Rebecca-Ann looks between our table and the tables out front where the parents and grandparents are setting up shop and unfortunately chooses to join us, Jackson following right behind like a puppy nipping at her heals.

Great. Two of my favorite people.

Rebecca-Ann takes a seat directly across from Apollo, Jackson sitting down immediately next to her.

"Hi, Apollo," she says, and then, honest to God, she twirls her hair around her finger. Jesus Christ. I'm living in a sitcom.

I notice she doesn't say hello to me. No problem. Saves me the trouble of having to pretend to like her.

I was worried things would be awkward with Apollo in the daytime after the way our time in the snow ended, but he seems content to pretend it never happened, so I'm following his lead.

"You know, I'm starting a weekly Bible study," Rebecca-Ann says, her gaze trained on Apollo. "Saturday mornings at ten a.m. Teens for God. You'd be welcome to come, if you wanted." *Oh God.* Is she flirting? I want to gag.

Apollo gives her a small smile that doesn't reach his eyes. "Cool, thanks. I'll consider it," he says in a voice that tells me he will literally never think about this again.

Or maybe that's just me projecting.

Jackson glares at Apollo, and everyone ignores me. I feel like one of the many Jesuses on the wall, here just to observe and judge.

Now that everyone has taken their food, the meeting is ready to begin. Rebecca-Ann is called back to the front by her parents to present the petition she was collecting signatures for at the beginning of the school year. Jackson, predictably, follows along after her.

I turn to Apollo once they're gone.

"Oh, Apollo," I say mockingly. "Let us pray. And then make beautiful, beautiful babies."

He frowns. "I don't think she likes me like that."

"Are you kidding? She was definitely planning her future wedding."

"Hmm," he says, as though genuinely considering this for the very first time. He looks toward the front of the room. We're far enough back, we can only sort of hear the discussion. "What do you think of all this?"

"The debate or the lawsuit?"

"Either. Both. The whole Wilbur situation."

I feel nervous suddenly. This is the first time we've discussed the lawsuit at all and therefore the closest we've ever come to discussing my own identity. I'd be lying if I didn't admit there was a part of me desperate to tell him, but that doesn't seem wise.

"I wish people would stop calling it 'the Wilbur situation,' like it's a case of rats in the kitchen or something," I say. "It's a real girl who just wants to use the bathroom, and she has to sue the school to do it because this town is so *goddamn* backward." I stop, suddenly aware of how much I've said and how passionately, as though I'm talking to Apollo at the circus rather than here in the daytime.

He looks taken aback, and I wonder if I should have said something else, something less, but then he says, "You're absolutely right," and I breathe a sigh of relief. "My parents haven't stopped talking about this all week. They're acting like it's some sort of crisis situation, but we don't even have any trans students at school."

"That you know of," I interject, and when he looks at me, I add, "I just mean, someone might be trans but is too scared to come out." My face feels hot, like I'm on the edge of walking into something I can't walk back from.

"You're right. Again. That was stupid of me to say. Who wouldn't be scared to come out around here?" He laughs bitterly. "Of all people, I should know better than to assume something like that." He cuts himself off, and I see the fear in his eyes as he realizes he almost outed himself to me, unaware that I'm already well aware of how he feels about guys.

Look at the two of us. Living in a town that has made us too scared to be honest with each other. I think of my grandparents, of his parents, of all the parents in this room today, scared to death of teenagers who just want to be themselves, and all I want is to scream at them and ask them if they know what they're really doing. Do they know they're killing us? Or do they just not care?

I meet Apollo's eyes, feeling suddenly emboldened. "I get it."

He swallows. "Do you—are you—"

Ask me, I say with my eyes. *Ask me.*

But he doesn't ask me. Not what I want him to ask me.

"How do you think she does it?" he asks. "The girl at Wilbur? How do you think she lives here and listens to everything people have to say and doesn't hate herself constantly?"

It's a good question, and I think the real answer is that, like everyone else, Kaycee sometimes does hate herself. She just loves herself more. I wonder now if Apollo is talking about his sexuality, which as far as I know isn't anything people have speculated about, or about the other rumors—of the fire and of going to juvie.

"Honesty, probably. I think she shows the world who she is and says 'Fuck you' to everyone who doesn't like it."

In short, she does exactly what I am incapable of doing for myself.

I'm not sure what Apollo thinks of that, because at that moment his parents call him to the front of the room, and once again I'm alone.

The small committee of parents decides to move forward with a proposal making it official that students must use the bathroom associated with their birth sex. Grandpa calls it an illogical decision but doesn't seem to have any disagreements with the idea itself. I wish I could text Moira and talk to her about the whole thing, but she still isn't speaking to me.

Friends are hard to come by these days.

THIRTY-THREE

I notice the feeling first. It's hard to put into words other than to call it a feeling of *wrongness*. It sits heavy in the air as I take my first step into the circus. I've made it almost all the way to the tent before it hits me.

The children.

There are no children tonight. I spin back around, confirm it for myself. Adults, everyone. And it's not just the lack of children that chills the air tonight. I shiver and wrap my arms around my chest, wishing my dream self were wearing warmer attire.

I hear shouting in the distance, and as I approach the main tent, I'm greeted by a group of past circus members, arms locked together in front of the entrance. Their leader appears to be the main clown harassing Seb a month ago. I guess he's still upset that Seb chose someone less terrible to replace Maisie.

What they're shouting becomes clear as I get closer. It's a call-and-response led by that annoying clown, like they're union workers on strike or something.

"No justice?"

"No peace!"

"No jobs?"

"No peace!"

Some curious audience members stop and look, but most continue on their way.

I spot Seb watching, arms crossed, and go join him.

"What are they doing?" I ask, though I realize the answer is rather obvious.

"Making a scene," Seb says. "They're refusing to move unless René puts them in the show."

"They do know there's a back entrance, right?" Seb doesn't answer. "Were they always like this, d'you think?" I ask. "So . . . mean-spirited? It just doesn't seem like the type of person who'd have been part of the circus, you know?"

Seb nods toward an Asian woman in her mid-fifties at the end of the row. "She's a singer," he says. "Voice like an angel. And the one next to her is a tightrope walker."

"How do you know that?" I ask.

"They were here when I first started," Seb says. I forget that as young as he is, he's been here longer than almost anyone else. "Su Lin was practically a mother to me. And Nikolas taught me how to play cards."

I look at both of them, arms linked with the other former performers, faces filled with anger, and then back at Seb, a weariness present in every inch of him that's so far from the energetic boy who first welcomed me to the circus just a few short months ago.

"What do you think happened to them?"

"The same thing that's happened to the rest of this place," he says, not sadly, just matter-of-factly, which might be worse. Then he sticks his hands into his pockets and walks away, head down.

I can't watch this anymore. I need to find Apollo.

I run into Jenni in the tent. "Asher!" she says. "I had to come in here to hide out. Everything out there is just . . ." She trails off, shivering with her whole body in lieu of words. I know exactly what she means. "Though things aren't that much better in here." She pointedly avoids looking toward Marko, who is doing Fizz's makeup. It's become a nightly occurrence, covering the myriad bruises that decorate his body. But even that isn't as bad as the sound coming from the other side of the dressing room, where Peter sits on a costume chest, his entire body hunched over as he's racked by coughs. Seb sits beside him, clearly trying to cheer him up, but I worry about what it's doing to him. The circus is supposed to be our escape from the world; what happens when the world becomes our escape from the circus?

I quickly change and head out to the trapeze ring, where I find Apollo, not stretching but flying, Tessa catching for him. I'm taken back to the first time I ever saw the rig, ever saw Apollo, and I'm struck once again by his beauty. Only now I know it's so much more than just physical beauty.

I think I might love him.

I watch until he spots me and signals to Tessa that he's going to come down. I meet him at the edge of the net, kissing him as soon as he's back on the ground. He pulls me into a hug, and I never want to let go.

Despite the protesters at the front of the tent, the show goes on. René and Jenni lead the crowd through the dressing room to their seats, a profoundly strange experience for those of us used to that space being our private sanctum. The lack of children further compounds the unpleasantness of the experience.

Not even the show itself is immune from the strangeness of the evening. One thing goes wrong after another, and by the time Apollo and I are set to close out the individual acts, it seems to be less a matter of *if* something will go wrong than *what*, which is a terrifying feeling to have when you're about to throw yourself off a platform twenty-five feet above the ground.

"Are you ready for this?" I ask Apollo.

"Nope," he says, as the music cues us on. "Let's do this."

We run out into the lights, and I try to keep my attention focused only on the task at hand but even the cheers from the audience feel different tonight. Less cheerful, more . . . ominous. At the same time that I'm scaling the ladder to the board on one side of the rig, Apollo is scurrying up to the catch trap, getting into position. I dip my hands into the bag of chalk, hoping I don't sweat through and fall mid-act. Though at least the net will catch me if I do.

I run quickly through the act in my head before I pull the catcher's bar forward and indicate to Apollo that I'm ready to go. He starts his swing, getting into the catcher's lock, and when he's almost in position yells *Ready!* And then *Hup!*

I jump, and all my worries fall away. My body and Apollo's are fully in sync, perhaps better than they've ever been before. I hit every move like I was born to do only this, every turn, every flip, every catch. And when Apollo and I lock hands? Magic.

It's that magic that I want to keep alive when we're back on the ground, and once the show has ended. Put aside all that's wrong and focus on one of the few things going right—my relationship with Apollo.

After we've taken off our costumes and scrubbed our faces clean of makeup, I take Apollo behind the tent and kiss him with a hunger hard to capture in words.

"So," I say when we finally break apart, "what will it be tonight? Carnival games? Try to win that stuffed elephant you won't be able to take with you when you wake up?"

Apollo takes my hand and squeezes it gently. "How about we go somewhere quieter? Look at the stars?"

We find a spot out behind the tent and lay out a blanket. He's quiet, and I wonder what he's thinking as he looks toward the sky. He runs his hand through a patch of clover.

"Have you ever found a four-leaf clover?" he asks me.

I shake my head.

He rolls over onto his side. "I did," he says, "once. It was after my great-grandfather died, my grandmother's father. I was young, six or seven maybe. All us kids were sent outside to play while the adults made the funeral arrangements, and I looked down and saw two right next to each other. I picked them and gave them to my grandmother and she started crying. It was the first time she'd cried since he died, and I thought I'd done something wrong, so I started crying too." He smiles faintly at the memory. "But then she told me they were happy tears because she knew they were sent by my great-grandfather to let us know he was okay."

Something seizes up inside me as he tells his story, and I try not to think about the extended family Apollo's talked so much about. Try not to think about how our relationship exists only within the confines of our dreams.

"I've never found a four-leaf clover," I say, letting the lump in my throat settle, "but I always thought the day I did would be the best day ever."

Apollo returns his gaze to the stars, and I switch mine to him.

I feel like I know his freckles the way I know the constellations, and even though so much has gone wrong, he makes me happier than I've ever been in my life.

"Hey," I say softly, reaching over and running my thumb along Apollo's jaw. He sits up, leaning back, hands on the grass beside him, and looks at me. I smile, but he doesn't return it.

"Everything okay?" I ask, and I want him to laugh and tackle me to the ground so he can kiss me beneath the night sky, but he doesn't, and I feel my heart sink further and further the longer the silence stretches on.

"I think I love you, Asher," Apollo says finally, and I don't know how to respond because he sounds so sad, and in none of my deepest fantasies was this how it was supposed to sound to hear those words. I want to say it back, but my voice has dried up and no words come out.

"I have a friend," he continues. "She's a lesbian, I think, and she told me something today, gave me some advice while we were talking. She said if I wanted to be happy, I needed to be honest, and I haven't been honest. Not for a long time. And I realized I've been using the circus as a crutch, but I can't keep doing that, because it's not real. You're not real. I made you and all of this up because I couldn't deal with who I am. And I need to start dealing with it. That's why I can't do this anymore."

"Of course it's real," I say, desperate for him to believe me. "I'm real." The words feel distant, like someone else is speaking them for me.

"It's a dream," he says, "Just a beautiful dream. But I can't live in a dream forever. I'm sorry."

I can't speak. At the edges of my vision, the world dims and

I feel like I'm drowning, gasping for air in the one place that always had all the oxygen. Apollo leans over, kisses me gently on the lips, then stands up and walks away.

I watch him as he goes, watch as he gets smaller and smaller, pausing only once to stop and look over the midway and the tent, and then watch as he disappears from my sight entirely.

I pull handfuls of clovers from the ground, and when I've torn up a large patch, I look down and see the clover in my hand. It has four leaves, my first.

I break.

When I can stand again, I stumble out onto the midway just in time to hear the most horrific wrenching sound, like nails on a chalkboard times infinity, and I freeze as the Ferris wheel breaks free of its axis and comes crashing to the ground, followed by screaming. So much screaming.

Everything after that seem to happens both in slow motion and hyperspeed. My feet move almost of their own accord, not away but toward. It's only later that I'll realize how lucky it was that René shut down all the rides back after the first incident, and that there were no children at the circus to get caught in the wreckage.

For now, I see none of that, think none of those thoughts. My body runs on pure adrenaline as I help pull the few unlucky circus-goers from the debris, as my mind takes in but doesn't process the blood, the arm bent at an unnatural angle, the water poured into my mouth by a hand attached to a body I don't see. I process nothing until the last person is safe, until I go to scale the debris once again and find myself pulled back by hands that grab on to me and don't let go.

"It's over, 'mano, it's over," Seb says. "Everyone is safe. You got them all."

It's as if he said the magic words, because at that moment the weight of everything that's happened, of everything I've done, comes crashing down upon me, and I fall to my knees. Nothing is okay, and I'm not sure it ever will be again.

René gathers us together once the last patron has been evacuated from the circus, sent back to wherever it was they came from. I wonder if they'll wake up in their beds grateful to be alive. Perhaps they'll forget what they saw—a nightmare that simply fades into the background of their otherwise mundane day.

If only I could be so lucky.

He clears his throat, and the crowd quiets down. This is the weariest I've ever seen him. I fear the slightest breeze might topple him over, but still we look toward him for guidance, look toward him to say the words, whatever those words are, to fix all this.

"Friends—" he starts, pauses, shakes his head, unable to continue.

Someone, Seb I suspect, begins to cheer for René, and soon everyone else has joined in. He looks overwhelmed by gratitude.

"Friends," he says again, stronger this time. "There are no words. The circus is supposed to be a place of joy, a place for all of us to call home. Tonight, I've failed you all, and for that I'm sorry."

"It's not your fault René!" another voice shouts.

René puts a hand to his heart in gratitude. "I need to think about what comes next. I'm going to be in my trailer for the rest of the evening. If anyone needs to speak to me, you can find me there." I swear, but perhaps I am just imagining it, that René focuses his attention on me.

When he's gone, leaving the rest of us to do who knows what, I turn to Seb.

"I need to talk to you," I say. He seems reluctant to leave Peter, but Peter reassures him he'll be fine. We walk away from the rest of the crowd, and I try to figure out where to begin. "Do you remember the day René told me I could switch to trapeze?"

"You mean the day you stabbed me in the heart," Seb says jokingly. He pretends to fall back as though having been actually stabbed. "That hurt, 'mano!"

And this is going to hurt more. I take a deep breath.

"Well . . . it turns out that wasn't really René's idea."

I tell him everything. About meeting Jean for the first time and wanting to fly. About taking the book and then trying to use it to improve the circus, and then about giving the book over to Jean after the Masquerade, when I realized he was kicking out Tessa and Jenni.

I tell him about the conversations that came later, about confronting Jean after everything started to fall apart, and when I'm done, I go silent, waiting for his response.

"How could you?" he says, all traces of humor gone from his face, which is not what I was expecting. I don't know what I was expecting. Sympathy perhaps, or anger at René for kicking people out of the circus in the first place. Certainly not the rage now being directed at me.

"But he was kicking people out of the circus! Peter came back because of me."

271

"Well, thank you so much. There's nothing I wanted more than to watch my mentor dying!"

"That's not my fault!"

"Is anything? Did you ever even think of talking to René? Asking him why people don't stay forever? Or were you so blinded by your own selfishness that it never occurred to you?"

He's right. I just assumed René was being cruel, but I never allowed him the chance to explain.

"Maisie left because of you. Because she felt like there wasn't a space for her here anymore. And what about me? Have you ever wondered why I've been here longer than anyone else? Why everyone else leaves, but never Seb? Well, you didn't ask, but I'll tell you anyways, 'mano." That word, one he'd always used in friendship from the first moment he laid eyes on me, he spits out now, and just when I think I can't feel worse, I do. "Seventeen foster homes in eight years. The circus is the only stable thing I have. Do you know what it feels like to be *that* unwanted? Maybe you do. I don't know. But I do know I'd never assume to be the only person who needs this place. Tell René, or I'll do it myself."

He shakes his head, disgusted, and as I watch him walk away, I wish I could just wake up.

The tent village is empty as I make my way through. Half-dealt card games lie on overturned crates beside bottles of soda not yet consumed. Bottles of soda that won't ever be consumed.

René's trailer comes into view, and I stop at the steps. Take a deep breath. Something lands on my shoulder as I step up to the door. I could laugh. It's my butterfly friend, returned once more. He rests on my shoulder, giving me strength as I knock and step inside.

"Ah, Asher. What can I do for you?" René gestures toward an old couch for me to take a seat. "Tea?"

I nod, and he pours me a cup. I hold it between my hands, watching the steam rise, and when I take a sip it's the perfect temperature. Not too hot, not too cold. It's exactly as Apollo said.

A beautiful dream.

And I've turned it into a nightmare.

"I took your notebook." I force myself to look up and meet René's eyes. "I stole it when you were out of your trailer because I wanted to fly. And then I gave it to a man named Jean after the Masquerade because he said he would bring Tessa and Jenni back. I thought I was doing something good, but it was really something selfish.

"I know sorry doesn't begin to cover it," I say, voice cracking, "but I am. Truly. But now that you know, you can find Jean, get the notebook back, and fix everything."

René listens silently. When I'm done, he finally speaks. "Thank you for telling me the truth, Asher, but I'm afraid it's not so simple. I know Jean, and he's not going to give the journal back. You should go. I need to sort out a few things here before I make the announcement."

Announcement?

"What are you going to do?"

René meets my eyes, and for the first time I realize he's much older than I thought. Can see it in the weariness of his eyes, in the utter exhaustion living in every line of his face, and I realize

I did this to him. Suddenly the face of Mr. Roberts pops into my head. I couldn't save him then, and I can't save René now.

"I'm going to shut down the circus," he says finally. My heart nearly stops.

"What? But you can't!"

"Alas, it's the one thing I *can* do. And it's the only way to stop him," he says. "You should go and spend the remainder of your time with your friends. I would appreciate if you didn't tell them what I've told you. I'll make my announcement just before dawn."

I can tell there's nothing more I can say to change his mind. I take one last look at his trailer, and then I turn and exit. I have one more thing to try.

Jean arrives before I can try to call for him, at the edge of the woods where we met for the first time, almost as soon as I've drawn the breath I'd need to do so.

"René's going to shut down the circus."

He takes a moment to consider this. He can't want this. He's going to have to negotiate with me. I can still make this right.

"Faster than I expected. Hmm. Well, good. Thank you for letting me know." He turns and begins to walk away.

"Wait!"

He stops, turns back.

He's bluffing. He has to be bluffing.

"You can't want this! If you wanted the circus shut down, you would've done it already. As soon as I gave you the note-book. This isn't what you want."

The gaze I receive, as best I can guess, is one of pity. "On the contrary. Shutting down the circus is all I wanted, and it's the one thing only René could do. I'm sorry, but it's too late to fix this. René and I made our beds long ago."

"So that's it then?" My voice cracks, and I don't know if it's a result of me or the circus breaking down.

"You should go say goodbye to your friends," is all he says, before he too leaves me alone.

I close my eyes, imaging the sights, sounds, and smells of my beloved circus for the last time. I see the tent, that beautiful blue and gold tent where I learned how to fly. I smell Gino's popcorn, hear the sounds of music and the laughter of children. See the faces of my friends, and then when I can't take it anymore, can't take the guilt or the sadness, I open my eyes. When I'm afraid I'll fall to my knees and never be able to stand back up, I say goodbye and good night for the last time, and I pass through the woods.

When I wake up in my bed, it's still dark, and when I fall back asleep, I dream of nothing.

THIRTY-FOUR

I'm awakened by the light shining through my open blinds, and it's disorienting because I'm always awake before sunrise, so it takes me a few moments to remember what happened last night. And as soon as I do remember, I wish desperately I hadn't. I lean over my bed, grab my trash can, and proceed to throw up stomach acid and bile until my throat burns and my eyes water. I've lost everything. I've lost Apollo, the circus, Seb, Fizz, and Gemma. Worse still is knowing they've lost everything too, and it's entirely my fault.

I pass the day in a fog, unable to concentrate. At least it's a weekend, and I don't have to get ready for school. My thoughts are a jumble, my stomach in knots. Mom's worried enough she takes my temperature, but it's normal. What's wrong with me can't be fixed with anything as simple as Tylenol and a long nap. I wish desperately that it could.

Not even drawing helps. Just the thought of illustrating the circus in any form makes me feel nauseous, so instead I lounge on the couch, grimy and unwashed as I eat cold leftover pizza and watch *Judge Judy*.

I nod off and dream I'm on trial in her courtroom, Apollo as my lawyer. Someone throws a tomato at me from the audience, and when I turn around, I see Seb juggling four more. "Catch," he says before pelting me rapid fire with the rest of them. The audience is filled with my fellow performers, all of them jeering at me, except Tessa, who looks at me with disappointment.

From the front of the courtroom, Judge Judy decides she's come to a verdict. She bangs her gavel, but all I hear is a shrill *beepbeepbeepbeep*. I open my eyes and realize the beeping is coming from the fire alarm in the kitchen. Mom's standing on a chair trying to make it stop. Finally, she gives up and yanks the whole thing from the ceiling.

"Low battery," she says. "I need to pick some up at the store." She steps down from the chair and brings it back to the table. "Mail came while you were napping. You've got something from UNH."

It's a large envelope, the universal sign of good things when it comes to colleges. Either Mom doesn't know or she's trying to keep her cool, because she's not even looking as I rip it open, hands shaking as I read the opening lines of the letter.

Congratulations!

That's all I have to read because *holy shit*. I got into college. I hadn't expected a response anywhere near this soon, but it's the one bright spot in this otherwise hellish day.

"What's the letter say?"

When I don't answer, she turns and walks over. All I can do is hand it to her to read and watch as she bursts into tears.

"Mom?" I say hesitantly. If there's one thing I know about my mother, it's that she doesn't cry. She probably did when my dad died, but I was too young to remember. So it's shocking to me now to watch her cry over a piece of paper in her hand.

"We have to celebrate," she says.

"I should probably call Grandma and Grandpa. They'll want to know."

"Later," she says. "After we celebrate. Let them find out

something second for once. Come on, we'll go out to eat. Wherever you want."

Well, I can hardly say no to *that*.

Mom and I end up at Friendly's. It's not the fanciest restaurant; in fact it's not at all fancy, which is part of the appeal. It's not the type of place my grandparents would take me to.

But Friendly's. Glorious, glorious Friendly's, with its plates of chicken tenders and ice cream sundaes with the tiny gummy bears that are vastly superior to all others. Back when I was a kid, Mom would sometimes take me here for breakfast while we did our laundry at the laundromat down the street, and I'd order the pancakes they made look like a face; M&Ms for eyes and whipped cream for hair.

I go to the bathroom as soon as we get inside, and when I come back, Mom's grinning. "I got your favorite table," she says. "Over by the mural."

The mural. As a kid, I couldn't get enough of it. I even begged my mom to paint a replica on my bedroom wall, despite the fact that she has no artistic talent of any kind. In fact, if I were to look back at the path of my life, my becoming an artist, my ending up at the Midnight Circus, I think perhaps I could trace it all back to this mural on this wall of this Friendly's in this small town in New Hampshire.

The mural in question, the mural I'm now forced to stare up at as I order my meal, is of a carnival. An old man walks around selling bright balloons, a little girl with her blond hair in a ponytail waves down to someone on the ground from a flying plane ride, a worker sells ice cream from a small stand, a mother purchases cotton candy for her child, a group of teenagers try their luck in a carnival game, and this is where I have to laugh—the pièce de résistance, a giant carousel with a blue and gold awning.

Blue and gold. And a goddamn carnival.

I refocus my attention on the menu. It's not Mom's fault the mural is the last thing I want to see right now. It's not her fault I forgot all about it when I chose this restaurant.

"Get whatever you want," Mom says.

The waiter comes to take our orders, and I'm reluctant to hand over my menu when we're done. Mom asks how school is, I tell her it's fine. She asks about Moira, I tell her she's fine too.

"I haven't seen her around much lately," she says, almost hesitantly, as though she realizes we've been fighting but isn't confident enough to ask me about it. That seems to be a recurring theme in our relationship.

"Just busy," I say. "College applications, babysitting her siblings. All that."

Mom nods, and fortunately the waiter comes over with our food, sparing us the need to continue a steady back-and-forth dialogue.

"What about our new neighbor. Apollo?"

"What about Apollo?" I ask.

I dip a chicken tender in the honey mustard and then in the barbecue sauce and take a bite. The mural taunts me. I would actually prefer to look up and see a giant crucifix, which is really saying something.

"It seems like you've grown close. I've noticed him giving you rides to school."

I shrug. "Convenience," I say, then, "You're full of questions all of a sudden."

Mom frowns. "I'm making conversation."

"I'm just saying, all the questions. It's new."

I go back to eating my chicken nuggets, but Mom isn't done yet.

"I care," she says. "I always care, and I always want to know what's going on in your life."

A snort comes out of me before I can stop it.

She looks hurt. "I don't know what's gotten into you, but I don't like it."

"Sorry," I say. "Go on, keep asking questions."

Ask me. Ask me what happened that day at school. Ask me how my eye was injured.

"No, I'm done," she says, shaking her head. "I'm just going to sit and enjoy my meal in silence."

"Fine," I reply.

She doesn't respond. We eat in silence, and when the waiter comes to take our plates and see if we want dessert, I shake my head. I've lost my appetite.

THIRTY-FIVE

Saturday bleeds into Sunday, and Sunday into Monday, but the circus doesn't come for me. I didn't expect it would, but the reality is worse than the expectation. The world without the circus is devoid of color. Sleep, when I get it, is fleeting and restless. I wake up sweating and screaming from nightmares of which I have no memory. The only dreams I do remember involve Mr. Roberts. Every time they're exactly the same. I enter the shop, which is in complete disarray, art supplies strewn across the floor, shelves tipped onto their sides, and find Mr. Roberts rummaging through the mess searching for something. And each time he looks up at me and asks where it is. The only problem is that I have no idea what *it* is.

School passes in a fog. Apollo still drives me, and every morning it's a reminder of all that I've lost. The only thing keeping me going is my art. Drawing the circus causes me pain, but I can't stop. I doodle on every free scrap of paper, and when I get home each afternoon, I return to the graphic novel I've started working on.

Where before I used to look forward to sleep, used to rush off into bed in the hopes that the circus would find me sooner, I now stay up later and later each night. The mere thought of climbing into my bed and surrendering myself to the black depths of unconsciousness makes me break out in cold sweats, and I take to walking at night, the sting of the harsh December air penance for everything I've done.

Occasionally I wander through the empty field that lies

behind the thin stretch of trees in our backyard, the field that once housed the Midnight Circus. Maybe. Sort of. I can't explain how the magic worked, whether I really climbed out of bed some nights and walked through these trees, or whether that was just a dream too. I look for signs that it was here, it was real, but all I find is the field as it's always been. I could start a lost-and-found with everything I find here, and everything I don't.

Found: beer cans (six), cigarette stubs (thirteen-plus), lacy black panties (two), sock (one), a half-burned copy of *Macbeth*, one nonfunctioning lighter, a single ballet slipper, a box of crayons and a soggy coloring book, one wallet (empty, except a single still-wrapped condom), two empty cans of Pringles, and a partridge in a pear tree. Well, a Christmas card with a partridge in a pear tree on the front, and on the inside, a message from Dear Old Aunt Mauve—"To Timmy, May Santa Claus bring you everything you wish for. Merry Christmas!" Beside the message, someone has scribbled a giant hairy dick. It's unclear whether that was what Timmy wished for.

Lost: one tent, blue and gold and shimmering under the light of the moon, popcorn (kernels: many, innumerable), not just popcorn, the *best* damn popcorn you've ever tasted, clowns (two, no, revise that, three; don't think too hard about how that happened), Ferris wheel (one, may be broken; ride with caution), friends (zero, but it used to be more), notebooks (one, long, long gone, also not really lost because how can something be lost if you know exactly where it is?), balloons (many), balloon animals (varies in both number and type), train car (one, good for screaming and/or kissing atop), also my heart and my sanity. If found, please return to Asher Sullivan.

I don't have any particular plan when I leave my house tonight, except to not be in my house, so by that metric, I've accomplished my goal as soon as I step foot outside. It's snowing, a light, fluffy snow that coats the trees and ground and makes everything look pretty. I'm busy thinking about how I might try my hand at capturing the image, when I see some movement from Apollo's driveway.

All the lights in his house are off, which is unsurprising given the hour of the evening.

Quietly, I move closer, my footsteps muffled by the snow, and realize someone is attempting to break into Apollo's car.

"Stop!" I yell, running closer.

The person jumps back, trips, then falls to the ground.

"Shit. It's me!"

Apollo pulls out a small flashlight and shines it so I can see. I help him to his feet.

"What are you doing?" I ask him. "Where's your key? And what are you doing in the dark?"

"My key was confiscated by my parents. Along with my cell phone and my computer and damn near everything else. And I was trying to break into my car and hot-wire it, but obviously that was a stupid fucking idea." He kicks his tire a few times, then sinks down to the ground. I squat beside him.

"Do you want to know where I really was this summer?" Apollo asks. "Why I didn't move in with my parents in the spring?"

I don't respond. I don't know how. The truth is I am curious, but I don't want to say that.

He laughs bitterly. "It wasn't juvie, in case you were wondering. Though it might have been better if it was. No, instead

I spent a summer, how did they advertise it—reconnecting with God and nature in the rustic foothills of the Alleghany Mountains as I came to terms with my developing manhood. Or some bullshit that sounds a lot better than digging poop holes in the woods while some middle-aged man tried to get me to "pray the gay away." I didn't even know it was that type of camp until I got there and I was halfway up a damn mountain. And the only reason I'm not still there is because I managed to sufficiently convince my parents I was 'cured,' or at least would no longer succumb to my 'same-sex attraction.' My old school burning down at the same time was either a convenient or an inconvenient coincidence, depending on how you look at it. I can either admit my parents sent me away because they caught me kissing another boy or continue letting everyone think I burned down our school." He turns to look at me for the first time. "I'm sure you understand why I haven't refuted the rumors now." He looks away again. "That didn't really answer your initial question though, did it? Why I was trying to break into my car in the dark or why my parents took away my keys and my phone? It was Halloween. They found out I wasn't staying at Bea's—that's my sister—and they're convinced I spent the night with a boy, so in an attempt to save my soul from going to hell, I'm now on permanent house arrest. So yeah," he says. "Now you know everything there is to know about me."

"Apollo . . ."

He turns back, and now I can see the tears in his eyes. "How do you do it?" he asks. "How do you live here and listen to everything they say and not hate yourself constantly?"

I remember what he said our last night at the circus. I know he thinks I'm a lesbian. "Apollo," I say, "I'm not . . . I don't . . ." My heart races. I want to tell him the truth. I want him to know he's not alone. That the boy he knows only from his dreams is right here beside him. I want him to know I love him. That I think he's perfect the way he is. That no one has the right to make him feel anything less.

"There's something I need to tell you," I manage to get out. "It's not what you think. I don't like girls, not like that." I reach out a hand to rest it on his knee, heart racing. "I—"

He pulls away. Sniffs and wipes his eyes dry. "Right, no, sorry," he says. "I shouldn't have assumed. I thought—well, it doesn't matter, I'm sorry. I should get back inside before my parents realize." He stands up. I scramble to my feet.

"Wait."

He turns back around. I want to tell him. I feel blood rushing to my head like I'm going to pass out, but the words are on the tip of my tongue and I want to get them out.

"I'm—"

"You're?"

"I'm not—" I can't say it. I need to say it.

"I get it," he says, voice chilled now. "You're not gay. I shouldn't have assumed you were. I have to go."

He runs back into his house, and when he's gone, I fall to my knees.

"I'm not a girl," I whisper, but it's too late.

THIRTY-SIX

There's no mention of our midnight meeting when Apollo gives me a ride to school the next morning. He asks me about a homework assignment, and that's about the extent of our conversation. I'm considering dropping out and going to live as a hermit in the woods somewhere far, far away, because it seems like everything I say recently makes one of my relationships worse.

There's a reporter standing in front of the school when we arrive, speaking, of course, to Rebecca-Ann. I don't even want to know what that's about, but I'm forced to find out when the reporter turns to me and Apollo.

"Would you two like to make a comment?"

"About what?" Apollo asks before I can stop him. Now I actually have to pause and listen.

"It seems that the school board at Our Lady of Mercy Academy has moved to institute a more official bathroom policy in response to the lawsuit at Wilbur High. As students at this school, do either of you have any thoughts you'd like to share?"

Frankly, I don't know how this is news at all. We're at a Catholic school for God's sake. The Catholic Church isn't exactly known for its progressive views on gender.

"No comment," I say to the reporter, then to Apollo, "Come on."

"What about the petition?" the reporter says, running to

keep pace with Apollo and me. "Do you care to share why you signed it in favor of Wilbur High?"

This stops me dead in my tracks. "Excuse me?"

Rebecca-Ann has already gone inside, so it's just Apollo, the reporter, and me in front of the school as the first bell rings.

"You are seniors, yes?"

"Yeah, and?"

"I was speaking to your class president, Rebecca-Ann, and she said she was proud to have gotten the signatures of the entire senior class on her petition in support of such a policy. So my question is this: Why did you decide to sign the petition?"

I'm fuming. How dare she say that? "No comment," I say again, and then I take Apollo by the arm and drag him inside before he can say anything else to the reporter.

As soon as we get inside, I storm over to Rebecca-Ann, who is standing by her locker chatting with Jackson. "What the *fuck* is wrong with you? How dare you tell that reporter everyone signed your stupid petition? You know that's not true at all."

Rebecca-Ann's face is the picture of innocence. "I didn't say that. I said I was proud to have the overwhelming support of the senior class."

"Come on," Apollo says. "Let's just go."

But I'm not ready to go, because I don't believe a word she says. I don't care how wide she's able to make her eyes. I can see straight through her fakeness.

"Why didn't you sign the petition?" Jackson asks. He smirks. "Actually, neither of you did. Why is that, I wonder? Are you a couple of fags? Is that why—" He doesn't get to finish that sentence before he finds a fist in his face. My fist, to be precise, which immediately throbs. Totally worth it.

Rebecca-Ann screams, and Apollo tries to hold me back as I attempt to go back for more. "Stop it, Ash!" he says, but I can't stop. I want to kill him. I want to tackle him to the ground and pummel his face until it bleeds, until he can't open his stupid mouth, until all the pain in my life is concentrated in my hand and nowhere else.

"Enough!" Our fight is broken up by a voice I know well. "My office. Now," says Principal Walker.

"What were you thinking?" Apollo whispers to me furiously. We're sitting outside Principal Walker's office while he calls our parents, and probably my grandparents, to come to the school. Jackson and Rebecca-Ann are sitting all the way on the other side of the receptionist's area; Jackson, I note, sporting a pretty nice shiner.

"What was I thinking? What were *you* thinking? You should've let me go at him. I can't believe you of all people were the one holding me back."

Where does Apollo come off lecturing me about punching someone? The first thing he did when he got to this school was get into a fight with Jackson and Ricky.

"You don't need to defend me," he says coolly. "I don't need a straight savior. What are my parents going to think?"

"What? I'm not—that's not—" I'm stuttering, unable to get out what I want to say because he's got it all wrong.

Principal Walker comes out of his office, face grim. He leads all of us to a large conference room as we wait for our parents to come. Rebecca-Ann's arrive first and immediately proceed to wrap their daughter in a huge hug. I have to resist the urge to roll my eyes. It's not like I punched *her*.

Apollo's arrive next. They do not wrap their son in a hug, huge or otherwise. In fact, they barely spare him a glance, faces set like stone as they walk right past and pull Principal Walker to the side of the room for a private conversation. I don't know what would be worse—having parents clearly angry at me, or ones who ignore me altogether. Apollo stares down at the table in front of him, avoiding my attempts at eye contact. I can't hear what his parents are saying, but the harsh tone of their voices makes their displeasure clear.

Jackson's mom walks in at the same time as my grandparents, and Principal Walker looks visibly relieved to be spared the direct assault from Apollo's parents.

"Great," he says, once everyone has crowded in. "Let's begin."

It doesn't take long for the adults in the room to devolve into children. It's almost impressive, really. Rebecca-Ann's parents accuse Apollo and me of being menaces to society (despite the fact that Apollo was the one trying to stop me from punching Jackson). Jackson's mom fawns over her son, in a way that might make one believe he was on the brink of death. Principal Walker begins talking about an extended suspension for both Apollo and me, when Grandpa interrupts.

"What did Jackson say to you?" he asks finally. It's surprising it's taken this long to get to that question, but there hasn't really been much of an opportunity to speak.

"He called Apollo and me fags."

The room goes quiet. Grandpa turns back to Principal

Walker and raises an eyebrow. "Is this the kind of institution you're running here? I was promised there was a strict anti-bullying policy at this school when I enrolled my granddaughter and donated, *very generously*, I might add. Why are we not discussing suspension for this young man here?"

Principal Walker sputters, and it's just the opportunity Apollo's parents have been waiting for.

"Frankly, I'm not sure suspension is enough!" Apollo's father interjects. "We're talking about slander. If expulsion isn't on the table, I'm of half a mind to get our lawyers involved."

The room erupts anew at this sudden escalation, and I'm worried it's the adults who are about to get physical as Apollo's mother adds her voice to the mix.

"Our son is certainly not gay," she says, voice high, as though the person she's trying to convince is herself.

"I am, though." That voice comes in quiet, so quiet it's almost not overheard among the others, but I hear it. He looks to me and I nod, heart breaking for him as I try to imbue him with the courage I've never had. "I am gay," he says louder this time.

His parents go silent. "Son, be quiet," his father says, but Apollo shakes his head.

"I am gay," he repeats. "It's not something that's going to go away. It's not something you can get rid of or change. I am gay."

My heart races. No one seems to know what to do next. Principal Walker rubs his temple as though a massive migraine is coming on.

"Suspension," he says finally. "All four of you. Until the start of Christmas break. That's only two days. And that will be the end of this."

"Uncle—"

"No. Enough."

Uncle? Jackson is Principal Walker's nephew? That explains so much.

Grandpa rests a hand on my shoulder. "Let's go," he says. I stand. I want to say something to Apollo, want to tell him how proud of him I am, but he's focused on his parents, and now is not the time, so reluctantly I follow my grandparents out of the room, then out of the school, where we run straight into my mother.

"Mom?" I say, confused. She's still in her scrubs, clearly having come straight from work.

My grandfather nods curtly in her direction.

"What's going on?" she asks. "Why are you leaving the school? I just arrived."

"Everything's been taken care of, dear," my grandmother says. "No need to trouble yourself."

"Trouble myself?" Mom says, clearly furious. "This is my child. You should have called me." She turns her attention to me. "The secretary said you *punched* someone? Is that true?"

Grandpa's hand tightens on my shoulder. Grandma smiles at me, then turns to my mother. "One of her classmates made some utterly inappropriate accusations calling into question her sexual preferences. She was merely defending herself." Grandma tsks. "Of course it seems that boy wasn't entirely wrong about that neighbor of yours. But I'm sure your daughter will be keeping her distance from him from now on."

At pretty much that exact moment, Apollo walks by, followed by his parents. I try to make eye contact, but he avoids looking at me. I wish more than anything I could melt into the pavement.

"My daughter is perfectly capable of defending herself with her words, not her fists," Mom says. "And I'll ask you to not to encourage her otherwise. I take it you've been suspended?"

"Until the winter holidays," my grandpa says. Perhaps realizing they've overstepped, or just eager not to have his business aired in the school parking lot, my grandpa speaks before my grandma can say anything else. "I thought I'd take her to work with me the next few days. A bit of hard work seems appropriate, and it will be a good chance to introduce her to the business."

I know how my mother feels about *the business*, but I also know she can't afford to take work off to stay home with me, and it's clear she has no intention of letting me spend the next few days enjoying an early vacation.

She nods. "Work her hard." She doesn't look at me before turning away and heading back toward her car.

We drop my grandmother off and then drive to my house in silence, and when we get there, Grandpa tells me to go inside and change. Professional clothes. He doesn't say anything about the fact that I punched a kid in the face. Maybe he's afraid if he does, I'll make a confession like Apollo. Fat chance of that happening.

I spend the rest of the day at Grandpa's office assisting his rather chatty secretary, Marisa, with making photocopies and answering the phone. I think about Apollo, wonder what happened to him after I left. I hope he's okay.

Five o'clock takes its sweet time to roll around, and it's only after everyone else has left for the day that I feel able to gently prod Grandpa into driving me home.

"I don't condone violence," he says along the way.

"I'm sorry."

I'm not particularly sorry, except that I was unable to get in a few more punches before I was done. I don't say that part out loud.

"I'll be having a chat with Principal Walker about how they can do better. We pulled you out of one school for bullying. I was promised that wouldn't happen here."

Grandpa glances at me from the corner of his eye, either inviting me to say more or praying I won't.

I don't.

He pulls into the driveway and comes to a stop. "I'll pick you up at seven thirty sharp," he says. I nod, climb out of the car, and watch him drive away.

As soon as he's gone, I run over to Apollo's house. His car is in the driveway, but I need to see him for myself, to know he's okay. I knock on the door, then ring once for good measure.

His mother answers, frowning when she sees who it is.

"Is Apollo here?" I ask before she can say anything.

"No, he's not here."

But his car's here, I want to say but don't. "Will he be back soon?" I try to keep the desperation from my voice. They can't have sent him back to that place. Not this quickly.

She purses her lips. "I doubt that very much. Now, I'm sorry, but you interrupted my dinner with my husband, and I would like to return to it."

She shuts the door, leaving me alone on their porch in the cold.

THIRTY-SEVEN

I text Apollo but get no response. Every morning, evening, and pretty much any other time I'm in my room while I'm out of school, I look out my window to see if I can spot the light in his bedroom, but it remains dark. I'm terrified for him, terrified his parents have shipped him back to the conversion camp where they had him this summer.

The only solace in my anxiety is my artwork. I put everything I have into my graphic novel. I draw until my hand cramps, and then I crack my knuckles, squeeze a stress ball a couple of times, and get back to work.

I don't make the decision to apply to SAIC until the moment I step up to the counter at the post office on January 2, application envelope in my hand. Despite writing the required essays, despite drawing an entire graphic novel and photocopying it at the local library page by page by page and packaging it all together in one large envelope, despite being here this morning in the freezing cold and standing in line behind all the other people sending off their Christmas thank-yous and belated holiday gifts, despite all that, I almost turn back around and head home.

I've already been accepted into UNH. With my grandparents' promise, I can have a guaranteed four-year education, a law school degree, and a solid career with a well-paying salary for the rest of my life. And my grandparents will die eventually, and maybe then I can come out. Or I could take my four years of college and then do it, eschew the law degree and the comfortable salary. But there's no path forward I can see where I drop all that to move to Chicago and pursue an art degree no one is going to pay for. Mom certainly doesn't have that kind of money, and it's not just about the cost of the school itself. There are flights to think about, books and supplies to purchase, new clothes if I decided to come out and live as myself, and what would be the point of going all the way to Chicago if not to do that?

So it's a pipe dream and almost certainly a waste of the $50 application fee and the additional ten in shipping I took from my savings box under my bed, and yet when I step up to the counter at the post office, I find I can't do anything other than send it in. And when I head back out, receipt with tracking number in hand, I fold it carefully and put it into my pocket.

On the first Monday of the new year, I realize I have no ride to school. Fortunately, Mom doesn't have to work until the evening, so she's able to drive me, but I realize that's not always going to be the case. I wonder how Moira's doing; whether she had a good Christmas, whether she and Kaycee are still together. I thought about texting her a dozen times, even typed out a message on a handful of occasions, but each time I deleted it. I'm glad there's no way for Mom to see how many texts I send and receive in a given month. Zero is a pretty pathetic number.

As soon as I get inside the school, I spot Apollo. I rush over, pull him into a hug before thinking about what I'm doing, and when I realize, I pull away, embarrassed. I wonder if he's still angry at me, but he gives me a small smile and I know we're okay.

"I was so worried about you!" I say. "I went to your house, but your parents said—"

"They kicked me out." He rubs the back of his head as if he's self-conscious saying it.

"So where are you—"

"With my sister. Sorry I couldn't give you a ride to school. I wanted to text, but my parents took my phone back, and I haven't had a chance to get a new one yet."

I don't know what to say.

"They, uh, they wanted me to go to therapy. Someone they've heard of who deals with, you know, people like me, I guess, but I told them I wouldn't do it. I'm done being ashamed of who I am. And I'm eighteen now, as of Christmas officially, so they couldn't make me. And they'd already paid for my last semester here, and it's nonrefundable, so"—he shrugs—"here I am."

"God, Apollo, I'm so sorry. If I hadn't said—if I hadn't punched—"

He shakes his head. "It's not your fault. It was always building to this. I'm okay. Or, I will be."

I want to cry for him. I want to tell him I love him. Instead I just nod. He starts to walk away. "Do you regret it?"

Apollo turns back. He doesn't answer right away, and then finally he shakes his head. "No," he says. "I don't regret it. It's like"—he pauses, as if trying to find the words—"it's like I spent all year letting people hate me for something that wasn't true. And if they hate me now, at least they hate me for who I really am. And I can't do anything about those people, but now I'm able to see the people who still love me and know they love the real me. I spent a long time convinced there'd be no one left once I came out, but I'm starting to realize that isn't true. It's made me realize it's okay to move forward with my life. And my parents have already done the worst they can do, so I no longer have to fear it." He shrugs. "I don't know if that makes any sense."

I nod. "It does," I say. "Thank you."

A month passes, then two and three. Winter turns to spring, then back to winter again briefly, before it begins to release us from its clutches. Life moves on without the circus. Sometimes I think I see it out of the corner of my eye when I nod off in class. I see Fizz on the street, but when he turns around, I realize it's not him. I hang out with Apollo at school, but it's harder when we aren't there, now that he's living in a different town with his sister. Moira's still not speaking to me. I think about getting a new job, something to fill the lonely evening hours, but it feels like accepting that Mr. Roberts will never wake up. Soon I'll hear back from SAIC. I don't put much stock in an acceptance, but the daydream gives me hope, and I could use a bit of that at the moment.

My grandparents pick me up early from school one spring Friday so I can help them set up for their annual welcome for regional admits to UNH, which this year includes me. Somehow, even though Mom provided my grandparents with her work schedule weeks in advance, the entire thing is scheduled during one of her shifts. Knowing that nothing good ever comes from the mixed presence of my mom and grandparents, I choose to bite my tongue and let it go.

They've already brought in professionals to clean the house

and make it spotless, but my grandma doesn't trust anyone else to rearrange the furniture or put together flower arrangements or cook all the food, so it's a long and busy day. Fortunately she determines I have a particular talent for flower arrangement and leaves me to it. It's nice to be doing something artistic, and it keeps my mind off everything else in my life.

The waitstaff show up at five thirty and are immediately whisked away to the kitchen, while the first guests show up at six thirty. I'm put on door-welcoming duty.

By seven the house is full and I'm sent to mingle with my future classmates. A waiter, whose name tag says James, comes over and offers me a drink. I accept, and as he's pouring it, he says, "You look like you needed a break."

I take it gratefully. "I definitely did, thank you."

I look at James. He's young, maybe a college student himself, with naturally dark hair and blond tips. His fingernails are painted black to match the shirt and pants he's wearing, and I think in another life he's someone I could be friends with, maybe even more.

Not this life.

I'm about to ask James whether he's in college, when the room goes momentarily silent. I turn, thinking maybe my grandparents are going to make a toast, when I see instead what's happened.

Kaycee's here. And Moira, whose hand she's holding. In her other hand she holds up an invitation. I guess at least one of them must've been accepted to UNH.

My throat goes dry. "Excuse me," I say to James.

I walk over to them. "Hi," I say. The rest of the room, many of whom likely recognize Kaycee either from going to school with her or from the newspaper articles, eventually return to their conversations.

"Can I talk to you?" I ask. "Both of you. Please."

I'm worried they're going to reject me right here and now, in front of everyone, and I know I'd deserve it, but they don't, and I breathe a sigh of relief. I lead them through the house, through the crowds of people and into the kitchen, then out to the enclosed porch out back.

Moira crosses her arms across her chest. "What did you want to say?"

What do I want to say? I've thought about this exhaustively since Apollo got kicked out and since our conversation afterward. I've already lost most of my friends. It's no longer something I can fear.

I turn to Kaycee first. "I'm transgender," I say. I can see Kaycee's face shift through a range of emotions as she processes what I've said, from confusion and then, after a nod of confirmation from Moira, to anger.

"You knew the whole time?" she asks. "The whole time we were friends?"

I nod.

"But that—but that means . . ."

"Yeah," I say.

"You didn't stand up for me!" she yells, crying now. We're both crying. "You let me go into that bathroom and you let them say those terrible things to me and you said nothing. How could you say nothing?"

"Because I was terrified!"

There's silence.

"I was terrified," I say again. "I'm not like you, Kaycee. I'm not brave. When they said those things, I froze up. I'm sorry. I'm so sorry."

"You think I'm not scared?" She laughs bitterly. "I'm scared *all the time*."

"Then how do you do it?" I ask. I want so desperately to know the answer so I can do it too.

"Because the alternative would kill me," she says softly.

I turn to Moira. "I'm so sorry," I say, voice breaking as I try to hold back the tears that threaten to spill out. "I lied about knowing Kaycee because I was ashamed. Not of being her friend, but of myself. I should've stood up for her in the bathroom that day. I should've been a better friend—to both of you. I let myself think that I was the only one struggling and lost the two people I cared about the most. I miss you. I miss both of you."

Just then the door from the kitchen opens and James pokes his head in. "Your grandparents are looking for you. I think they're going to speak."

I take one last look at Moira and Kaycee, and then I head inside.

"Oh, good," Grandpa says when he spots me. "Your grandma and I wanted to say a few words but weren't sure where you'd wandered off to."

I've dreaded this part of the evening all night. Being paraded in front of everyone and put on display. I'd rather pretend to be another one of the admits, sink into the background and clap politely, and then go back to chowing down on food.

Grandpa steers me to the front of the living room, where Grandma stands waiting. When she sees us, she clinks her fork against her glass until the room quiets down.

"Welcome!" she says. "It is so good to have you all here with us tonight. My husband and I are honored to serve as regional chairs of the UNH alumni organization. This is our tenth year hosting this event welcoming all the recent admits, and for us, it's a particularly special year. Our granddaughter is here with us tonight, and she'll be joining the upcoming freshman class at UNH."

There's some whooping and cheering, and I'm feeling more than a little mortified.

I notice Kaycee and Moira standing out back. I avoid their gaze.

"We've put together a little something, if you'll indulge us a bit." My grandma steps aside, and my grandpa dims the lights. There's a projector set up behind us, and I suddenly realize what's about to happen, but it starts before I can do anything about it.

A slideshow set to "I Hope You Dance" begins playing, as pictures of me flash up on the screen in front of some sixty or more folks. Each picture is like a stab in the heart. Me at my first Communion in a white gown looking like a miniature bride. I hated that dress. I kicked and screamed, and Grandma spanked me just to get it on. But you can't see that in the picture. All you see is the forced smile. I look at the crowd, see the parents dabbing their eyes as they think of their own children, and suddenly it feels incredibly hot.

The pictures continue. The pink tutu from that dance class I was forced to stay in for a year because I had asked to take

301

lessons. I'd seen a boy doing ballet one day as I was walking past a dance studio, and I wanted to be him. But I didn't get to be like him. I had to be like *them*. All the girls in the class. And when I'd come home crying and saying I wanted to quit, I was told I needed to suck it up because that class had cost a lot of money.

I look out into the crowd and see Kaycee, and something in me snaps and I can't do it anymore. I can't be here, looking at the worst memories of my lifetime and pretending they were anything other than traumatizing.

I push through the crowd until I'm outside, the cool air bringing me back to myself.

My grandpa finds me less than a minute later.

"Are you okay?" he asks, and I can tell he thinks I'm the regular kind of sick, not the publicly-confronted-with-dysphoria-inducing-photos kind of sick. And I know it would be so easy to confirm that. To apologize and tell him I over-heated in the crowd and will be fine after a glass of water, but I think of Kaycee and how good it felt to be honest with her. And how sick I am of lying.

"Those pictures," I say, voice cracking, "they aren't—that's not who I am. That little girl? I *hated* her. I've always hated her. She's not me because I'm a boy, Grandpa. I'm a boy. I don't want to go to UNH, and I don't want to be a lawyer. I want to be an artist. And I'm sorry I never told you any of this before, but I can't keep pretending to be someone I'm not." I suddenly feel light-headed, like I might float into the air and blow away in the wind, now that I've released the weight I've carried for so long.

Grandpa doesn't say anything for a moment, and then

suddenly he slaps me across the face, hard. The sting and the shock bring tears to my eyes, and I take a step backward.

"You ungrateful child," he says. "After everything your grandma and I have done for you, and you embarrass us like this? Saying nonsense like you're a boy? Running out in front of all our guests? If your father was still here—"

"Well, he's not!" I shout, and I don't care that inside there are dozens of people who can probably hear me. "He's dead, and I'm all you have left, so you can go ahead and disown me if you want, but you can't change who I am!"

Grandpa clenches then unclenches his fist, lips pursed tight.

"You have two minutes to get back inside that house and apologize to your grandmother," he says. "And never say a word of that nonsense again, do you hear me?" He pulls open the screen door with excessive force. "Two minutes."

The door rattles shut, and my legs feel like jelly. I grip the railing for support as the world dims around me.

And then—

Arms wrap around me, propping me up, holding me tight.

"I've got you," Moira says. "We've got you."

THIRTY-EIGHT

Kaycee, fearful but dauntless, retrieves my coat and bag from inside. Moira wraps it around me, helps me to her truck, pulls out the driveway and down the street, far enough that I can't see my grandparents' house. But not far enough that I can't feel it. There is no distance far enough away for that.

We sit in silence for some time. It could be minutes or hours. My body feels numb. It also feels . . . lighter. I burst into laughter, which turns into a flood of tears. I move through all five stages of grief and back again, and my friends sit and rub my back, hold my hand, until finally Moira speaks.

"We need to get you drunk."

Moira drives us to her older brother's apartment. He's a sophomore at the community college two towns away and, for a small bribe, is convinced to provide us with alcohol and use of the apartment. It smells like boy; like dirty socks and stale laundry, but a few drinks in, that fades away. I feel . . . buzzy.

Kaycee sits on the couch, feet tucked beneath her. Moira rests her head on Kaycee's leg as Kaycee runs her fingers through Moira's hair. I hold out my empty glass, and she refills it.

I take a sip of the wine. "This is gross," I say, then take another sip. "It tastes like vomit. *Vomit wine!*" I giggle, which turns into hiccups.

Kaycee jumps to her feet, her knee knocking into Moira's

head. "I know how to stop that!" she says while Moira rubs her head and sits back up. "You gotta do this, look."

She holds her wineglass up to her chest, then bends over and puts her lips on the far side of it and starts tipping the glass forward. She gets a few sips in before she starts coughing, spraying wine everywhere.

I laugh so hard I start to cry. Moira grabs a handful of tissues and starts dabbing the wine from the rug. "Hey!" I say when I stop laughing. My hiccups are gone. "It worked!"

I take another sip of wine. It's so giggly. I'm bubbly.

Hehehehe

"I didn't do that right," Kaycee says. "Lemme try again."

Moira takes her hand, the only sober one of us. "Sit down," she says. "Jesus, I wish I didn't have to drive so I could stop babysitting your drunk asses."

"Asses, *hehehehe*."

Kaycee snorts. I giggle. Moira sighs.

"I've missed you guys," I say. Moira's expression softens.

"Missed you too, bestie."

This is good. This is fun. This wine is gross.

I take another sip.

"Hey," Kaycee says. "Do you still draw?"

I put down my wine and reach for my backpack. I pull out my graphic novel, still in my bag from photocopying it.

"I'll hold it, babe," Moira says, taking it from me.

"*Flyboy*," Kaycee says, reading the title.

I think of Seb and Apollo. I smile. Drunk is good. Drunk doesn't hurt.

"Asher," Moira says as they flip through the book. "This is really good. Like *really, really good*."

"Where did you get the idea for this?" Kaycee asks.

That's a funny question. "I had a dream," I say, "'cept it wasn't a dream. Not really. And first I was a clown, except I wasn't supposed to be a clown cuz I *sucked*. I was very unfunny. And so I told René that, and I said, 'René, I can't be a clown, I need to fly,' and he said, 'Okay.' Well, first he said no, but then he said, 'Okay', and so I flew. Except my flying partner was a real dick. And his name is Apollo, which is kind of a funny name." I snort and take a large swig of vomit wine. "And *then* he showed up in real life! Just like that! And then we kind of became friends, and we kissed and he liked me, except he didn't actually know it was *me* me because he thinks I'm a girl, 'cept I'm not. But I messed everything up anyways when I stole the book so I wouldn't have to leave, ever. But then I broke everything and now here I am."

Moira and Kaycee stare blankly.

"Boy, you are wasted," Moira says.

I nod. I go to take another sip, but my glass is empty. I frown, hold out my glass. "More, please."

Shit.

I wake up feeling like absolute death. My head is pounding, and my mouth feels like I spent the night sucking on cotton balls. Something tickles my head, and I reach up and grab a dirty sock. Gross.

Moira and Kaycee lie sprawled out across the pullout couch. At some point in the evening, Moira decided she was sick of not drinking and we were too drunk to deliver back home anyway, so we should just sleep over. Her brother only took another twenty dollars' worth of convincing to give up the apartment for the rest of the night.

I drag myself to my feet and go off in search of water. And some ibuprofen.

Slowly the rest of the evening comes back to me. Coming out to Kaycee. Apologizing to her and Moira. Coming out to my grandfather. Getting slapped. Deciding not to go back inside.

I find some pills, only recently expired, behind the bathroom mirror and wash them down with a handful of water.

I wonder if my grandparents called my mother. Probably not. I pull out my phone from my pocket. No missed messages.

There's some noise from the other room. In the kitchen, Kaycee's started making a pot of coffee. Moira's still asleep on the couch.

I take a seat at the table. She sits down across from me.

"How are you feeling?" she asks, kind enough to speak softly, though I don't know if it's for me, for her, or so as not to wake Moira. Regardless, I'm grateful.

"I feel like my head was driven over by a bus."

"Sounds about right."

Behind us the coffeemaker drips. I rest my head in my hands as I try to will the medicine to do something. The coffee finishes a few minutes later, and Kaycee pours us each a mug. She gives the milk a sniff and makes a face before dumping it down the drain. I don't wait to see if she finds any sugar before taking a sip.

Finding no sugar, Kaycee gives up and sits back down. She glances back toward the living room. "She could be out for a while."

I chuckle. Moira's not an early riser. I take another sip of coffee. I'm not sure if it's the caffeine or the medicine, but my head is beginning to feel slightly better. "I'm happy for you,"

I say. "I'm happy you found each other. I'd say you better not hurt her, but, well, I'm hardly one to talk."

"She's missed you. She didn't want to talk about it, but I know she has."

"Well, she's pretty stubborn."

Kaycee smiles. "Yeah, she is."

"Why didn't you tell her?" I ask. "About what happened that day? She was already mad at me. You could have made her hate me more."

"She never hated you. I don't think she could ever hate you. And I didn't want her to. But that's not why I didn't tell her."

"So why didn't you tell her?"

"I didn't want her to hate me."

I frown. I'm not following. "Why would she hate *you*?"

"For what I did to your eye?"

I reach up instinctually, feel the small scar. All that remains of the four stitches I had to get.

"I can't believe you don't hate me!" she continues. "I was so terrified. All I could think about was the narrative they tell about us. About the *scary trans person in the bathroom* and how I was the reason you needed stitches. I thought she'd hate me, and I was ashamed."

"Wait, Kaycee, stop," I say. She looks shaken. I grab her arm. "Stop. That's not what happened. Is that what you remember?"

"I don't know," she says. "It all happened so fast. I went into the bathroom and you came in after me and those two girls were there and then they started saying I didn't belong and that I wasn't really a girl, and when they asked you how you felt about a boy using their bathroom, you didn't say anything.

You just stood there. And as I was leaving, I shoved you into the sink. It's my fault you had to transfer schools."

"That's not what happened," I say again, coming to a new understanding of what Kaycee must have been putting herself through since then. "You didn't push me. You didn't even touch me. Almost as soon as you started to leave, I tried to run after you, and I slipped on some water and hit my eye on the sink. It was an accident. You didn't do this to me."

Kaycee sniffles, wipes her eyes with her sleeve. "You aren't just saying that to make me feel better?"

I shake my head. "No, trust me. I remember every bit of it quite clearly."

She closes her eyes, takes a deep breath to steady herself. "I thought—"

I take her hand. "You didn't do anything wrong. I'm sorry I wasn't a better friend."

"No, I'm sorry," she says. "I should've known you weren't comfortable with the plan. I never stopped to think that I'd been wrong about your identity. If I'd known—"

"How could you have? I never told you."

We sit in silence for a moment, each seeing the other a bit differently. "I'm glad we're talking again," Kaycee says.

I smile. "Me too. I missed you."

There's a loud snore from the other room, and then a groggy voice says, "Do I smell coffee?"

I let go of Kaycee's hand. We both laugh.

"Coming, babe," she says.

I watch her as she pours Moira a mug, as she takes it into the other room. I'm not okay. But I think I will be.

THIRTY-NINE

Once we've all sufficiently sobered up, Moira and Kaycee drive me home. Mom's car is in the driveway, and I take a deep breath.

"Do you want us to hang out here for a little bit," Moira asks. "Just in case?"

She doesn't need to specify in case of what.

I shake my head. Whatever happens when I walk through those doors, I know my mom isn't my grandfather. Besides, I don't even know that he would have called her. Almost all their communication goes through me.

As I watch my friends pull out of the driveway, I check my phone one last time. No missed messages from my grandparents or my mother. Here goes nothing.

I don't know what I expect to find when I walk inside, but Mom sitting at the table with a bouquet of flowers, some balloons, and a cake is definitely not it.

"Surprise!" Mom exclaims as I stand frozen in place, unsure what could possibly be going on. Did Grandpa call her?

"What—"

I don't get a chance to finish before Mom cuts me off. "Okay, okay, I know I shouldn't have opened it, but it came in the mail yesterday, and I was pretty sure that a big envelope was good news, and I wanted to surprise you, so I got the cake, and then I saw the balloons and the flowers and thought, well, what the heck, why not get some—"

I'm so confused. "Mom, what—"

"—and then I got home and thought, well, what if it isn't really what I think it is. I mean, I didn't even know you were applying anywhere other than UNH and—"

"Mom!" I finally manage to cut in. "What are you talking about?"

She stops and holds up a large folder with the black box and white-lettered logo of the School of the Art Institute of Chicago on it.

"My daughter, the artist," she says with such pride in her voice that I can't help but feel immense love despite the whiplash of being misgendered at what I'd briefly thought might be a coming-out celebration.

Mom hands me the folder, and I open it with shaking hands. I barely even process my deadname as I read the one-word sentence immediately following it.

Congratulations!

I'm in shock. I did it. I got into one of the best art schools in the country, and it's in *Chicago*.

I could leave here. I could actually leave this place.

"Well, go on!" Mom says. "Read it out loud! I made myself stop after the first sentence, and you don't know how much it's been killing me waiting for you to get home."

I read the rest of the letter out loud, trying to let it sink in. And then I see an envelope behind the acceptance letter.

FINANCIAL AID PACKAGE

I stumble over the last sentence of the letter, but Mom doesn't seem to notice. She's too busy beaming in my general direction. When I finish, I close the folder before she can see the envelope.

"I'm so proud of you!" she says. "Why don't I cut you the

first piece of cake. I got your favorite—double vanilla with strawberry jam."

I smile. "Sounds good," I say. "I just need to use the bathroom first."

Mom doesn't notice as I slip the financial aid letter out of the folder and take it with me. Once I'm in the bathroom, I sit on the toilet and open it. I start with the letter.

> On behalf of the School of the Art Institute of Chicago's Admissions and Financial Aid Committees, I am pleased to award you a Presidential Merit Scholarship in the amount of $25,000.

My breath hitches as I read the rest of the letter, but it's mostly logistical information. With a silent prayer, I turn the page to the cost breakdown and I almost cry.

It's still expensive, like astronomical levels of expensive, but between the merit award, FAFSA, and some additional need-based aid, it's pretty much on par with UNH minus my grandparents' contribution. And even if that were still a guarantee after yesterday, I'm no longer sure that I would accept it.

There's a knock on the bathroom door. "I'm going to eat this entire cake without you if you aren't out soon!"

I laugh. "Coming!" I flush the toilet, take a moment to compose myself in front of the mirror, and walk out.

Once we've filled up on cake, I ask Mom to drive me to the hospital. There's someone else I want to share my news with. She checks me in at the front desk and then walks me to Mr. Roberts's room. "Do you want me to stay?"

I shake my head. "I'll be okay," I say.

"Okay," she says. "Have the nurse's station page me when you're done." She kisses me on the forehead, and then I'm alone.

I take a deep breath and open the door. It's not at all what I imagined. The room is bright and warm—sun shines in through large windows and paintings of flowers decorate the walls. And while I'd pictured Mr. Roberts hooked up to a dozen different machines, there're just a few, monitoring his heart rate and oxygen levels. I watch from the doorway as his chest rises and falls beneath the light blue sheets and think that he could just be sleeping.

"You can go on in," a voice says from behind me, and I realize it's one of the nurses, coming in to check on him. She gestures for me to take a seat beside his bed while she notes some things on a clipboard after checking the monitor beside him.

"I thought he'd have . . ." I gesture to my face, forgetting the name of the machine that helps people breathe.

The nurse clicks her tongue. "Strangest thing really," she says. "Breathing just fine on his own. Like he's sleeping and just doesn't know it's time to wake up."

The nurse leaves a glass of water for me on the bedside table. I take a sip, pretending it's because I'm thirsty and not because I'm stalling, unsure what to say. Mr. Roberts looks thinner, though not by much. His face is scruffy, white and gray hairs interspersed with a few ginger ones, and I wonder if they'll let it keep growing or if someone will shave him.

"Hi, Mr. Roberts," I say eventually. There's no reply, obviously. "It's me, Ash." I take another sip of water. My hand shakes, and I put it down. "Mom said you might be able to hear me. I hope you can. I'm sorry I didn't visit before. I thought it would be too hard, but I realized recently that I do that a lot. Avoid stuff that's hard, I mean. And I've hurt a lot of people because of it. So, I'm sorry."

I pause. He doesn't respond. Obviously.

"I got into art school," I tell him. "Chicago." I sniffle, wipe my nose with my sleeve. "You were right." I chuckle. "You usually were. I can't stay here. I need to live my own life, for me. And I think I'm ready to stop hiding."

I pause, take a deep breath. "My name is Asher," I tell him. "And I'm a boy."

Maybe because he can't respond, or just because I need to get it out, I end up telling Mr. Roberts everything while he lies in front of me. About discovering the circus for the first time, about Apollo being a jerk and then becoming my neighbor and later my dream boyfriend, about Moira and Kaycee and how I messed up and almost lost them both, and how I lost both the circus and Apollo and then my grandparents when I came out as trans at their party.

Being able to finally say everything out loud is cathartic, but also dehydrating. I stop and take a drink of water. "Right, ummm, I also brought you something." I take the sketchbook I've been holding on my lap and place it on the bed beside him. "I found it while I was helping Samantha clean out the shop. I was going to hold on to it until you woke up, but you've been in my dreams lately. Looking for something. I know it's probably stupid and that it's probably just a dream, but I've had some experiences lately that are making me question that, and anyways, yeah."

I start to put the sketchbook on the table when a different nurse than before walks in.

"Don't stop talking because of me," she says as she walks around to the far side of Mr. Roberts's bed. "I'm just taking a quick look at Jean-René, and then I'll be out of your hair."

It takes me a moment to process what she said, and then as soon as she's gone, I jump up from my chair and go to the end of the bed, where Mr. Roberts's medical chart is hanging.

There it is. Jean-René Roberts. Jean, like the Masked Man, and René like, well, René. I look over at the elderly man lying in his bed, and so desperately wish I could ask him if it's simply a coincidence or something more. It has to be something more. I feel the loss of the circus, of Seb and Fizz and Tessa and Apollo so acutely in this moment, it's like I should be the one lying in that bed.

I have so many questions and no way to get them answered. Who is this man I thought I knew?

I let the medical chart fall back against the foot of the bed and return to my seat beside Mr. Roberts. "Who are you?" I whisper. There's no answer, not that I expected there would be. I take Mr. Roberts's hand in mine as though I can will him awake.

It doesn't work. I feel so stupid thinking I could just wish him awake. He's been in a coma for months. He's not just going to magically wake up the second I visit.

Wait. Magic. That's it!

I turn back to the sketchbook sitting on the bedside table, then look at Mr. Roberts. *Please, please let this work*, I think as I pick up the book and place it beneath his hand.

I wait a few seconds, but nothing happens. The breath I was holding rushes out of me. I feel deflated, like one of Gemma's balloons with the air sucked out of it. I sniff, rubbing my nose on my sleeve. Of course it wasn't going to work. Magic died with the circus.

I killed it. I stand up. I've been here long enough. I should go find Mom.

"Wait."

The voice is so faint I'm sure I'm imagining it, but then when I turn back to Mr. Roberts, I see his eyes flutter open. I should get a nurse, get someone, but I'm frozen in place. Too stunned to move. It worked. I could cry. It really worked.

"Water."

I grab the glass of water from the side table. Mr. Roberts tries to hold it, but his hands shake, and I have to hold it for him as he takes small sips.

"Mr. Roberts?"

"Mmm, that's good," he whispers, his voice beginning to regain its strength. He takes a few breaths, then he lifts his eyes to mine and smiles. "Ah," he says, "Asher," and I realize it's the first time he's used my real name. I take a deep breath, trying not to totally lose it, but a few stray tears still escape. Mr. Roberts pats the sketchbook beneath his hand, and I realize he wants me to take it. "Open it," he says, voice still faint from months of disuse.

SKETCHBOOK OF J. R. ROBERTS. PRiVATE! KEEP OUT!

That's where I stopped last time, out of respect for a man who's meant so much to me, but now with his permission I turn the page, and there it is.

The circus. My circus.

Our circus.

It starts with a drawing, a tent beneath a dark night sky, sketched in black and white, but with a few color palettes sampled beneath. Red and blue, red and yellow, blue and purple, and then, circled repeatedly, blue and gold. Hand shaking slightly, I turn the page. On the right side, there's another tent, this time in the colors I'm intimately familiar with. On the left, a list of names. Most are crossed out, though still legible— Cirque de la Nuit, The Night Circus, The Dream Circus, Circus of Dreams, and finally, this one underlined repeatedly, The Midnight Circus.

Each page reveals something new, yet intimately familiar. Detailed sketches of items as small as the ballet slippers worn by one performer, or as large as the Ferris wheel that towers above the rest of the circus, interspersed with notes and half-completed thoughts, such as *trapeze?* and *too many clowns?*

That last one makes me think of Seb, and I can't help but laugh. While most of the pages are done in black and white, some, like the drawing of the circus tent, are in full color. One in particular takes my breath away. It's a multipage, full-color spread of the Masquerade, everything from the lush forest, lights floating amidst the brilliant fall canopy, to sketches of individual masks. Like so many of the other pages, this one is accompanied by a smattering of notes, this time explaining the purpose of Masquerade. Here I see the birth of the idea that set so many of the past months' events in motion; the idea that the circus will be only a temporary refuge, taken as quickly and easily as it was given.

I turn the page and find a folded newspaper clipping tucked inside. I take it out and look at the picture drawn on the page beside it first—a detailed drawing of a young man, and though it's unlabeled, and I've never seen his face without a mask on, I know this young man is Jimmy. The boy young René was unable to hold on to. I unfold the newspaper next. An obituary. *James "Jimmy" Hirschfeld, age seventy-eight.* I skim the rest. He passed away only a few years ago, leaving behind his husband and partner of thirty-seven years. Gently, I refold the obituary and place it back into the sketchbook. I guess that explains why Jimmy didn't return to the circus with everyone else.

"I'm sure you have questions," Mr. Roberts says when I finish looking through the rest of the book. Then, "Water." I hand him the glass, and this time he's able to hold it himself as he drinks.

I have nothing but questions, but I hardly know where to start.

Mr. Roberts starts for me. "I was young," he says, eyes as far away as the past he's recalling. "Fifteen or sixteen. It was a different time then. Not like it is now." He meets my eyes, and I know he's talking about being queer. "It was a fantasy, a dream. Some place I could be myself. Some place we all could be. And then one day it was real." He smiles, clearly reminiscing. "I think perhaps you know what that felt like."

I do.

He continues. "It wasn't long before it became the most important part of my life. Surviving the days to live for the nights." He gives me a pointed look. "I think you also know what that is like."

I do.

"It worked, for a time. Until it didn't. It's why nobody gets to stay forever."

"Nobody except you," I can't help but say.

He nods. "Nobody except me." He sighs. "Perhaps this is for the best. Shutting it down for good. I lived so long in a dream that I forgot that life happens when you're awake."

"No!" I don't mean to shout, particularly not at an old man who's just woken from a coma, but I can't help it. "You were right that the circus shouldn't be forever. But it's still needed. What about Fizz? And Seb? You can't just take it away from them all."

"You know, I'd always intended for Seb to take over the circus someday." He chuckles. "I don't know if that was one of my best or worst ideas."

"You have to bring it back," I beg. "Please."

"I can't." He raises a hand before I can protest. "It's not that I don't want to. But I can't. I don't know how. I didn't know what I was doing the first time, and I certainly don't know how to do it again. I'm sorry."

I have more I want to say, more I want to ask, but it's at this moment that the nurse comes back into the room and, upon seeing that Mr. Roberts has woken up, rushes to his side.

"I'm sorry," she says, "but you'll need to come back later." As she pages for a doctor to come and check Mr. Roberts out, he catches my eye and mouths an apology. Reluctantly, I stand up and head to the nurse's station so I can share the good news with Mom, who is quite literally speechless when I tell her.

"I need to call Samantha!" she says, once she finally finds her words.

We make our way out of the hospital toward the car as Mom calls Mr. Roberts's niece, and I think about what he said about living so long in a dream he forgot that life happens when

319

you're awake. The memory of the Thanksgiving football game comes to mind, and I realize how easily that could have been me. Trapped in this small town, in a body that isn't my own, pretending to be someone I'm not. All because I was too scared to take the next step. If Apollo hadn't left me, and if René hadn't shut down the circus, would I have become like Mr. Roberts? Never living my truth in the daytime world because I had the circus as a crutch?

I think I probably would have. But I also know that I never would've taken that next step without the circus. Never would have stood up to my grandparents or admitted the truth to Kaycee. And I'm just one person. The circus helps so many, and that's why I know that it's still needed.

As we reach the car, Mom finishes her call with Samantha. I spot a flier on our windshield, some local dance recital or something. I fold the flier and stick it into my pocket.

"Ready?" Mom asks.

I nod. I am ready. Because I suddenly know what I need to do to bring the circus back.

FORTY

I stay up late into the night, until the sun rises, and my stomach grumbles with hunger at barely half past five. I break for a quick breakfast and then return to work. My new colored pencils come in handy, as does the pad of paper. A book that could—should—easily take months to fill up fills up in hours as I work.

It doesn't matter how unfeasible my plan is, how impractical, how much of it depends on an understanding of something that is by definition beyond such things. But if Mr. Roberts's art could bring a magical circus to life, perhaps mine can bring it back. I've got nothing more than a prayer and a dream, but I hope it's enough.

I've certainly got to try.

Seven posters. Each featuring a different aspect of the circus. I've got one for the clowns, Seb and Maisie juggling a series of colorful objects; Ivan and Isla and their knife-throwing act; Gino selling popcorn and Gemma making balloon animals; Vikram lying on his stomach, legs folded back over his head next to LaTanya, about to pirouette; one features the tent, a second the Ferris wheel; and finally, the last—two boys flying through the air, high above an adoring audience.

I take a look at the clock when I finish. It's ten o'clock. Church is starting, but I'm not there. It's the first Sunday I haven't been at church in, well, honestly I can't remember how long. My grandparents still haven't called my mom, which means they aren't going to. At least not before they've given me a few weeks to get over what they probably think is some kind of temper tantrum.

I thought about coming out to Mom after we got back from the hospital last night as we sat on the couch watching *Judge Judy* reruns and eating celebratory Chinese takeout. But it wasn't how I wanted to do it, and after my experience with my grandfather, that's important to me. I deserve to come out on my own terms. And just like I've got a plan to bring the circus back, I've got a plan for that too.

I shoot Moira a text and soon after she arrives with a much-needed large coffee, which I practically inhale. I've got the posters spread across the floor of my room. She takes them in slowly.

"I'm confused," Moira says. "Is it some kind of performance art? Something to help you get into art school? Because you know I'm down for that, but I'm also a little confused."

"Well, about that . . ." I reach under my pillow, pull out my acceptance folder from where I've hidden it, and hand it to Moira.

She takes a second to process, skimming the acceptance letter and then the one from the financial aid office, and then—

"OHMYGODASHERHOLYSHITYOUMOTHER-FUCKINGLEGEND!!!" Moira screams as she practically tackles me with a hug.

"Careful of the posters!" I say with a laugh. Moira climbs off me and looks at the posters again, with a renewed sense of confusion.

"Wait," she says. "So, if this isn't for getting into art school, then what is it exactly?"

"Good question," I reply. "Let's just say this. It's something that will ultimately either explain itself or leave you seriously questioning my sanity. You in?"

Moira looks offended. "Umm, have you met me? Please. Where do we start?"

We make multiple copies of each poster, and then we hit storefronts and telephone poles across town with our guerrilla postering campaign.

One Night Only
Witness the Magic
The Midnight Circus
Friday, April 16, doors open at 11 p.m.
McCloud Field

"You'll be there?" I ask Moira as we tack up the last poster.

"I wouldn't miss it," she says. "I still don't fully understand what you expect to happen, inviting the entire town to the empty field behind your house, but I figure worst case is you've trolled the entire town, and you know that's something I can get behind."

I smile, then sink down to the ground in front of Mr. Robert's—René's—now-emptied storefront. I'm exhausted, running on no sleep and too much coffee.

There's just one more thing to do. I send a quick text to a number I grabbed from my mother, and then I stand back up and tape a poster to the door. It's one of the flying-trapeze ones.

I hope this works.

✦✦✦

The next five days are some of the longest of my life. With school being on April break, it's hard to know if people are talking about the posters. But then Mom comes home on Thursday and asks if I've seen them. "It's all anyone is talking about at work," she says. "And it's practically in our backyard! Maybe we could go?"

I grin. "Yeah," I say. "Yeah, that would be fun."

Mom has work until the evening on Friday. In the morning, Moira picks me up, Kaycee in tow.

"Are you ready for this?" Moira asks. "If you do this, you can't really go back."

I look at Kaycee. She smiles reassuringly. "I know," I say. "But it's time."

We pull into the parking lot of the Good 'Do, the hair salon where Moira's older sister, Jessalyn, works.

I'm anxious and excited as we walk inside, and I see Jessalyn getting her station prepared for me.

She gives all of us hugs when she sees us, then sits me down in the chair.

"I'm proud of you," Kaycee says. She holds my hand as Jessalyn cuts my hair, a weight lifted with each chop of the scissors, each buzz of the razor. I've given her a picture I drew showing the haircut I wanted. When she's done, she brushes away the little hairs at the nape of my neck and holds up a mirror to show me the back.

I run a hand through my hair. I can't stop touching it.

I don't cry, not until I turn and face Moira and see her wiping away her own tears.

"Why are you crying?" I say.

"It's you," she says. "This, it's the real you."

I start crying too as I look again in the mirror. She's right. This is me.

For the first time ever in the daylight hours, I look into the mirror, and I recognize the person looking back at me.

FORTY-ONE

The hours tick by. Six, then seven, and there's still nothing.

At eight, I hear the front door open.

"I'm home!" Mom shouts. "I brought pizza."

I take one last look in the mirror, run my hands through the short hairs on the back of my head. Deep breath in, and out.

I can do this.

Mom is sitting at the kitchen table, slice of pepperoni pizza already partially in her mouth when she sees me. She takes a bigger bite than I can tell she intended to and starts frantically waving her hands in front of her mouth as her eyes water and she searches for a napkin.

When she's done chewing, she turns to me and says, "That haircut looks good on you."

I absolutely lose it. I laugh so hard I struggle to breathe. Tears stream down my face, and it's like the absurdity of the moment wipes away not just my carefully planned coming-out conversation, but all the fears I had about it in the first place.

When I regain control, I flop down into a chair, take a slice of pizza, and say simply, "I'm a boy. My name is Asher. And I would appreciate if you used he/him pronouns for me going forward." And then I eat my slice as Mom processes what I've just said.

She says nothing for a moment and then softly, "Asher," not addressing me so much as trying the name out for herself, and even after months of hearing it at the circus, I'm still

326

unprepared for how much it affects me to hear my mother say it.

Her expression suddenly changes, as though realizing something, and with a look of horror she says, "That day in the bathroom at Wilbur. Was that because you were . . ." She trails off, and I realize what she's thinking and shake my head vehemently.

"No," I say. I no longer have a reason to hold back the truth of that day, so I tell her about Kaycee, about our friendship, about being asked to accompany her into the girls' room for the first time and being terrified because I didn't want anyone to find out the truth about me. "But I really did slip on water," I say. "That part wasn't a lie."

Mom exhales deeply. "When I got that phone call . . ." she says, voice going quiet for just a moment before she continues. "When I got the phone call from the hospital that there had been an accident, that you needed stitches, all I could think of was your father." Her voice cracks. "You've always been different. Always marched to the beat of your own drum. You were a sensitive kid, always so aware of everything and everyone around you. I knew living here was never going to be easy for you, but after your father died, I didn't have any other choice. I always hoped you'd be comfortable enough to share things with me, but I also know I haven't been around for you the way I wanted to." She pauses, cracks a lopsided smile. "I thought you were a lesbian. I never asked because I didn't want you to feel pressured to come out before you were ready, but when I got that phone call from the hospital, all I could think about was losing your father and how I couldn't lose you too. When your teacher told me what she saw—two girls running out of

327

the bathroom, and you stumbling behind, blood dripping down your face, I thought it was because you were gay. I thought that if I sent you to Catholic school, if you dressed the same as all the other girls, if you had Moira there to look after you, that it would be better. Safer." She sniffles, and I reach across the table, take her hand in mine. "You should've told me."

"I thought you might not love me anymore." It's the first time I've voiced that fear out loud. The fear at the heart of everything. The fear that came true when I came out to Grandpa.

"Listen to me," Mom says suddenly, fiercely. "There is nothing, *nothing*, you could do that would make me stop loving you. You're my child. You are my *son*, and I love you exactly the way you are."

I break down. Mom stands up, brings over a box of tissues. I blow my nose. It's loud.

"You know," Mom says, "you never did blow your nose like a girl."

I stop crying, stare at her for a second, and then we both burst out laughing.

Afterward, once we've returned to our now-cold pizza, I realize there's something else still bothering me. Something I need Mom to know.

"I came out to Grandpa," I say. "At the UNH party." I pause. "It . . . didn't go well." The memory of his hand against my cheek comes rushing back, and I wonder if it will ever leave me. "I don't think they want to see me anymore."

I'm not sure I've ever seen rage on my mother's face like I see it now. Nor have I ever heard more colorful language from her mouth.

"I should've taken you away from them when I had the chance," Mom says. "I should've never let them back into our lives."

Now I'm just confused. Mom seems to realize what she's said and sighs. "Come to the couch," she says. "I think it's time you hear this."

I follow Mom from the table over to the living room, where she pats the space beside her. I sit down, crossing my legs and tucking myself into the corner of the worn leather couch as I always did when I was a child.

"As you know, I was only seventeen when I got pregnant with you. It was the summer before my senior year of high school. Peter, your father, had just graduated and was on his way to Yale. We'd always talked about staying together, getting married one day, starting a family, but not like this. Not so soon." Mom pauses, as though gathering the courage to continue. I reach out and take her hand. She squeezes it gratefully. "I scheduled an abortion, took the money from my bank account, and made a plan to go to Vermont. I didn't tell anyone, not even Peter."

I had no idea. Mom's never spoken about any of this before.

"So what happened?"

"My parents found out. They got a notification about my withdrawal from the bank. They tore my room apart, found the pregnancy test, and kicked me out the same day. I had nowhere else to go, no one else to call except Peter. His parents took me in. They were so kind—I clung to it. I should've known better. They'd never liked us dating, saw me as a distraction from Peter's potential. But when they heard I was pregnant with Peter's child, all that changed.

"Peter wanted to defer for a year, but I didn't want that for him. It's why I hadn't told him about the pregnancy in the first place. And I wasn't ready to be a mom. I was too young."

"So why didn't you have an abortion?"

"Your grandparents," Mom says. "They were so kind, and for a time everything was so perfect that I didn't want to break the spell. Your grandmother doted on me, told me it had taken them so many years to get pregnant with Peter, that they'd tried to have another, but that it was never in the cards for them.

"My own parents"—Mom winces, squeezes my hand, and I realize this is the most she's ever talked about her own family— "let's just say that month was the most peace I'd ever known. The longer I waited to get an abortion, the more attached to you I became. We'd go to the store and your grandmother would walk us past the baby clothes, point out how cute they were. Or she'd mention how they had the space to turn one of the spare rooms into a nursery.

"The month flew by, and soon it was only a week before Peter was supposed to leave for school, and I knew I had to make a decision. I decided to go through with the abortion, but before I could tell everyone, your grandparents announced that they wanted to adopt you."

My jaw drops.

"I was too taken aback to say anything. Eventually I told her I'd need some time to think about it. I remember exactly what she said next." Mom's grip on my hand increases to semi-bone-crushing levels, and I can only imagine what's coming. "'As you know, Abigail,'" she says, voice even taking on that same lilt as my grandmother's voice, "'abortion is against our faith. I'm sure you don't want to end up without a home again, so please do consider your options carefully.'"

"They threatened to kick you out?" Just when I thought I couldn't possibly despise my grandparents more.

Mom nods, but then her expression becomes fierce. "But I want you to know that's not why I didn't do it. I chose to have you. I chose you. And your father did too. We made the decision together. Your father signed up for classes at the local community college, began applying for a job to support us while I finished high school and worked on the side. No matter what happened, we knew we weren't going to let your grandparents adopt you and raise you as their own. No chance in hell. Your father never even wanted to be a lawyer—that was his parents' dream. He was still figuring out his own.

"We got our own apartment the day he was supposed to leave for Yale. Your grandparents were furious. But he was eighteen, and by that point so was I. There was nothing they could do. We had almost no contact with them the first few years of your life.

"You were only three and a half when the accident happened. It was January, and the streets were icy from freezing rain. Peter was coming home from a night class when he lost control of the car, crashed into a tree. Doctors said he died instantly. Your grandparents stepped in immediately. I didn't have the money for a funeral or a plot, so they paid for that. We were barely getting by as it was. They offered to take us in, but I refused. It was a huge gamble, but it worked. They bought this house, under the condition that they get to play a role in your life. I didn't want to say yes, not after everything they'd done, but I had no choice.

"I knew I didn't want to spend the rest of my life in their debt, so I studied my ass off to get into the nursing program, worked as many jobs as I could handle, and stood my ground with you as much as I could. It's why I never let them put you into Catholic school before this year, even though I knew you'd get a better education there. It was hard watching them take you to Mass every Sunday, even though Peter and I swore we wanted nothing to do with the Church that had caused us both so much pain, but I had no choice. I had to give them something, or we'd have nothing."

Mom finally breaks down. "I'm sorry," she says. "I'm so sorry. I knew what kind of people they were and should've taken you away from them sooner. I should've stepped in."

I squeeze Mom's hand and shake my head. "No," I say. "You can't blame yourself for their actions. You did everything you could, Mom." I'm sniffling now too, and with my free hand I wipe the snot from my nose. I'm so angry at my grandparents. All my grandparents. The ones who abandoned my mom when she needed them most, and the grandparents who've spent the past eighteen years manipulating my mom for their own gain. I look at the woman on the other end of the couch as though I'm seeing her for the first time.

And when she pulls me into a hug and whispers, "I love you, son," I know she's finally seeing me too. The real me.

FORTY-TWO

I nearly forget all about the circus after Mom's confession. We sit on the couch together and watch *Jeopardy!* reruns as we both process the revelations of the evening. It's only when Mom stands up, makes her way to the kitchen, and peers out into the backyard that I remember my coming out to her was not intended to be the night's main event.

"Hmm," she says, glancing toward the clock, which reads 10:00. She yawns. "Are you sure there's supposed to be a circus back there? I still don't see anything, and it's getting late."

"It'll come," I say. I know it will.

It has to.

She climbs back onto the couch, curls up on her side, and closes her eyes. "I'm going to close my eyes for a bit," she says. "Wake me if something happens."

I move to the back door, watching. Waiting.

I stand for ten minutes, then pull over a chair. I must doze off at some point, because when I open my eyes, the clock says 10:58. I rub my eyes, stand up, and look out the window again.

"Mom!" I yell. "Mom, wake up!"

She comes to the back door a minute later and joins me in looking out. "Wow," she says. "That was quick! Almost like magic."

Magic indeed.

Mom decides to have a smoke first, so I go ahead, stopping only to put my shoes on before I run out the back door into the dark night.

This is it. I stand at the end of our backyard, at the edge of the trees that separate our yard from the normally empty McCloud Field and am brought to my knees by the sight of my beloved circus.

It's been four months since I was last here. Four months since I destroyed the place I felt most at home, since I lost some of my closest friends, since Apollo told me he loved me, then walked away. Four months since I ruined the best gift I've ever been given, and now I have one more chance to make things right.

I was worried nobody would show, but everything's as it's always been. Gino scoops popcorn into large bags, his face split into a giant grin. I spot Gemma creating a balloon animal for a little girl, and I'm pretty sure one of the people I see in the crowd is Sister Rosa from Our Lady of Mercy. I want to say hi, to run over and pull Gemma into a hug, but there's someone I need to find first.

I find him on top of the train car. He says nothing when I climb up to sit beside him.

"Seb," I say finally, hypercognizant of the way my voice sounds.

It's higher than it normally is at the circus, which I suppose makes sense since this isn't the dream version of me, but I push past my discomfort, because it's the last thing that matters right now. "Please," I say, voice cracking, "look at me."

He turns his head.

"I'm sorry," I say to him. "I'm so, so, so sorry. And I know words can't make up for what I did, but I'm sorry. And I don't expect you to forgive me ever, but I still needed to apologize. And—" I swallow, "and show you the real me." I gesture to my body. My fat in all the wrong places, high voice, sports-bra-bound body.

"I already know the real you, 'mano," Seb says, and just hearing his voice again makes me want to start crying, which is another thing I hate about this body. It cries too much. "And I already forgave you."

I look up. "What?"

He meets my eyes. "Not at first, I didn't," he says. "Not when you ran away before René told us he was shutting down the circus. I thought you were a coward, and I was *so* angry. But I've had a lot of time to think about it the past few months, and I realized I could never hate you more than you probably hated yourself." He pauses, gazing off into the distance. "Peter passed away. Not long after René shut everything down. I came across his obituary online. He told me something, the last night we were here. He said he was grateful that he got to see me again. See that I was okay. And I wouldn't have gotten that if it wasn't for you." He wipes his eyes and looks up at me. "I missed you, flyboy."

I sniffle and wipe my eyes. "I missed you too."

We make our way to the performers' entrance of the tent. I spot Apollo in the distance, looking out over the crowds of people. "You go ahead," I tell Seb, and then I take a deep breath and walk over to Apollo.

"Hi, Apollo."

He turns. "Hey, Ash—" He stops before I can tell which me he was addressing. I wonder who he's seeing right now. He shakes his head. "I don't understand."

Watching as he tries to take in what he's seeing, watching

335

as his face takes on a look of confusion breaks my heart, but I steady myself. I've had enough of hiding.

"It's me," I say. "Asher. This is the real me. I'm sorry I didn't tell you sooner. I was scared if you knew who I really was, you'd hate me."

Understanding dawns on him. "You're trans," he whispers. I nod. I feel like I can see his mind at work as he connects the dots, as he rethinks every moment we've spent together, both in the day and at night. "So the whole time you knew who I was?"

I nod.

"I'm going to need some time to process this," he says. I dig my nails into my thigh. Don't cry. Don't cry.

"Of course," I say, trying to keep my voice steady. "We should probably get ready anyways. For the show. You will perform, right?"

He nods but doesn't move.

"I'll go on ahead," I say, and then before he can say anything further, I run away.

Marko cries when he sees me. Well, more accurately, he continues crying. He's a complete mess, telling every performer how much he's missed them. I'm able to pass off my tears as a natural reaction to the circus being back, because there's hardly a dry eye in the dressing room. Everyone is hugging and crying and talking over each other, then saying, "No, sorry, you go, you go," and it's like Christmas and New Year's rolled into one.

When I finally sit down, Marko begins working on my stage makeup, and soon I'm back into costume and it's like no time has passed. Everything is the same and somehow completely different. Before I warm up, I take a moment just to look around. There's

Seb, cracking jokes and juggling whatever objects are closest to him. There's LaTanya dancing and Ivan and Isla back together again. And there's Maisie, who I almost don't recognize when she first walks in because she's gotten so much taller. As soon as Seb spots her, he drops everything and pulls her into a huge hug, and I'm not sure the grin on my face can get much larger.

I spot Tessa standing by the performers' entrance watching and go over to say hi. She hugs me, and I'm reminded once again that for such a small woman, she's got some incredible strength in her arms. When we pull away, I spot Apollo over by the costume rack, looking over at us—at me. I flinch, and Tessa turns to see what I'm looking at.

She gestures toward Apollo—for me to go to him.

I shake my head. "He hates me," I say, facing Tessa and trying to enunciate clearly, though I'm pretty sure my facial expression says it all.

She shakes her head then points to Apollo and taps on my chest just above my heart.

Thank you, I sign.

I hope she's right.

The anticipation backstage is through the roof as we hear the fireworks shoot off indicating five minutes until showtime. Seb's bouncing up and down on the balls of his feet while I run through my routine in my head. It's been four months since I've been in the air. Four months since any of us has performed or had a rehearsal, and I know everyone is feeling similarly. A determination to do this right, for the audience and for our-selves. And speaking at least for myself, feeling a little bit of terror as well.

The show begins, and as the first group of performers runs out to the applause of the audience, I wonder how many of them I know. I wonder if any of them will recognize me when I perform. I wonder if my mom will.

Apollo stretches silently beside me. He hasn't said anything else to me since my confession, but I can't think of that now. There will be time later.

We wait in the wings as Vikram performs, and when I hear the final shouts and applause, I look at Apollo and nod.

This is it.

Go time.

The energy in the crowd is electric as Apollo and I run out onto the stage, and I borrow some of that fire to fuel my performance. Everything returns as easily as breathing, and as I scale the ladder and climb up onto the platform, my body takes over.

Oh, flying, how I have missed you!

My hands on the wooden bar, fingers covered in chalk.

A rush of air, a pump of the legs.

Fingers wrapped around Apollo's wrist.

Moments and fragments of moments rush by as I jump and fall and twist and turn, but there's no time to pause and reflect. We are a machine, an automaton dedicated to beauty and wonder.

I fly as I've never flown before, and when it's time for my last trick, I know what I need to do.

Hup!

I JUMP, swing out, then FORCE OUT at the front and back again, legs behind, then STAND and swing forward, higher and faster, then let go and

ROLL

ROLL

ROLL

ROLL

CATCH.

Then spin back to the bar and dismount into the net.

Then, only then, do I let myself laugh, because I did it. We did it.

But I'm not done yet. I climb down from the net. Join Apollo, clasp hands, raise them up and then bow once, twice before an audience who has jumped to their feet. I see Moira and Kaycee, Zoe and Julian and other classmates, and maybe they see me too. Really see me. I spot one other guest as well. She gives me a wave, and I grin. Maybe my plan will work after all.

When we're done taking our bows, Apollo drops my hand. I didn't expect him to keep holding on to it, but even still, it hurts. "Please," I say. "Let me explain. I just need to take care of something first, but then I'll come find you."

He doesn't yes, but he doesn't say no either. I choose to take it as a good sign. "I'll come find you," I say again and then dash off before he can say anything at all.

I don't know who I'll find inside the trailer when I knock on the door, but it's René who is sitting behind the desk when I walk inside. In the week since Mr. Roberts woke up, I've been back to visit a couple of times, and what's become clear to me through those conversations is that while Mr. Roberts is both Jean and René, Jean and René are not Mr. Roberts. At least not as I know him now. They're what happened to Mr. Roberts when his heart was broken by Jimmy leaving the circus. René, the part of Mr. Roberts determined to hide here forever, and Jean, the part determined to break free. Trapped in the past, unable to move on.

Despite the more-festive-than-normal atmosphere at the circus tonight, René sits behind his desk, fingers steepled as he stares ahead blankly.

I had an entire monologue planned, but what comes out of my mouth instead is, "It's not too late, you know."

René looks up, and though this body is young, I can see his true age in his eyes.

"Ahh," he says. "The optimism of youth is a wonderful thing. I'm glad to see things worked out for you. It makes me feel like perhaps I've done something right after all. If the circus is to have one last hurrah, I'm glad this was it."

Seeing him like this, knowing now who René truly is, makes me angry. "I'm not talking about the circus. I'm talking about you."

"Oh, it's much too late for me."

"It's not!"

I don't mean to shout, and it takes René by surprise almost as much as me. I regain control and start again. "It's not too late for you. Don't you see? I couldn't have done any of this without you. And you want this too—I know you do! It's the whole reason any of this started. You need to stop fighting yourself. You're braver than you believe."

I realize I've just stolen that line from Winnie the Pooh, but it seems to do the trick, because René doesn't argue.

"Come on," I say. "There's someone you should see."

Samantha is waiting right where I asked her to, at the base of the Ferris wheel, but René stops well short as soon as he spots her.

"I can't," he says.

"You can," I say. I turn toward the woods. "Jean," I say. "It's your turn." It doesn't take long. I have a feeling he's been lurking the entire night. He comes out of the forest, wearing the plague mask I first encountered him in.

"I think it's time to take the mask off, don't you?"

Jean looks toward me and slowly removes the mask. The man beneath isn't the smooth talking, angry man I've come to know, but an even younger version of the René standing beside me.

The two men, each part of a larger whole, turn and look at Samantha, standing off in the distance enjoying her cotton candy as she stands beneath the Ferris wheel. René then turns and looks back at me, as though seeking strength. I don't know that strength is something you can give, but I nod anyway. I think of Apollo, and Moira, and Kaycee as I do. Sometimes it's knowing that someone will catch you if you fall that gives you the strength to carry on. Sometimes it's the inspiration of others who've come before you.

René turns back and, together with Jean, takes the first step forward. I watch them go, walking closer and closer together until there's a shimmer or a trick of the light and they come back together. No longer Jean and René, but Jean-René, or as I know him best, Mr. Roberts. I watch only long enough to see Samantha pull her uncle into a big hug, before turning away to give them their privacy.

While Mr. Roberts speaks his truth, it's time to speak mine. Whatever happens next, Apollo deserves my honesty, and for the first time I know I'm strong enough to give it.

FORTY-THREE

I find Apollo sitting atop the train car where we first kissed, knees tucked to his chest as he looks out over the midway. The same spot where I apologized to Seb earlier in the night. Where I sat and looked over the circus on my first full night here. This spot holds a lot of memories.

I climb up and take a seat beside him. Not too close. I can feel the heat radiating from his body. All I want is to kiss him, to take his hand in mine and tell him I love him, but I know I can't.

"I suppose you'd like some answers," I say. He doesn't meet my gaze, but he nods, so I start talking.

I talk until my voice is hoarse, and then I keep talking. I tell him about being a kid and hating being a girl, how I cried and threw a fit every time Mom or Grandma tried to put me in a dress. I tell him about trying to join the Boy Scouts, about cutting my own hair off with dull scissors and doing such a poor job of it that Moira had to take me into the bathroom at the rectory and clean up the mess I'd made. I tell him about the first time I learned what being trans was and how I knew that was me. That I was really a boy, not just a girl who wanted to be a boy. I tell him about Jason Reed, the first boy I ever kissed, and how he never came back after learning the truth of who I was.

"And then the circus came," I say. "And I thought, here is this place where I can just be me and nobody will see me any differently. And I thought it was just a dream, until you showed up at school one day. I didn't even like you then, but then that changed too, and by the time it did, it felt like it was too late to say something. And I was scared. What if you didn't want to be with me anymore? What if you didn't want to be my friend? I almost told you so many times. I'm sorry I didn't tell you sooner."

"Asher—" Apollo starts to speak, when we're interrupted by Moira. She reaches the top of the ladder but doesn't climb up next to us.

She's out of breath and looks panicked. "Fire!" she shouts as she points toward the woods.

Toward my house, where smoke now billows out.

We sprint toward my house, my legs threatening to give out with each step. All I can think about is my mom. I haven't seen her yet.

Please, I think, sending up a silent prayer to whoever might be listening. *Please don't let her be inside.* We run past the Ferris wheel, the popcorn stand, the cotton candy machine. Past the face-painting booth and the carnival games, and when we reach the line of trees, I feel the heat on my face.

My house is on fire. Moira pulls out her cell phone and then swears. "Shit, no service." Flames burst through the windows of the first floor, and I'm frozen in place. "I'm going to run to your neighbors' and call 911." She runs off, but we stay.

Mom.

My knees buckle and then I feel arms around my waist holding me up, realize it's Apollo.

"What if she's in there?" I say. "I need to go help her!" I try to pull away but he's holding me back and I'm too weak to protest because I know there's nothing I can do. I can't run through the flames and pull her out.

Then—

"Asher!" I turn, and my heart skips a beat because she's here and she's pulling me into a hug and I'm holding on for dear life.

"Mom! I thought you were inside. I thought—" She pulls away, starts coughing. Sparks fly from the house, and Apollo steers us farther back, but Mom still doesn't stop coughing. She doubles over trying to catch her breath, but she can't. "Mom!" I yell, and I'm hitting her on the back, but it's not helping. I turn to Apollo for assistance, but he looks as helpless as me.

Mom falls to the ground, gasping for breath as I start coughing too. Only Apollo is spared from the fits overtaking Mom and me. The air feels shallow and my lungs burn and with a horrible sinking feeling, I realize what's happening.

This is the Midnight Circus.

A magical *dream* circus.

I've spent this entire evening operating under the assumption I summoned the circus to my town because my real-life friends were in the audience, but then I think about Seb and Fizz and Gemma and everyone else and realize that doesn't make any sense.

I've made a horrible miscalculation. The Midnight Circus isn't really in my town.

This is a dream and we're asleep. All of us—me, Moira, Seb, Apollo, my mom, everyone. Mom and I are asleep in a house that's currently engulfed in flames.

I turn to Apollo and tell him what I've realized.

"I'm going to try to wake myself up," I say. "I need you to wake up and call 911."

Mom is now lying on the ground, unconscious.

Apollo shakes his head, and I can see the panic in his face. "This isn't real. This is just a nightmare. Asher isn't real. This isn't—"

I grab his hands and squeeze them tight, forcing him to meet my eyes.

"Please," I say. "If you ever loved me—ever loved Asher— I need you to trust that this is real. I'm real. And I need your help."

It's getting harder to breathe. I don't know what will happen if I pass out before waking myself up. I don't have time to wait and find out.

"I trust you," I say, and then I close my eyes and my world shifts.

I immediately sit up and inhale before I can stop myself.

Smoke, thick and black and acrid, burns my eyes, my throat, my lungs. I roll out of bed and fall to the floor, coughing and choking.

Don't panic.

So much easier said than done when you're in a house that's literally on fire. But panic means death, and I'm not ready to die. I crawl along the floor where the smoke is least thick, feeling blindly for the doorway, and when I find it, it's open.

My bedroom is upstairs, but Mom's is downstairs in the back of the house. Unless she's fallen asleep on the couch again, in which case she might be in the living room.

I think of her at the circus, falling unconscious, and I know I need to get to her, but when I get into the hallway, I feel the flames shooting up the stairs before I see them.

Shit.

I crawl back into my room and shut the door. I can't stay here, but I can't get down the stairs. I'm going to have to go out the window.

I make my way to the window facing Apollo's house and try to open it from down on the floor, but it's locked and I have to stand to unlock it. It's so hot, I feel like every bit of me is on fire even though the flames themselves haven't reached my room. The floor beneath me burns my bare feet as I pull open the window. When I finally do, I stick my head outside, eagerly sucking in the oxygen-rich air.

I climb out onto the roof, my small sanctuary all that's keeping me from the flames that have now reached my room. I suddenly remember the box under my bed, the thousand dollars painstakingly saved up over years, but I can't go back. Smoke billows out the window, and my back burns from the heat. I don't hear any sirens, have no way of knowing if Apollo actually woke and called 911. If he were still living at his parents', he could have woken up and looked out and seen the fire, but he's not, which means any emergency call would have to be made on faith alone.

There's no time to wait for rescue. I'm going to need to jump.

As I look down from my second-story roof, I try to tell myself it's not any higher than the trapeze platform. Only this time there won't be a net to cushion my fall.

I can do this. No one knows how to fall better than me. I position myself at the edge of the roof, lying on my stomach and lowering my legs down slowly until I'm supporting my weight on my forearms alone. In this position I'm closer to the ground, and closer means a safer fall. My arms aren't as strong as at the circus—they burn under the weight of my body.

I take a deep breath. I need to relax. Just like trapeze.

I let go.

Push away from wall, feet first and together, knees and body relaxed. *Don't tense up.* Then

IMPACT

feet hit the ground, knees bend then extend and stomach tight and

ROLL

too close to the house to roll forward, so I roll back, over my shoulder, protect my head and then

Stop.

I take a moment to breathe, take stock of my body, mentally scan for injuries. I sit up, bruised and battered but alive.

I hear the sirens as I pull myself to my feet and run around to the front of the house just in time to see a train of trucks and lights and people. It takes all my energy just to wave and point as I try to let them know that Mom is still inside. Someone tries to put an oxygen mask over my face, but I push it away.

"My mom!" I manage to gasp. "She's inside."

"Is there anyone else in the house?"

I shake my head. "Please . . . my mom . . ." The woman nods, relays the information to the fire chief, and then I'm sitting in the back of the ambulance, oxygen mask over my face, mylar blanket wrapped around my body. I can still feel it, the heat singing the tiny hairs on my arms, and when I close my eyes I see the flames.

✦ ✦ ✦

Breathe in
and
Breathe out

The paramedics ask me questions, but I can't understand what they're saying. It's like they're underwater and everything is garbled, so I stare blankly and I think I hear the word *shock* and then the questions stop and they leave me be.

And all I want to know is, did they get her? Did they get her out, and will she be okay? But I can't speak, I can't move or do anything but

Breathe in
and
Breathe out

As my world falls apart around me.

Then there's commotion outside, and I see a flurry of movement and I hear

Smoke inhalation
and
Second-degree burns
and
Female, mid-thirties

And I rip off the oxygen mask and try to leave, but the paramedic holds me back.

"There's nothing you can do right now," she says. "They'll take care of her, don't you worry." She helps me put the oxygen mask back on, and I sit helpless and wait.

The sky is clear and the moon barely a sliver in the sky on the night I watch my home burn down to the ground. Later, when they're done investigating, they'll tell us the fire started in the living room. A lit cigarette and an old couch and fire detectors with the batteries removed. They'll say it was pure luck Mom survived at all, that if the 911 call hadn't come in so quickly, she definitely wouldn't have.

But for now, I just sit and watch as the paramedics rush my mom off to the hospital, and the firefighters battle a blaze that was once my home.

"Asher!"

Apollo.

He runs over and pulls me into a hug, undeterred by the paramedic asking him to step back, and I cling on and refuse to let go, and when I pull off my oxygen mask, I give the woman a look that dares her to do anything about it.

His eyes stare into mine and then he's kissing me and his hands are running through my hair and I pull away only because I'm dizzy and I need to breathe. I hold the oxygen mask up to my face and take a few long, deep breaths while Apollo steps back sheepishly, but I take his hand.

Please don't go, I say with a squeeze, and he moves closer so he can sit beside me in the back of the ambulance as I

Breathe in

and

Breathe out.

When it's all done, when the house is reduced to ash, I'm asked if there's someone else they can call, an adult or a relative other than my mother. I think of my grandparents briefly, then tell them there's no other family and give them the number for Moira's house. She arrives with her dad not five minutes later, despite living fifteen minutes away. They're still in their pajamas, and when Moira sees me she pulls me into a hug, crying the entire time, while her dad speaks with the paramedics and the fire chief. I have some minor smoke inhalation and a few cuts and bruises from my fall, but am otherwise medically sound and cleared to spend the night at Moira's house. They say I can be checked out at the hospital tomorrow once I've gotten some sleep.

Moira's dad looks at me, then at Apollo, who still sits beside me holding my hand, and says, "Let's go." He doesn't say anything when Apollo follows me into their car or when Moira takes Apollo's keys and drives his car behind us all the way back to their house.

And he doesn't say anything when Apollo leans into me and whispers, "I love you."

FORTY-FOUR

After the fire, Moira's family buys me a cell phone and adds me to their family plan, since Mom is still in the hospital, and my old phone was lost in the fire. It's a smartphone, and Moira takes great pleasure in her ability to text me constantly. More than once she's sent me a lengthy paragraph of nonsense, or some absurd meme from across the room, just because she can. It almost makes me miss my old flip phone.

My eighteenth birthday falls a little over a week after the fire, and the plan is to visit my mom and then come back and have a small celebration at Moira's with a handful of friends. I have the number of everyone who we've invited to the party already programmed into my phone, which is why I know I shouldn't answer when an unknown caller pops onto the screen, but I do anyway.

"Hello?"

There's no immediate response, and I'm about to hang up, when I hear a voice.

"Hello . . . it's me. It's Grandpa."

The pause where my name would—should—be doesn't go unnoticed.

"What do you want?"

There was a time in my life when even the thought of speaking to Grandpa like this would make me break out in hives, but that time is long past. That version of me died in the fire that took our house and nearly took Mom's life.

"I wasn't sure you'd pick up," he pauses. "I'm glad you did."

"I didn't recognize the number," I say. "If I had, I don't know if I would've."

He doesn't respond to that. Just clears his throat and moves on. "Your grandmother wanted me to call and wish you a happy birthday, and tell you that she's got your room all ready for you. And I spoke to the dean of admissions this morning at UNH. He said you turned down your spot, but given the extenuating circumstances, they're willing to reopen it for you."

I almost laugh. It's like nothing has changed.

"What's my name?" I ask.

A pause. "I'm sorry—what are you—"

"What. Is. My. Name."

I don't even flinch as he says my deadname. "Your grandmother and I know you've been under a lot of stress this year. Perhaps switching schools senior year was a poor decision, and I take some responsibility for that. I should've seen that your outburst at the party was a cry for help and—"

"Grandpa," I say, cutting him off. "Don't call me again." I hang up the phone, not realizing that Moira is standing in the doorway until she comes over and pulls me into a hug.

"Are you okay?" she asks, and I realize that I am.

"Yeah," I say. "Yeah, I'm good."

I visit Mom at the hospital most days after school. It's been a month since the fire. She's recovering but still has a long way to go. As I sit beside her bed, I tell her stories of the circus. I don't know how much she remembers from the night of the fire. She spends a lot of her time asleep, but the nurses tell me she's always in a better mood after I visit. I'm hoping she'll be well enough to come to my graduation at the end of the month. At least one good thing has come out of this—she's vowed to quit smoking.

I also visit Mr. Roberts. He's still in the hospital but getting stronger every day. The nurses haven't stopped talking about how miraculous it was, how they've never seen anything like it before. If only they knew the full extent. It's going to be a tough road to recovery—coming out of a months-long coma in your mid-seventies is pretty much unheard of. But then I see Samantha sitting at his bedside and Mr. Roberts showing her drawings from his sketchbook, and I think that he's already lived through worse.

It was a funny thing, returning to school after the fire, not just because I'd chopped all my hair off. It was also the first time since the circus, the memory of which floated at the edges of most everyone's memory like a weird fever dream half remembered. No one had any explanation for what had happened, or whether anything had happened at all. All the posters advertising the circus had mysteriously vanished across the town by the morning after as completely as the circus itself, which has yet to come for either Apollo or me since the night of the fire.

I've made my peace with it. Mostly. Apollo said he knew when he chose to wake up to call 911 that it would mean the end of the circus for him. "It was just this feeling I had," he said. I had felt the same way. But I like to think it's still out there, still helping others.

The night before graduation, Moira, Apollo, Kaycee, and I take a drive. We end up at the abandoned housing development overlooking town that Apollo and I came to on the day we ditched school back in November. This time, however, there's no snow in the forecast.

We've come prepared this time too. Moira's packed us a picnic blanket and some snacks, and we set up camp on the hill facing the White Mountains. I lie back and stare up at the stars, my best friend and her girlfriend to my right, my boyfriend to my left, and I marvel at how much has changed since the last time we were here.

"Are you ready for tomorrow?" I ask.

"Ready to read the most cliché graduation speech ever, you mean?" Moira asks.

"Okay, smarty-pants. I'm sure your speech will be fine."

"Your speech is great, babe," Kaycee says.

"It was fine until Mrs. Johnson sucked all the life out of it."

The rest of us laugh.

"Your sister's still coming to the party tomorrow, Apollo? And your mom, Asher?"

"Yup," Apollo says. "Wouldn't miss it. And I think one of my cousins might come."

I smile. Though still cut off from his parents and grandparents, it seems like the younger generation has been supportive. I know how important that is for Apollo.

"She's planning on it," I say, in regard to my own mom. "She'll definitely be at graduation, and we'll have to see how she's feeling after."

"I'm sure she'll be glad to get out of the hospital and into the new apartment in a few weeks," Moira says.

"Already trying to kick me out of your room?" I joke.

"Never!"

Kaycee raises an eyebrow, and Moira blushes. "Well, it wouldn't be the *worst* thing to have my room back."

I pretend pout while everyone laughs. Apollo leans into me and whispers into my ear, "I wouldn't mind you finally having your own room again either."

I flush, but he's not wrong. His sister's house is too far away to be convenient, and Moira's house is too crowded for any privacy. It makes me miss the convenience of the circus, though I wouldn't trade being out, and being together in the real world, for anything.

Not anymore.

"I'm envious you all graduate tomorrow. I want mine to be over and done with," Kaycee says, changing the subject.

"I know the feeling," I say. "But at least they're letting me wear pants. Going to play the pity card for all it's worth. I'm sure they'll be glad to get rid of me, though."

"Oh! That reminds me," Moira says, sitting up suddenly. She rifles through her bag and pulls something out. "For you, my good sir," she says, handing the object over. "A souvenir."

I look at what I hold in my hands and start laughing. It's a crucifix, like the ones hung throughout the school, only this has a sign around his neck that reads *Jesus Says Trans Rights*.

"Stole it from the third-floor bathroom. It was really a public service."

"You stole bathroom Jesus?"

Moira looks quite proud of herself. "I didn't want you forgetting about me when you're in Chicago."

"And bathroom Jesus is what's supposed to remind me—"

"I'm sorry," Kaycee interrupts. "But what exactly do you mean by 'bathroom Jesus'?"

Moira, Apollo, and I exchange glances and then burst into laughter.

Tomorrow three of us graduate. In two months, we go our separate ways. Moira and Kaycee are both off to UNH, Kaycee to study to become a teacher, Moira an engineer. Or a fashion designer. Or a film studies major. Knowing Moira, she'll find a way to do all three.

Apollo was accepted to the pre-vet program at the University of Vermont. He got a few scholarships but will have to take out loans for the rest. And I officially accepted my place at SAIC. I'm excited for a fresh start.

As the four of us sit on this hill on the verge of the rest of our lives, I contemplate all the shit we've gone through to make it this far—Apollo moving in with his sister, me living with Moira while my mom works each day to recover from the fire that took everything; Kaycee fighting her school for future generations of trans kids, and both of us fighting just to survive. But we made it. We're here and we're alive and we're ready to take on the fucking world.

And I can't wait.

ACKNOWLEDGMENTS

Flyboy would not be even half the book it is today without the support of GrubStreet's Novel Incubator Program. To Michelle Hoover, our brilliant, generous leader, and my Year 9 classmates: Aube Rey Lescure, John McClure, Sara Shukla, Juliet Faithfull, Nicole Vecchiotti, Cameron Dryden, Joan Nichols, Michael Giddings, and Susan Larkin. From home-baked pastries to late nights closing down the bar, Zoom workshops and backyard reunions, there's no group I'd rather discuss the fates of imaginary people with than all of you.

To the Novel Incubator alumni community who have provided friendship and support these past few years. To Milo Todd—meeting you at the Boston Book Festival changed my life. Thank you for your mentorship, your friendship, and all you do for the queer writing community. To Julie Carrick Dalton, Kelly Ford, Elizabeth Chiles Shelburne, Desmond Hall, and honorary incubee E.B. Bartels for your support and advice on navigating these pre-pub/post-deal years. To Rachel Barenbaum for all the above and more—thank you for welcoming me into your home for Shabbat dinners and for showing so many of us what it means to be a good literary citizen.

To my host parents, Kevin and Diane—thank you for welcoming this Massachusetts kid into your home, your lives, and being the best #hostfam I could possibly hope for. Thank you for all your support, in ways too innumerable to list, but especially for your unwavering belief in my writing dreams and that first crucial introduction to GrubStreet's writing community.

To Katie Bayerl and the members of her fall 2018 YA Novel-in-Progress course: Ellie Moreton, Laura Wareck, Angie Mouradian, Emily Coleman, Alex Rivas, Connor Hager, and Michael Lindquist for all your help workshopping early pages of *Flyboy*.

To Laura Wareck and Ellie Moreton, my Drama Llama Beach Bums, thank you for your continued support and friendship and all the dining room/beach house/Zestfriendz (RIP) writing sessions.

To my agent, Mollie Glick, an absolute powerhouse and the best champion *Flyboy* could have hoped for. From our first phone call, I knew that you truly got Asher and his story. I'm so grateful to have you in my corner. And to my wonderful editor, Alessandra Balzer, for taking a chance not just on *Flyboy*, but on me. Thank you can never cover it.

To everyone else at Balzer + Bray/HarperCollins who has worked on my book: Caitlin Johnson, Alison Donalty, John Sellers, Audrey Diestelkamp, Patty Rosati, Mimi Rankin, Kerry Moynagh, Kathy Faber, and Jen Wygand, as well as anybody I may have missed—the work you do is invaluable. Thank you. Extra-special thanks to Julia Feingold who designed *Flyboy*'s cover, and Colin Verdi who brought that vision to life with his art—I know I might be biased, but I truly think I have one of the most beautiful covers in existence.

To Sonora Reyes—for your beautiful blurb and for helping pave the way for a story like Asher's.

To everyone at Cabot House who helped me call it home for

so many years: to Stephanie and Rakesh Khurana for allowing me to stay on as a house aide after graduation and giving me one of the most precious gifts an author could ask for—time to write my book—as well as for always embodying the spirit of Semper Cor. To Jai Khurana—thank you for begging your parents to hire me after graduation, and for being an early reader on *Flyboy* and my (now-abandoned) middle grade novel. Special thanks as well to Amanda Pepper, Mike Russell, the HUDS staff who kept us nourished, and the custodial and maintenance workers who do the dirty work (literally!) that keeps the house running.

To Therese Walsh—thank you for inviting me into the Writer Unboxed community, and for your support in helping me attend the 2023 UnConference. The community you've cultivated is truly something special.

To Merlin Butler—thank you not just for being an early reader of *Flyboy*, but for my first ever fan art! When I struggled to see the finish line, the pictures you drew of Asher and Apollo made me feel like a real author.

To Kris King for your support and the work you do for our trans+ community.

To the Levi Heywood Memorial Library and all its librarians—thank you for being my childhood literary home.

To my fellow 2024 debut authors, but especially Aube Rey Lescure, Sara Shukla, and Sydney Shields—thank you for being on this ride with me.

To my Jewish community, especially my friends and Rabbi Andrew Oberstein from Temple Israel of Boston/the Riverway community, CJP Spark Israel trip, Rachel Barenbaum and family, and my Jewish debut solidarity group chat—I don't know what I would have done without you these past few months. Am Yisrael Chai.

Thank you to all those already listed who generously provided the financial support needed to pursue my writing, as well as to Alice Hoffman whose Novel Incubator fellowship I was a recipient of.

To the friends, family, teachers, classmates, and communities throughout my life who have helped me in my journey to where I am today, thank you.

And finally, to my parents, Paul and Denise LeBlanc. To Mom—for all the books you read to me as a child, and the near-daily trips to the library, thank you for helping me fall in love with reading (as well as making sure I put down my books once in a while and went outside to play!). And to Dad—my biggest supporter in everything I do. I hope you enjoy reading *Flyboy* for the third time. I love you both.